# ALTA

# ALTA

## MERCEDES LACKEY

# DAW BOOKS, INC.

**DONALD A. WOLLHEIM, FOUNDER**

375 Hudson Street, New York, NY 10014

**ELIZABETH R. WOLLHEIM**
**SHEILA E. GILBERT**
**PUBLISHERS**

http://www.dawbooks.com

First Printing, March 2004

1  2  3  4  5  6  7  8  9

DAW TRADEMARK REGISTERED
U.S. PAT. OFF. AND FOREIGN COUNTRIES
—MARCA REGISTRADA
HECHO EN U.S.A.

PRINTED IN THE U.S.A.

To Jemima Parry-Jones and Mozart

# ALTA

ONE

**O**VERHEAD, the stars that filled the night sky, the ornaments upon the robe of the Goddess of the Night, seemed close enough to touch. The *kamiseen* wind whined in the tops of the trees of the oasis beside him; even at night, it never completely ceased. It smelled of baked stone, with a hint of desiccated plants.

He had come to learn that the desert was not all one sort of landscape; he had escaped over stony hills into the pure sand of the desert dune country; now he was in yet another sort of desert, a place of marginal life. The sand beneath Vetch was not as comfortable to sit in as one might suppose; since this wasn't dune country, the ground was hard beneath a surface mix of dust, sand, and pebbles. He was glad of his bedroll now since it provided a layer of softness between himself and the ground. Strange. When he had been Khefti-the-Fat's serf, he wouldn't have noticed how hard it was; in so short a time he had gotten used to certain comforts.

Yes, it was the time of the *kamiseen,* and the ever-present wind whined over the desert, carrying with it a film of dust and sucking away moisture. But this was an oasis, with carefully tended date

1

palms, and Vetch's camp was downwind of the palm grove. The Bedu camped within the oasis, permitting Vetch the downwind side for his own camp, so the *kamiseen* would not trouble him much tonight.

Vetch's scarlet dragon Avatre slumbered at his back, her body warm inside the pit he had dug in the sand and lined with stones heated in his fire. Fuel was as precious out here as water, but tonight no one begrudged the effort of collecting it for him. Firstly, this clan of Veiled Ones boasted many camels and could afford the dried dung for the fire. And secondly, Avatre had earned the right to her fuel and more.

She had eaten well today, taking down four of the desert gazelles. The first time had been this afternoon, twice in rapid succession, enough to feed her well at midday. The second time had been with the help of Vetch's sling, and enabled the two of them to provide an evening meal not only for Avatre herself but for Vetch and the clan of Veiled Ones who were hosting him on this last evening in the desert. There was a faint scent of roasting meat on the *kamiseen* tonight, the last remains of the evening feast.

He was within striking distance of the goal he had sought for so long. Soon he would cross the border that divided Tian lands from Altan. Soon he would be among his own people, and although he probably looked outwardly calm, inside he was afire with excitement—and at the same time, afraid. This moment was one he had dreamed about for so long, but dreams were one thing—reality another.

Once, he had dreamed of having a dragon, too. Now he had one, and Avatre was so much more than he had been able to imagine. She gave him freedom—and tied him to her with bonds of responsibility and love. He had never envisaged how much she would mean to him. It was a glorious burden he would never have given up for the world, but it meant that he was no longer beholden only to himself. In fact, when given a choice between his own welfare and hers—and there had been many such choices on this journey—he would always choose hers. He could not help himself. She was his beloved, after all.

Now, faced with the prospect of crossing into the land he had once thought of as his goal, he knew that no matter what his dreams had been, they could not possibly replicate what he would encounter.

Those dreams might be better than what he actually found, or they might be worse. But they would probably be different, and that alone was a reason for fear.

But this was as far as the talismans that the Veiled Ones had provided as a series of guides would take him. Tomorrow, one of them would personally take him to within sight of the Altan border, the lands where the desert ended and the swampy delta began, and leave him there.

Tonight, unlike previous evenings, he was not alone at his fire. He shared it with one of the Mouths of the Bedu nomads, an enigmatic and apparently sexless creature covered from head to toe in one of their characteristic, belted blue robes and over-vest, dyed with indigo. As all of the others, the Mouth was veiled by a drape of cloth that showed only the eyes. Both sexes wore the veils; a practical consideration when one lived in a land where the wind never stopped, and neither did the dust. He had never heard of any of the Bedu going without their veils, but then, he had never heard of the Bedu going outside the desert. That the costume made the Veiled Ones even more enigmatic to outsiders was, he was sure at this point, a source of endless amusement to them.

He still could not tell whether these Mouths were male or female. Perhaps they were neither; it was altogether possible that they were a kind of eunuch. He didn't find that idea as discomfiting as he might have once; if the Mouths *were* a sort of eunuch, it was not something that had happened against their will. And certainly there were priests of certain obscure gods even among his own people who volunteered for such a sacrifice. Some believed that those who had done so obtained the special favor of their god; others that to remove sex from one's life opened one to visions, or granted great magical power. For some, such a sacrifice was worth the gain.

This particular Mouth was regarding Vetch from the other side of a smaller fire than the one that had heated Avatre's rocks, watching with a direct and clear-eyed gaze over the veil. The Mouth had asked Vetch to tell his tale in full, and now had been simply regarding him quietly for some time now, but Vetch hadn't made any effort to ask why. The Mouth would tell him—or not—in good time. Vetch still wasn't entirely certain what role the Mouths played in the lives of the Veiled Ones; they didn't seem to be priests, quite. They weren't exactly magicians, either, although they did work magic, the magic that created the talismans that guided him from clan to clan, for instance. They certainly were the only ones who spoke to outsiders, but they weren't precisely interpreters, nor were they ambassadors. All bargaining with outsiders was conducted by them, yet they were not traders. And they weren't leaders of their people either.

In fact, if he could have guessed *anything* at this point, it would have been that they were, literally, the voices of their clans, that somehow they knew what everyone in the clan thought, or wanted, with regard to an outsider, and they were the tool through which these wants, thoughts, and needs were expressed.

But they certainly had their own personalities, for every single one he had encountered so far was as different from the last as any two individuals could be. Some had barely spoken at all and held themselves coldly aloof from him; others had been positively garrulous, interested to hear whatever of his own story he cared to impart, and forthcoming with news of the world outside the desert, if not of details of their own lives and customs. Some had been terrified of Avatre, others treated her like a kind of giant falcon—with the respect that talons and teeth deserved, but no fear at all.

This one was somewhere in between, but operating on the "helpful" side of the accounting. The Mouth had been wary of

Avatre and inclined to keep Vetch and his charge far away from the Bedu camp, but otherwise friendly enough. The Mouth had asked careful questions about Vetch's life as a serf as well as his treatment by the Tian Jousters—Ari in particular—and about the journey that had brought them here. Perhaps Avatre's gift of meat had paved the way for that. And this Mouth sat at Vetch's fire now as if wishing to be there, and not as if mounting guard over the "outsider."

"You call yourself Kiron, son of Kiron," the Mouth said abruptly, although the voice did not break the silence so much as insinuate itself into the silence and part it. "So you have asked us to address you. And yet, you do not think of yourself as that person."

*How does the Mouth know that?* It was something that Vetch himself had not realized until the moment it was pointed out.

Vetch considered that statement in silence without retorting immediately, giving himself time to analyze the thought. He had, over the course of these travels, also learned to keep his mouth shut and think about what a Mouth said before he responded to it, having shoved his foot rather neatly into his own mouth a time or two in the early part of his journey. "I have been Vetch, the serf, far longer than I have been Kiron, the keeper of Avatre and dragon rider," he said at last.

"And yet, if you enter into your native land thinking of yourself as Vetch, your own people will treat you thuswise," said the Mouth, with a touch of warning in the tone. "Vetch the serf is a person of no worth and no account, deserving of no consideration or special treatment."

He felt a kind of stillness settle into his gut. This was important. He wasn't certain why it was important, but it *felt* important. Once again, Vetch considered the words. Carefully. What was the Mouth trying to say to him? "And?" he ventured.

"And, perhaps, they will try to take the dragon from you."

"She won't go," Vetch replied, with some heat, and yet sure of himself. She wouldn't, of course, and this was absolutely the one thing he had no fear of. Unlike the dragons that were captured as fledglings and tamed, he had raised Avatre from the egg. She was as bonded to him as any creature could be—as no other dragon, save one, had ever been bonded to another human.

That one, and that other human, were perhaps the most important part of his past that there was. Kashet, and his former Master, the Jouster Ari. They flew in the service of the Great King of Tia. Both of them were his enemies in name, now, and yet were his friends in fact. It was Ari who had engineered his escape when Avatre had made her First Flight with him clinging to her back, all hope of concealing her existence anymore gone off on the *kami-seen* winds.

Ari and Kashet lay behind him somewhere, in the lands claimed by the High King of Tia. He could not think of them without gratitude, and yet it was a gratitude tinged with pain. If he could have, he would have never left them. And yet—

And yet they were Tians, and he was Altan, and if they ever met again, they would probably have to fight each other, and possibly to the death.

Still, Kashet would permit no other to ride him but Ari—and Avatre would be the same with Vetch. He had absolutely no doubt of that, for Avatre had actually tried to face down Kashet—who was many times her size—when she thought the great blue was threatening Vetch.

"Nevertheless," persisted the Mouth, "they will try. They may starve her until she eats *tala*-treated meat, and is drugged into submission. Unless you *make* yourself into Kiron, son of Kiron, Altan Jouster. Unless you come to *believe* that you are that person. Then, no one will presume to doubt that you are entitled to ride her."

Vetch closed his eyes for a moment. A Mouth never, ever said something as an idle observation. And along with all of the passage-rights that Ari had purchased for him with his Gold of Honor, had come another—the right to be instructed in whatever any Mouth thought might be useful. Some of the Mouths had honored this more in the breach than the observance, but this one seemed to be offering sound advice. "Can you teach me to believe?" he asked finally, opening his eyes.

The Mouth regarded him with solemn dark eyes above the veil. "Perhaps. I can, at least, give you a guide to teach yourself. First—among our people we have a saying. 'Assume the attitude of prayer, and in time, the attitude will become the prayer.' I put this to you. Already you are aware of how you hold yourself, for this tells your dragon much, and instructs her on what she should be thinking about what is around her."

Vetch nodded; that was plain enough. Dragons were supremely sensitive to the language of body and posture.

"So—mind, now, Kiron, son of Kiron. Put yourself in the attitude of a freeborn man, or even one of wealth or noble birth. Recall how the masters of your master held themselves, and hold yourself in like manner. Behave in all ways as the Jouster-in-training of Tia would, and within Alta you will be taken as one who has authority by right. Behave in all ways in that manner, and as this becomes second nature, your spirit will come to believe what your body tells it." A pause, as those dark, enigmatic eyes gazed at him. "To begin with, you might raise your head that you may look down your nose at those who are inferior to you. Such a posture conveys a great deal."

He blinked at that, and self-consciously straightened. No more hunched shoulders; no more deference. He must look people in the eye as if they were at least his equals, and possibly his inferiors. And, yes—down his nose.

"Good," said the Mouth approvingly. "Another thing. The Jousters of Alta, like those of Tia, are permitted to take what they need within reason. If you offer to pay for anything, once you cross that border, there will be suspicion. If your dragon hungers then, find a great estate, land, and take what she needs. Do not permit anyone to question you. Say you are a Jouster in training if need be, but no more."

"But—am I properly garbed for such a thing?" he asked doubtfully. Doubt; it still ate at him, made him think, *Sooner or later, they're going to find out I'm an imposter, a thief. Sooner or later—* After all, he had no armor, no helm, nothing but a selection of common kilts. He did not look the part—

Although he could not see anything but the eyes, there was a softening there that suggested the Mouth was smiling. "The chances are, the larger the estate, the less likely there will be anyone of rank about who might even consider questioning you or your rights. Go in, demand food and water, and even clothing if you will, and leave. Jousters of Alta are ranked as lesser nobles; there are fewer of them, and they are valued higher." The Mouth's eyes closed for a moment, as if listening to a voice only the Mouth could hear. "I *believe*," the Mouth added, "Although I do not *know*, that this is the only way, save through the priesthood, that a man of the common folk may become ennobled."

Vetch nodded; this was more good advice, and not something he would have thought of.

"If I were in your position—" A pause. "This is speculation. But if I were in your position, I would feign to be offended if anyone were to question my rights."

Vetch sighed. That was going to be hard; what were the odds he'd be able to continue this charade for very long? He wasn't ready for this. He had been so long the lowest of the low—

Yet, for Avatre's sake, he would try.

No, he would not try. He would succeed. He *must* succeed; he had nowhere else to go right now. She was barely half grown, and they could not continue to live in the wilderness. She was doing all right, but she wasn't prospering, and the bigger she got, the more food she would need. To raise her properly, he either needed to turn her loose among others of her kind, or take her to a Jouster's Compound. There was no other choice.

"Do not hunt unless there are no large estates, for this will be a waste of your effort, and you should be making for Alta City, not wandering about," the Mouth concluded. "Though I think you will find estates in plenty. And remember to *act* as an Altan of rank! The dragon conveys the rank—you *have* the dragon, therefore, you have the rank, by the very laws of the land."

*I have the rank. The dragon confers the rank. And I must do this for her.* "Have you any other advice?" he asked quietly.

The Mouth's eyes closed for a moment, as if considering. "Ah. In one thing the ruling of Alta differs from Tia. The Great Kings and Great Queens rule jointly, and there are always four of them, two sets of Sacred Twins. So refer to the Great Ones, not the Great King. In all other ways, rulership is similar. And until you come to Alta City and reveal yourself for what you are, the tongues of Alta and Tia are similar enough that you should have no difficulty in passing yourself as some Jouster in training from a distant province. And now, it is time for sleep. Since I must come with you on the morrow, the journey to where I must leave you will be long in time if not in distance. To save time you might need to spend in hunting, I will have a child bring a beast for your dragon's meal."

As abruptly as the conversation started, the Mouth rose and left.

And there seemed no reason to do anything other than follow the Mouth's advice, and sleep.

The last leg of this part of his journey began before dawn. Avatre woke and nudged him; he, after all, was supposed to get her breakfast! He sat up and blinked sleepily at a bit of movement, lighter shadow against dark, at the edge of the oasis.

The predawn light slowly turned the world from shades of darkness to a world painted in tones of blue-gray. And the Mouth had told him the truth last night; there was already a small boy with a goat waiting for him to awaken.

The Mouth had not told him to pay for the goat, and yet—yet it seemed churlish in the extreme not to do so. These people fought the desert, and fought it with all their strength and cunning, to wrest a living from it. It was not fair to take and give nothing in return. He rummaged through the coins that Ari had left with him and which he had not yet used, and offered what *he* considered to be a fair price for the beast. It must have been, for without a word, the child pushed the halter rope at him, took the coins, and ran off. He hadn't been required to pay for Avatre's food the times when their hunting had been without success— that was one of the rights that Ari had bargained for—but some- how it just seemed polite to do so now, especially when he was passing out of their guidance. Being fed on the way because he had failed at hunting was somehow different from this, though he could not put his finger on how.

Avatre was not used to having her breakfast delivered alive if she was not hunting it, but she was obviously not averse to the notion. The goat, however, was petrified; feeling rather sorry for it, Vetch dragged it by the halter rope with all four hooves making furrows in the ground until Avatre got tired of waiting, levered herself up out of her pit, stalked over to them both and dispatched the beast with a single, impatient blow of her foreclaw before it had a chance to bleat in terror.

He left her alone with it, and made his own preparations for leaving; there was bread from last night, and onions and a little meat. He did not have a great deal to pack either. By the time she was finished—leaving nothing but the halter rope this morn- ing!—so was he.

And so, apparently, was the Mouth. Vetch looked up to see the Mouth waiting in the shelter of the date palms, the halter of a camel in one hand. Once Vetch was aware of the preparations, the Mouth made the camel kneel, and mounted, curling one leg over the front of the saddle and locking a foot behind the other knee, then giving the beast the command to rise. With a groan of complaint, the camel climbed back up to his feet and the Mouth started off, tapping the camel's shoulder with a crop to make it trot.

The *kamiseen* whined, filling the silence that the Mouth left be- hind; carried on it were the smokes of cooking fires, and the breath of the deeper desert where even the Bedu did not venture.

Vetch took his time in harnessing Avatre; it wasn't as if they would have any trouble finding their guide once they were in the air! In fact, they would probably spend a lot of time circling overhead as the camel crossed the desert beneath them at what would seem to be the pace of a tortoise compared to that of the dragon.

And that was, in fact, exactly what happened. Although the rider was out of sight by the time Avatre pushed off the ground with Vetch on her back, it was not long before Vetch spotted their guide, and it took relatively little effort to catch up.

Avatre was a fine flyer now, and Vetch was used to the bounding wingbeats that left the stomach somewhere behind. In fact, unless he actually thought about it, he never even noticed it; he was so in tune with her, it sometimes felt to him as if they were part of a single, united creature, conqueror of the air.

At first, Avatre had to do a great deal of actual *flying*, doubling back and forth across their guide's path in that peculiar combination of flying and gliding that the dragons used when there were no thermals to ride. And the air of early dawn was cold enough to numb the feet and hands and nose; Avatre didn't like it much, and to tell the truth, neither did Vetch. He shivered in the chill, and was just grateful that the *kamiseen* gave Avatre something to ride. If this had been still air, she'd have had to work a lot harder. It was the gods' own gift that she had made her First Flight at the beginning of the *kamiseen*, for the wind had aided them all across the desert. Had it not been the season of the wind, he had the feeling that they would be making old bones together in the sand, even now.

But as the sun rose and the sand began to heat up, he stopped shivering and Avatre was able to switch from tacking back and forth on the wind to flying as hawks and falcons of the desert did, spiraling passively up one thermal, then gliding down until she found another to repeat the process, following roughly the same course as their guide. For his part, as far as Vetch could tell from above, the Mouth was singularly unperturbed about whether or not they were keeping up, but kept the camel at a steady, ground-eating lope. Fast enough to make good time and the sort of pace a camel could keep up indefinitely.

Vetch was keeping an eye on the horizon as well as on their guide, and when, shortly after midday, a thin line of green appeared along it, he was not at all surprised that their guide chose the shelter of a thicket of acacia trees to stop at, and dismounted. The Mouth didn't wave to Vetch from below, but then again, he didn't need to, for the message of the green horizon was clear enough. The Mouth had brought them to within sight of land claimed only by Alta; peaceful land, where he could not run into either fighting, or Tian Jousters. It was time for him to leave the desert and his guide.

Avatre drifted down to the waiting Bedu, and backwinged to a graceful landing—she'd gotten a great deal better at them than she used to be! And the Mouth nodded toward the horizon as soon as she had folded her wings.

"Half a day, and you will be where you wished to be—across the border, in Alta. I hope that this proves to be truly what you desired," the Mouth said.

*Half a day*— That seemed about right. In the clear air of the desert, things were a lot farther away than they seemed to be to one who had been born in the land reclaimed from the swamp. He shaded his eyes with one hand and peered out into the western distance, the faint haze that marked the beginning of land where things could grow. He licked dry lips. "It has to be what I truly desire, doesn't it?" he replied, as straightforward as the Bedu had been. "There's no place else for me to go."

"You undertake a different sort of trial, when you cross that border, young Kiron," the Mouth persisted. "And perhaps things will not always be to your liking. We of the desert know little of the dwellers in the marshy delta of the Great Mother River, for they have little to do with us, and we have nothing at all to do with those of the Seven-Ringed City itself. I cannot tell you what to expect other than the advice I have already given you. It may be that you go only from one hazard to another."

"But I will be free," he said softly, with one hand on Avatre's neck. "And so will she. Perhaps we need remain only long enough for her to grow to her full strength and size, and if things are not as I had hoped—well, it will be easier for us to escape again, should it come to that."

The Mouth's head bowed slightly. "This is so." The other stared with Vetch to that distant haze of green. "Then, I can only say, your gods go with you."

Kiron touched his brow, his lips, and his heart in thanks and farewell. He gave Avatre the signal and, with a tremendous shove of her legs, she launched for the sky.

When he looked back over his shoulder, he saw that the Mouth had already turned the camel and was heading back in the direction of the clan's encampment. Which was just as well, since he had no intention of following the advice about not hunting to the letter. While he and Avatre were still in the desert, they still had hunting-rights, and he was not going to assume that once they crossed into that belt of green, they would immediately find a place where he could obtain the tremendous amount of meat that she needed to sustain her.

So long as he kept that green in sight, they had a goal. They had already come so far north before turning back toward Altan lands that any interception by Tian Jousters on patrol was next to impossible. So while they would probably camp tonight inside that belt of green, before they reached it, he would be certain that Avatre had eaten her fill.

When they found an exceptionally strong thermal, he sent her up as high as she could go, remembering how the first time he had been carried a-dragonback he had sworn he would never, ever set foot off the ground again. It had been an utterly terrifying experience for one who had never been any farther from the ground than the flat roof of his father's farmhouse. To have that experience while lying face-down over Ari's saddle, when he had never seen either a Jouster or a dragon up close before, had only made it worse.

And to tell the truth, the first few flights with Avatre had been almost as frightening. But he had known very well that he should not and could not *walk* across the desert, so he had gritted his teeth and tried to guide her, and somehow, they had learned to fly together.

Only on the latter half of the journey had they actually learned to hunt together, however. Their first few efforts, singly and together, had been less than stellar, and for a while, he had relied on the Bedu more than he had liked.

Now, though—he was actually rather proud of their ability to feed themselves. They had even worked out more than one technique, and Avatre had learned how to dive, rake with her claws, strike, and hover on commands that could be either physical or verbal. She had even learned to tow or carry something on the other end of a rope; a hard lesson to master, when her natural instinct was to either fight it or give in and flop down at the end of the tether.

This sort of desert—on the very edge of the fertile lands—had a lot more in the way of game than it might appear. There were wild camels, asses, and goats, animals that had escaped from the Bedu; there were also herds of gazelle (Avatre's favorite) and smaller game.

And lions. And Kiron (he *must* learn to think of himself as Kiron!) had learned that he could often rely on the lions to show him where the other game was.

So when, as they circled up the thermal, he saw a pride of lions trotting purposefully toward the north, far below them, he raised his eyes and looked for the cloud of dust that might be telling *them* where the game was.

Avatre had learned the same signs, and her eyes were keener than his. Before he had seen the telltale plume of slightly thicker dust carried on the *kamiseen* wind, she had made her turn out of the thermal and was gliding down in a new direction, north and a bit west, bringing them closer to the green horizon.

It took two more thermals, and they had left the lions far behind, when the herd of wild asses came into view, grazing slowly on the scrubby vegetation that hardly anything else could stomach. They must never have been hunted by a dragon, for they did not even seem to notice them in the sky above. Too bad for them, then.

He got out his sling, and readied a stone. One thing that had certainly made hunting easier was that the farther he and Avatre got from Tia and the wild dragons that lived and bred in the mountain valleys beyond the river, the easier it was to find unwary game. Yesterday had been unusual in that they had found two herds in the same day, but when the grazers weren't spooked by the dragon above them, it was almost too easy to take at least one of them down, now that his skill with the sling had improved.

He picked his target carefully; wild asses were smart and tenacious and the last thing he wanted was to take a jenny with a foal at her side. The herd generally fought harder for one of those.

He gave Avatre the signal, and she began a long, slow glide at very near landing speed that would take them directly over the herd. His chosen target actually looked up, ears swiveling toward them curiously as they neared, making a perfect target.

He let fly.

The stone struck the young jack directly in the middle of the forehead; stunned, it stumbled and went down.

The rest of the herd shied away from the jack for a moment for they did not yet realize what had happened. But the moment that they worked out that this was an attack and not an accident, they could turn at bay, ready to fight for the downed member of the herd. Kiron's stomach tightened and his pulse began to race; Avatre pumped her wings, then, fighting for height, as he stowed his sling in his belt and changed his grip to hang onto the saddle with both hands. For now, it was her turn.

Abruptly, she did a wingover, folded her wings, and plunged toward the ass herd.

*Now* they were spooked, if only by the sight of something so large coming straight down on them. Snorting and tossing their heads, they galloped away from the fallen one for that crucial moment as he struggled to regain his feet and rejoin them. If he somehow managed to get back to the herd, they would have lost their chance.

But he didn't, and as Kiron held tight to the saddle, Avatre made her strike.

The hawks of the desert took rabbits in this way, plunging down on them to strike and bind with their talons, though the actual kill was usually made with a bite to the spine behind the head. Avatre struck in much the same way, though she had four sets of talons, not two. She hit the staggering ass with a force both beautiful and terrible; Kiron was thrown forward in the saddle over her neck by the impact, and only the Jousting straps holding him there kept him on her back as she grasped the jack's hindquarters and chest.

The jack was far from finished, however. Braying frantically with pain, he bucked and kicked, trying to shake her off. They were nearly a match in body size, and the jack actually might outweigh her—in the wild, dragons hunted in pairs at least, in order to be sure of finishing off quarry that was struck.

But if Avatre did not have a dragon hunting partner, she had Kiron.

She clamped her wings tightly to her sides, and threw herself over sideways, and the jack went over with her. This gave Kiron the chance to kick free of the restraining straps and roll clear of the tangle of dragon and ass. As he came up, he had one of his knives in his hand, and he waited only a moment before dashing in, avoiding the thrashing hooves that lashed so near to his head that he felt one of them graze his shoulder, to slash the ass's throat.

"Avatre!" he shouted. "Loose!'

And there was the true measure of her trust for him, for she did just that; she loosened her grip and allowed the ass to break free, leaping back out of reach of its potentially lethal kick. No wild-caught dragon would ever have trusted her rider enough to let go of game she had caught on command.

But the wounded beast staggered away only a few paces before going to its knees, blood spurting from the gash in its throat, pouring down its leg, and staining the ground crimson.

A moment more, and it was down again for the last time, kicking out the last of its life as the herd, scenting the blood, turned and fled. And again Avatre showed the depth of her trust, waiting until he gave the signal before pouncing on the quivering carcass. The blood scent filled the *kamiseen* wind; it would carry for miles. Avatre would need to eat quickly, before the lions and jackals arrived. She might be able to take one or two lionesses or jackals, but not a whole pride or pack.

Then she hunched over the body, fanning her wings out to either side in an echo of the way a hawk mantled over her prey, as she tore loose great mouthfuls of flesh and gulped them down. The metallic tang of hot blood joined that of dust and baked earth as she feasted.

This was why he and Avatre were able to take down game like wild ox and ass; beasts that could break a dragon's leg or wing with a well-placed kick. Now that their hunting skill had matured to this point, she was eating nearly as much as she would have gotten in the Jousters' compound. Anything bigger than that ass, though, would have needed a different sort of attack. Kiron felt they'd mastered it, but it had been something he'd been loath to use too often—he thought that if they found the right victim, he could drop a rope over its head and neck and Avatre could pull it tight until the wild ox choked. He'd even taught her how to pull something up off the ground with that rope attached to the back of his saddle, and he wasn't sure even Kashet had been taught that particular trick.

She gorged herself; he let her feast to repletion. When she finally turned and walked away from the stripped carcass, there was not much left but the head and some bones. This was the way that dragons ate in the wild, and had she been in a compound, she might have eaten even more than this.

In a compound, she would have followed her feast with a nap; sometimes he had allowed her such a rest on this journey, but he could not today. The sun was past zenith and there were lions coming. It was time to be on their way.

He approached her, and patted her neck in the signal to kneel. She turned her long neck to look at him mournfully.

"I know, my love," he said apologetically. "But we need to be gone."

She sighed, a long-suffering sigh; but she knelt and let him take his place in her saddle again.

Heavy with her meal, however, she did not so much launch herself into the air as lumber skyward, and she made slow going until she found a thermal strong enough to allow her to soar upward with less effort.

He had not eaten; he was used to that, though his stomach growled sadly and hurt a little. Water from his waterskin would have to do for now.

From slow spiral up, to long glide down, to slow spiral up again, Avatre lazed her way over the desert, with that green belt growing ever nearer and clearer as the afternoon progressed. Kiron was keeping her working her way in at an angle, for he had decided, now that she'd had a proper meal, that it might not be a bad notion to look for signs of one of those great estates that the Mouth had urged him to seek. The worst that would happen would be that they would have to retreat, or even flee. But the best that would happen would be that they would be able to successfully claim the rights of an Altan Jouster and dragon.

Finally, he spotted what he was looking for in late afternoon, just as Avatre began to be a bit less lethargic and show more energy.

He spotted it when Avatre was at the top of one of her thermals: a walled compound far too large to be that of a mere farmer. It was certainly the size of a village, though it was shaped nothing at all like a village; no streets, nothing that looked like individual houses. So it must be the great house and grounds of one of those great estates that the Mouth had described.

He pointed Avatre's head toward it with a tug on her guide rein. Obedient as ever, she broke out of the thermal and began her long glide in the direction of the estate.

Kiron gulped back fear, and straightened his back.

*Now,* he thought. *Now. Or it will be never.*

And he sent Avatre in.

# TWO

**B**ENEATH him was a green landscape, so green that after all his time in the desert, it dazzled his senses. Still, he was able to make out what the crops were, even while he adjusted to the change. *Date palms. Barley fields. Onions?* The closer they got to the compound and the lands around it, the more Kiron recognized, and the more certain he became that this was, indeed, a Great Estate, and not a village. Villagers each had their own little plots and usually grew mixed sets of crops, so that a field was a patchwork of little bits of this and that. The great estates had enormous fields of single crops. And now he could see people working in those fields, none of whom had the look of villagers, for all were men, and they worked in teams. A villager would work his own fields with his wife and those children who were old enough to help. No, these were servants, or, perhaps, slaves. And it gave him a moment of hot satisfaction to think that some of these slaves might be captured Tians, laboring as he had labored to the profit of someone other than themselves, owning nothing, not even the cloth wrapped around their loins. Altans did not have serfs, who were linked to the land they had once owned, for the oft-broken treaty with Tia that created the serf class applied only to those people who had once owned the captured land that they were now tied to. The Altans had been losing land, not taking it, for a very long time now. So there were no serfs inside Alta and any captured Tians became slaves, who could be bought and sold at will.

The air here *smelled* different; different from Tia, different from the desert. This was water-rich air, heavy with humidity, and with the scents of lushly growing plants, the scent of mud and the *latas* that was blooming profusely everywhere. And Kiron felt something strange stirring inside him, a feeling that made him clutch Avatre's saddle and gulp back a lump in his throat.

This was the scent of *home,* of childhood. Except that his home was gone, his family divided.

No. No matter what that scent promised to his heart, his head knew that he was not coming home.

He shook off his melancholy; time enough for brooding later, when he wasn't about to perpetrate a fraud. He clenched his jaw, and concentrated on the fields below. As Avatre's shadow passed over them, the men looked up, shading their eyes with their hands. He wished he knew what they were thinking.

*Not in the fields. Not near the cattle. Not too near the Great House either.* He decided to send Avatre to land in a large yard near a herd of penned goats. Goats were not expensive, and Avatre was no longer spoiled with feeding on tender beef, sent to the altars of the gods. After her feed at their kill, she would need no more than one or two of those goats to satisfy her. He would not be greedy; he would demand animals that were easily replaced.

As she backwinged to a landing—an exceptionally good and graceful one, and he felt a thrill of pride in her—the goats milled and bleated in panic, and a man in a striped headcloth came out of a nearby building to see what was agitating them.

The striped headcloth, and the fact that he was wearing a kilt rather than a loincloth, marked him as someone with more authority than a field hand. As he approached, his face already creasing into a frown, Kiron slid down over Avatre's shoulder and stood with one hand on her foreleg, waiting for him.

*Stand like the new Jousters,* he reminded himself. *You are Kiron, son of Kiron, rider of Avatre. Raise your chin. Look down your nose. . . .*

"What—" the man began, and Kiron interrupted him, hoping he could keep his voice from shaking or going shrill with nervousness. "Three goats for my beast, date wine and food for me," he snapped. "Quickly! We have far to go."

The man reddened at Kiron's tone, and looked as if he was going to challenge Kiron's right to anything, but at that moment, Avatre, sensing her rider's nervousness, stretched out her neck and hissed at him. The man paled and took a step backward.

"You had better hurry," Kiron said, narrowing his eyes, feigning annoyance, though what he really felt was a tight fear in his gut that the man would, even now, challenge them. "Or she might choose for herself. She is *very* hungry."

With two goats inside of Avatre, and one slung behind Kiron's saddle for her breakfast, together with a skin of wine and a bundle that presumably contained food, they launched into the air again, heading north and a little west, angling in toward Alta City. He was filled with elation at his success, almost dizzy with relief that he had actually managed to pull off the scam, and had to restrain himself to keep from shouting his triumph as she surged into the sky. Once in the air, Kiron picked up the river, the Red Daughter of Great Mother River, and they followed it until, just as the sun began to set, he spotted an island.

It was exactly what he wanted; mostly rock, and covered with the detritus of past floods. There was a lot of dead wood there, and that meant a lot of fuel for a fire to warm the rocks for Avatre's bed. She was not at all loath to land, and waited with commendable patience while he picked out a hollow among the rocks for her, built the fire, lit it, tended it, let it die, and finally, with the

stars bright overhead, tested the rocks to make sure they weren't
too warm for her.

Here along the river the night didn't get nearly as cold as it did
in the desert, anyway, and these rocks had been baking in the sun
all day already. She settled right in and went to sleep, while he
investigated his "loot."

It wasn't a princely feast by any means. In fact, it was basic
laborer's food of coarse barley bread, onions and goat cheese, and
the wine was just short of becoming vinegar. Nevertheless, the
man hadn't shorted him, and it was entirely possible, given where
he'd landed, that this was the best there was to be had without
recourse to the Great Lord's kitchens.

It was quite a change from the diet of the nomads, however,
which was mostly stringy meat and unleavened flatbread, and on
that basis alone, he made a good meal out of it. And perhaps, as
he got better at demanding what he needed, what he got would
also improve. He ate quickly and settled in at Avatre's side,
among her warm rocks. It had been a long, long day, and as he
relaxed, he realized how *tired* he was.

*Excitement*, he decided. *All the excitement. Making it as far as
Alta, coming out of the desert, fooling that overseer. I feel as if I've
been running all day.* He yawned hugely, and felt his muscles going
slack as the tension came out of them. He tried to keep his eyes
open a little longer, but the warmth of the rocks was so good, and
for the first time since he'd left the compound he had a completely
full stomach, and before he knew it, his eyes closed of their own
accord.

He was awakened before dawn, not by Avatre, but by a dead
duck falling on his head.

He had always been in the habit of coming awake all at once; a
good idea, since Khefti-the-Fat had enjoyed sneaking up and kicking the unwary awake in the morning. The habit had stood him
in good stead in the desert; twice during their journey, lions had
attempted to steal up on them in the night. Avatre had scented

them in her sleep and he had driven them off with a burning brand from his fire. But a dead duck falling on him—that was different.

He jumped to his feet automatically, shaking the sleep from his eyes, and saw, all in the same moment, the duck at his feet with an arrow through it, a flight of more ducks overhead, and, coming up out of the mist, a small boat with two men in it, one paddling and one holding a bow.

They seemed surprised to see him; he was no less surprised to see *them*, and was not particularly happy to note that the one with the bow was sporting a pair of enameled armbands. "You!" the archer called, with the self-assured arrogance of someone of rank. "Have you seen—"

Avatre's head came up behind him; she took one look at the men in the boat—she had never seen a boat before, after all, at least not one that was on the same level with her—and snorted in surprise.

The man with the armbands yelped with a surprise that equaled hers, and fell backward into the boat, and the man with the paddle had all he could do to keep it from capsizing.

Kiron bent and picked up the duck by the arrow. "I believe," he said, neutrally, "this must be yours."

"Ah. Yes," the archer stammered.

Kiron tossed it; it fell at the rower's feet. Neither man made any move to pick it up, and Avatre snorted again.

"You had probably better get what sport you can before the sun gets much higher," Kiron went on, hoping he sounded less nervous than he felt. "When my dragon rises, she'll probably frighten every duck in the marsh."

"Ah. Indeed. Pardon us," the archer said, and tapped the rower on the shoulder. The rower started, as if being wakened from a trance, and began digging at the water with his oars as if he could not get away from there fast enough. Soon they vanished into the mist again, and Kiron rubbed his head ruefully.

"Now I wish I hadn't given back that duck," he said wistfully. "It would have tasted fine for my breakfast."

Then he remembered the fishing line in his gear; unused since it had been given to him (or rather, sent to become part of his grave goods!), it occurred to him that it was going to take Avatre some time to wake up properly, eat, and warm herself up enough to fly, and while she was doing so, he might just as well try his luck. He hadn't had fish since the last Tian festival.

His luck, apparently, was in. With a bit of bread left over from his supper, he soon had several fish baking in the ashes of his fire, and both he and Avatre took off with full bellies that morning.

North and a little west; they followed the river while it meandered in that direction, lost it as he had expected, then picked up the Great Mother River's second daughter shortly around noon. This was the branch known as the White Daughter, the middle of the three; for there were three, all told: Red, White, and Black, so named for the color of their water, tinted by the mud they carried. This time of year, the White Daughter was more of a pale green; she was shallow, shrunken within her banks, waiting for the rains to make her full again.

From the Red Daughter to the White, they flew over cultivated lands that were vastly better watered and more fertile looking than the corresponding properties in Tia, and between the fields was a lattice of irrigation ditches, some of them as wide as a cart and deeper than a man was tall. This fertility was no illusion, but Kiron knew it had come at a cost; every hand of farmland had been claimed from the swamp by *someone*, building the ditches to help drain the land, dredging up baskets of silt from the bottoms of the ditches and building fields, bringing in earth from the edge of the desert to do the same, or extending the reach of the river with a further network of irrigation ditches beyond the land that had been swamp.

He looked down on these fertile lands and their tenders, and it came to him that he had dared the bluff twice now. Twice he had passed himself off as an Altan Jouster, and twice he had succeeded; dared he try a third time? The nearer he drew to Alta

City, the less likely it seemed that his ruse would pass muster, no matter what the Mouth said.

And there was that saying that his father used to use, "Third time pays for all," that you might get away with something twice, but when you were caught the third time, the reckoning would be high.

Safer not to try again, perhaps.

And it seemed that his caution was appropriate when, as noon approached and he knew Avatre was getting hungry, he spotted the fresh carcass of a cow washed up on another of those rock islands. He knew it was fresh because it wasn't at all bloated, and when he brought Avatre down on the island to investigate it, the gaping wound in its stomach told what it had died of.

That was a crocodile bite. Perhaps it had waded in too deep for a drink; perhaps it had been one of a herd that some farmer had sent across a ford. It could have been carried downstream by the beast that wounded it, and kicked free only to die and wash up here. For whatever reason it had gotten here, he was thankful; he let Avatre have her fill, then doze in the sun while he fished again, this time encasing the gutted fish in mud to bake in a fire until she had finished her nap. He ate one on the spot, and stowed the rest; when Avatre woke, they continued their journey.

He wished he had a map. He wished that he knew how far it was going to be before he reached Alta City. Going dragonback was infinitely faster than any other way to travel, but Alta was big; Tia was long, but it was narrow, with most of the population confined to either bank of the Great Mother River. Alta was wide; he had heard that if a man tried to walk it from the Eastern Desert to the Western Desert it would take him at least a full moon, depending on the time of year, and there were many flood-swollen streams and ditches he would have to cross.

And his goal was Alta City, which lay on the coast of the Great Salt Sea that bordered Alta on the north. He knew that he could reach it by following this, the White Daughter of Great Mother

River, but how much farther would it be? Dragons flew fast—and far, in a day. Two days? Three?

His luck was out as sunset neared; there were no more islands, only sandbars, and the Great Estates were more numerous than he liked. But Avatre was hungry again. What was he to do?

It was the sight of a temple that decided him; it was a large one, and there were bulls penned for sacrifice nearby. Tian dragons were fed from the remains of Tian sacrifices; it was reasonable to think that the Altans might do the same. He signaled Avatre to land; he could hardly escape notice at a temple at sunset, and he was not at all surprised that not one, but several shaven-headed priests in their white linen kilts and enameled pectoral collars hurried up to him as he slid down from Avatre's back. They looked nervous and apprehensive.

"Food for my lady-dragon and for me," he said, shortly.

One of them brightened. "You are come auspiciously, Jouster," he said, "For on this Feast of Abydesus, more sons of the Hare Nome have become men than usual, and many cattle have spilled their blood in His honor. Wait, and we will bring it, that your great lady may eat her fill."

*The Feast of Abydesus!* He had completely lost track of time, out there in the desert. It had been one of his favorite feast days as a child, for the Ram God favored children, especially boy children, and those who could afford it sent bulls to be sacrificed when their sons had their child locks shaved and became men. That meant meat for a feast to which friends and relations were invited, while those who were still considered children got honey cakes and the priests' blessings to carry them through another year toward manhood.

Though the god only required the blood, it was considered inauspicious to waste the meat of the bulls that were offered to him—and in the season of the *kamiseen* it could not be kept for long. Some went to the homes of those new-made men for their feasts, of course, and some to the larders of the priests. But the larders could only hold so much, and anything left outside the cold-magic could only be burned or dried. It was possible that such a small temple did not have anyone who could make cold-magic, and in such humid weather, he had the notion that beef would not necessarily dry well.

And while the scent of the burning might be sweet in the nostrils of the gods, it generally offended the neighbors downwind. The poor might get their share of the inferior cuts, but if enough bulls died on the altars, there could be a small problem with disposal.

Soon enough, several acolytes arrived trundling barrows, and at the sight of so familiar an object, Avatre actually began to dance with impatience. To the startlement of the acolyte bringing the first barrow, she shot her head out in the trick that Ari's Kashet had used to pull on Kiron, and snatched the top piece before the poor, shocked acolyte could set the barrow down for Kiron to take.

With a yell, he jumped back, and the barrow thudded to the ground, overturning and spilling half its contents.

Avatre gave the boy a very hurt look.

"Peace!" Kiron said, holding back a laugh, and patting Avatre on the shoulder. "My lady is possessed of gentleness, if not good manners. She would not harm you for the world."

The acolytes said nothing, though their looks of doubt told Kiron that they would rather err on the side of caution. So Kiron came and took the other two barrows while Avatre polished off the contents of the third, and brought them to her himself.

So she ate to her heart's content, while the priests and acolytes gazed on her from a respectful distance.

"If you would care to stay the night at the sanctuary, young lord," one of them called, "there is a room where your sky warrior may sleep warm. It is not often used, for we are a modest temple, but—"

"You make us feel welcome," Kiron said immediately. "Our thanks, and we will stay."

From the pleasure on the priests' faces, although he could not

recall the Ram God having any particular association with dragons, he got the feeling that the arrival of a Jouster on a feast day
was considered to be a sign of great favor. If that was the case,
he was going to take shameless advantage of the fact.

So he and Avatre were led to a roofless chamber where the
floor was heated from below by fire, and although it was not the
hot sands that she preferred, she settled down with a contented
grunt. Then he was taken to a bathing chamber where he was
able to give himself a good scrub for the first time in far too long,
given a clean loincloth, and a proper, soft-wrapped Altan kilt (in
contrast to the stiff, starched Tian variety that anyone of rank
wore). His hands remembered how to wrap it, even if his mind
didn't; an acolyte braided his hair for him, Altan fashion, in a
clubbed plait down the back of his neck. Then he was conducted
to the feast that the priests themselves held.

And that was when he very nearly bolted; when he saw the
couches arrayed around the dining chamber and realized that he
was going to be a guest. And he was *supposed* to be an Altan
Jouster!

Panic took him for a moment, and he sat down woodenly on
his couch, expecting at any moment that someone would realize
that he was a fraud—

But once again, his luck saved him, for the priests not only did
not question him, they did not seem to expect him to be much of
a conversationalist. Or, perhaps, they assumed that no Jouster
would be conversant with what was, after all, merely local gossip.
A few remarks were directed to him, which he answered cautiously and briefly—but most of the conversation went merrily
on without him, and seemed to concern the intertemple political
maneuvering here in the Nome of the Hare. In fact, the only sig-
nificance his presence had was that his (and Avatre's) appearance
at this particular moment was going to put *this* temple up a notch
or two in the ever-changing pecking order, at least for a while.
Probably if he had come at a time when there was no overabundance of meat, he might have been less welcome.

And these men were truly only interested in what lay within the borders of this Nome; they were remarkably incurious about either Alta City or even their neighboring Nomes. All this worked to his advantage; all he needed to do was to be a courteous and agreeable guest.

Yet surely, before he left, he was going to be expected to make an offering to the god—and unlike a real Jouster, he didn't have a lot to his name.

He cast his mind over his poor possessions, trying to decide if there was anything among them that was *worth* offering. And then it struck him.

"I have with me the captured amulets of enemy Jousters," he said to the Chief Priest with great diffidence as the feast drew to a close. "If the God would deign to accept them as a worthy sacrifice and a sign of His power over the gods of the enemy—"

"Deign?" the Chief Priest said, throwing up pudgy little hands in delight (he was a small, round man who was clearly fonder of the pleasures of the table than he was of political machinations). "Good young Lord Kiron, it would be an honor to offer them for you! Let me send for your baggage, so that we can make the sacrifice before the midnight hour!"

It was with no small sense of irony that Kiron watched the Priest lay out the line of faience amulets upon the Ram God's altar with a reverence more suited to objects of gold than simple glazed clay. All of those amulets, sent to be Kiron's own grave offerings by the terrified dragon boys to prevent his haunting them. . . .

Still, most of them were Haras-hawk amulets, sign of the Jousters of Tia, and as such, were powerful symbols of an Altan victory over a Tian, if not valuable in themselves.

And, presumably, they were something no other temple within the Nome of the Hare could boast of having.

They wanted to send him to the guest quarters, but he was adamant about having a couch placed in the same chamber as Avatre. He had not slept a night away from her side since she was hatched, and he did not intend to start now.

He was escorted to his couch by yet another acolyte, who apologized so many times for the simplicity of the quarters that Kiron was weary of reassuring him and glad when he took himself out. And if the quarters were bare, well, that was his choice, wasn't it?

And besides, when the lamp was blown out, all quarters were the same. As long as they held Avatre, he could not have cared if he slept on rock, or in the Great King's palace.

It had been a little difficult to judge accurately, but if the Ram God's priests were to be believed in *their* guesses of how far it was to Alta City, he and Avatre would be there by nightfall at the very latest, and mid-afternoon at the earliest.

He did not have much of a plan, but then, perhaps he would not need one. His "plan," such as it was, consisted of finding the Altan Jousters' Compound, landing there, and telling his story. Or at least, an edited version of the story.

This version featured him purposefully (rather than accidentally) making his escape flight and working his way in short stages around the edge of the desert, instead of involving the Bedu. In the first place, he did not want any rumor of the Veiled Ones' involvement to get back to Tia, and in the second place, he did not want any rumor of *Ari's* involvement to get back either. Everything would be true up to the point of Avatre's First Flight; everything would be true after the point at which he crossed the border into Alta. In fact, the stories about the happenings in between would be partly true. He could tell a great many truths about learning to hunt with Avatre, the things he had taught her, about sandstorms they had been forced to fly above, about finding tiny wilderness water sources not even the Bedu had known were there. He would just be a little vague about the locations where these things had happened. . . .

He was pretty certain it would work. And if the Altans were mistrustful of him at first, that was no great loss. Avatre was not even in the first stages of Jousting training, and neither was he. It would be years before he would actually be ready to fight, and by that time, he should be accepted without question.

Only the acolytes were awake when he and Avatre were up and ready to fly. This was not exactly a surprise; the serious inroads into the offerings of palm wine and date wine were just being made when he had left the feast, and none of those priests had looked particularly ascetic. There would be aching heads this day—which was all to the good, since he wanted to be well away before anyone thought of any questions they wanted to ask about just why such a young-looking boy was riding a dragon toward Alta City. And why such a one would have Tian amulets in his possession that he *claimed* to have been captured from the enemy.

Avatre ate her fill; she seemed supremely content with the chamber they'd shared, and was ready, even anxious, to be off. Perhaps she picked that up from him; with the end of the journey now in sight, he wanted it to be over. They were in the sky just as the sun crested the horizon; with the chamber heated all night long, there had been little need for the dragon to warm up her muscles before she flew.

They made excellent speed; the wind was favorable, the way clear, and there was no real need to stop until Avatre hungered again.

Below, the White Daughter showed her true nature; the water the curious color of watered-down milk, the sandy shores as white as reed paper. She seemed a placid enough river; the shortest (and hence, termed the "youngest") of the Three Daughters. During the flood season, her waters spread out over the land gently and predictably, and she returned to her bed just as gently. In fact, the worst that could be said of her was that she was a veritable nursery for crocodiles and river horses.

For along much of her length, it was easier to dig irrigation channels than to fill or drain her swamps. And if those swamps were a haven for ducks, geese, and other desirable things, they were also the chosen shelters for the two most terrible forms of death by water other than drowning itself.

As he and Avatre flew over the marshes, it was easy to see the great river horses in their herds, looking like slowly moving boulders that would sometimes submerge altogether. The huge, fat beasts were deceptively placid-looking, and yet they could be more deadly than the crocodile. Like the crocodile, they could swim swiftly, hidden underwater for a surprising amount of time, and in the White Daughter's murky current they were nearly impossible to see. Their huge jaws could crush a boat literally in half, or rip a man's leg off at the hip, and their uncertain tempers meant that there was no telling if, or when, one would choose to attack. And for all their bulk, even on land, they could move very swiftly for a short distance.

And yet they were considered fine eating in certain seasons, and in both Tia and Alta it was considered a mark of great courage to take part in a hunt.

Crocodiles were harder to spot, except where they sunbathed on the banks or on sandbars. The White Daughter hid them even more effectively. The best that one could do, with regard to crocodiles, was to try to clear a ford with nets before crossing it. Still, except with the very largest of the beasts, it *was* possible to win in a fight with one, if you could get its jaws clamped or tied shut, for though the muscles that closed those jaws were immensely strong, the ones that opened them were weak. But one man against a river horse did not stand a chance.

Still. both tended to keep to the swamp rather than the open river. It was rare for either to attack in broad daylight.

Rare. But not impossible. Especially not when provoked.

*We can't be far now,* Kiron thought, looking down at the vast swamp beneath him. The White Daughter was visible—oh, yes, clearly visible—cutting her path through the heart of the swamp, but for as far as he could see was nothing but a sea of reeds. The scent that rose from this swamp was perilously close to a stink; it smelled of stagnant water and rotting reeds, and things he couldn't name. This was the first of the Seven-Ringed City's defenses; Alta City had never permitted the swamp here to be filled in or drained, because it was too effective as a passive defense. There were only two ways to the city—down the White Daughter to the sea, and by ship from the port side of the city.

And the swamp itself was a source of more than just defensive measures. Papyrus cutters worked here endlessly, cutting the reeds for the paper for which the city was justly famous. Geese and ducks were actually farmed here by keeping their wing feathers clipped; wild ones were hunted. There must be a hundred sorts of fish to be hooked or netted.

As Kiron looked down, admiring the flight of a flock of birds beneath him, he saw something else; two small boats of exceptionally fine design. The reason he saw them was that the gilded prows caught the light and his attention.

There were two men in each boat; out of purest curiosity, for he could not imagine what they were doing, he sent Avatre to circle a little lower.

Two spearmen, two rowers. The rowers were in Altan kilts, but the spearmen were in short, knee-length tunics. He caught another glint of gold from each of the spearmen. Nobles?

He snorted to himself, and was about to give the signal to Avatre to circle back north and onward. Nobles, out spear fishing! In the swamp, no less! What idiocy—he hoped the midges and mosquitoes ate them alive—

But then he heard a splash, and a shout—

—and a scream.

It was not the scream of a young man, it was the scream of a *girl*.

Startled, he glanced down, just in time to see the huge jaws of a river horse smash down on the aft of one of the boats, crushing it and engulfing the head and upper torso of the rower who had been sitting there; he bellowed in agony, a cry swiftly cut off. The boat went over; the spearman—the *girl*—was thrown into the water.

With the river horse.

A crocodile would take a single victim, carry it under, and drown it, then eat it at leisure. A river horse, if maddened, would take as many victims as it could get; it would not eat them, for it was a vegetarian. No, it would maim them, crush them, kill them if it could, until it was dead, it tired of the carnage, or all the possible victims were gone.

And these were Altans. *His* people. He had to save them! Or save the girl, anyway; the rower was dead, or as good as, for nothing that escaped the savage jaws of a river horse lived for long.

He signaled Avatre with knees and hands; she turned, and circled back, her muscles tensing under him as she sensed his intention. There was another maneuver besides the "strike and bind" that he and Avatre had practiced out there in the desert—but not on living things that could fight back as a river horse would, only on potential prey. No matter. They had to try it now.

The river horse still had the rower in its jaws, tossing its enormous, blocky head back and forth while muffled screaming came from inside that terrible maw. The girl in the water, sensibly, was saving her breath, trying to swim away from the river horse as fast as she could before it noticed her. The river horse was between her and the other boat; the spearman was cursing the rower for trying to escape, while *he* tried to take aim with his flimsy little fish spear at the river horse's head. Blood flowed from the river horse's jaws, turning the milky water pink.

All this, Kiron saw in that single moment when he gave Avatre one of her new hunting commands.

"Avatre!" he shouted. *"Rake!"*

One half-grown dragon could not hope to take down anything much larger than an ass with the strike-and-bind attack she knew instinctively. But the desert falcons used a different technique to drive an enemy away—they would attack with outstretched talons, but would *not* close once they had struck. Instead, they would leave bloody furrows across their victim's head; with luck, blinding it, but at least inflicting a lot of pain and giving it something else to think about than, say, a nest or a newly fledged youngster.

Kiron had not known whether dragons used this same ploy until he'd tried it with Avatre. Apparently, they did. Now she had a command word to go with the attack—but this was the first time they were using it against something that could turn on them.

And if the river horse got one of Avatre's feet—

Too late to worry about that now. Avatre understood instantly what she was supposed to do; she folded her wings and went into a dive; Kiron leaned over her shoulder, eyes narrowed against the wind of her passage.

She struck.

She *hit*.

There was no shock, as there was when she hit and bound. Instead, she slowed for just a moment, as a bellow of rage erupted just below her feet, then she surged upward with a great beat of her wings.

It sounded like thunder in his ears, each wingbeat pounding the air, and the bellowing of the river horse still ringing below them. But Avatre knew she was not done, not yet. Her blood was up now, and the prey was audibly still alive. She got just enough height to stoop again, and did a wingover that left Kiron's stomach still hanging in the air behind them, as she dove for another raking maneuver.

The girl was still in the water, fighting her way through the reeds. The river horse was only wounded; it had shook what was left of the rower out of its jaws, and was peering around with its little piggy eyes to see what had hurt it so. But before it could catch sight of the girl's thrashing arms, Avatre struck again.

More bellows; again that surge of wings. As they climbed, Kiron looked down again.

No good. The other rower was getting away from the area as

fast as his arms could take him, despite the curses of the spearman, who had somehow lost his spear. The river horse was still
between them and the girl. The girl's arms weren't moving as
fast; she was tiring. And there was blood in the water, plenty of
it. It would not be long before there were crocodiles, or worse,
more river horses.

They couldn't keep raking the beast; at any moment, it would
understand that attack was coming from above and dive, and then
it might find and seize the girl. Time for another trick.

Except that the girl didn't know it. So *he* would have to get into
the water.

He signaled Avatre with hands and legs not to make a third
attack, and turned her toward where the girl was. If he could just
reach that coil of rope behind him—

His hand found it; he pulled it off the pack, and looped it around
himself just under his armpits, and tied it in place. The other end
was still fastened to the packs. He hoped he had fastened it securely. This would be a bad time to discover that he had not.

As Avatre swooped low over the girl, who ducked instinctively,
then came up in a hover, he threw himself out of the saddle, tuck-
ing himself into a ball to protect his head and stomach.

He hit the water with a splash that stung his arms and legs and
drove him under for a moment. He unfolded his limbs and forced
himself upward, tossing his head and gasping as he broke the surface of the water and looked around for the girl.

Unbelievably, she was no more than an arm's-length away, and
before the rope could tighten around him, he had her, wrapping
both his arms around her just under her arms, and clasping his
hands on his own wrists.

"Pull!" he screamed at the dragon above him, and obediently,
Avatre surged upward.

The rope around his chest cut into him as the dragon turned
her hover into flight; the dead weight of the girl threatened to pull
his arms out of their sockets, and reeds lashed his back and head
as Avatre pulled them both through the swamp backward. It felt

as if Khefti-the-Fat was giving him the worst lashing of his life, while trying to squeeze him in half, and tear him limb from limb, all at the same time. And meanwhile, the weight of the girl threatened to drag him underwater. It was a total, painful assault on all his senses. He couldn't think. He couldn't even see, not really. All he could do was to hold on, grim as a hungry ghost, hold on, and hope that Avatre would find somewhere solid to land.

Soon.

*Please. Oh, gods. Soon.*

He couldn't see; he could only feel. Couldn't let go. Wouldn't let go. Pain turned his arms and back into hot agony, his lungs burned with the water he'd inhaled—

*Don't let go—*

Hard to breathe—the rope tightening over his chest—

*Don't let go!*

The world grew darker—redder—darker—as he sobbed to get a breath, just one, just another, then—

Then it stopped. The motion, anyway, if not the pain.

He gasped for a breath that didn't have water in it; agony burned across his chest. Thought he heard something like a curse.

The wire of pain around his chest snapped, and he could breathe again, and he gasped in one huge, blessed breath of air.

Felt someone tugging at his arms, his poor, wrenched arms. "Get up!" said the high voice urgently in his ear. "Please, get up!"

"Can't," he said thickly and tried to shake the water, hair, and mud out of his face. He opened his eyes; everything seemed blurred.

"Orest!" the high voice called. "He can't get up! You have to help me!"

He tried to move his leaden legs then; found that they would work, a little, so that when a second person came splashing through the shallows, he was able to at least get his own feet under him. With one person on each side, they got him to the side of a boat, and he half-fell and was half-pushed, into it. Wind buffeted them all. Somehow he rolled over and saw a blur of scarlet above as the other two clambered in beside him.

"Avatre!" he called, and coughed. It hurt to call—hurt to breathe again, but he didn't want her attacking— "Avatre! Follow!" he managed. "Follow!"

He fell into a fit of coughing again, and his vision grayed for a moment. Small hands pounded his back, until he coughed up some muddy water, which seemed to help a little, and the high voice said, "It's all right. She's following us."

"And hanged if I know how he's making her do that," said a new voice, admiringly. "I've never seen any Jouster who could make his dragon do *anything* like he did. Who are you?"

"Kiron," he managed, around pain-filled gasps. "Son of Kiron—"

"Never mind that. Never mind any of that," the young girl's voice said firmly. "You just rest. We'll get you back, you and your dragon. Just rest. We'll get you help and take you to where you belong."

*Where I belong!* he thought wonderingly, around the pain. *Where I belong—*

And he closed his eyes, lying curled in the bottom of the boat, and let them take him wherever they were going to. Because wherever it was—it was going to be home, where he belonged, at long last.

# THREE

H E MUST have hurt himself more than he'd thought—he'd thought his life had hardened him against any and all punishments, but apparently being dragged backward through a swamp, over submerged logs and sharp sedges and who knew what all else, was a little more than even he could handle. Something happened to him after he was hauled into that little boat, because he lost a significant slice of time. One moment, he was curled with his cheek against the reed bundles of the bottom of that boat, and the next—he wasn't.

Probably he blacked out for a while; at least, that was the only conclusion his pain-fogged mind could come up with, because the next thing he knew, he was being picked up with surprising care by two enormous men, one at his head and the other at his knees, while the girl babbled and fussed at them. And all he could think was that Avatre would surely think he was being attacked.

"Wait!" he gasped, "My dragon will—"

"Here's the Healer!" interrupted the boy's voice, just as the two men set Kiron down carefully on a warm, rough surface that felt like stone. And it hurt anyway. His back screamed at him, until he rolled over on his side to get what was obviously lacerated skin off that rough stone.

Kiron blinked his eyes hard to clear them from the tears of pain; as he got them to focus, he saw he *was* lying on stone, on a little pier, in fact, and the mud-spattered girl and boy had been joined by two enormous men in plain rough-spun tunics, probably the ones who had gotten him out of the boat. Bending over him was a woman with her hair hanging loose; she was dressed in a flowing white linen gown with no jewels at all, and only a soft white belt at the waist. Avatre had already landed at the very end of the stone pier, and was eyeing the proceedings with anxiety. He tried to say something—to warn them that Avatre could be dangerous in this situation—

But then, to his astonishment, the girl walked fearlessly up to the dragon and stretched out her hand.

Avatre started back, eyes wide—then, cautiously, eased her head forward, sniffing suspiciously at the outstretched palm.

And the most astonishing thing of all happened; the moment that Avatre's nose touched the girl's hand, the dragon relaxed. Relaxed *entirely,* in fact, and went from a pose that warned she was ready to fight, to looking as if she was back in her own sand pit with only Kiron beside her.

And she sat, then stretched out at full length on the stone. She kept her eyes fixed on Kiron, but with no signs of concern at all, as if she knew that no one was going to hurt either of them.

"She'll be all right now, Tef-talla," the girl said, confidently laying her hand on Avatre's shoulder and reaching up to scratch under her chin.

Kiron would have experienced a surge of betrayal and jealousy at that moment, except that was the exact moment that the Healer chose to place both hands on his chest, and he was far too busy thinking about how much it hurt—

And then, once again, he wasn't thinking of anything at all.

\* \* \*

When he came to himself a second time, he was lying in a bed. It was not the sort of hard, flat couch that the Tians used; this was more like the fabric frames on low legs that the *tala* fruit was dried on, but much stronger, of course. And instead of a hard neck rest, there was a soft pillow beneath his head. That, and the sultry breath of a breeze that moved over his face, full of the scent of greenery and water, told him that he was not in Tia, even before his mind caught up with his wakefulness and he remembered *why* he was lying on a bed.

In fact, this was the sort of bed he had used as a child, when his father Kiron was master of his own farmlands, and those farmlands had been in Alta, not Tia.

There was a linen sheet over him, which was a very good thing, since he quickly discovered that he'd been cleaned up, which was good, but also that he wasn't wearing anything beneath that sheet, which could have been embarrassing.

Well, that wasn't entirely true; his chest and presumably his back had been expertly bandaged, so he was "wearing" bandages. But when he opened his eyes, the first thing that he saw was that the girl he had rescued was in the same room with him, and he was glad that they'd given him *something* to cover his nakedness.

Then his second realization was that he wasn't in a room, it was a courtyard, open to the sky, which was made necessary by the fact that—his third realization and a great relief—Avatre was also with him. She looked as pleased with herself as could be, and she'd been unharnessed, wiped down, and seemed too contented to be hungry, so someone must have fed her.

And besides the girl and Avatre, there were three men in this courtyard, all standing at his bedside, conversing with one another in low tones.

The first had one hand resting on the girl's shoulder as she sat beside the head of Kiron's cot; since the familial resemblance between them was strong, he quickly assumed that this was her father. If so, well—from the gold collar and armbands, the fine linen tunic, the belt of gold plaques, and the gold circlet around his close-cropped hair, he was wealthy at the least.

The second man was robed much like the woman-Healer had been, and there wasn't much else to note about him, except that he had kind eyes. And the third—

Well, the third wore leather arm-bracers and a wide leather belt over his soft kilt, and carried a leather helmet that was enough like the ones that the Tian Jousters wore to make Kiron think that this must be an Altan Jouster. The first, in fact, that he had ever seen.

"Oh, good!" the girl said, seeing that his eyes were open. "He's awake! Kiron, son of Kiron?"

"That," Kiron croaked, finding his throat strangely raw, "would be me, yes."

The Jouster looked as if he wanted to speak, but the man dressed as a Healer held up a hand. "One at a time, please, and I believe Lord Ya-tiren has precedence?"

The man with his hand on the girl's shoulder coughed, and looked embarrassed. "I—ah—whatever we learn here, I wish to make it plain that for saving my daughter's life, this young man has the protection of my house. That's all."

The Jouster looked pained. "Lord Ya-tiren, you surely do not think—"

"A strange, bedraggled youngster appears out of nowhere with a dragon that acts like his puppy; he saves my daughter from a river horse, and all that we know of him is that his few possessions appear to be Tian?" Lord Ya-tiren replied pettishly. "And then *you* appear before he's even been brought to my house? Well, what is anyone to think? Except that I do not want *you* people hauling him off to be 'questioned' as if he was a spy or a—well, I don't know what. But he's surely no older than my son, and I doubt he's a spy. The last that I heard, the Tians were hardly so desperate that they needed to send boys northward to spy for them!"

Kiron decided that he liked Lord Ya-tiren; the man might not be altogether certain of who and what *he* was, but was willing to protect him from less delicate ways of finding out than simply asking—

"I am—I was—born Altan, and made a Tian serf and served as a dragon boy among the Jousters of Tia," Kiron interrupted, taking tiny breaths often, to keep his chest from moving too much. "I suppose you could say I stole Avatre from them, except that without me, she'd never have hatched at all. The rest is a long story." He eyed the strangers; the Healer looked resigned, Lord Ya-tiren interested, the girl fascinated, and the Jouster skeptical, but willing to be convinced. "If you want to hear it—"

The Healer sighed. "Send for the chairs you wanted, my lord. I can see that my patient will be allowed no rest until this 'long story' is told."

So Kiron told his carefully edited tale, beginning from the time that his father's land was taken—a little more judicious editing with *those* facts left them with no real idea how much, or how little, land had belonged to his family. Let them assume whatever they wished to, but if they assumed that the elder Kiron had been the holder of a large estate, well, it would do no harm to *his* cause. It was a cold fact that a man of wealth and noble blood would look with far more sympathy on someone of his own class than he would on someone far below him, but in a similar plight. Would Ari have been nearly so friendly to him, if Ari had been noble-born rather than common-born? While he would like to think "yes," experience taught him otherwise.

He spoke bitterly of his father's death, of the division of his family as a sop to the treaty agreements that meant that Tians could not own land they had taken outright without also "caring" for those to whom it had once belonged. He described his life as a serf under Khefti-the-Fat, and Lord Ya-tiren had the grace to wince more than once. He told of how Jouster Ari had plucked him from under Khefti's nose—

And then went on at length about Ari and Kashet.

"We know this Jouster, too well," said the Altan Jouster thoughtfully. "There were rumors that he had done something very different with his dragon—certainly the results he has are remarkable. Most said it was magic."

"Not magic," Kiron objected. "Just—wisdom, study, observation and a great deal of thought and care. And he made it clear that any man who was willing to do as he had done, and raise a dragon from the egg, would have the same result. Well, look!"

He pointed at Avatre, lying at her leisure, unbound, and calm as could be. "As he had done, I decided to do," he continued, and described how he had purloined the egg from the mating of two Jousting dragons, incubated and hatched it, and raised Avatre to First Flight.

And edited again, making it seem that his escape had been planned, making no further mention of Ari, nor of the Bedu, except to claim he had traded with isolated clans, once or twice, for water-rights or food. He had to pause frequently for rest, and to let the muscles of his chest relax again; he suspected there were cracked ribs under those bandages. The sun had just about set by the time he finished, and servants had come bearing torches and lamps to illuminate the entire courtyard.

The Jouster sucked on his lower lip, consideringly. "It is a fantastic tale," he said, judiciously. "And I would have said, fantasy tale, if this dragon's own behavior were not just as fantastic."

"She loves him, Lord Khumun," the girl said simply, the first time she had spoken since she'd announced that Kiron was awake. "She loves this boy Kiron as if he was her nestmate. When have you ever heard of a dragon who *loved* her rider?"

*And how does she know that?* Kiron thought, startled. For the girl had spoken with the authority of someone who really *knew* what Avatre felt.

"Never. And that alone settles it, I think," the Jouster said, and stood up. "Very well. My Lord, I leave this boy and his dragon in your care—though the Jousters will see that the dragon's ration is brought every day—until he is well enough for me to return and enroll him. After that, his disposition will be up to you."

Lord Ya-tiren bowed his head a little. "Thank you, Lord Khu-mun," he replied.

"No *tala!*" Kiron interrupted, a stab of concern matching that of the pain in his chest lancing through him, as he realized *why* the Jousters would be providing food for Avatre. They would assume that she needed the calming, taming effects of the *tala*, and that was the very last thing she needed! "Avatre is to have no *tala* on her food! Please!"

"No *tala.*" The Jouster looked from Kiron to Avatre, who was now watching them all calmly, and shook his head. "Very well. I cannot argue with results. No *tala.* Has she eaten since I arrived?"

The girl giggled. "She told me she was hungry while the Healer was with this boy, and I took care of it, Jouster. I unharnessed her and wiped as much mud and dirt off her as I could manage to reach. She tells me she will want a morning feed, but wishes to sleep now."

The Jouster shook his head again. "And she speaks to a Nestling-Priestess, as if she were a tame thing. No *tala,* then. I believe I can leave it all safely in your household, my Lord, and by your leave, I will report this to the House of Jousters and the Great Ones."

The Lord Ya-tiren nodded, and the man rose, and took himself out of the courtyard.

"And you, Healer?" Lord Ya-tiren asked.

"I am satisfied, my Lord," the Healer said, with a little smile. "This boy is stouter than I had judged. Call upon me if you wish, but I believe my services will not be needed anymore. If I, too, may go?"

The Lord Ya-Tiren nodded, and the Healer departed as well.

That left the girl and her father, who regarded Kiron benevolently. "Well, my young rescuer," the lord said. "Do you think you could manage to eat something? Or is that a foolish question?"

Kiron's stomach growled before he could answer, and the girl chuckled. Her father smiled.

"In that case, I will summon you a servant and a meal, and go about *my* duties. Aket-ten, I leave him in your hands. Do not overtire him, but I suspect that between you, there are several *kilons* of unanswered questions, and most of them are things that would not interest me. Goodnight, my children." And with that, Lord Ya-tiren rose and followed in the wake of the Jouster and the Healer, leaving Kiron alone with the girl, who still sat like a little miniature oracle on her three-legged stool.

She had changed from her short tunic of the swamp into a robe very like those of the priestesses he was familiar with, although there were some differences. There was no elaborate wig, for instance; she wore her own black hair cut short, like a helmet that framed her face and skimmed the nape of her neck. And the robe was not pleated tightly to her slim body; it hung loosely from her shoulders and was confined with a beaded belt. Around her neck was an enameled and beaded collar that depicted a flame with two wings, like the wings of the Haras-falcon.

"Um," Kiron said, feeling tongue-tied. Then the one thing he really wanted to know just burst out of him. "How can you know about Avatre?"

"What she's thinking, you mean?" the girl replied. "I'm a Nestling-Priestess; I have the Gifts. I mean, I *will* have the Gifts when I get older and more training and if they come to me, but I've always had the Gift of Silent Speech with animals. That's how they knew I was going to be a Winged One when I grew up."

He blinked. A Winged One? "You mean—you're going to be a sea witch?" he blurted, then blushed. "I mean, that's what they call—the Tians—"

She giggled again; she had a charming laugh, and he was relieved that she seemed to be the sort of girl who refused to take herself too seriously. "I know that, silly! I know that's what the Tians call us! But no, I'm not going to be one of the Magi, people

that have real magic. I'm going to be the kind that can see and
hear and know things that people without the Gifts can't. That's
what a Winged One is. The others aren't really priests and priestesses at all. Magi, we call them. They serve the Great Ones. We
serve the gods."

He digested that for a moment, trying to sort it all in terms of
the things that he was familiar with. He'd never heard of anyone
who could "speak" with animals, but that might not mean anything. He wasn't exactly conversant with the ways of priests.
"It's a good thing you can talk to Avatre. I mean, thank you for
trying, and getting her calm. She must have been really scared."

"She was, but she was fine as soon as I told her we were going
to take care of you," the girl said, with complete equanimity, as if
she "spoke" to dragons every day. Well, if she "spoke" to animals
all the time, perhaps that wasn't such a stretch! "Then she was
all right, but she wouldn't be parted from you, so that's why
you're in my courtyard instead of in a proper room. She's very
nice, a little like a hunting cat, and a little like a falcon, and I talk
to those all the time. Father likes to hunt, and he relies on me to
find out how his cats and birds are feeling." She looked up at the
sky, now dark, and filling with stars. "I hope it doesn't rain—"

That was the least of his concerns. "During *kamiseen?* Surely
not!"

She laughed. "Oh, of course not. You're right. So—you're
Kiron, and I'm Aket-ten. And you saved my life! That was terribly
brave and clever of you, and I hope you realize that I really am
awfully grateful, and so is my father, and we're terribly in your
debt." She flushed. "You really did, you know, even though I have
Silent Speech. I *can't* talk to beasts unless I touch them, and I
think that the river horse would have bitten me in two before I
could have made it calm down, so you really did save me." She
took a deep breath, her flush faded, and she sobered and bit her
lip. "Poor Larion-al. I wish you could have saved him, too."

He gulped, recalling that poor rower, engulfed and being shaken like a dog shook a rag. "So do I. What were you *doing* out there, anyway?"

Now, for the first time, she frowned. "We were sent to catch a special sort of fish for Magus Kephret. That is, *I* was sent, and my brother Orest wouldn't let me go alone. The Nestlings all take training together, you see, so the Winged Ones or the Magi that are teachers can give assignments to whomever they wish. He said that with my Gifts I should be able to know where the fish were, and get them to come to my spear. I tried to tell him that my Gift wasn't that strong yet, and anyway, I wasn't sure it could be used for something like that, but he said how could I know if I didn't try—" Now she paused, and seeing the odd expression on her face, Kiron got a strange feeling in the pit of his stomach.

*She has a bad feeling about that Magus, and about why he sent her, but she can't put a finger on what's wrong.*

"Anyway, Father went straight to the Teachers, the Teachers went to the Pedagogues who are in charge of all Nestling and Fledgling training, and *they've* said that there is to be no more sending of Nestlings out on dangerous errands like that again," she continued, her face clearing. "I mean, it wasn't as if it was time for my ordeals or anything, I'm not nearly old enough! So, anyway, that was why we were out in the swamp. And I didn't realize that our boat had gotten between a river horse and her calf until it was too late, and she was charging us."

He sighed as she gave him a long look. "I'm glad we were there when we were," he said sincerely, and just then, several servants arrived, burdened with food, and for a time, he and Aket-ten were too busy eating for many more questions.

He was absolutely ravenous, but there was still time between bites to have a look at his surroundings. As a courtyard, this was a singularly austere spot. There was no ornamental pool, such as the Jousters of Tia shared, and hardly any plantings, just a tree in each corner in a big stone box. He was beneath the branches of one of these trees, an orange tree, he thought. Avatre was in the barren middle of the courtyard, surrounded by charcoal braziers, which must have been keeping her warm enough or she would surely be complaining. The walls around the courtyard were white stone, and there was one door in the middle of each of the four walls, making it enough like Avatre's former pen that she probably felt perfectly secure here.

The meal was delicious; spiced lamb, hot and oozing juice, and chickpea paste with herbs in it, goat cheese pungent and tangy, sharp onions and some green stuff he wasn't at all familiar with that went well with all of it. It came with a flat round of something that Aket-ten used to scoop up the chickpea paste and wrap around the lamb and vegetables. He followed her example and found it was a sort of chewy bread. There were also dates in honey, and a much better date wine than he'd gotten from that overseer. The head of his bed could be propped up, as she showed him, even though it made him dizzy to sit up at first. It felt quite luxurious to be sitting, eating in bed, with servants to wait on him.

Aket-ten quite sensibly concentrated on eating rather than chattering, which was something of a relief. From what Kiron vaguely recalled of his sisters, they had spent a good half of the time at every meal gabbling like a flock of hens.

She didn't seem much like a typical girl. On the other hand, he didn't know a great deal about girls, other than the little that he remembered of his sisters. The fact was, the only females that Kiron had even seen much of once he'd been taken into Ari's service were the serfs, slaves, and servants in the compound's kitchen area. And most of those weren't *girls*, but women old enough to be his mother. He really didn't know what to expect from this one; Altan *and* noble *and* female. And he certainly didn't know what to say to her.

Fortunately, he was saved from having to make any attempt at conversation by the arrival of her brother.

"Father says our hero is awake!" called a cheerful voice from the darkened door nearest them, and the young man himself sauntered out into the courtyard a moment later. "And so you are! Did you leave me any dates, little oracle?"

"Yes, if you want them, unless Kiron needs them," Aket-ten said.

"No, no, they're too sweet for me," he replied—the truth, since he wasn't used to anything as sweet as a honeyed date after all that time in the desert.

"Hmm! Thank you! My brothers always gobble them up like locusts on a wheat field, and I never get my share!" Orest said with a grin, helping himself to a bit of flatbread and a sticky-sweet handful of dates before a servant could offer them. Orest looked like a lanky male version of his sister; they even wore their hair the same length, though he had a tunic like his father's instead of a gown, and his pectoral collar was of plain gold and turquoise beads without the winged flame.

"Brothers?" Kiron replied, a little surprised. "There are more of you?"

"Five more boys; Aket-ten is the youngest and the only girl. And the only Winged One." Orest made a face at her. "Well, if she *had* to be a girl, at least she's going to be doing something useful with herself and her time. Not one of those stupid creatures that spends all her time giggling with a claque of others like her."

Aket-ten sniffed disdainfully at him; this was apparently a joke of long standing between them. She tossed her head. "Whereas unless *you* stop skipping your lessons with your tutors, you aren't going to be of any use whatsoever!"

"Ought to be glad I skipped today, little oracle!" he retorted gaily, and turned to Kiron with a face full of avid curiosity. "So, just *how* did you get a dragon? I mean, you weren't exactly dressed like a noble or even a Tian Jouster, so how did you get a dragon like *her*? She's *wonderful!*"

Avatre muttered sleepily, as if in agreement with that sentiment.

"I stole an egg, and hatched her myself," he said, and found himself telling the whole story all over again. Not that he minded. There was nothing he would rather talk about than Avatre. This time, since the adults weren't around, Aket-ten asked several of her own questions, and it was perfectly obvious from them that she hadn't been in the least exaggerating her ability to communicate with animals. The things she asked proved to Kiron that, if she wasn't actually speaking in words as such, she was surely getting the general tenor of Avatre's thoughts.

And that could be very, very useful, he suddenly realized. In further training, he wouldn't have to teach Avatre what he wanted in tiny little increments. Oh, no—he could have Aket-ten or someone like her actually *tell* Avatre what he wanted!

"Look," he said, finally, after another of her questions. "I want to know something. If you can talk to the dragons, why aren't you Winged Ones helping with the training for the Altan Jousters? It seems as if your dragons are a lot more dangerous than the Tian ones, and if you could—"

"Because we don't have any tame dragons," Orest answered for her. "Ours are really, really wild, maybe wilder even than the Tian dragons, because we trap ours fully grown. Truth to tell, they're more than wild, they're dangerous, and some of them have been killers when they aren't drugged with *tala*. They're kept muzzled when they aren't eating."

He blinked at that. No wonder there were fewer of them than Tian dragons! He digested the ramifications of such a system, slowly. Fewer dragons; harder to manage. Less cooperative than the wildest of the Tian dragons. Which meant the Jouster had to spend more time controlling his mount and less time in fighting.

"The only time they can be handled is when they're full of *tala*," Aket-ten added. "And then, not only is it still very hard for anyone but their Jousters and dragon boys to get near them, their minds are too dull to talk to. I'd have to touch one, anyway, and everyone says that's too dangerous for me to try. I don't know anyone with the Gift of Silent Speech that can talk to an animal without being really near to it."

"Oh, she won't say it, but young and silly as she is, she's the one with the strongest Gift of Silent Speech they've seen in two generations," Orest chuckled, poking at his sister with his elbow.

"She's afraid it'll sound like boasting if she says it. They expect great things from her."

She wrinkled her nose. "They can *expect* all they like, but if the Gods don't put more Gifts in my hands, you'll probably find me explaining to the horses in the Great Ones' stables why they need to pull the chariots properly in battle."

"But if you're in training to be a priestess, why aren't you living at a temple?" Kiron asked, as another question occurred to him. What was she doing *here?* All the girls connected with the temples in Tia were kept carefully behind the temple walls at all times. And nobody would have sent one into a swamp after fish!

"Because I'm a *Nestling*," she replied patiently. "Oh, if I were from quite far away, or if my parents were poor, I'd live there. But Nestlings stay with their parents. That's why we're called Nestlings, you see? I won't move into the Temple of the Twins until I become a Fledgling."

"And I can't wait. I'll finally have the courtyard all to myself, and then I can have the servants build a ball court—" Orest began, a teasing look to his eyes that told Kiron that this was another joke of long standing between them.

And it relieved him to know that this was not "Aket-ten's courtyard," or at least, not hers solely.

"Don't you dare even think of it!" she scolded back, her face turning pink. "It's not just your courtyard, and I won't be spending all my time at the temple and when I'm at home, I want to be able to enjoy *our* courtyard without having to worry about being hit with a hard leather ball every time I cross it or listening to you and your friends playing your stupid games of court ball! Why, you might as well move a dragon in—"

Kiron had never actually seen an idea "dawn" on anyone before this moment, but it was clear from their faces, and the look they exchanged, that at that moment they had the exact same idea.

Orest spoke first. "Kiron, what would it take to hatch a dragon egg?"

He snorted. "First, you'd have to *get* one." But from the look on Orest's face, he knew that the young Altan lord had just had an epiphany. Orest had seen what Avatre was all about, and no matter what he said, Orest was not going to give up on his new dream of having a dragon just like her.

Before his own exhaustion made him beg them to leave him in peace long enough to sleep, he knew that Orest not only wanted to hatch and train a dragon like Avatre, he was willing, and proba- bly able, to do everything it was going to take in order to make it all happen. And despite all of his sister's scolding, the moment she realized what Orest meant, she was as eager for him to have a dragon as her brother was.

And he knew why.

Orest was the youngest son of Lord Ya-tiren, and the only one with no clear future ahead of him. The eldest son was the heir, of course, and spent all of his time at Lord Ya-tiren's side or with his overseer, learning all that he could about managing the estates. His next-oldest brother was well on the way to a sterling career as an architect and builder, working as the right-hand man of one of the most respected architects in Alta City. Although not a Winged One, the third brother was very much a mystic and was already a priest, and the fourth enrolled in training to be an army officer. Only Orest had had no clear idea of where his place was in the world.

Until now, that is.

His one pleasure, and his single talent, was in working with ani- mals of all sorts, though he did not have any discernable Gift. He was as good a falconer as anyone in his father's service, was trusted by both the Houndmaster and the Horsemaster to do anything he liked with any animal in the kennel or stable, and had been thinking seriously about getting a cheetah to train to hunt as well. Being a Jouster, *forcing* his will upon a half-drugged, wild dragon, had held no appeal for him at all. But working with a dragon like Avatre—

Looking at him, Kiron remembered only too clearly how he had lusted for a dragon like Kashet.

His last thought on falling into sleep, and his first thought on waking with the dawn, was that if the thing could be done, then he could, and would, help Orest to do it.

The young Altan Lord must have sat up half the night thinking about it, too, for as a servant arrived with the dawn, leading another with a cartload of meat for Avatre and a kilt and loinwrap (at last!) for Kiron, he heard stirring from Orest's side of the courtyard.

With the servant's help, and with much wincing, Kiron managed to get up and get properly clothed. The servants did not want to get anywhere near Avatre, and given what he now knew about Altan dragons, he didn't blame them. But Avatre was on her very best behavior, as if she understood that her continued presence here depended on good manners, and she ate her breakfast carefully, slowly, even daintily, looking up now and again at the nervous servants and trying out different looks and silly little noises until at last she startled a laugh out of them with what looked like a full-on, flirtatious wink. It probably wasn't anything of the sort, but that was what it looked like, and she repeated it until she got some sort of relaxation from them.

"I think she likes you," Kiron said, and the servants laughed nervously, as if they were still not quite sure if Avatre "liked" them because she wanted to eat them. Nevertheless, they began to relax a little more around her, and in the end they were no longer afraid when she was done to take the cart away, nor to turn their backs on her. So that was progress, and another step to making certain that Avatre would actually be welcome here for as long as they needed to stay.

But as soon as the servants were gone, Orest came popping out of his door, looking as if he had not slept well at all last night. "Kiron," he said without preamble, "I want to—"

"I'll help," Kiron said instantly. "However I can."

Orest stopped dead in mid-sentence. Obviously, he had been

working up to a speech all last night, which accounted for his current appearance, and to have it cut short was clearly a surprise. His jaw dropped, and he gave Kiron a goggle-eyed look that made Kiron want to laugh. "But you don't even know what I wanted to ask you!" he exclaimed.

Kiron shrugged—carefully—and smiled. "It's as plain to me as the sun rising. You want to try hatching out your own dragon and training it. I'll help, as long as your father agrees. I could see it in your face last night, and everything you said to me just made me more certain; you want an Avatre of your own the same way I wanted a Kashet of *my* own."

Orest sighed, looking immensely relieved that he wasn't going to have to talk Kiron into helping him. "You're right, of course. For a moment, I was afraid you were a Winged One yourself! Was I *that* obvious?"

"Like a fountain in the desert," Kiron laughed. "But what I want to know is, how do you propose to get yourself an egg?"

"I don't know yet," Orest admitted. "But I know who to ask."

"Well, the first person to *ask* is Lord Ya-tiren," Kiron admonished him. "I've had my fill of sneaking around, trying to hide a baby dragon, and that was when there were other babies around to help disguise that she was there! Besides, you need both your father's help, and possibly that of the Jousters themselves. No, you ask your father first if he's willing to let you try this project and become a Jouster. Then I'll help, if he says yes."

Orest stuck around then, to help him give Avatre a cursory grooming (the best he could do without proper sand and oil, and he wondered how hard Aket-ten had worked in order to get her as clean as she was), then harness her and help him onto her back. "I'm going to take her for—well, take her out like a dog," he said to Orest. "I'm fit enough to do that much, and she needs both the exercise and to keep from soiling your courtyard."

"Then take her to the waste ground just past the fruit trees that way," Orest said, pointing eastward. "It will be just a hop for her. I have to go to my tutor now, but I'll be back."

Avatre had been sorely puzzled by the lack of sand or a proper corner to use; she was glad enough to see the bit of waste ground, for the ashes and cinders that were dumped there were enough like sand for her to be content to use them. It was just a hop, but by the time Kiron returned, Orest was nowhere to be seen.

Somewhat to his shock, later that morning, Lord Ya-tiren himself appeared at the courtyard, just as he returned with Avatre after another short flight so that she would *not* leave her droppings on the pristine stone of the courtyard.

The Altan lord watched in fascination as Avatre backwinged to a soft and graceful landing, and Kiron slid off her back, wincing, but not without patting her affectionately. She turned and nuzzled his hair as he unharnessed her.

"My guest," called the Altan lord, a prudent distance from both of them, "My son tells me he wishes to emulate you, and hatch a dragon. Here. He tells me you can help him do so."

Kiron took a deep breath. "If an intact egg can be brought here, warm, he should be able to," he admitted. "And I have promised to help. But only if he got your permission first."

Now Lord Ya-tiren's expression was a curious mixture of emotions; wistful, as he looked at Avatre, resigned as he looked at Kiron.

*He would rather not see Orest becoming a Jouster—Jousting is dangerous, as dangerous as any other fighting. But he can understand why Orest wants to do this, and if he were younger, I bet he would do the same.*

"Well," he said at last, and his words were an uncanny echo of Kiron's own thoughts. "Though it means sending my youngest son into great danger once he is a Jouster, how can I deny him the chance to try what *I* would try were I younger?" He sighed. "All right," he continued, after a long pause. "You have it. You have my permission. And may the gods grant you success."

# FOUR

O F COURSE, it wasn't going to be as easy as all that. Putting a dream into action never was.

Complicating this was that it soon became apparent that Orest was not the only person in Alta City to want to raise a dragon from the egg. Furthermore, once Kiron's existence was made public, he and Avatre ranked as the curiosities of the moment, and it wasn't only Jousters who wished to see these curiosities for themselves.

In fact, beginning that afternoon, and all through the rest of the day until the evening meal, Lord Ya-tiren admitted a parade of guests who wished to see the tame dragon and the boy who rode her for themselves.

Avatre was on her best behavior, although she could not resist showing off, preening under all the attention. For most of her life, she had only had one person around; nevertheless, she was still young, and on the journey she had gotten used to seeing many who would come and look at her from a near distance when they had stopped with the Bedu clans. Now, however, there were others, who came much nearer (though none of them cared to touch her) and made admiring noises.

She loved it. Although Kiron couldn't give her a proper grooming, he, Orest and Aket-ten had given her a good wash (though at the expense of a fair amount of pain from his cracked ribs) and he had oiled the more sensitive skin with almond-oil from the kitchen. She glowed in the sunshine as if she'd been made of jewels, the ruby of her body shading into the topaz of her extremities, her gorgeous golden eyes more beautiful than anything made by a jeweler.

Some of the visitors were Altan Jousters, and although all of them were interested in the concept of raising a tame dragon, for the most part their interest faded quickly when they discovered how much work was involved in tending to a dragon like Avatre. As Ari had already discovered among the Tian Jousters, when the aristocratic Jousters of Alta learned that all of this work had to be undertaken by the man who wished to bond with the dragon, they were very much inclined to go back to their current ways.

For a very few, it was not the work that was involved, it was the fact that a man who was already fighting would have to spend so much time out of combat. "Two to three years before she'll be fit to fly combat!" snorted one, when Kiron told him Avatre's age. "We can't afford to have Jousters out for that long! The old way may be hard, but—no. Better to have as many trained men on the battlefield as we can. The old way works; imperfectly, but it works."

But the last visitor of the day, before Lord Ya-tiren let it gently be known that he was wearied of the stream of strangers and near-strangers trotting through his courtyard, was not just any Jouster. It was the same man who had first come to look at Kiron and his dragon, but this time, he came in an official capacity, and looking so splendid that at first Kiron did not realize it was the same man.

He came strolling—not striding—in, at Lord Ya-tiren's side. Kiron had not been in any condition to pay close attention to his visitors when he had first awakened, but that had been yesterday.

Today he felt a hundred times better, and there was no doubt in his mind that he had *better* pay attention to this man.

The visitor was a fine figure of a man, with a nose like the beak of an eagle, high cheekbones, deep-set eyes beneath a craggy brow, and he wore his own jet-black hair cut sensibly short to fit under his helmet. This set him in stark contrast to many of the other visitors, who wore theirs fashionably long and braided into a club if they did not sport wigs. By now, Kiron could recognize the Jousters' "uniform" of a soft, wrapped kilt, buskins to protect the shins, wide leather belt, and a leather chest harness; this man wore a completely different variation on that uniform today. His chest-harness was ornamented in bronze, and sported a medallion of a ram's head right where the straps crossed at his breastbone. He had bronze armor plates that could not possibly serve any practical function fastened to the harness over each shoulder, and bronze vambraces. His kilt had a band of embroidery about the bottom, and the leather helmet he carried was gilded and ornamented with bronze plaques that matched the one on his chest. It came to Kiron then that one of the subtle oddities that had been nagging at the back of his mind was that thus far, everyone he had met had been several shades paler than the Tians. He had been used to being the freak among the darker dragon boys. Now, neither his longer hair, nor his lighter skin marked him as different.

This then was the man he had to impress, and his stomach tightened with tension.

"Kiron, rider of Avatre," said Lord Ya-tiren as Kiron made a low bow to both of them. "I would like to make you formally known to Lord Khumun-thetus, Lord of the Jousters and responsible for their training and that of the dragons."

Lord Khumun-thetus was not paying any attention to Kiron. All his attention was on Avatre, who knew a true admirer when she saw one. Kiron's tension eased a little. If their welcome here rested on Avatre's shoulders, then there was very little to worry about.

"You know, she gets better on second viewing, when she's

rested, fed, and clean," said the Lord of the Altan Jousters. "I'd like to see her after a proper sand bath and oiling. And when she's full-grown, she'll be amazing. I don't suppose she'd let me touch her, would she, young Kiron?"

This was the first of the Jousters, the first of any of the visitors save Orest and Aket-ten who had asked to touch Avatre, and given how positively she was acting, Kiron saw no reason to forbid the contact. "I believe she will accept that, my Lord. The soft facial skin is particularly sensitive."

Khumun-thetus approached confidently, but with care, holding out his hand to Avatre, who stretched out her neck and sniffed it before permitting him to lay hands on her. From his demeanor, Kiron had no doubt that this man enjoyed working with animals and was good with them, and his next comment told the truth of that. "I was a cavalry officer before I became a Jouster," he said, to no one in particular. "Though I was not reluctant to give over my dragon when I was made Lord of the Jousters, if I had a dragon like *this*, there would have been a fight! What a wonderful creature this lady of yours is!" As she stretched out her neck so that he could reach the soft skin just under her jawline, he chuckled. "She's very like a horse in her enjoyment of being petted."

"More like a great hunting cat crossed with a falcon, my Lord," said Kiron diffidently. "She has much of the independent nature of both. I tended the adult dragon who was raised as she was. I found that Kashet was strong-willed and sometimes needed to be humored, and he was given to sly pranks, but on the whole he was as intelligent as a dog but without a dog's fawning nature."

"And she has the pleasure-loving nature of a great cat, too, I see." Again the Lord of the Jousters chuckled. "It is a great pity that so few of my men are willing to invest three years of their dignity and lives in order to attain an achievement of this sort. If I had a wing of just ten fighters—"

Kiron refrained from mentioning that the same was true among the Tian Jousters. But Khumun-thetus was not finished. "However, as I have made some inquiries among the young, I have found some few who find it no hardship to become the slaves of an egg and a dragonet. Your host's son is one among them, I am told."

"So he told me, my Lord," Kiron agreed, concealing his relief. Well, it appeared that they had been accepted, just as he had hoped, and with remarkably little interrogation.

"And among the young, who would not in any case be fit to fight for almost as long as three years, the loss of fighting time is of no moment." Now he turned his head to look straight at Kiron, although he did not stop scratching Avatre. "So tell me, Kiron, son of Kiron, what does one need to hatch a dragon's egg?"

Kiron could not help smiling in his relief. "First, my Lord," he pointed out, "you need the egg."

"Then come, sit, and tell me about the eggs," the Jouster invited. Kiron took a stool from beside his cot, and began.

Carefully, and in great detail, he described what kind of egg was needed—gathered and transported carefully from where it had been laid, so as not to addle it. Brought still warm, so as not to kill the incubating creature inside, or taken freshly laid so that incubation would not yet have begun. He described the hatching sands to the best of his ability, and how the egg was mostly buried in them, yet turned at least twice daily. "The heat is brought to the sands by magic in Tia," he added. "I am told that the heat is moved from places where things are wanted to be kept cold—storage rooms for meat, for instance, or the Royal Residences at midsummer—and moved to the sands. I did see the ceremony by which such a thing is done, but—" he shrugged. "I am no priest; I could not tell you anything except that it involves a great deal of chanting by numerous assistants, and four priests, and must be renewed periodically."

"Hmm," Khumun-thetus said speculatively. "Well, I expect the Great Ones will be able to persuade some of the Magi that such a task would be in their best interest. We *have* been using other means to heat the sands of our desert dragons, but it is clear that will not be hot enough to incubate the eggs. The Magi will complain that it is beneath them, of course, so I will have to approach the Great Ones when they are in a good mood."

Since there was no graceful answer to such a statement, Kiron wisely kept his mouth shut.

"So. And when the dragon hatches?" the Lord of the Jousters continued his careful and exacting questions. And when Kiron finally answered all the questions that he could, the lord seemed pleased.

"Not as difficult as I had thought," he began, and as Avatre delivered a reproachful look, he stopped scratching and began to pace. "I believe that I can find candidates for as many eggs as I can obtain. Which will be few! I must warn you that it will be difficult to collect these precious eggs of yours, but nevertheless, I believe I can get more than one. Can you train the candidates and the young dragonets if I do?"

"I can try, my Lord," Kiron replied, feeling stunned. *Me? A trainer? But—*

"I am hoping we can learn something as you train the tame dragons that we can use to help us make our captured dragons tamer," the Jouster continued, giving Kiron a penetrating look.

*So, he wants to know if I really do know what I'm talking about, and if I can give him something he can use* now. *I can't blame him. With the Tians building up the numbers of their Jousters, and the Altans already fewer, he needs help.*

"If you think it might be valuable, perhaps I can offer you some advice on the older dragons as well," he said, after a moment of hesitation. "Now, I do not know if this will make a difference with your current beasts, but any new ones that you trap—well, there was a trainer among the Tian Jousters, newly arrived, who had impressive success in treating newly caught dragons as if they were falcons."

"Falcons!" exclaimed Khumun-thetus. "That had never occurred to us! He kept them hooded, then?"

"Day and night, and fed them through the hood until they accepted the presence of men. Then he harnessed them, and flew them on a rope in one of the landing courtyards, giving them food rewards, until they accepted the harness, the weight, and the commands without complaint." He took a deep breath, then regretted it, as his chest muscles complained. "My Lord, there were a great many new dragons being trained in this way when we escaped. Almost all of the pens were full. Mind, the Tians trap only newly fledged dragons, not the adults, which they deem too dangerous—but the pens were almost all full. The Tian King has ordered that the numbers of Jousters be increased dramatically."

Khumun-thetus frowned. "That is ill hearing. In two or three years, then, we could see double the number of Tian Jousters?"

"Or more," Kiron replied. "But if you have men who train hawks and hounds and great cats—all of which this trainer had done—especially those who train hawks trapped as adults—you may have some success with adult-caught dragons."

"I must see what is to be done." Khumun-thetus' expression had darkened. "In the meantime, if I get you eggs, hatching pens, and boys, can you show them what to do?"

"Yes, my Lord, I can," Kiron replied confidently, knowing that none of this would happen any time soon.

"And in the meanwhile—" Khumun-thetus eyed him critically. "My Lord Ya-tiren, you extended the invitation for this boy to take lessons with your son's tutors. Until he is needed by the Jousters, and perhaps afterward, I should like to take advantage of that invitation. Well-born he may be, and a dragon rider already, but through no fault of his own he has been educated not at all, and if he is to take a place of authority over well-born boys, he must be able to match them."

"Surely," said Lord Ya-tiren, as Kiron forced an impassive expression on his face. Lessons? What sort of lessons? What on earth did the Lord of the Jousters think he needed to know?

He had not been here two days, and already someone else was taking charge of his life.

Whether he liked it or not.

* * *

"Oh, it won't be so bad," said Orest, when he appeared with servants at sundown, bearing Kiron's dinner. "You'll have to learn to read, of course, but Father's stopped *my* mathematica lessons now that I'm going to be a Jouster, so I expect the tutor will be let go. The rest of it is mostly listening to philosophers lecture. And answering questions afterward. And asking questions yourself. Actually, it's better to jump right in and start asking questions; philosophers are only too happy to hear themselves talking. If you can get them going again, you usually escape having to give any answers yourself altogether."

Well, that didn't sound so bad. *I wouldn't mind being able to read,* he thought to himself, with a wistful longing. *If I could read, I could properly recite the prayers for the dead.* His father had one shrine, now, but—well, it would not be bad to have another, here. As long as he didn't end up like the boys who learned to be priests or scribes, bent over a lap-desk all day, copying texts onto potsherds until he went mad. But no, that was stupid; they wanted him to train Jousters, not copy records or write letters.

"I like lessons," Aket-ten said, coming into the courtyard. Today, it appeared, she was trying to look more grown-up; she had on a slim-fitting yellow dress instead of a boyish tunic. For the first time, he wondered just how old she was. Eleven? Twelve?

"Well, that's only because you know you wouldn't be getting any lessons if you weren't a Nestling," Orest countered. "So just to keep getting them, you'd say you liked them even if you didn't."

"That's not true! And you know that Father said after the last report from your tutors that it didn't matter I was a girl, if I hadn't been a Nestling, he'd have given me the same tutors as you, and I probably would have done better than you because I *apply* myself, so there!" There was a fight brewing, and Kiron hastened to end it before it began.

"The Lord of the Jousters was here," he said, interrupting it. "He asked if I could teach others how to hatch and raise a dragonet, and then said that he'd get all of it organized. So I guess there's your answer, Orest. It isn't going to be just you, but at least you're not going to have to try and get an egg all by yourself."

"They might just let a couple of the fighting dragons mate," Orest observed, popping a little dainty that he had told Kiron was a stuffed grape-leaf into his mouth. Kiron had tried them himself; they were spicy, but good, full of chopped meat and bread crumbs. "That would be the easiest."

"No, it wouldn't," Aket-ten countered. "In fact, it would be stupid and dangerous! The easiest would be to tie out one of the female fighting dragons, and let a male come to her. That's how they trap the males already, anyway, they just don't let them mate."

"And just what do you know about it?" Orest asked heatedly.

"I *read*," she shot back. "I've been reading about dragons all day, in fact! Which *you* could have done, if you hadn't been spending all your time telling your friends what a great Jouster you're going to be, and how your egg is going to hatch out the biggest dragon there ever was!"

"Oh, you read all about it, did you?" Orest, his ears getting red. "And just who let a Nestling back into the restricted scrolls?"

"The librarian of the Temple of the Twins, of course," Aket-ten said primly. "The temple has just as many scrolls as the Great Library, and no Nestling is ever restricted from reading any of them. So there." She folded her arms over her chest and gave him a look of triumph. "I probably know more about dragons than anyone but a Jouster. I could probably be a Jouster if I wanted to."

"No, you couldn't," Orest said, with such a look of smug superiority on his face that his sister flushed. "They don't let girls be Jousters."

"I could go in disguise," she retorted, and looked hurt when both Orest and Kiron laughed at her. "Well, I could!"

"The Jousters train and bathe together when they aren't fighting," Orest said. "They wrestle naked and bathe naked. So how are you going to disguise what you don't have?"

"It's a stupid rule," she said, going from triumphant to sullen sulk all in a moment. "I could raise a dragon just as easily as you."

"No, you couldn't," Orest and Kiron said together. They exchanged a look, and Orest nodded.

"Dragonets eat lots and lots of raw meat," Kiron said. "Piles of it. And *hearts* and *livers* and *lungs*." Aket-ten was looking a little green at the thought, and he drove it home. "The dragonets need bone in with all of that, so you have to break up the bone so they can swallow it. And you would have to feed the baby this stuff by hand, yourself, or she won't bond with you. By the time I got done giving Avatre her first feedings, I was bloody up to the elbows, it was in my hair, under my nails—"

"All right!" she interrupted, looking as if she was going to be sick. But her brother hadn't had his say yet.

"And then, the bigger the dragon gets, the more it eats. *And* you have to clean up her messes, too, because you don't want anyone else in the pen until she's bonded to you! You don't even like to clean out the cat's sand pan, so how do you think you'd manage with a dragon?"

"*All right!*" she said forcefully, hot anger making her flush, her queasiness forgotten. "You've made your point! But I still *know* more about dragons than you," she added, glaring at her brother.

"*Girls,*" Orest muttered under his breath to Kiron. Kiron just nodded slightly. "She is just not going to give it up," Orest added, with a resentful glance at his sister.

Kiron nodded again. He remembered enough about his sisters to be on Orest's side this time. Girls just got onto a fellow and wouldn't let him alone if they got an advantage over him. He needed to distract Aket-ten, or she was just going to keep on baiting Orest.

"All right, then, since you've been reading all morning," Kiron said, deciding to pacify her and learn something at the same time.

"I know about the Tian dragons, tell me about the Altan ones. Where are they trapped?"

"*Well.*" Aket-ten bounced a little in her seat, once again looking very well pleased with herself. "You know that dragons need heat to hatch their eggs. We have two kinds of dragons, actually; we have some that use the hot sand in the desert, like yours do, and we have a smaller kind that makes a big mound of rotting plants the way the crocodiles do to bury their eggs in. Those are the swamp dragons. They're easier to trap, so they're the ones we have the most of, but we have some desert dragons too. In fact, we have a couple of Tian dragons that lost their riders and that we managed to catch. Both of those are female, and when the Jousters want a wild desert dragon, they take one of those two females and stake her out at the edge of the desert and wait for another one to find her. A female will come to fight her, a male will come to mate with her."

"So the smart thing *would* be to take both of those females out and let them mate," Kiron mused. "You wouldn't have the risk of losing a mating pair, and you might even be able to trap the male after the mating is over. What about taking swamp dragon eggs, though, from wild nests?"

"You'd have to drive off the mother somehow, and instead of sand, you'd have to come up with a place that was hot and damp to incubate the eggs," Orest said. "That wouldn't be hard, though; there are a lots and lots of hot springs around here, or you could use rotting reeds like the dragons do themselves. It's taking the eggs that would be difficult. Even if you took a lot of people, trying to drive a mother dragon off her eggs could get them killed. A trapped dragon is bad; a mother protecting a nest is ten times worse. The swamp dragons may be smaller, but they aren't *that* much smaller." He scratched his head in perplexity. "I don't know; maybe at night, when they're torpid?"

"Trying to do it at night would be worse," put in Aket-ten. "At night, both parents come and lay on the nest. They might be torpid, but there would be two of them. And it would be in the dark, too, when the river horses come out to feed, and the crocodiles, too. If the dragons didn't get you—" She shivered.

Kiron was just grateful that it wasn't his problem. "If I was going to choose, I'd stake out those females," he said. "The one mating I saw was in the sky, but I bet they don't always mate that way."

"Was that Avatre's parents?" Orest asked. "I know you told us that you'd taken an egg from one of the Jousting dragons. What happened?"

"Partly it was not enough *tala* in their food, and partly it was stupidity from the dragon boys and the Jousters both," he said with scorn. "Nobody bothered to notice that they were—" he glanced at Aket-ten and modified the rather coarse language he had been going to use. "—getting interested. Finally during a practice, everything just went bad at once. The Jousters were new and kept missing strokes, and finally when one connected, because the female chose that moment to turn the practice into a mating flight, the male's rider hit wrong. He knocked the female's rider out of his saddle, and another Jouster, Kashet's rider, caught him before he hit the ground and got killed. Meanwhile the female was flying free now, and the male's rider lost control and they went into a full mating flight. He couldn't get control of his dragon until the mating was over, and when the female tried to fly off to the hills, Kashet and his rider managed to herd her back."

That was a very dry version of the whole incident, that had been both tremendously exciting and terrifying at the same time. If he closed his eyes, he could still see the horrifying plunge of the injured Jouster out of his saddle, and the incredible dive that Kashet made to catch him, saving him from a certain death.

"I wouldn't have wanted to be the male's rider," Orest muttered, his eyes round.

"You wouldn't have wanted to be either of them," Kiron corrected. "The female's rider almost died anyway; would have, if there hadn't been a Healer there quick. And by the time it was over, *both* of them had their dragons taken away and given to other Jousters. They were sent back down to train all over again. The Overseer was very angry, and so was the General in charge of the Jousters."

"Glory!" Orest exclaimed, seriously impressed now. "But how did you get the egg?"

"Because after she was mated, she got aggressive and her dragon boy actually walked out rather than tend her." Once again, Kiron allowed his voice to drip with scorn. "I'll tell you the truth, he was an idiot. He was at fault and in trouble in the first place for letting her go without a full *tala* ration and for not noticing she'd come into season. Then he decided she was trying to kill him when all that was really wrong was that she was *hungry*. He got so hysterical over it that he had every other dragon boy in the compound standing around him by the time he walked out. The Overseer was so angry he swore he'd see to it that the boy never got an apprenticeship with *anyone*, but he'd made the others so frightened before he was done that nobody wanted to take her. So I said I would, as long as they took all my other duties off my hands, and it turned out that the fool had been short-feeding her all along; if he didn't feel like carrying as much food as she wanted, he just didn't, and let her go hungry. So she wasn't getting enough food *or* enough *tala*. As soon as she realized that I was going to haul enough food that she could eat until she popped if that was what she wanted, she stopped being aggressive, and the *tala* took care of the rest. I figured, so what if she got fat? She wasn't going to get a rider until she'd laid those eggs, and while they were waiting for that, they weren't going to get a new dragon boy for her either. Or, at least, not until I'd civilized her again. So I knew when she'd laid the eggs, and I stole the first one. There was an empty pen next to Kashet—they liked to keep dragons separated by empty pens before they started getting so many—so that was where I put the egg, and you know the rest."

"That was smart," Aket-ten said admiringly.

He shrugged. "I had a lot of time to think about what I would do if I got the chance."

"Well, we won't have to do all of that," Orest said with relief.

For the first time since he came here, he had a moment of resentment. "We won't have to do all of that" didn't even begin to cover all of the backbreaking work he had put into caring for the breeding dragon, Ari's Kashet, *and* Avatre. Orest was soft—and spoiled. A nice boy, who probably didn't know he was spoiled, but—spoiled. He had never been beaten, never gone hungry, never been worked so hard he staggered with fatigue. *You haven't got the first idea of what I went through,* he thought, as Orest and his sister argued about whether it would be better to have swamp dragons or desert dragons. He thought about the long process of getting Avatre's mother to accept him; about watching her anxiously for the first of the eggs to appear, then agonizing over whether it would be better to take the first-laid, or the last-laid. The night he stole the egg was still vivid in his mind: slipping into the pen in the darkness, trundling the egg in a barrow down the corridor and praying that no one would happen to come along just then, and that no hungry ghosts would choose that moment to appear.

And only then did the *real* worries begin, of hiding the egg from anyone who might glance into the pen, of keeping it safe from the strange storms that the Altan Magi had sent, of the ever-more difficult task of hiding and feeding the hatched dragonet. And, of course, of pulling double duty, tending not only to Kashet and Ari, but to Avatre on the sly. He hadn't had a sound night of sleep, frankly, until his first night with the Bedu clan.

No, no matter how hard Orest and his friends worked for their dragons, they would never match the effort that he had put in for Avatre.

"So how sore are you still?" Orest asked, breaking into his brooding.

"Sore enough," he admitted, though the fact was that getting around at the moment often hurt as badly as if he was being beaten by Khefti-the-Fat, and he found himself sleeping a lot. It was quite strange, actually; though he didn't actually remember it, all he could guess was that he had hit a great many obstacles in being pulled through the water, and had probably broken several ribs in the process. And perhaps he had dislocated his arms at the shoulder as well; the joints ached enough for it. The reeds had certainly lacerated his back; he'd seen the rags left of what he *had* been wearing. Fortunately, the Healer had made those cuts close over; evidently dealing with broken bones took longer.

It was equally fortunate that his body had protected Aket-ten, or she would have been as injured as he was. And he was glad he had an Altan-style cot rather than a Tian bed that would have required him to sleep on his back. He could lie on his stomach to sleep on the cot, which was the least uncomfortable of all of the possible positions.

*I don't believe I will try that sort of rescue again,* he thought. *Or at least, not quite in that way.*

Orest sighed. "I was hoping you might be able to start lessons tomorrow," he said mournfully. "I was supposed to have read some wretched scroll today, and I didn't, and if you were getting your first reading lesson, my tutor Arit-on-senes might forget I was supposed to have read it. Or maybe I'd get a chance to read it while you were getting the lesson."

"That's what you get for spending all day next to the round pool telling your friends what a great Jouster you're going to be," Aket-ten said smugly.

"Look!" Orest burst out, "Just how do *you* know what I did all day?"

"I have ways," Aket-ten replied, looking superior. "And don't try to deny it, because I *know*, and I even know who you were talking to, and when."

Orest crossed his arms over his chest. "All right, then," he said belligerently. "Prove it."

"Right after your reading lesson you met with Leto. After Leto, but before luncheon, you talked with Ka-afet and Pe-katis. Then your mathematica tutor caught you and dragged you off to lessons, and he must have passed you directly to your philosophy tutor because you didn't get back to the pool until after that, but then—"

"Stop!" Orest cried, and threw up his hands. "You really have use the Far-Watcher Gift yet, and I know you didn't bribe anyone who does—"

"Because I wouldn't!" Aket-ten said, scandalized. "That is a sacred Gift, and not to be used for things like sneaking a look at a bad brother!"

"So who told you?" he demanded, ignoring her outrage.

"No one. I have ways," was all she said, looking smug again.

But Kiron had an idea that the library that she had said she used all day probably stood right near this pool that Orest seemed to favor as a meeting place. Altan buildings were not all like the Tian ones with few windows, but with slits parallel to and up near the ceiling to allow cooler air inside—but he would bet that some of them were. Such slits were very good, under some conditions, for conducting sound inside a quiet room from the outside. A quiet room such as—inside a library, for instance.

But this time he was not going to help Orest out. He liked Orest a great deal, but he already had the impression that Orest was a bit of a shirker when it came to doing his work. If he thought that his sister had some special means of knowing where he went and who he talked to, and even what he said and did, he might get into the habit of being a little more diligent. Kiron did not intend to nursemaid Orest through the hatching and raising of his dragon, and he especially did not intend to "help" him by doing the tasks he had "forgotten" because he wanted to go socialize with his friends.

But he wasn't going to say that—at least, not yet—and he might never have to if Orest thought that his sister was able to tell what he'd been up to and was apt to tell tales to their father.

Orest frowned at her. She sniffed.

"I'm not going to tell on you this time," she warned, "But you'd better start being more serious if you expect to be a Jouster. The scrolls I read said that the Joust-Masters are allowed to beat shirkers, no matter how high-born they are. With staves," she added wickedly. "Like a slave."

"What?" Orest exclaimed, taken strongly aback.

"So if you don't start to act serious about your studies, you could find yourself with a set of stripes like a slave," she continued. She ate a last grape then, and stood up. "Good night, brother mine," she said. "Consider yourself warned. Good night, Kiron, I hope you're less sore in the morning. I think you'll quite enjoy reading when you've learned to." Then she turned to the dragon in her circle of braziers. "Good night, Avatre," she said, fondly.

The dragon open one eye, and sighed gustily. Aket-ten laughed, and padded across the courtyard to the door that must lead to her rooms.

Orest looked after her, baffled. "Where does she find out these things?" he asked no one in particular. Then he looked at Kiron, who shrugged.

"But if she's right about those Joust-Masters, she's also right about getting out of the habit of slipping away from lessons whenever you feel like it," he pointed out. "Look, I've been a serf, and I *know* what a real beating feels like. I'll show you my back at some point. Khefti-the-Fat left scars. It's not something you want to find out for yourself."

Orest groaned. "You're right, and I know you're right, but . . . well, a fellow likes to talk to his friends now and again."

"Maybe, but all day? Or most of it, anyway." Orest couldn't be much older than Kiron was, but somehow Kiron felt as if he was as old as Ari, and Orest was as young as that newly liberated serf taken from Khefti-the-Fat. Younger. He hadn't needed encouragement to do his duty once he wasn't being abused anymore. Orest was certainly spoiled, and it was time for him to start picking up his responsibilities.

"But there was you—and Avatre—and the dragon-egg idea—" Orest protested weakly. "Everyone wanted to hear about it!"

"And tomorrow, and tomorrow, and for a lot more tomorrows *I* am still going to be here, and so will Avatre, and so will the dragon egg idea." It was utterly ridiculous on the face of it, that he should be acting like a mentor and elder to one no older than he himself.

But Orest had gotten his own way quite enough—not enough to make him into an overindulged monster, but enough that he was too careless and carefree. And Kiron—

*I've lived through a hundred times more than he has. Maybe I'm right to feel old.*

"How would you feel if you 'forgot' to feed your dragonet because you were chatting with your friends, and she became ill with hunger?" he demanded. "Or worse, you weren't looking in on her, and something bad happened to her? She could tear a wing membrane and bleed to death, she could break a wing bone and cripple herself, she could even wander out of her pen and into the pen of one of the Jousting dragons and be killed and eaten!"

Orest hung his head. "I know," he mumbled. "I know you're right. It's just—a fellow likes to have friends."

"Well, if they can't adjust to you working harder, they aren't friends worth having," Kiron replied. "You don't want friends who'll encourage you to be a layabout if you want to raise a dragon and be a Jouster, Orest. You want friends who'll say, 'listen, why don't we get together after you've done what you need to do?' Those are the ones worth hanging onto."

Orest raised his head and smiled wanly. "You sound like one of my tutors. So why do I like you so much?"

"Maybe because *I* want you to have a dragon, and *I* want you to be a Jouster, at least as much as you do," Kiron replied warmly. "And maybe because I might be the right kind of friend?"

"That might be the answer. Good night, Kiron. If I'm going to be virtuous, I had better get my sleep so I can read that blasted scroll over breakfast." Orest stood up, and motioned to the servants to clear away the remains of dinner.

"Good night, Orest," he replied warmly. And once he was alone again, he got up and went to his cot, which today had been placed behind a woven grass screen for a bit more privacy, and beneath a canopy for shelter from weather. As he lay down on it, he wondered at the strength of his feelings for Orest—and yes, even Orest's rather overbearing little sister. He liked both of them a very great deal; liked them in a way that he had not felt for anyone except perhaps Ari. Was this what it felt like, to have a good friend? If so, well—it was a good feeling. And with Orest and Aket-ten, he didn't have to worry about much of a difference in age, the way he had with Ari.

And as for a difference in rank, well—maybe he hadn't been born into the noble class, but the Mouth of the Bedu had said that having a dragon conferred nobility, and what the Lord of the Jousters said seemed to confirm that, so there wasn't any real difference there either.

He still didn't own more than he could pack onto Avatre's back, but—

But possessions weren't everything. Look at all that Ari had owned, and how he had just given away the Gold of Honor as if it were nothing more than a lot of cheap clay amulets!

If only Ari could have come along. . . .

The regret was just as much of an ache as the pain in his shoulders, and just as real.

The latter would heal. Somehow he doubted that the former ever would.

# FIVE

OREST was as good as his word. He awoke—or rather, had his servant awaken him—as soon as the meat was delivered to Kiron to feed Avatre. By that time, of course, Kiron was already up and dressed in yesterday's tunic (for there was no point in putting on a new one that was only going to get blood on it) and Avatre was stretching her wings and making inquisitive noises in the direction of the barrow. Orest made a great deal of noise himself, groaning and grousing about it being so early, though by Kiron's standards, he'd been sleeping quite late of a morning, and Orest was positively lounging about.

The thing was, in Tia, it had been easy to tell when dawn was coming long before it actually arrived. The air changed, the bitter cold of desert night lost its edge. Here, there was no change of that sort; the night never got all that cold, and so it was the light, and not the change in temperature, that woke him. This place was softer than Tia, with softer air and softer beds.

The scents were softer, too, but heavier; they wafted in and clung. Perhaps that was because of the humidity. And there were more of them. He wondered why it didn't bother Avatre—but perhaps dragons had a different sort of sense of smell.

By the time Kiron was ready to bathe and change into a clean tunic and loinwrap, the servants had brought breakfast and a sleepy-eyed Orest was eating with one hand while he read his scroll with the other. Kiron hastened to get himself clean while the bread was still warm enough to be at its best, tender and not tough.

At least Tians and Altans both shared proper ideas about bathing. He'd sorely missed his twice-daily baths in the desert, and here, if he'd wanted to, he could have a bath five times a day.

"What's that about?" Kiron asked, joining him. The servant had even brought a table and stools. How strange to be waited on, rather than being the one doing the serving.

"It's sacred poetry," Orest said, making a face. "All about Teoth, the god of the scribes. Fifteen stanzas, if you please, on the glory of the god and on the superiority of those who master language and writing!"

"Maybe your tutor is trying to tell you something," Kiron suggested, slathering honey onto some bread and taking a bite.

"He's telling me that sacred poetry is a dead bore, that's what he's telling me," Orest complained, reaching for more grapes. "But at least he isn't making me memorize it. All I have to do is tell him in general what it's about." He sighed. "I hate memorizing."

"Maybe now that you're going to be a Jouster he'll assign you those scrolls your sister was reading yesterday about dragons, instead of the things you have been reading," Kiron pointed out. "Where is she, by the way?"

"Up and out before dawn, and hanged if I know how she can stand it," Orest replied. "The Nestlings don't *have* to attend Dawn Rites, but she does, and she's wretchedly perky about it, too." He glanced at the sun, then at a series of lines carved into the courtyard paving. It was only at that moment that Kiron realized they were the marks of a sundial that used the shadows of the courtyard walls to mark the time. The whole courtyard was one enormous sundial! No wonder the courtyard was bare! And no wonder Orest had his rooms here, if he required a reminder of the time that was so impossible to ignore. "Well, if you're done, we might as well go take our punishment. At least you'll be there to share it with me."

With a great deal less trepidation than his new friend, Kiron rose and left the servants to clean up after them.

*Servants!* he marveled, as they left. *What wonderful things servants are! No wonder everyone wants them!* Oh, he'd had people to bring him food and clean his table back at the Tian Jousters' Compound, but in everything else, *he* had been the servant. It was quite a different matter to be the one who was waited on.

He'd taken the precaution of having the servants bring a large kapok-stuffed leather ball, a couple of enormous leg bones, and one of the bells that were often used as wind chimes to leave with Avatre by way of toys. "I'll be back later, love," he called to her as he left; she gave no evidence that she was concerned by him leaving her alone, but then, she was used to being left alone by now. In fact, she seemed more interested in the leather ball than in his leaving. He hoped that she would play with it, and not rip it to bits.

They didn't have to go far. Orest's tutor Arit-on-senes was waiting for him in a large, airy room with good lighting from a southern-facing window that was just off the next courtyard. There were two small carpets in front of where he sat on a leather-padded stool, with a cushion on each little carpet, a lap-desk in front of it, and a jar of scrolls beside it. His appearance surprised Kiron; he wasn't Altan or Tian. His hair was yellow and curly, and his eyes were blue. He was astonishingly handsome, and far more athletic-looking than Kiron had expected a scholar to be. His good looks were only slightly marred by the sardonic smile he wore when he saw Orest entering first, and reluctantly.

He was also clean-shaven, and his hair was cut even shorter than a Jouster's. Kiron wondered if he was a slave—but if he was, he certainly didn't act like one. He acted like a lord, actually.

"Well, Orest," he drawled as they entered the room. Kiron

noted a faint accent there, different from his own. "I suppose I can count on the fact that you read your assigned scroll?"

He sounded as if he meant the opposite, that he could count on Orest *not* having read the scroll.

"It is fifteen stanzas in praise of Te-oth, the god of scribes and the bringer of writing to mankind," Orest replied, taking his seat on the cushion, and settling his desk on his lap. Kiron followed his example, a little awkwardly. "There are two initial stanzas about Te-oth specifically, several on how much a blessing writing and being able to write are, several more in praise of the profession of scribes and contrasting that profession with the misery of all others. I did notice that the author did not mention either Jouster or Councilor to the Great Ones as being inferior to the position of scribe, however."

"Ah, but a Jouster is a sort of soldier, and a Councilor to the Great Ones has had to learn the craft of the scribe, so they are implied," Arit retorted.

Orest shrugged. "The final two stanzas praise Te-oth for being the god who most *consistently* blesses mankind."

All during this recitation, the tutor's left eyebrow rose until it had climbed halfway up his forehead. "Well," he said, when Orest was finished. "I must admit I am pleasantly surprised. If this new diligence is as a result of your association with my new pupil, I am going to revise my initial negative expectations of his influence on you. And as a reward—" Here he bent down, removed the jar of scrolls that had been at Orest's side, and replaced it with a different one. "—here is literature you will find much more to your liking. Pick any of the three, you'll be reading all of them and more eventually. I want you to read and then copy each of them, and since you will be needing them in your new career, I suggest you be more careful than you usually are in your copying."

At that, Orest eagerly plucked a scroll out of the jar, unrolled it, and began scanning it. His face lit up. "Te-karna's Natural History of Swamp Dragons! Thank you, Master!"

"Don't thank me, thank your sister," said the tutor, "and the

Lord of Jousters. She's the one who suggested that you would probably be more attentive if you were to concentrate on this particular subject, *and* she is the one who ran over after Dawn Rites with these scrolls borrowed from the temple librarian. What is more, by this time she has already spoken to the Lord of the Jousters about getting the loan of more scrolls. I fully expect him to agree. I believe he will be charmed by her audacity, which is just as well, since he is a man whom *I* would not care to cross."

"Nor I," Kiron murmured, earning himself a glance of approval from the tutor.

Orest's face was a study in shock and chagrin. "I guess I owe her my thanks," he said slowly.

"*And* an apology," Kiron muttered, feeling as if Aket-ten was due more respect from her brother than he had seen. He had been very patronizing last night, even if she had been acting like a know-it-all, and this was how she had responded.

"You owe her more than that. You owe her the courtesy of being diligent from now on. Now, get to your work." The tutor made an impatient gesture. "And remember when it comes to your copying, if you mar the original—"

"—you have Father's permission to beat me," Orest said, with an air of having heard that before.

"No. I have the temple librarian's orders to beat you until you will have to stand to eat," the tutor said grimly. "She said, 'A boy's brains are in his buttocks; he learns better when beaten.' I suggest that it would prove wise to take extra care and not force me to prove that theorem."

Kiron was very glad that he'd had so much practice in keeping his feelings from showing, or he would probably have destroyed this new friendship by laughing at the expression on Orest's face until he was sick.

But now it was his turn, as Orest bent over the scroll and the tutor turned to him. "So, boy, what do you know?"

"Nothing, master," Kiron replied truthfully. "Or practically nothing. The little script I know is Tian."

"Ah, chicken scratches." The tutor dismissed Tian writing with an airy wave of his hand. "Just as well, then, you have nothing to unlearn. Well, here is your scroll, and here is a box of potsherds, and this is your pen. Take your scroll, and lay it out before you with the weights."

It was a very short scroll, and fit perfectly across the top of his lap-desk. The weights were handsome ones, carved pale-brown soapstone images of—such a coincidence—the god Te-oth, in his bird-headed human form, his long, curved ibis bill poking out from beneath his wig.

"That's right," the tutor said approvingly. "Now take your pen in your hand as you see Orest doing. Good. Dip it in the ink. Not so much that you will drip, not so little that you will make an unreadable scratch."

That was a little trickier; the reed pen had to be dipped several times before the tutor was happy.

"Now," he said, pointing to the first symbol on the scroll with a longer reed. "This is *aht.*"

Slowly, the tutor took Kiron through the signs and hieratic shapes for the sounds of words. There were a great many of them, but fortunately the signs were all things that were easy to recognize, pictures of things which began with the sound in question, and the hieratic shapes were each a kind of sketch of that picture. Slowly, and with infinite care, he copied the hieratic shapes onto his potsherds. Over and over and over. When he came to the end of the scroll, he was required to go back to the beginning and copy again, forming the sound in his mind as he did so, melding shape, picture, and sound in his head. When he ran out of potsherds, it came as no great surprise to him that the tutor had another box ready for him. Bits of broken pottery were the logical thing to use to practice on; there were always plenty of them, and they served much better than precious papyrus.

It was harder work than it sounded, and by the time the lesson was over, he had a much greater respect for scribes than he had ever had before. Such a lot of shapes! He was certain he would never get them all right. And somehow, he was going to learn how to put those shapes together into words, and words into meaning. . . . Well, if Orest could manage, so could he.

Now he understood why the work of scribes was so important. Words, written words, must be magic, it took so much effort to set them down correctly. And he wondered, did scribes define the world and keep it from spinning off into other shapes with their hedge of words?

He was absolutely so mind-weary by the time the tutor declared that they were finished that he felt as if he had just done a week's worth of work in a mere morning—

But there were, it seemed, to be a new set of lessons to replace the "mathematica" lessons that Orest had so despised.

As Orest carefully rolled up his scroll, and Kiron capped his pot of ink, the tutor addressed them both. "This will be something new for both of you, I think. You, Kiron, should have no difficulties, even injured as you are, but it is the opinion of the Lord of the Jousters that you, Orest, are in need of conditioning before you undertake to tame a dragon. Therefore, you are both to follow me, now, and I am to deliver you to the *kymnasi*."

Now Kiron had not the faintest idea what the tutor was talking about; this was an Altan word that he had never heard before. But Orest looked considerably happier at that moment, so Kiron assumed that whatever it meant, it was not going to involve more scrolls and pens.

The tutor marched them out of the room, through several of the house's public rooms, and straight out the door.

This was the first time that Kiron had been outside of Lord Ya-tiren's house, for the ash pit where he took Avatre was well inside the garden walls. This was certainly the first time he had seen Alta City except for fleeting glances as he guided Avatre in that tricky bit of a hop, and he had to stop dead in his tracks and just *look* for a moment.

Lord Ya-tiren's home was evidently in one of the outer rings of the city and stood, like its neighbors, on the top of a ridge. The ground sloped away toward the canal from this point. From here, Kiron got a good look at the area surrounding this—well, it was a minor palace, apparently. It stood among other fine homes; to the left was another palace like it, and to the right was a temple surrounded by a walled garden. He suspected that this was the temple to which Aket-ten was attached as a Nestling. These structures all stood along one side of a spacious avenue wide enough for several chariots to pass side by side. Beyond the avenue was one of the seven canals that ringed the city, and on the other side of the canal were more buildings, which seemed to be a bit smaller and crowded more closely together than those on this side of the canal. But beyond that, in the distance, was the heart and core of the city, a hill upon which the Palace of the Great Ones stood, as well as the Great Temple of Khum the Light-Bringer, and several other important buildings and temples. Built of alabaster and limestone, they shone in the sunlight as if they were gilded. And Kiron suddenly understood in that moment that no matter how big Mefis had been, Alta City was ten, a hundred times larger.

"Come along," the tutor said, a little impatiently, but not without a look of understanding. Kiron followed down the stairs of the villa to the avenue, feeling dwarfed and altogether insignificant in the throng of humanity swirling around him. The thick walls of the villa had kept out the noises of the traffic, and the hum of hundreds and thousands of voices, but now it all surrounded him, and he for just a moment he found it a little hard to breathe.

But it appeared that this segment of the ring was a little city unto itself, for once they got past the next-door villa, there were markets, with shops and craftsmen. So everything that might be needed was here, within reach. And from the way people were acting, they were anything but strangers to one another.

*All right, then,* he told himself. *This is just like a* lot *of villages all running into one another. It's not just a giant hive.* And some people recognized either the tutor or Orest as they passed, and smiled, or nodded a greeting.

Still, there were a lot of people. It looked as if, where the population of Tia was strung out along the Great Mother River, the population of Alta was mostly concentrated here. He was going to have to think about that, and what it might mean.

Meanwhile, they continued their brisk walk down the avenue, with the occasional cart or chariot passing by, and plenty of people being taken here and there in covered or even enclosed litters. There were a hundred scents in the air, and few of them were unpleasant; the ever-present scent of water, of course, and various cooking odors, and hot stone, and fires, and the scents of flowers that Kiron couldn't identify. Most people seemed to be wearing perfume as well. There were differences from Tia, but truth to tell, Kiron would have said that there were more similarities than differences. The accent and some of the words differed, of course, enough that he had to *think* to understand people, though Altan was the tongue of his childhood, and he was falling back into the accent far faster than he would have thought.

They passed a cook shop, with a beer shop beside it; there were a couple of men arguing heatedly over something, while several bystanders listened as if their debate was some sort of entertainment. The tutor turned into what appeared to be another temple building, and they followed.

It turned out to be something quite different. There was a sort of entrance hall that they passed straight through; on the other side of that hall was an enormous courtyard, open to the sky, with a pool in the middle of it. Except for the pool, it looked like one of the Jousters' landing courtyards, but this one was covered in turf, and there were young men engaged in all manner of sports spread out all over it, and more were swimming back and forth through the water.

Orest looked positively eager as the tutor summoned a white-kilted servant and requested the presence of At-alon. The servant hurried off, and came back with a middle-aged man who was as thoroughly Altan as the tutor was not; black-haired and dark-eyed, with a jutting chin, stocky and incredibly muscular.

"Ya-tiren's boys, eh?" he said, and looked them up and down. "Thank you, Master Arit. I expect they'll be able to find their way here from now on, when you're done with them for the day."

"I expect they will," the tutor said dryly. "I'll leave them here with you, then. Lord Ya-tiren expects them back in time for the noon meal."

With that, the tutor left them; Kiron shifted his weight from foot to foot, wondering what was to come next.

"You," the trainer said, pointing at Kiron, "are going to go do *very light* work until those ribs heal. I'll have you myself. But *you*," he continued, looking at Orest, "need all-around conditioning. See those boys over there?" he pointed to a group of boys of mixed ages, stretching and bending nearby, at the direction of another white-kilted man. "You go join them. They'll be your work group until I say differently, or the Lord of the Jousters has orders. Hop!"

Orest hopped, without a single word of question or complaint, running off to join the group. He stopped only long enough to explain his presence to the man in charge, then took his place among the other boys. At-alon beckoned, and Kiron followed; they went around the outside of the huge courtyard until At-alon entered one of the doorways into it.

"Now don't be alarmed; I'm not the sort that's looking for a pretty boy," the trainer said gruffly. "But I have to find out just where you're hurt, and how, which means that I'll be feeling you all over and pulling on you a bit to see what's wrong. Hold your arms up, stand still, and if you feel pain—that's *pain*, not general aches—say so."

So Kiron was felt and poked and prodded, and it was soon ascertained that the *pain* was in his shoulders (still) and the rib cage at his back and left side.

"Good enough," said At-alon. "Dislocated shoulders that are healing, and cracked ribs that are setting. Healers did a good job on your cuts, from the look of it. You've got fine muscle, boy, you're going to need it, and we don't want you to lose it while you heal up. So, since there's nothing wrong with your legs, let's see you do running rounds of the court until I say stop. Begin at a walk, and when you feel warmed up, increase speed to a run."

Kiron obeyed, although it felt very, very strange to be running without having a place to be running to, and a duty at the end of the run. Still, in theory at least, he understood what At-alon was doing; since he wasn't undergoing the strenuous work of a dragon-boy anymore, he knew that he'd better be getting some form of exercise or he'd lose all of the muscle he'd put on. So he ran.

He wasn't the only runner; there were several boys and men doing the same thing. Some were faster than he, some slower; after a while, he began to feel a sort of pleasure in the exercise. The soft turf kept his ribs from jarring too much, and though he couldn't run as freely or as fast as he used to because of the pain, it was still good to stretch the muscles of his legs. He could even feel them loosening as he ran.

Finally, the instructor beckoned to him to come into the center area where he was waiting. And then he did some strange arm movements with bags of sand in his hands; he supposed that they must be strengthening exercises, though for someone used to flinging big chunks of meat about and wheeling heavy barrows, they seemed a bit—feeble. After those, he did some bending and stretching, though not too much of those, because it put pressure on his rib cage. Then—carefully—some different things with bags of sand in his hands, only this time, when it began to hurt, he was to stop.

Orest was doing pretty much the same sort of things, only not as long, and not as hard, and he was getting tired much faster than Kiron was. It gave Kiron a feeling of wry satisfaction; at least here he was better than Orest at something. Or he would be until Orest toughened up.

Finally, they were sent to the baths, where they were bathed by yet more servants, massaged with oil with a crisp scent to it, and in Kiron's case, rebandaged. Their tunics were taken away and brought back freshly cleaned. Then they were sent home, and it was time for the noon meal and a much-needed rest, for Altans, like Tians, took a rest, or even a nap, after the noon meal at the heat of the day. And today, Kiron was very happy to have that privilege that he never enjoyed as a dragon boy except during the rainy season.

They took their noon meal with the rest of the household; Lord Ya-tiren and those of his older sons who were still living at home. Orest came in for a great deal of teasing but some serious congratulation that he had been—tentatively at least—accepted as this new sort of Jouster in training. Kiron kept very quiet, and simply observed, though he caught Lord Ya-tiren watching him with approval now and again. Evidently Orest's father felt that he, Kiron, was a good influence! Aket-ten was also much in evidence, reporting with triumph that the Lord of the Jousters had promised to lend copies of every scroll of Jousting training and dragon lore that the Jousters possessed. Kiron sighed. This was a little like hearing that the cooks were preparing a feast of every favorite food one had, at a time when toothache kept one from eating any of it!

He resolved to put more effort into learning to read.

Finally, with stomach full and the strong palm wine the lord favored at his table making Kiron a bit drowsy, he returned to the courtyard where Avatre was to discover that someone had cleverly set up a box of sand where she could deposit her leavings.

And before he could clean it out, a servant appeared.

*Are they hovering just out of sight?* he wondered, startled, *Or are they able to know what I'm thinking?* Either way, it made him uneasy; Orest might take such things for granted, but he wasn't used to having people appear out of nowhere to take a task out of his hands before he started it.

"It is by the direction of the Order of Magi, my Lord, that the dragon's—droppings—be taken to them, as the Jousting dragons' are," said the servant, with great politeness, relieving him of the shovel he had picked up. "That is my assignment, and your dragon seems not to mind."

"Oh, she's safe enough," Kiron said blankly. "But I thought that—well, she looks dangerous, and your Jousting dragons *are* dangerous, so I thought—"

"That we would be afraid?" the servant replied, and smiled. "No, my Lord. The Lady Aket-ten told us that we need not fear the little dragon. This is all the assurance we need."

"Well—ah—thank you, then," Kiron replied, and once the servant and his burden were gone, after giving Avatre a great deal of attention and scratching, he went to lie down on his cot in the shade.

His dreams were full of hieroglyphs and hieratic script at first, but then the sign for *"wah,"* which was a pair of wings, swept under him and carried him off, and the wings turned into Avatre.

And then his dreams were full of flying.

The afternoon was given over, as Orest had said, to listening to philosophers and historians teach. Except that Avatre needed *some* flying exercise (though not nearly as much as a fully grown Jousting dragon did). And since Orest was going to have to learn this anyway, Kiron decided to help his friend out by recruiting him to learn how to put the harness on a dragon, using Avatre, who would by far be the easiest he would ever handle until his own dragon got used to the weight and feel of it. The philosophers and historians would still be there when Avatre had been exercised.

"Later I'll let you fly her, too, if she'll take you," he said, "But not until I'm healed, and she's stronger, and not until I'm sure, really *sure,* that she'll always obey me if I'm on the ground."

Orest looked disappointed, but he didn't voice it, which Kiron thought was very much to his credit.

Avatre was practically quivering with excitement, and the need to get into the sky. Kiron had to use a stool to get onto her back; his ribs hurt him too much when he tried to climb up the usual way, even with her lying down.

Finally he gave her the signal she was longing for, and she leaped up like an arrow from a fully pulled bow. And she jarred him so that he sucked in his breath in a hiss to keep from yelping and startling her. This wasn't going to be easy. . . .

And, in fact, until she reached the height that pleased her and found a thermal to soar with, it was damnably painful.

But once she spread her wings to the warm, rising air and stopped jouncing him, and he was able to look down—he found himself thinking that the view was worth some pain.

The hot wind of the *kamiseen* held them aloft; up here it tasted of the arid desert, a little. Avatre stretched her wings and her neck and he could swear that he saw her smiling. From here he could see the innermost two canals of the seven that ringed Alta City, and a good part of the third. And from here, it was quite clear how the city had grown. The first canal must have been dug around a relatively high spot in the delta marshlands, and everything that was dug up had been deposited in the center, building up what eventually became the hill upon which the Great Ones' Palace and all the important temples stood, as well as the minor palaces of all of the most important nobles of Alta. Probably everyone in Alta City had once lived there, but eventually, as the city grew, and those of rank and wealth wished more and more land, the common folk were pushed across the canal to the other side.

Where they promptly built themselves another circular canal to protect themselves, depositing what they dug out on the land they intended to occupy, exactly as the Altan farmers were doing out in the marshlands even now. So this second ring of houses, markets, and craftsmen also had its own hill, or rather, ridge, not as tall as the Royal Hill, but certainly enough to give those who lived on top of it a slightly more panoramic view than those who did not.

Then, as the nobles and wealthy grew more numerous, and there began to be divisions of rank even among the notable, the lesser nobility found *themselves* being pushed off the Royal Hill. They certainly would not have chosen to live among the commoners of the First Ring, and the commoners had no intentions of surrendering what they had a second time, so—a third canal was dug, forming the Second Ring, where those who could not claim divine blood in their veins settled. And again, this ring had a raised ridge of its own running down the center of the ring, which was where Lord Ya-tiren's villa stood, as well as the temples that could not compete for status on Royal Hill.

By this time, of course, Kiron could guess the next part of the tale. With nobility now living in the outermost ring, there would be a call for protection—

He peered in the direction of the Third Canal; although the air was much hazier here than in Tia, he thought he saw a dragon in the distance. He gave Avatre the signal to send her in that direction—which was, in any case, a safer one than allowing her to head in the one she wanted, which was to try the thermals and updrafts of Royal Hill. He had an idea that overflying the Palace of the Great Ones might get him in a spot of trouble.

How she read the air, he could not guess, but she seemed to be able to see thermals somehow. She spiraled up the one she was in, then began a long glide down over the Third Canal, and caught another on the opposite side. And just as Kiron had guessed, down below were the barracks of the army, the shops and cook shops and drink shops that catered to them, the homes of those who ran and served in those shops, and the whole support structure of armories and stables, forges and supply warehouses, Healers and training grounds and practice fields that an army needed.

And here, too, were the temples of those gods that loved soldiers, and that soldiers loved, and the pens of animals waiting to be sacrificed.

And, as he had expected, the Jousters' Compound.

It looked very like its Tian counterpart, with some differences. Three fourths of the pens had hot water wallows, not sand pits. And in those pens that had wallows, the dragons were a little smaller than those he was used to, their colors darker. They looked up as soon as they spotted him, of course, their heads weaving back and forth on their long necks. The familiar sounds of slightly irritated dragons drifted up to him from below.

Well, he didn't want to make any trouble for anyone, especially not the dragon boys who might have to calm their charges if they got any more restless, so he angled Avatre away, curious though she was to look at these odd and unfamiliar relatives.

The Third Ring did not have a hill; whether this was by accident or chance, Kiron could not tell. It might merely have been that the Third Ring covered so much area that the ground that had been dug to make the Fourth Canal was barely enough to raise it all above flood level. Then again, since the Third Ring was devoted entirely to Alta's military, it could be that no one had felt the need to be physically higher than anyone else.

Beyond the Fourth Canal it was quite clear that the land had been given over to farming, and Kiron had no real interest in seeing what lay there. He knew that three more canals lay beyond the Fourth, probably settled as farmers prospered and their sons desired farms of their own, and continued what had now become habit and custom, of building up farmland by digging out a canal that was as much for drainage as for protection. The canals were all linked by subchannels that cut across the rings like the spokes of a wheel; more spokes were formed by the bridges that linked the roads of the Rings. It was unexpectedly beautiful, and when he thought about all of the labor that had gone into creating the city, his head just swam.

Other than the dragons of the Jousters' Compound, no one looked up when the shadow of a flying dragon passed over them. Avatre soared from thermal to thermal above the Third Ring to her heart's content. There were boats out in the canals; little fishing boats, larger barges. Some were hauling cargo from the outer to the inner rings; some were clearly pleasure boats, or the boats carrying officials about on their duties. As he watched, he even saw a species of small boat that seemed to be coming in to land whenever someone on shore hailed it. After a moment, it came to him that these boats must be for hire, to take people wherever in the Rings they wished to go, like hired litters or chariots. That would be much faster than walking, though he doubted that it would be faster than driving a chariot.

The sound of a gong below him startled him, and he looked straight down to discover that he was directly above one of the temples, where a ritual was just beginning, the gong being the signal for the worshipers to gather. And that reminded him that he had an appointment of his own to keep; more lessons. He sent Avatre angling back the way she had come, crossed the Third Canal, and soon spotted Lord Ya-tiren's manor, with Orest watching anxiously down in one of the minor courtyards. A servant was just arriving with a barrowload of meat, and seeing that, Avatre was not at all loath to land.

Nor, truth to tell, was Kiron; flying required a great deal of the rider, as he shifted his weight and balance to help his dragon. Between that exertion and the exercises of the morning, he was sore.

On the whole, he was going to welcome these lessons, if it meant he might sit at his leisure and merely listen.

Orest hurried to help him take off Avatre's harness; all of her attention was on that barrow, and when Kiron wheeled it close enough to her that she could reach it, she dove in. He knew that when she was sated, she would want to sleep, so she would not miss him for the rest of the afternoon.

"I was beginning to wonder if you'd decided to fly off again, after seeing all the lessons you were going to have to do," Orest said, only half teasing, as they made their way out of the manor again, this time going toward the temple next door.

"Why, because you would have?" Kiron teased.

Orest made a face. "Well, yes, actually. We're going to the temple where my sister is a Nestling; they hold lectures on philosophy and history in the courtyards there. Which do you want first?"

Kiron shrugged as much as he could without further jarring his rib cage. "It's all one to me; you pick."

Orest sighed. "History, then. Philosophers go on *forever* unless it's close to dinnertime."

Kiron laughed, and followed his friend in through the gates of the temple, which featured a pair of rainbow-colored wings supporting a slender golden flame. Despite Orest's glum face, he had a notion that this was going to be interesting. He was beginning to have the impression that Orest was not, and never would be interested in anything that required exercise of his mind, but Kiron felt rather like a sponge that had been dry all of its life and had suddenly been put into water. Let Orest sigh and look gloomy; *he* was going to enjoy all this "tutoring."

# SIX

**K**IRON remained as still as a hungry crocodile lying in wait, as Lord Khumun-thetus surveyed the group of youngsters before him in the antechamber to the Jousters' Compound. He did not yet want to draw attention to himself. Soon enough, these boys, some of whom were actually older than he, would discover that *he*, Kiron-son-of-unknown-Kiron, was to be, in essence, their trainer, their Overseer, and ultimately, the one who would pass judgment on their ability to raise a dragonet. Or not. That was going to cause some resentment, he feared, but it couldn't be helped. In all of Alta City there was only one person who knew how to raise a dragon from the egg, and that person was not going to entrust a precious dragonet to careless hands.

It was a mixed lot, drawn from every possible class. There were several boys who had been animal handlers—Kiron had high hopes for the one who had been tending to lions and cheetahs, and the one who had been taking care of some high-ranking noble's hawks. There were, of course, quite a few nobly born youngsters, of whom one was Orest.

And there was a prince.

Or at least, Toreth-aket was a prince as Kiron understood the term. Toreth and his brother had been frequent visitors to Orest, for Toreth had been Orest's friend long before Ya-tiren's son had the lodestone of a dragon in his courtyard. Kiron had been astonished when he learned just who and what Orest's friend was.

Here in Alta, succession to rule was not in a direct line, nor was it even matrilineal as it was in Tia, where the man who married the firstborn daughter of the Great King was the man who succeeded to the throne. There were *several* royal families or clans here, and the thrones went to the two sets of married twins in the Royal Houses who were oldest when the thrones became vacant.

Toreth-aket and his brother Kaleth-aket were currently the oldest set of male twins within the Royal Houses, and they had been betrothed in their cradles to the oldest pair of female twins (who were actually three years older than they were). When one of the current set of Great Ones died or became incapacitated, it would mean that the rest of the group would have to step down. When that happened, Toreth and Kaleth, if not already married, would be wedded and crowned all on the same day, and take over the ruling of Alta.

Now, it might seem that Toreth would have been forbidden to take his place among the Jousters on that account alone, but if Kiron understood things correctly, the Altans had very specific requirements for their princes. One of the male twins was always to be a scribe or a priest, while the other was always to take some sort of military training. Becoming a Jouster counted, evidently.

If Kiron had not known that the two were twins, he would never have guessed it. He would have known that they were brothers, of course, for there was that much familial resemblance there, but otherwise they were nothing alike. Both had eyes of the same deep brown, and thin, angular faces, and both wore their own hair and wore it long, past their shoulders, braided with hundreds of tiny braids.

For anyone other than scion of a royal family or a merchant of dazzling wealth, this little quirk would have been impossible. Such a labor-intensive hairstyle required several body servants and was a sign that the wearer was of higher status than even someone who could afford the finest of wigs. The wig always remained perfect; one's own hair needed unbraiding and rebraiding all the time.

So both had the "royal" hairstyle. But there the resemblance ended. Toreth was strong, tall, supremely athletic, and able to make lightning judgments. Kaleth was shorter than his twin, did not give a toss for games but was a brilliant scholar, who already read and spoke five languages fluently, and would ponder every question for hours before making a decision. Both were good-natured and hard-working, and generous to a fault. If Kiron had been asked to choose the people he would most trust, next to Aket-ten and Orest, it would have been Toreth and Kaleth.

Nevertheless, Toreth might face failure here for the first time in his life, for he would have to impress Lord Khumun of his sincerity. Might—though truth to tell, Kiron didn't think it likely that Toreth would fail.

"You are here today," said Lord Khumun, "because all of you want to be Jousters. I suspect that eventually all of you *will* become Jousters, but this is a group who will become a very particular set of Jousters—you will be beginning your training years earlier than any other Altan ever has, and you will be raising your own dragons, literally from the egg."

There were nods all around, and some sighs. Of course, all the boys here knew this; it was why they had petitioned, begged, pleaded—some of them—to be allowed to join this group. But other than Orest and the two animal handlers, Kiron didn't think any of them had any notion how much work was going to be involved.

"This means," Lord Khumun continued, "that you will be doing things that no Jouster of Alta has ever had to do before. And I do not," he went on, raising an eyebrow at one particularly enthusiastic-looking lad, "mean what you *think* I mean. No. What I mean, just to begin with, is that you who win the way to a dragon egg, will, at least in the first year, be doing all of the work that a dragon boy normally would perform and doing it by yourselves. This means feeding, tending, cleaning out the pen, exercising, grooming, training. All of it. While a dragon boy or other servant will be assigned to you to bring the dragonet's food to you and tend to your quarters, *you* will be doing all of the work in the pen. There will be no exceptions, unless you are so ill or injured that you cannot move from your bed."

From the look of shock on one or two faces, Kiron knew that this revelation had come as a complete, and entirely unpleasant, surprise.

"I have it on the authority of the second of only two men ever to accomplish this feat that this sort of thing is an absolute require-ment to achieve the goal we want, which is a tame and bonded dragon," Lord Khumun went on, "And from my own studies of animals, I am in complete agreement with him. So, if there are any of you for whom this requirement is too distasteful to con-template, please, feel free to take your leave of us." He paused, and looked straight at those who had been looking the most shocked or unhappy. "You will not be considered a failure in any sense. We will need true volunteers for this, young men who will find it no burden, will even find some pleasure in taking care of their charge's every need. Dragons are immensely sensitive crea-tures and they will know and react to unhappiness on the part of their riders—especially since this group will be handled completely without the use of *tala*. So if you have misgivings, please take yourself from the group. There will continue to be wild dragons trapped, and we will continue to train and recruit Jousters of the old sort for some time. And this will not be the first wing formed from tame dragons, so if you decide you want to try, say, next year, there will be another wing recruited. Just because you elect not to join this wing means only that you will have to wait until you are older before you can volunteer to train with the traditional

Jousters, and if you change your minds, there will be other chances with tame dragons in the future."

There was a shuffling of feet, and then, almost as if they had read one another's minds and found reinforcement in numbers, a group of five separated from the main group. Lord Khumun gave them a perfectly friendly little nod, and heartened by this, they filed out of the room.

"Now, as for the rest of you, for those of you who do not know this young man, this is Jouster Kiron, rider of Avatre, who will be supervising you, guiding you, and training you." Now Lord Khumun gestured to Kiron, who came forward from where he had been standing off to one side. He was wearing the Altan Jouster's "uniform" now: the soft, wrapped kilt that covered a hardened leather, groin-protecting loin cup such as the ones that bull dancers wore; the leather harness with hardened-leather shoulder and bicep armor; the wide stiff leather belt; the hardened shin guards. His hair had been cut at chin-length, and he carried his helmet, hoping that he did not look as young as he felt.

"Kiron, rider of Avatre, only the second bonded and tame dragon in all the world, will now describe to you exactly what your duties will be—in detail—for the next year or so. And once again, any of you who believe this to be beneath their dignity, please, remove yourselves." Lord Khumun looked them over and heaved a theatrical sigh. "I have undertaken to supply an egg to every boy who remains and passes through the initial training. Frankly, I would be just as pleased to see your ranks thinned a little further."

There was a weak chuckle at that, as Kiron took a deep breath, reminded himself that he, at this moment, as he stood, was the equal to any of the boys here in rank. Yes, even the prince. *I am a Jouster, even if I have never ridden to combat. I have a dragon who answers only to me. And without me, there will be no tame dragons to Joust for Alta.* He was a unique and valuable weapon in the Altan arsenal. There were several pairs of princes. There was only one Kiron, one Avatre.

"First," he said, "you're going to start by becoming dragon

boys yourselves, serving dragons we already have. You will take the place of the dragon boys in this compound until such time as you understand the serving of a dragon completely."

A couple of the boys gulped. He didn't blame them. Three of the dragons that had been here had been actual killers; they could only be handled with their jaws muzzled, which had made feeding them—exciting. These three had been handled only by men, two of them, at all times.

"There are no more killer dragons in the compound," he announced. "Lord Khumun and I have had some success with retraining the dragons that are currently here using falconry techniques." Was he sweating? He hoped not. He wanted to look confident. He *had* to get their respect now, or he could have trouble with them later. "It has taken us most of a moon, but even the killers are now on reasonably good behavior, for wild-caught dragons."

And *that* had been an ordeal! But the results had been striking. Or at least, it was now possible for the dragons to be handled and groomed without the risk of a dragon boy losing life or limbs.

"But although they are no longer killers, you must remember at all times that they are still dangerous." He swallowed, and was very glad that his voice had broken during the moon he and Lord Khumun had been doing the retraining. Having his voice crack and squeak would have done nothing to add to his air of authority. "We will be handling them with choking chains, and you will never actually be alone with your charge; the current dragon boy will always be with you to help get you out of difficulty. But make no mistake about it, you will be doing the work. And once your egg hatches, you will still be doing most of the work. We have decided that the first several moons with the dragonet are absolutely crucial, and if your dragonet sees someone else, or worse, is fed by someone else, we don't know if she or he will bond properly to you. So you are going to have to be comfortable with doing a great deal of manual labor." He tried to look apologetic, but he had the feeling he wasn't succeeding. When he thought about what he'd had to go through—feeding and tending *three* dragons at once, one of them secretly—he couldn't feel at all sorry for them. "So, until the eggs get here, this is how your days will go—"

He'd practiced this speech in front of Aket-ten so many times that he didn't have to think about it anymore. He just told them, clearly and precisely, how much work they would be doing. And although they would not be tending to the Jouster as well as the dragon, nor would they be required to do all the work of repairing harness and weapons and drying *tala* and the rest, they would be continuing whatever studies their fathers deemed necessary. He had to hide his grin when he saw Orest's face fall at that news—nor was Orest the only one to look disappointed.

"There will be tutors coming here, to avoid the waste of time it would take for you to come to them. Most of us will share tutors and lectures."

*But not me. I get Master Arit to myself. Lord Ya-tiren said so.* He was getting a tutor all to himself to accelerate his reading ability; Lord Khumun had decided that until he knew how to read well, he would be getting the extra tutoring. Master Arit was pleased with his progress. He could read simple things now. He had a new shrine to his father's spirit, and he could read the prayers for the dead inscribed on its side. Master Arit was certain that with the full attention of a very good tutor—and his own determination —he would pass for a boy as well educated as Orest within a year.

"Your day will begin when you rise about dawn. This is when your dragon will rise. It will take your dragon some little time to come out of the torpor of sleep, and you will take this time to ready his morning meal."

He continued describing what their days would be like; when he was done, four more boys decided that this project was not to their taste. That left them with eight, of which the prince, looking more eager than ever, was still one. Kiron was surprised, a little, and yet, considering what he had heard about Toreth, perhaps he shouldn't have been. He had never, ever heard anyone say that either of the princes was afraid of a little hard work.

"You're sure, now," Lord Khumun said earnestly, looking each and every one of them in the eyes. "You're absolutely sure that you can undertake this, and that in fact, you *want* to?"

Each of them nodded soberly but with a glow of anticipation. Even Orest.

"All right." He looked over at Kiron. "Four eggs in a clutch, you say?"

"That's what I was told, and that was what I observed, my Lord," he replied firmly. "Mature females always lay four eggs."

"Then we'll stake out our two female desert dragons and hope for the best," the Lord of the Jousters decided. "We'll wait to see if we need to go after swamp dragon eggs only after we find out what is going to happen with the desert dragons."

Kiron nodded; that would be his choice, too. The swamp drag-ons had proved to be a bit more reptilian in nature than the desert dragons, and a bit more difficult to handle, although it had been the wild-caught male desert dragons that had proven to be the killers.

*Maybe because they once ate a man.* That was always problem-atic; once a wild dragon tasted human blood, it always knew that eating a human was an option.

The two desert dragon females that had been taken from Tian Jousters were lazy—half the reason they'd been caught was that they very much preferred to be fed rather than to hunt. Being lazy was an advantage now on a number of counts. In the past, they had proved that they were unlikely to fight their chains when staked out as "bait." This meant, when they were taken off the heavier dose of *tala*, so that they would come into season prop-erly, it would still be possible to handle them. They would proba-bly not try to fight off their would-be mates, and in fact, might well be quite responsive. And when they finally began laying their eggs, they were less likely to be aggressive about defending the newly laid eggs than a more active dragon.

The last advantage was that Kiron knew exactly what to expect and how to incubate a desert dragon egg. Swamp dragons—that was going to be a matter of experimentation, as far as he was concerned. If they could get eight fertile desert dragon eggs—

Eight boys, eight eggs. Nine was a good size for a wing. They could learn and drill together, learn to fight as a group.

"If the gods are kind, both dragons will mate, and all the eggs will be fertile," he replied.

"I will be making sacrifices today, and every day until hatching," Lord Khumun said firmly, and cast a now-steely eye over his new volunteers. "And so should you all."

And so they did. But not before Kiron put them through their first day with utter disregard for their comfort.

They drew lots for which boy was assigned to which dragon, that way no one could claim that Kiron had shown any favoritism in his assignments. As it happened, Orest and Toreth got the two easiest to handle, saving only the two captured females, which had already gone to the edge of the desert to await their suitors. One was a huge swamp dragon that Kiron suspected was actually a cross-breed, terribly lazy; the other was a small male desert dragon that, provided you didn't move too quickly and made certain he had his full ration of *tala*, was no worse than any of the fledgling-caught desert dragons. The rest, however, were typical Altan Jousting dragons, which was to say, by Tian standards, difficult.

Kiron introduced the boys to their charges slowly, one each day, while the remaining boys watched during the entire day. He kept Orest and Toreth for last, so that when they actually got their dragons, they had seen (and helped with) virtually every problem that the draconic mind could come up with saving only illness and injury. They were both prepared for the worst, probably expecting that Kiron had saved the worst for last, so as a result, they were completely on their guard and unlikely to let their guard down for the moon or so it would take before the eggs were laid. Of all things, Kiron did not want them to trust their dragons *at all*. It had been his experience that injuries happened when dragon boys took the tameness of their charges for granted, and became just a little careless in their presence. Perhaps they pressed their charges in a way that they would never have considered with a wilder dragon. Perhaps they turned their backs one too many times. Or perhaps they made a slip they would have been too wary to do in the presence of a more dangerous beast. It did always seem to be the ones that everyone considered the best behaved who inflicted the worst injuries.

He was far from idle himself; besides keeping track of every one of the boys of his new wing, he was training Avatre, twice a day, every day. He knew at this point that there was no choice in the matter; if he was going to train the others, he had to work out how to train them himself.

He counted himself lucky that Avatre was, if anything, more sweet-tempered than Kashet. She put up with indignities from his clumsy experiments that would have left him kicking his legs as he went down the throat of a less-patient dragon.

And she was growing apace; he'd already had to have new harness and saddle made for her, and it looked as if she was going to need another set of kit before two moons had passed. Ah well, the old rig certainly wasn't going to go to waste; the leatherworkers were using it as the pattern for eight more harnesses, and the benefit was, if the dragon fit the first harness, they'd know it was big enough to fly with a rider.

It occurred to him when he'd let out her cinches as far as he could, that *he* was growing, too . . . a growth spurt that had begun when he had joined the dragon boys and was still going. Lack of food had kept him stunted; plentiful food had set him growing like a weed. He doubted that he would ever be very tall, but—

*And my voice just broke.* Girls were beginning to look a bit more interesting to him as well.

And he wondered, in the dark of the night, just how old he really was. Older than even he had thought, he suspected, or his voice wouldn't have broken already. *Could I be fifteen Floods old now? Fourteen, anyway?* He had lost track of the Floods once he'd been made into a serf; no one ever celebrated his birthday, for what was there to celebrate in another year in captivity? One day had been like another, varying only in degrees of misery. Maybe he was fifteen Floods old now. That would make him as old as most of the others.

That would do no harm; the others would accept him as trainer and leader more readily if he was older than he'd thought.

He grew to know the boys during this time, and somewhat to his surprise, there was not a single one that he was not happy to have as a friend, and that realization, made one day as he was helping Toreth harness his charge, nearly stunned him. He, who had never had a real friend before, now had eight—nine, counting Aket-ten—

It was at that moment that he also realized that for the first time in his life, he was happy. And the revelation left him stunned for the rest of the evening.

As for Orest, his first friend had truly found his passion. He had flung himself into the work with his dragon to the point where Kiron sometimes had to order him to rest. When he wasn't tending his dragon—which was so immaculately groomed that his scales gleamed like gems—he was reading about them, asking advice of the other dragon boys, and even (when he dared) querying the Jousters about combat. His father, from being resigned, was now as proud of his youngest son as he was of his eldest.

Where Orest was vocal and single-minded in his passion, Toreth was a little more divided. Then again, he had to be; as the likeliest heirs to the thrones, he and his brother perforce spent a lot of time in learning governance. And, though this was not what Kiron would have expected, mastering the tasks of dragon care came as easily to the prince as breathing. Perhaps it was his calmness, which seemed to have as much of a tranquilizing effect on his charge as the *tala* did. After the first day, Toreth had come to the pens with the royal hairstyle gone; he had opted for a cut like

Aket-ten's, just at chin length. He said nothing about it, and nothing was ever said to him, but Kiron knew that he was serious after that day.

The remaining six were a mixed bag indeed, but none of them was in any danger of failing this final test before they were given custody of a precious egg.

Two had turned out to be as competent as Kiron had expected. Ka-lenteth, the falconer, had the most fractious of the beasts, and as a result, took longer than the others to accustom it to his hand. It even tried his immense store of patience a time or two, and he was the only one to be injured. Not badly, but his dragon had learned the use of his tail to intimidate, and Kiron finally had to get the young falconer fitted with actual boots before the moon was over. Kalen (as he liked to be called) was the smallest of the boys, thin and wiry, and seldom spoke. When he did, it was in a low, soft voice. Kiron only heard him shout the once, when he got the first lash of a tail across his shins.

Pe-atep, the cat keeper, was Kalen's match in patience, but was his exact opposite physically. He was taller and broader than the prince, with an equally broad, flat face and a booming voice when he raised it in conversation. He had no trouble with his fractious charge, actually staring it down during their first confrontation—something he said also worked on lions. He and Kalen were often found experimenting with minute changes in the dragons' diets to see if there was any corresponding change in their behavior. Not varying the *tala* ration, of course, but changing the kinds of meat and the mix of meat to organs, adding things like hide and hair.

Huras was a friend of Pe-atep, though not an animal keeper. The son of a baker, he was the lowest-born of the lot. And was second to no one in his intelligence. He tore through the scrolls on dragons, Jousting, and dragon keeping twice as fast as anyone else, and anything he read stayed in his memory forever. Otherwise, he was average-looking in appearance; he probably would have run to fat if he hadn't been working so hard.

Then there was Gan. Ganek-at-kel-te-ronet would have been the highest ranking member of their group, if the prince had not been one of them. Gan was tall, lanky, and had a languid air about him that gave the impression that he didn't care a great deal for anything except, perhaps, food and gossip. Nothing could have been farther from the truth. He was the oldest, no longer a boy, but a young man—and his airs concealed a passion as fervent as Orest's. Kiron had the feeling that, like Orest, he had been looking for something for his entire life without knowing what it was. And now he had found it.

Equally deceptive was Oset-re, the peacock of the group, and a friend of Orest's. He was, to put it bluntly, the most beautiful human being that Kiron had ever seen, of either sex. No matter what the time of day or the task he was engaged in, he was always impeccably, flawlessly groomed and clothed. Whenever he ventured outside the compound, women flirted with him covertly or openly, and like Ari, there were even women who pursued him shamelessly. And he wore his peacock persona like the mask it was. Beneath the seeming vanity was a hard purpose, honed to razor sharpness. He had seen what Kiron had with Avatre on an early visit, and he was determined to have something like that bond for himself. But not at "all" costs; he would have it with honor or not at all. Even if it meant ruining his finest kilts to achieve it. He had already made one great sacrifice; the day after Toreth cut his hair, so did Oset-re.

Last was shy Menet-ka, who never spoke above a whisper or unless he was first spoken to, who hung at the back of any group, and who seldom made eye contact. He was so successful at self-effacement that most people who knew him would have had a hard time describing him, and if there were three other people in a room, would forget he was there. He had never yet demonstrated why he was here, for it must have taken an extraordinary act of will for him to put himself forward, but part of it might have been that he had been one of Oset-re's best friends from childhood. And the other was, without a doubt, that he, too, had seen the bond that Kiron shared with Avatre, and wanted something like that for himself with all his heart.

This was his wing; as different as it was possible for individuals to be, yet as they shared food and work, they began to forge a friendship among themselves that defied both stereotype and description.

As the eight sat together over supper, nearly a full moon into their "trial" period, Kiron approached their table carrying a jar. They all looked up immediately at the sound of his now familiar step, even Menet-ka. He put the jar down in the middle of the table.

"That doesn't look like beer or wine to me," said Gan lazily. "So what is it doing on our table, estimable wing leader?"

"You are each going to draw two of the pebbles from that jar to determine what your colors are going to be," Kiron explained. "We're going to need a way to tell each other apart in the air; the regular Jousters don't do this, but they also don't fight as a group because they daren't get their dragons too close to one another. *We* are going to be very different; but we'll have to know who is who in order to play to everyone's individual strengths. So you'll all wear your colors on your armor and harness, and we'll probably fly streamers or something."

"And your colors?" asked Orest.

"I pulled rank on you and chose black and scarlet," he admitted, with a grin. "Because they go well with Avatre's colors. You'll get whatever you get—though, if you really *hate* the combination you choose, you can swap among yourselves."

"I suspect I'll be forced to," moaned Oset-re. "I would rather die than be seen in colors that clashed with my dragon."

The rest snickered, and Kiron laughed out loud. "In that case, draw first," he suggested. "That way you'll have the best odds for the best choices."

He didn't have to ask Oset-re twice; the handsome lad stood up and plunged his hand into the jar up to the elbow. And when he opened his closed fist, he heaved an exaggerated sigh of relief as the painted pebbles in his hand were revealed.

"Black and white!" he said, sitting down. "What a relief! Black and white go with everything; I can't even imagine a swamp dragon that those colors would clash with. Well, I won't have to kill myself after all."

Orest was next to take the plunge into the jar, and emerged with blue and scarlet. "Well, you'll certainly be able to see me," was his only comment.

Toreth came up with yellow and white; Gan got green and brown. Pe-atep's pick was black and yellow, and his friend Kalen ended up as yellow and brown. Huras got blue and black, and Menet-ka, who predictably chose last, did not seem unhappy with his green and white.

"So, why are we taking colors right now?" asked Gan. "Why not wait to see what color dragons hatch out?"

Kiron grinned; he couldn't help it. He had some very good news for them. "Partly because of the training games I'm going to be giving you," he said, "but mostly because Lord Khumun told me today that both females have mated with three different males, which ought to pretty much guarantee that all four eggs each lays will be fertile."

Heads at the other tables turned as all eight of the wing broke into a cheer—even Menet-ka. "When are they coming back?" Orest asked excitedly.

"Their Jousters are flying the ladies back tomorrow," Kiron told them, now allowing his grin to show. "They'll be sequestered in their pens and stuffed full of as much as they'll eat to nourish the eggs to come. Three males were also trapped, so there will be three new Jousters training with them, which will allow us to try falcon training right from the start instead of having a dragon that needs to unlearn a lot of bad habits. You'll be observing that, by the way; no point in missing the opportunity. So, the reason you've gotten your colors *now* is because you're going to draw lots for who gets the eggs in what order."

He took the pebbles from each boy, and put them back in the jar. This was going to be a complicated system, but it guaranteed random chance. "Everyone take a pebble. If you don't get one of your colors, put it back but don't take a new one until the next round."

Only Menet-ka got one of his colors the first time; on the second round, Gan and Orest got one of theirs, and on the third, Menet-ka made the first combination. So Menet-ka, who always hung back, was going to get the first egg. It seemed to Kiron there was a certain justice in that.

The jar went around enough times for everyone to be impatient before it was over. Orest's egg came in the middle, and it was Peatep who would get the last of the eggs. Although everyone except Menet-ka moaned about the wait, no one really seemed unhappy. And Kiron was very proud of them all when Menet-ka offered to trade his place with any of the rest of them and no one took him up on the offer.

"You're as ready as any of us, and more ready than I am," said Orest stoutly, even though Kiron knew he was afire to have that egg in his possession.

"So, let's go look at the pens, and get your colors up outside them," Kiron urged; eager to put their imprint on what would be the centers of their worlds for the next several moons, they filed after him, going out into the torch-lit, open-topped corridors to a newly built section of pens.

Here were ten of the sand-pit pens (one would stay empty for now), all along the same corridor, five on either side. Avatre's was the first, and already had a block of four squares of red and black inside a lozenge-outline painted on the wall outside it. A servant with brushes and paints waited for them at the entrance to Avatre's pen.

They got pens in the order in which they would get their eggs; this meant that a hatching dragon would only have noise on one wall, keeping disturbances as minimal as possible. Kiron was not sure what Lord Khumun had done, but despite initial objections, the Magi had agreed to create spells that moved the heat from some of the hot springs that created water too hot and too sulfurous to use into the sands of the pens. While the adult dragons could cope with the shifting levels of heat in sand pits warmed by ovens or other means, hatching eggs needed a constant temperature. Kiron hoped he had gotten that temperature absolutely right, but the only way to tell would be if the eggs all hatched.

From the beginning, these pens had been set up with living quarters as part of them; there would be no makeshift pallets for the boys of Kiron's wing. Eventually, of course, the dragons would be old enough to be able to sleep alone, as Kashet did, but until then, they would need their boys—their "mothers"—with them. Especially at night.

When Lord Khumun wanted something done, apparently it got done; here were thick-walled pens, (with walls, not of mud brick, but of stone) with roofed living quarters, running water (every two pens shared a room for bathing where, presumably, the boys would also get water for their dragons), heated sands, and a better canvas roof arrangement for the rainy season than the Tian Jousters had. And it had all been constructed within a moon or so.

The boys were impressed, and well they should be, for this was nothing short of amazing. The only time Kiron had heard of construction going up faster was when a Royal Tomb was being built.

"After the eggs are hatched, we will begin constructing more pens for the next lot of volunteers," Lord Khumun had said to Kiron, "But I do not want to chance anything that might disturb the eggs."

"Well," Kiron said to his new wing. "Will this do?"

"I should like to move in now, if I might," said Toreth. He looked around at the others, who nodded agreement.

"I don't have any objections," Kiron told them, though secretly, he was pleased. The boys were all living at their homes now; he wanted them at the compound as soon as he could get them here. The sooner they settled into their new way of life, the better, but they could hardly have gone in with the existing dragon boys. For one thing, there wasn't really room, and for another, there was bound to be tension there before long. The dragon boys were freeborn, as in Tia, but they were mostly from extremely poor families, and there was not a single one of the new wing that wasn't at least from the caste of craftsmen. And as for Toreth—

Well, while Kiron doubted that the prince himself would have any objections to being put in with boys from the lowest levels of society, anyone with so much as a single drop of noble blood in his veins would probably have a fit the moment word got out that a prince was being housed with the peasantry. And the screams of outrage would be heard on the top of the Great Tower of the Royal Palace.

"You could move in at any point, including tonight," Kiron told them all.

Toreth grinned. "Then I am sending a runner for my things. Mother has an entire herd of female relatives visiting her, and the gabble and cackle is like to drive me mad."

"And I believe I shall do likewise," Gan drawled. "It's going to take me a quarter moon to get these quarters comfortable anyway, and I might as well start now."

That started the stampede, and before long, as Kiron joined Avatre in their quarters, he could hear the coming and going of numerous servants, bringing the boys' belongings from their homes. He even overheard Toreth generously sending his servants after the belongings of Huras, Kalen, and Pe-atep, who obviously had no servants of their own.

And shortly after that, he heard much coming and going from Gan's quarters, and heard that familiar, lazy drawl cheerfully distributing "extra" comforts "that there just is no room for, hang it!" among his wingmates. Soon, there were trades going on, as what had been personal belongings (or "supplies" pressed upon sons by anxious mothers) were distributed, through the alchemy of friendship, across the entire group.

"Listen to them! They're acting as a unit," he told Avatre, wonderingly. "They haven't even got dragons yet, and already they're a real wing!"

She nodded quite as if she understood, and dug herself a little further down into the warm sands. As far as she was concerned, life was perfect, for the hot sand was a great deal more comfortable for her than the stone of the courtyard she had been using.

And as the excited chatter and the other sounds of eight boys settling into new quarters died away, Kiron settled down himself for the night. It was an auspicious beginning, a good foundation to build on.

And with that cheerful thought in his mind, he allowed himself to drift into sleep.

# SEVEN

EIGHT eggs were cradled in the hot sands of their pens. Eight anxious young men watched and brooded over them quite as if they had laid the eggs and not the dragon mothers. No longer were they playing dragon boy to the dragons of other Jousters; they knew what they needed to know about the tending of ordinary dragons. With plenty of time on their hands, they were now studying every scroll on dragons that they could get their hands on in good earnest—and short of getting their hands on the scrolls in the keeping of the Magi, they had access to every other scrap of papyrus on the subject in Alta.

Nor was that all, for thanks to Toreth's family, there was a set of two tutors, one of them a noted scholar of history, who arrived every day to teach all the boys. As what they were learning was the history of the war with Tia, plain and unvarnished, and the history of mankind's use of dragons, none of them objected, not even Orest.

Two things, however, had sorely puzzled Kiron since he had begun to move about the city and get to know these people who were his own. Both puzzles seemed such an accepted part of Altan life that he was not entirely sure how to ask about them.

The first was not so much a puzzle as a *non-sequitur*. When he first realized it, it had been something so entirely alien to his way of thinking that it had come as a shock.

And yet, it was a simple fact. The Priests of the Gods were not the ultimate authority in Alta. They did not even rank as a close second. The very notion seemed blasphemous, and yet everyone here took it for granted.

In Tia, even the Great King consulted with the Priests of the Gods on every occasion, and woe betide him if he failed to heed their words! Terrible things could, and did, happen to one who went against the will of the temples. Kings had been toppled from their thrones in the past, and it was not always the hand of a god that did the pushing.

Of course, the Great King himself was a priest, and a High Priest at that, but so far as Kiron been aware, he was a magicless man, and that made all the difference. The priests controlled all magic, for all those born with magic were swiftly taken into one temple or another as soon as their talents became evident. That included Healers, who were, in Tia, Priests and Priestesses of Te-oth, or rather, his Tian equivalent.

In Alta, Healers were a separate class that included those who Healed with herbs, with the knife, and with prayer, as well as those who Healed with their own special magic.

Things were very different here.

The only "magicians" who were not among the priestly caste in Tia were charlatans, street performers, who accomplished their "wonders" with trickery and sleight-of-hand. Male and female, young or old, whether or not they or their families were willing, once someone showed the signs or was detected by another magician, into a temple he went. So, although the priests seldom overtly exercised their power, *they*, and not the Great King, were the ultimate authority in Tia.

But here, it seemed, things were very different. There were those who went into the temples who had certain Gifts and Callings—the ability to see the future or what was happening at a distance, to hear the thoughts of beasts (like Aket-ten) or even the thoughts of men. There were rumors of those who were able to speak with the dead who went into the Temple of the Twins. And that was the end of priestly magicians. All the rest of the priests were entirely without magic, either devoted by reason of avocation, or having more in common with the scribes than the magicians.

As for the Healers, they stood apart from all and served no one god, but served all of them, collectively. Their enclaves, something like temples, but with less than a tenth of their space devoted to a sanctuary filled with images of every god and goddess in Alta, were distributed all across the city. And that was a shock all by itself; it was hardly to be thought of that one didn't run to the Temple of Te-oth when one needed a Healer!

But there was a greater shock as far as Kiron was concerned, because not only did the practitioners of magic *not* belong to the priests, they had their very own caste. And it its way, this caste was even more exalted than that of the rulers of Alta.

They were the Magi, those Tians called "sea witches" since so much of what the Magi had once done involved the sea and water-magic. That was no longer the case, it seemed.

A Magus was one who worked—well—*magic*. The Magi used spells to work their will upon the world, to channel strange powers; spells that were chanted over incense, sung from the tops of towers, or murmured in hidden chambers in the bowels of the earth. Spells that *did* things—like the spells that called up the fierce storms and flung them down the Great Mother River to drive the dragons and Jousters of Tia to earth and ravage the countryside.

There were rumors of other spells that they had not yet unleashed. Spells to call up fire from the earth or down from the sky. Spells that not only repelled the hungry dead, but compelled them to serve or to haunt those the Magus indicated. The curse of a priest was potent—but in Alta the curse of a Magus was doubly so and doubly feared, for the curse of a priest relied on whether or not his god was moved to implement the curse, but the curse of a Magus depended only on his own power and his own will.

It was the Magi, and not the priests, that the Great Ones of Alta listened to in Council. Oh, there was a High Priest sitting on the Council as well, taken by lot from among the priests of all of the temples once a season, but he was one, and the Magi were many. Unless he had a Foretelling from one of the Winged Ones, he might as well keep his mouth sewed shut when the Magi spoke. And according to Aket-ten, there had not been a Winged One with a truly powerful ability to Foretell the future in a very long time.

This revelation rocked his world to the foundations; he understood it, but it still came as a shock. Perhaps his village had been so remote, and so provincial, that none of this had reached him as a child.

Or, perhaps everyone had known this, and he had simply been too young to understand. After all, to a child, all figures of authority are equally powerful, and anyway, the Magi never left the safety of Alta City, so there never were any Magi to rival the priests for power in his old village. Then again, how would such a thing concern simple farmers near the border? Even if they had known, it would scarcely have affected any of them. No matter who ruled or made the decrees, the seasons would come and go, and some humorless official would arrive after harvest to collect the taxes, and it really didn't matter to a farmer where those taxes went after he turned them over. The Great Ones could have been a family of goats on the thrones for all he cared.

But for Kiron, steeped as he had been in the Tian hierarchy, it made no sense at all. And the more he learned from the scholar, the less sense it made, for in the past, the Great Ones had bowed to the will of the priests, just as in Tia. And all those who had any pretense to power had been within the temples. How had this come about? It was such an accepted part of life now that there seemed no way—and more importantly, no one—to ask.

But that was only a puzzle. And although it sometimes kept

him lying in bed, trying to understand it, the situation affected him no more now than it had when he had been a serf called Vetch. The Jousters had nothing to do with the Magi, except on the rare occasion when they were asked to perform some magic like warming the sand pits. Otherwise—the Jousters were as far removed from the Magi as the sea from Tia.

But the second thing that sorely puzzled Kiron was an attitude. And *that* affected him.

Now, Alta had been losing land and villages to the Tians steadily, for as long as he had been alive, and yet although there was outrage, and every Altan in the city wanted revenge and "their" land back, there was absolutely no fear that the Tians would ever come here. It was as if every Altan knew, beyond a shadow of a doubt, that the Tian army could not approach any nearer than the outermost canal.

Surely they weren't expecting the canals to hold their enemies at bay! They knew how many Jousters the Tians had! All it took was for the Jousters to command the air, and no matter how the Altans tried to prevent it, the Tian forces could, and would, bridge the canals, one by one. All it took was time and boats and you had a floating bridge that could carry armed men straight into the heart of Alta City. How could they not be afraid?

Was it simple, blind arrogance, a false sense of surety that they could not be conquered on their home ground?

Or was there something that they knew that he did not?

He never got an answer to the question of why the priests and the Magi were two different castes, but he finally got the first clue to his second question one day when he was listening to the historian scholar. For once, the subject was not the current state of the war, but the beginning of it.

Although it was interesting to hear the story from the Altan perspective, as he had already gotten the tale from Ari from the Tian point of view, it was nothing new . . . until the moment that the scholar said, ". . . and then, of course, the Magi created the

Eye of Light, and the direct threat against Alta City was ended and . . ."

That was when he woke up. *The Eye of Light? What in the name of all that is holy is the Eye of Light?* He couldn't imagine—was it some sort of Far-Seeing Eye that any Magus could use that allowed them to keep the land around Alta City under constant watch? But what good would that do? But by the time he gathered his wits, the scholar had finished his lecture, and it was time to feed Avatre. She was putting on another growth spurt of her own and was constantly hungry, and he knew that he didn't dare delay her dinner for even a single question.

So he hurried off, his curiosity a fire within his belly, his thoughts circling around that tantalizing bit of information. At least now he had a name for the reason why the Altans did not fear invasion of their city, even if he did not know what that name meant.

However, he was, by the gods, going to find out.

"The Eye of Light?" Orest said, and blinked. "Um—actually, I don't know what it is. I mean, I know what it *does,* but I don't know what it *is.* No one knows what it is, except the Magi. It's up in the Tower of Wisdom, and no one is allowed up there except the really powerful Magi."

Kiron sighed. "All right, what does it do, then?" he asked.

Orest licked his lips. "Mind you, I've never seen it myself. The Magi don't show it off all that often—by the gods, they don't *have* to! But Father has, and—you know that stretch of slag glass, right by the Ha-aras Bridge over the Fourth Canal?"

Kiron nodded; it was a strange feature, following the line of the canal itself, a slab of black vitrified earth about as wide as a chariot and as long as three dragons, nose to tail. He'd wondered if it was the remains of some terrible fire.

"The Eye made that," Orest said, with lowered voice and a sidelong glance, as if he feared being overheard. "Father said this beam of light came down out of the top of the Tower of Wisdom—that's the high tower in the middle of the Palace of the Magi—and just burned it there. They say it can reach all the way to the other side of the Seventh Canal and do the same thing there. There's supposed to be the burned footings of a ruined bridge they took down out there; I don't know, I haven't gone to look."

Kiron stared blankly at his friend; if he hadn't known that Orest wasn't any good at deception, he would have expected this to be some sort of joke. "Nothing can do that!" he objected. "I've never heard of anything that can do that!"

"Well, then, *nothing* melted the earth right where you can go and look at it yourself," Orest snapped, nettled. "I can tell you this—it's the reason why no one crosses a Magus! Once every few years, they decide to put on a show with the Eye, just to make sure that everyone remembers it, and let everyone know it still works. And that's why, when you deal with a Magus, you are very, very polite. If they can do *that*, what else can they do?"

Kiron licked his lips, picturing to himself a beam of light moving across the earth, burning everything in its path—or across the sky— "Can it be moved up?"

"Can it cut a dragon and a Jouster out of the sky, you mean?" Orest asked. "If they don't get out of its way, I should think so!"

Kiron thought about the dragons, ranked in their wings, and a light beam sweeping across the sky. Well. No wonder no one in Alta City was afraid of invasion. And no wonder the Magi were, in their way, the silent rulers of this land. He had to wonder if anyone in Tia knew about this thing. Surely they did—with all the spies and agents they had, with the Altans demonstrating it very publicly every few years, surely they knew about it!

It was very strange, though, that in all of the time he had been in Tia, he had not heard even a rumor of such a thing. So—why not? Why was it that the thing that had terrified people most was only that the Magi could send storms down on them?

*Maybe because the Great King and his advisers know that as long as they stay on the other side of the Seventh Canal, the Eye can't reach them—so unless they find a way to get rid of the Eye, or the Magi, they won't march on Alta City. And maybe the reason the storms scared them was that if the Magi could send storms, maybe they could reach past the Seventh Canal after all?*

Not that it mattered what they thought; at least, not to him. Except that he had a very uneasy sensation in the pit of his stomach, knowing that the Eye could reach anywhere inside Alta City. . . .

"They've been trying to make another Eye for years, one they could put on a wagon or something and carry around," Orest went on, "Or the Great Ones have asked them to, so they say. I mean, obviously, if we could put another Eye out there, maybe even with the army, it would change things completely. But for some reason they haven't been able to." He shrugged. "You should ask Aket-ten; she'll know ten times more about it than I do. I should think there isn't a scroll in that temple she hasn't read twice, and she's not shy about asking to read any piece of papyrus that crosses her path. Besides that, she's very good at not being noticed; she's sat in the same room with dozens of important people around, listening to things she had no business listening to, and no one ever noticed she was there even though she was in plain sight." He sounded rather cross about that; Kiron guessed, with some amusement, that his little sister had more than once been listening in on *him* in that way. And of course, she had also found her secret listening post as well, not that Orest was doing any lounging about these days! Still, this business of the Eye . . . he got the feeling that Orest went through life not listening to much, where as Aket-ten listened to everything. So she might well be the person to ask.

"Perhaps I will," he said slowly. He still found the mere idea hard to believe—and yet there was physical proof that the thing existed, and what it could do.

It gave him cold chills to think about; this was like one of the weapons of the gods! And there were plenty of tales about what happened when ordinary men got their hands on those . . . most of those tales ended badly.

Even more chilling was the thought that the Magi had made sure to demonstrate the thing within the limits of the Seven Canals, proving it could be used on chosen targets inside the city as well as against invaders. A potent means of silencing troublemakers who might want to know why the Magi had so much influence . . . a reminder that such a thing *was* possible.

Yes, he rather thought he would have a word or two with Aketten as soon as he got the chance.

The chance came sooner than he thought.

It was the beginning of the season of the rains; the welcome relief from the *kamiseen*.

As in Tia, runners had been sent around the compound last night to warn of the coming rains, and everyone had dutifully pulled the canvas covers over their dragon's sand pits—except for those who had swamp dragons, who would be perfectly happy to have rain pouring down into the pools of warm, sulfurous water. They'd have been even happier with mud, but wet dragons were hard enough to harness; muddy ones would have been impossible. Once in a great while they were allowed a mud wallow, but it wasn't often, and they were cleaned off almost immediately afterward. Last night, they had all gone to bed feeling the weather bearing down on them. The wind had changed direction, coming from the sea and the north, rather than the desert and the west. It was a slow, heavy wind, bringing yet more humidity to this city surrounded by marshes, and it carried a chill with it. Kiron was happy to roll up in a woolen blanket tonight, and Avatre, born amid the rain, was so buried in the sand she was nothing more than a hummock in her pit.

The sound of thunder rolling continuously overhead was what woke Kiron. He waited for it to stop—and waited—and waited—and still nothing happened.

He opened his eyes and rolled over with a groan. There was

light out there in Avatre's pen, but it wasn't very bright. Either the clouds were thicker than he thought, or it was just dawn. Both, perhaps. It was cold, a penetrating cold, and he knew he was going to need a woolen tunic today beneath his rain cape.

The thunder continued to growl overhead, yet there wasn't any rain pounding down on the canvas awning. That struck him as very odd, and it roused his curiosity enough that he decided to get up and have a look around. Besides, he was awake now. Until the rain started, he wasn't going to be able to get back to sleep. There was such heavy tension in the air, waiting for the storm to break, that dozing was impossible.

He pulled on a kilt and a tunic and tiptoed past Avatre, who was still sleeping. In fact, given how cool the air was, he doubted she'd be very happy about being awakened.

Not that he blamed her in the least; if he hadn't been so curious, he would be back in his cot, under his warm woolen blanket, thank you.

Once he got out from under the canvas and into the corridor, he still couldn't see anything, because the Altans sensibly had the same canvas roofs over the corridors that they strung over the dragon pens. He would have to get somewhere that was open to the sky, like the landing court.

No one else was awake and moving, though, which made him think that the continuous thunder was considered perfectly normal by the Altans. That was a bit of a comfort, anyway. He padded his way along the stone of the corridor, barefoot, until he came to the entrance into the landing court—and as he approached it, he saw, in the sky above the walls—

Lightning. Not striking the ground, but crawling across the base of the clouds, like veins of fire across charcoal-colored flesh. It wasn't like any lightning he'd ever seen before; this was reddish, and didn't seem at all inclined to strike the earth. Gingerly, he eased himself out from under the scant protection offered by the canvas and looked up to see that the reason why the thunder didn't stop was that there was never so much as a heartbeat of time when there *wasn't* any lightning crawling across some part of the sky.

Well, that certainly explained the thunder.

He moved out into the courtyard so he could see the whole sky, including the tops of the buildings on the central island. After a moment of watching it with the same fascination of a bird watching a snake, he noticed that it was all emanating from a central point. That point was just above the tip of the Tower of Wisdom. The clouds there were darker, much darker, completely black, in fact, and they swirled around that center point in a slow, somehow ominous, vortex. And even as he watched, a single lightning bolt, not just red-tinted but as red as blood, cracked upward from the tip of the tower into the center of that vortex. When it vanished, it seemed to Kiron that the clouds were spinning just a little faster.

There was one thing he was not mistaken about; there was a heaviness to the air, a drowsiness, warring with his sense that something was going to break loose at any moment. He had thought he could not possibly get back to sleep, but now—now he felt as if all he wanted to do was to get back into his bed.

*This storm—it's just strange,* he thought, and he wondered if there was anyone else but the Magi awake at the moment to watch this. Or was it just so commonplace for the Magi to control the storms of the rainy season that no one even thought about it?

Or had the Magi done something to ensure that all of the citizens of Alta City stayed in their beds while *they* did their work? That heaviness in the air felt as if it was weighing him down, as if he could and should just lie down right here in the courtyard and go back to sleep. . . .

And that was not right. At that moment, he knew that this was exactly what the Magi wanted. They did not want anyone to see what they were doing. He had been at the mercy of someone who did not want others to know his secrets—Khefti-the-Fat had many secrets—and he knew the signs.

He shook himself awake just as he felt his eyelids drooping. *Oh, no!* he thought, clenching his jaw. *If you don't want me to see this, then that's exactly what I want to watch!*

And so he did, watching with grim determination not to miss a single moment, as the thunder rolled and the lightning raced across the sky to the horizon, and as the clouds spun, faster and faster, until the moment when a final bolt, a *black* bolt scarcely visible against the clouds, arced upward.

A deafening avalanche of thunder threatened to flatten him where he stood.

Then the heavens opened up, and the rain poured out of the sky, very nearly managing to flatten him, which the thunder had not.

He scrambled back under cover of the canvas, and after standing there, dripping and cold, gazing out into the sheeting rain and listening to the now-ordinary peals of thunder, he decided that whatever it was that he was not supposed to watch was over. The rains had begun, and he might just as well go back to bed.

And yet—it felt as if there was something that he ought to do. He just didn't know what it was.

After a moment of indecision, he decided that he wasn't going to be able to get back to sleep anyway, so he might as well put on a rain cape and see if he couldn't find Aket-ten. She always attended the Dawn Rites at her temple, so he knew that she would be awake. He hadn't seen her since Orest got his egg; he had the feeling that she was tired of hearing about what might be inside it.

He went back to his quarters, checked on the sleeping dragon (who was as insensible as a stone), decided that he ought to change into something drier than he was wearing, and finally, with the compound *still* sleeping around him, went out into the rain.

Everyone in the city slumbered just as in heavily as in the Jousters' Compound, as far as he could tell. Then again, who would want to go out in this rain? He had the streets all to himself at any event, and he bent his head to the pounding water and sloshed barefoot down the road toward Aket-ten's temple.

This temple was devoted to a pair of twin deities that were unique to Alta as far as he knew; the Goddess Beshet of the Far-Seeing Eye, and the God Anut the Spirit Walker. Beshet presided over those Winged Ones who had visions—of the future, of the past, of events at a distance. He was the patron of those who spoke with the dead—but also those who could *act* at a distance, who did not just have visions of things far away, but who could, in spirit, travel there and perhaps act on them. Between the two, they oversaw everything—save magic—that a Winged One might do. Other than that, Kiron didn't know a great deal about the Twins; their rites were secret, reserved for the Winged Ones, the Fledglings, and the Nestlings. Interestingly, though their rites were secret, the temple was one of the most open in the city, with lectures and discussions going on in every open spot and corner, and all through the gardens, every day. There were even little side chapels devoted to some of the lesser deities: the patrons of lovers, of mothers, of luck and—hardly surprising—one to Te-oth, the god of writing. Only the sanctuary itself was closed to the public, and then only during the rites.

The water sluicing off the crest of the hill toward the canal was ankle-deep at times, and cold enough to numb his feet, but it would have been of no use to put on sandals. Not only would the rain have ruined them, but the leather soles would have been slippery; better to trust to his feet, which were harder than leather soles after all those years of going barefoot anyway.

It was just as well that he knew where he was going, since the rain was so heavy it was like trying to peer through a waterfall. The rain cape kept most of it off him, but there was a steady drip through the seam of his hood down the back of his head, trickling down his neck. It was with benumbed gratitude that he finally made out the bulk of the temple he wanted, and splashed his way up the three steps into the forecourt, where he shook out his cape in the torch-lit gloom.

He stood there uncertainly for a moment—not that he didn't know the layout of the temple, just that he wasn't sure where to begin looking for Aket-ten—when he heard the sound of feet run-ning lightly toward him from behind, and turned quickly.

And before he had time to react in any way except to recognize that the runner was exactly who he was looking for, Aket-ten careened into him. She had been looking back over her shoulder with an expression of absolute terror, and hadn't even noticed he was there.

He expected her to scream or at least gasp, but she must have recognized him the moment she touched him, for as he fought to keep his balance, she grabbed his shoulders with both hands. "Kiron!" she whispered, frantic with fear. "Help me! Hide me!"

He didn't even think; he just flung the folds of his rain cape over her, disguising her completely, for it was made for someone *his* height and it covered her down to the floor. Then he led her into a side chapel where he pushed her to her knees in front of the little image of Ater-oth, Goddess of Lovers, and knelt beside her, tak-ing both her hands in his.

Just in time, too, evidently, for a moment later, he heard heav-ier footsteps out in the forecourt. He wasn't worried; the only trace that had been left was the water dripping from the rain cape, and there was no way to tell whether that had been left by one person entering from outside, or two. He was wet enough to have come here without a cape.

The steps stopped for a moment—then moved toward the chapel. Aket-ten's hands trembled in his, and he was astonished; he would never have imagined *her* being afraid of anything or any-one! Yet clearly, whoever this was, she was petrified of him.

And that was enough to put a chill down his spine that had nothing to do with the storm outside.

He heard the steps stop again, just outside the entrance to the chapel. He did not turn around, and he clamped his hands down hard on Aket-ten's to keep her from moving. In the dim light here, with both of them kneeling, there was no way for anyone to tell how young they both were, much less what they looked like.

Nevertheless, he felt, rather than saw, the fierce glaring of someone's eyes, and the back of his neck prickled.

There was no sound but the rain outside and on the roof, and the thunder cutting across the sound of the downpour. He was deeply grateful for both sets of noises; otherwise, their unseen watcher would have been able to hear Aket-ten's frightened breathing.

Finally the footsteps began again, walking purposefully away. When there had been only silence for a long moment, he started to stand up.

This time it was Aket-ten who restrained him. "Not yet," she whispered in a shaky voice. "Not until they're gone."

So he waited, while his knees began to ache from kneeling on the stone. Then, at long last, he heard more footsteps. Quite a lot of them, in fact. They shuffled across the forecourt, then out the door into the rain.

What struck him as uncomfortable and even frightening, even as he listened to the newcomers, was the lack of voices. In a group that big, someone was always talking. Even if they had been prisoners, someone would have been saying something—complaining, whispering, whimpering.

Not a word, not a noise. Only the sound of feet going out into the rain. And once again, the hair on the back of his neck crawled.

Silence descended on the temple, and Aket-ten slowly stopped shaking. Finally she stood up, and so did he, grateful to at last be off his knees.

"What—" he began.

"That was the Chief Magus and six of his underlings," she said, fear warring with anger in her voice as she pushed back the cowl of the rain cape. "They came here to collect Winged Ones to 'assist' them in sending out the storms against Tia. Only they don't allow you to say 'no' to them, and there doesn't seem to be anything that the Chief Priestess, the Teachers, or the Pedagogues can do to stop them, because the Great Ones have said that we must do this. They took me yesterday, and—and when they were done, I found myself back here with no memory of coming back, no memory of where I had been, no memory *at all* of anything other than hearing that horrible man say, 'You're finally going to be of some use,' and grabbing my shoulders." She began to shake again. "And worst of all, I was practically faint with exhaustion, and it took until nightfall before I could Hear and See again! For a little while, it was as if I was as blind and deaf as—as Orest!"

From the way she had said "Hear" and "See," the inflection of her voice, Kiron was pretty certain she wasn't talking about ordinary hearing and vision. He felt his mouth firming into a grim line. "Did they just take Fledglings?" he asked. "Or do you know?"

She shook her head. "All the ones they collected before they got to me were Fledglings, but I don't know after that. I don't have *any* memory of it."

He felt a coldness in his stomach, but there was as much anger in it as fear. "I think we need to find out—but before we do anything else, I am going to escort you to your father's house." He placed a finger over her lips before she could object. "I know you don't live there anymore now that you're a Fledgling, but I think you should stay there for a while, at least until the Magi are done doing whatever it is they're doing with the storms. I don't think even they would dare take a girl out of her father's house, but—" He shook his head. "Let's find your father, and see if we can come up with a plan."

She nodded, and he wrapped the rain cape around both of them and they went out into the downpour.

They found Lord Ya-tiren just breaking his fast, with a scroll spread out before him and a steaming loaf beside him. "Young Kiron!" he exclaimed, getting to his feet, "It is good to see you—and Aket-ten—forgive me for greeting you in this state, but this rain seems to have made me oversleep—"

Then he peered at Aket-ten, and must have seen the fear in her eyes. "Daughter, what is wrong?" he asked softly.

She took a deep breath. "Yesterday the Magi came, and took

several of the Fledglings to 'assist' them in their work," she told him, her voice trembling only a little. "I was one, and I have no memory of what happened."

"Well, daughter, the need for secrecy—" the lord began, but sounding a little doubtful.

"And," she interrupted, her voice going a little shrill. "When I returned, I nearly fainted, and *my Powers did not work,* nor did they return until almost sunset!"

Lord Ya-tiren opened his mouth, closed it again, and looked thoughtful—and worried. "I like this not," he said finally. "I can do nothing against the Magi to protect any of the others, but you, my daughter, I *can* shield. I believe that until the rains are over, you are going to be ill. Quite ill. Something of the female nature, I think; we will have my Healer friend Akenem here to give weight to that claim. You will remain confined to your bed."

At Aket-ten's stricken look, he chuckled. "My dear, the servants come and go at will. If one of them happens to look like you, well, I doubt anyone will notice! Just keep away from the temple until I tell you it is safe to return."

She relaxed visibly.

"Far be it for me to interfere in this, my Lord," said Kiron quietly, "But I must ask you to consider that this may not be enough. The Magi may insist upon examining her themselves. Perhaps—" he hesitated. "Perhaps before that can happen, Aket-ten should be sent to some friend or relation to recover from her illness."

"Hmm. And a new young slave should enter my household? A wise plan. Surely no one looks twice at a slave."

"And a slave can pass to and from the temple without being noticed either," Kiron pointed out, "So Aket-ten can continue whatever instruction she needs from the Winged Ones."

They exchanged somber looks; Aket-ten still looked wan and frightened; her father looked angry. "Thank you for bringing her here, Jouster Kiron," the lord said, turning to Kiron. "You were quite right to do so. There is something about this that is deeply disturbing—yet where the Magi are concerned, it is dangerous to probe too deeply, too quickly." Then he smiled. "If I am able to take the measure of a man, I would venture to say that you have decided to find out just what the Magi are doing with the Fledglings. Eh?"

Red-faced, Kiron admitted that was exactly what he had been thinking of doing.

"Give a father leave to make his own attempts first," Lord Ya-tires said gently. "Gold is a potent weapon, and a loosener of tongues. The Magi have servants. Give me time, and I will find the one who can tell us what we want to know."

Kiron sighed, nodded, and bowed his head. Unsatisfying as it was, Lord Ya-Tiren's plan was the better one of the two. "I will, my Lord," he said. "And if Aket-ten wishes to go about the city, I will undertake to escort her, if she likes, just in case."

Aket-ten's cheeks began to glow, but she didn't look displeased with his offer. Nor did Lord Ya-Tiren. "Now that is an offer that I will be pleased to accept. Thank you—and now, I believe, I should escort my poor, ailing daughter to her quarters?"

Well, that was as graceful a dismissal as Kiron had ever heard; he bowed, and took his leave.

But though he left Aket-ten and her dilemma behind him, it was still very much in his mind as he returned to the Jousters' Compound, and a sleepy, but hungry, Avatre.

# EIGHT

**T**HREE days later, Orest was intercepted at breakfast by a servant with a message from his father, and Kiron saw him going about the compound shortly after with a worried face.

"Orest!" he called, intercepting his friend at the entrance to his pen. "What's wrong?"

"Father says that my sister's been sent to Aunt Re-keron in the farms beyond the Seventh Ring because she's ill," Orest told him. "I don't understand this—Aket-ten's never been ill a day in her life!"

It didn't take more than a moment for Kiron to figure out what was going on. So, the Lord Ya-Tiren *had* taken his advice! That was extremely satisfying.

*But either the lord learned something—or he discovered that the Magi were going to be impossible to refuse.* That was not so satisfying.

Orest looked torn between wanting to run back home to find out what was wrong, and staying with his egg. Kiron knew what the truth was—but it seemed that Orest hadn't been taken into his father's confidence.

*Do I tell him, or not?* Kiron weighed the decision in his mind. *No. No, I don't think I had better.* If Orest's father hadn't chosen to tell his son what was really afoot, it was not Kiron's place to enlighten him. Though perhaps the problem was that Lord Ya-Tiren had taken thought for his son's chattering and loose tongue. There was no telling who among Orest's friends, including the other boys here, might talk to someone that they shouldn't.

"Hmm." Kiron folded his arms over his chest and gave Orest a knowing look. "You know, I've heard that sometimes the female Fledglings have a lot of difficulty when they first become women." He actually had heard that often enough around the temple—though possibly Orest hadn't paid any attention to that sort of thing. He could be very single-minded, could Orest. Some might call him dense, but not Kiron; Orest could be absolutely brilliant when he chose to exercise his mind. The problem was convincing him of the need to do so. If Orest had a fault, it was that he concentrated only on what interested him and ignored or carelessly forgot everything else.

"What do you—" Orest began, then, to Kiron's great amusement, flushed a deep and painful-looking scarlet. "Oh. Ah. Yes, that might be it. I've—ah—heard the same thing—"

*Well. Maybe he does pay attention once in a while.*

"But of course your father wouldn't put it that baldly," Kiron continued, as bland as cream.

"Of course he wouldn't. And that must be it." Embarrassed though he might be, Orest must have been grateful for the explanation, for he seized on it with evident relief. "I hope she feels better, but if anyone can make her feel well, it will be Aunt Re. She's almost a Healer, she knows so much, and Aket-ten loves the farm."

Orest returned to the vigil over his egg with the air of someone who has had a great deal of concern lifted from him. Kiron, for his part, went to check on Avatre (who was not at all interested in stirring from her warm sand, so that she looked like a heap of rubies half-buried in it), and then went for a walk in the rain.

After that first torrential downpour, the rains were no heavier here than any ordinary rainy season—but rumor said that things were otherwise in the kingdom of the enemy. With exquisite timing, the Magi had—so it was claimed—arranged for terrible storms to lash the Tian countryside coinciding with the highest point of the Flood coming down Great Mother River from the lands above the Cataracts. The result—supposedly—was going to be a flood of epic proportions. Not only farmlands would be flooded, but whole villages, towns, even parts of the great cities that were too low to escape.

If this was true, Kiron felt unexpectedly sorry for the Tian farmers and villagers. The mud brick used for their homes could not stand against rising waters; people would return after the waters had receded only to find that their houses had melted away in the flood. This was going to cause a lot of hardship and it wouldn't be to the people who were waging this war, it would be to the poor farmers and craftsmen who just wanted to get on quietly with their lives and didn't give a toss about where the border was. In fact, it would impact the poor serfs on captured Altan land the most—their Tian overlords could escape the flooding, but they would have nowhere to go.

It seemed a very unfair way to wage a war, when the people who were responsible for it were not the people paying the price.

And he knew very well what others would say about that—it was too bad for all those farmers and serfs, but that was the way that war went. And maybe it was, but it still seemed very unfair to him.

It had seemed a fine thing when the Jousters of Tia were grounded by storms that hadn't affected anyone else so much—but this war on those who weren't even part of the fighting was just—wrong.

In fact, everything he had learned about the Magi in the last three days had that same faint aura of *wrongness* about it.

Not that he had been able to learn much.

The Magi kept pretty much to themselves, up there in their

"Palace of Wisdom" or whatever they called it. As if they were the only people in all of Alta to have a true grasp of wisdom. That seemed a case of monumental hubris to him. But you didn't see a Magus out beyond the First Canal very much; people said they were doing important things, too important to leave their stronghold. Kiron had the feeling, though, that it was because they didn't care to mix with those they felt were beneath them. It also seemed to him that they cultivated mystery and secrecy to the same extent that the Winged Ones eschewed it.

There was one time and place where he *was* seeing them though. Every morning, in the predawn, collecting Winged Fledglings. Every morning, the Fledglings lined up like a column of ants and marched silently out into the rain under the guidance of four Magi. By midmorning, they were returned, only they looked— drained. Blank-faced, pale, and stumbling with exhaustion. Kiron had a notion that this was exactly what they were—drained, that is. Hadn't there been a tale going around the Jousters' Compound in Tia that the sea witches had found a way to combine their power to send those new and powerful storms down on Tia? Well, it looked to him as if the Magi had indeed done just that. With one small addition to the story; it didn't look to him as if they were troubling themselves with the small detail of cooperation and willing partnership.

If the returned Fledglings felt as bad as they looked—if this was what had happened to Aket-ten—well, he didn't blame her one tiny bit for not wanting to be taken away a second time.

As he crossed the bridge from the Third Ring to the Second, he had the road mostly to himself. No one wanted to be out during the rains—except perhaps the swamp dragons. He wondered what being drained day after day was going to do to these Fledglings. It might make them stronger, but somehow he doubted it. It was far more likely to make them weaker, or burn them out altogether. Perhaps it was ungenerous of him, but nevertheless he had the feeling that such an outcome was not going to displease the Magi one bit. If the Magi had any real rivals for power and influence at all, it was the Winged Ones. Weakening the Winged Ones would only make the Magi stronger.

As for the rest, the only way to really find out anything was to get into the Magi's stronghold—

*As if I am likely to be able to get away with something like that!* he scoffed at himself, hunching his back against a gust of cold, rain-filled wind. *No, Lord Ya-tiren is right. Silver and gold will loosen tongues and I don't have much of either.*

What he *did* have, however, was a reason to go see Lord Ya-tiren. Not overtly to find out about Lord Ya-tiren's daughter, but to report on his son's excellent progress. Although he made no such similar reports to the other boys' fathers, there was a special bond of obligation on both sides between himself and Lord Ya-tiren, and no one would think twice about Kiron going to pay a visit to his patron's household during such an idle time, in order to tell him that the son he had been concerned about was thriving and making outstanding progress. So that was what he was ostensibly going to do now.

He said as much to the door servant, and his lordship's steward, and the servant who came to bring him into his lordship's presence. He was enthusiastic in his praise of Orest, which made all three servants smile, for Orest was a great favorite among them.

"Kiron, rider of Avatre!" Lord Ya-tiren greeted him, with a smile, as he entered the workroom where Ya-tiren was perusing a pile of letters. His lordship had a brazier burning beside his table to chase away the cold. On his table stood a fine alabaster lamp burning sweetly scented oil. The sound of the rain outside was muffled by the thick walls of his workroom, which were painted with scenes of duck hunting with cat and falcon. Kiron recalled Aket-ten telling him how she "spoke" to her father's cats and birds to make sure they were in good condition for just that sport. "Come and sit, and tell me how my son gets on!"

It was rather flattering to be invited to sit, as if he was an equal of Ya-tiren, both in age and in rank. He wasn't going to let it go to his head, though. He wasn't either of those things, and he had no intention of pretending that he was. He did take the proffered chair, though, and waited patiently while Ya-tiren finished the scroll, gave his scribe some instructions, and sent the man out of the room.

"Orest is flourishing, my lord," Kiron began. "He is most diligent in his duties."

"And in his studies as well, praise Te-oth; his tutors have never been so pleased. I was beginning to despair over him until he seized on this desire to become a Jouster, but it seems that being rewarded with his wish has given him the motivation he had been lacking until now," Lord Ya-tiren said, with a smile, and without changing either his expression or his tone of voice, went on, "and you were right to be concerned about my youngest. There have been visits and—pressure—which you were correct to anticipate. I was taken off guard. I shall not be so unwary again." And then, without missing a beat, he continued, "So when is the egg due to hatch? I assume that once it does, I shall not see much of Orest."

Lord Ya-tiren's eyes flicked, ever so briefly, to the door. Kiron took that as a warning that there might be someone listening there. "That is quite true, my Lord," he replied, as cheerfully as he could. "And I believe that the eggs will begin to hatch at the end of the rains, or thereabouts. You would be welcome to visit him, of course, if your duties permit you the leisure. The youngsters need a great deal of comforting from their surrogate mothers until they are old enough to begin amusing themselves with play."

"Play? Dragons play?" said Ya-tiren, momentarily diverted.

Since dragons in general and Avatre in particular were the dearest things in Kiron's heart, he could always be persuaded to talk about them, so he waxed eloquent on the subject of how tame dragons—which were not drugged and numb with *tala*, and so required things to do when they weren't fighting or flying patrols—entertained themselves. *I'm beginning to sound like Ari*, he thought, wryly, as he listened to himself babble. *Dragon obsessed!* But Ya-tiren gave every indication of being interested and asked many intelligent questions, until finally, a subtle relaxation and flicker of the eyes told Kiron that the unseen listener had gone.

*Probably bored. Just as well. Maybe the next time I come he won't be so keen to eavesdrop.*

"Well, I have taken enough of your time, Kiron," his lordship said, signaling that the interview was at an end—which was, in a way, frustrating, for Kiron had not learned anything much about Aket-ten. "I appreciate the time you have taken to tell me of my son's progress."

"It is not only my pleasure, my Lord," he said sincerely, covering his disappointment, "It is my honor to do so. I am in your debt."

"Not at all," Ya-tiren replied, as Kiron rose and prepared to leave. "And—oh, by the way," he added casually—*too* casually—as Kiron was halfway to the door, "I think you will find it highly profitable to pay a visit to the Temple of All Gods on this Ring. The Healers have a young female apprentice there who, they say, is learning to treat the ailments of dragons. It is said that she arrived very recently. My friends there are taking especial care of her, as she seems to be shy and reclusive. She could benefit from your experience, and perhaps you might find a way to introduce her into the Jousters' Compound."

*The one place where the Magi have little or no reason to go—the Temple of All Gods!* And furthermore, it was the one place that even the Magi would hesitate to invade with the intent of dragging someone unwillingly away. It was never wise to offend the Healers—for you might find yourself looking in vain for help the next time you were hurt or ill. Or if the help was forthcoming, it would be the *least* pleasant treatment available. Healers never forgot. Kiron bowed a little, but his smile of understanding won an answering smile from Lord Ya-tiren. "Thank you for that information, my Lord; it is *most* welcome. I shall seek out this apprentice immediately."

He collected his rain cape from the steward, and slogged out into the downpour; the Temple was about a quarter of the Ring away, and he was going to have plenty of time to think about his conversation with Lord Ya-tiren on the way there.

Kiron presented himself to the servant at the temple door, blessing the fact that the door had a generous overhang that shielded him from the rain. Unlike nearly every other temple in Alta, this one had a doorkeeper, rather than being open to anyone who cared to walk into the antechamber. It was the difference between being a place where worshipers needed to be persuaded inside and coaxed to part with their offerings, and being a place where those who came to the door truly needed what was on the other side of the portal and would fling offerings at whoever would accept them. But of course, this wasn't really a temple as such. It was a place where the sick and injured were brought, and because of that, it needed a doorkeeper to ensure that the sick and injured were taken care of by exactly the right people as soon as they crossed the threshold.

Actually, the place had more than one doorkeeper, as Kiron was quick to notice. There was the one that greeted him—a servant, or perhaps a slave, whose job must have been to intercept the hale and hearty casual visitor—and several more people waiting just inside, sitting on a long bench pushed up against a wall painted with scenes of men and women gathering herbs. Every one of those waiting was clad, perhaps in deference to the weather, in practical light woolen tunics that came to calf length, and there was not a hint of a wig or an elaborate hairstyle among them. All watched the door, with the look of alert anticipation of dogs about to be let loose to run.

The antechamber was relatively small, small enough for a single brazier to keep it reasonably warm. He took stock of those waiting as he explained what had brought him here to the doorkeeper. All were young, though a little older than he. Healers, newly made? Waiting for patients to be carried in, for urgent summons for those too ill or hurt to move? That surmise was borne out a moment later, when a panting slave arrived with a message of dire illness, and left a heartbeat later with one of the bench sitters, rain cape-enwrapped and a box of medicines and instruments in hand.

Kiron's own inquiry after the "apprentice dragon Healer" brought a nod and an invitation to take the seat just vacated. Now he found himself facing a wall painted with scenes of more men and women preparing medicines. At least it wasn't scenes of Healers working on patients. He stared at the painting for a while, then decided that he really didn't want to know what went into some of those medicines and dropped his eyes to stare at the polished sandstone of the floor. He didn't have to contemplate it for long, though. The slave that the doorkeeper sent off returned quickly, and beckoned him to follow.

They passed through a door in the right-hand wall of the antechamber. To his relief, they did not go anywhere near the treatment areas. A dragon boy quickly developed a strong stomach, but Kiron had the uneasy feeling that his "strong stomach" would not be proof against some of the more unpleasant aspects of human illness and injury and its treatment. Instead, the slave led him through the sanctuary with its row upon row of statues and shrines, none very large, but all carefully tended and each with an offering of flowers or incense in front of it. It was a bit disconcerting to see all these statues together, and realize just how many gods the Altans worshiped. There were no windows here; the room was lit by oil-burning, alabaster lamps that gave off a warm glow. The ceiling was painted in the image of the night sky, and the columns as giant *latas* flowers. They passed down the main aisle and through a small door on the other side of the room. It hadn't exactly been concealed, but unless you knew what to look for, it was rather hard to find, for it was in the midst of a wall painting of the door into the Judgment Chamber where the hearts of the dead were weighed. So, in fact, it looked like a door—a painted door.

His estimation of the cleverness of the Healers rose.

On the other side were what were clearly the Healers' private quarters; quiet, dim corridors lined with closed doors, painted with a long, continuous river scene that showed no humans, only birds, animals, and fish. And finally, after much traversing of corridors, the slave brought him to a small room overlooking a courtyard with a *latas* pool in the midst of it. It had a wide door standing open and on the other side, a window through which the pool was visible through the curtains of rain. A chair stood beside the window, and that was all he could see of the room from where he stood.

And seated in the chair, reading a scroll (as he might have expected) was Aket-ten. How he knew it was her, he could not have said, because the lady in the chair was nothing like the girl he knew.

She, who favored the simplest of robes and tunics, and wore her hair short, had been—well, the only appropriate term was *transformed*—rather thoroughly. The wig she wore was a copy of the "royal" hairstyle formerly sported by Toreth, made of thousands of tiny braids, each ending in three beads: one lapis, one turquoise, and one gold. Gone was her collar of a Winged One; in its place was a collar of gold, lapis, and turquoise with no representations woven into it. She wore a light woolen robe dyed a dark indigo blue that clung to her body, and a white woolen mantle embroidered with *latas* flowers pulled around her shoulders against the chill. In fact, she wore more jewelry than he ever remembered her wearing before; earrings, a beaded girdle that matched the collar, a beaded headband over the wig, armbands, wristbands. . . . That dress showed rather disconcertingly that she wasn't the "little girl" her brother thought she was.

As for her face—when she looked up at the sound of their footsteps in her door, he saw that she—who hardly had the patience to allow her servants to line her eyes of a morning—now had a full set of makeup; complete kohl lining to the eyes, powdered malachite to the lids, reddened cheeks, reddened lips—

If he hadn't *known*, by some inner alchemy, that it was Aket-ten, he probably wouldn't have recognized her. Which was, after all, the point. If those who were looking for her took thought about what Aket-ten was like, they just might go looking for her among the slaves and the servants. But they would never search for a fine young lady, and even if they believed that this lady really was Aket-ten, they would hesitate to seize someone dressed in the manner of a lady of rank and privilege.

But she leaped to her feet and flung her arms around his neck the moment he entered the room, the scroll she had been reading flung aside like a bit of scrap. "Kiron!" she sobbed into his ear, as the slave took himself discreetly out. "Oh, Kiron! I am so glad you came! Oh, thank you, thank you—"

His first impulse was to pry her arms from around his throat, but his second was to put his own around her and let her cry. He followed through on the second impulse. *I don't know what's been happening,* he thought, as surprise turned to a smoldering anger, *But Aket-ten doesn't frighten easily, and she's scared.* He knew who it was that was responsible, of course.

The Magi. Her father had said something about "pressure." Aket-ten's fear told him just how much pressure there must have been.

It was a very good thing that her dress was a dark blue, because the kohl lining her eyes was soon running down her cheeks in streaks, and would have ruined a white gown. He just let her cry; she had obviously been having a bad couple of days. And after a while, he began to enjoy holding her, in spite of her obvious distress. It made him feel unexpectedly strong and protective and capable. It made him feel—expectedly—very angry at whoever had frightened her so. And there were some rather new and entirely pleasant sensations stirring that he couldn't quite put a name to—

Finally, it was she who reluctantly disengaged herself from his arms and scrubbed at her eyes with the back of her hand (making the damage to her makeup much worse). She looked down at the mess on her hand and winced.

"Marit-ka is going to kill me," she said forlornly. "After all that work—"

"Marit-ka is just going to have to do it over," he replied, and steered her over to the chair she had been sitting on when he came in. He sat her down on it, looked about for a bit of cloth, spotted a towel beside an empty basin on a little table nearby, and took it out to hold it in the rain pouring down into the courtyard. When it was soaked, he brought it in and, with the expertise of someone who had been caring for the soft and tender skin of a dragonet for a year, scrubbed all of the streaked and ruined makeup from her face, taking care to get all of the malachite and kohl from around her red-rimmed, swollen eyes. He went out again for more of the cold rain, rinsing the towel as best as he could, and bathed her eyes again. She let him, holding still beneath his hands, her own clasped in her lap, her back rigid.

"There," he said at last, looking at his handiwork. "I've at least left Marit-ka with a clean surface to repaint. Now, why don't you tell me what has been happening to make you turn into Great Mother River in flood?"

She giggled weakly at that, which he took as a good sign. "It isn't so much that anything *happened*," she said at last. "It's that—Father had visitors, nasty and important visitors asking after me, and afterward he was frightened. I've never seen Father frightened before. That was the first time they came, and it was right after you brought me home, as if they knew where I had gone."

Kiron thought privately that the reason Aket-ten had never seen her father look frightened was probably only because Aket-ten hadn't actually been looking—or else, because Lord Ya-tiren had never brought himself to the attention of ruthless men before. He seemed to live a quiet life, there in his villa, as remote from the world as it was possible for a landed lord to be. Well, the world had come intruding. It was probably as much of a shock to him as it had been to his daughter.

But he said none of this to Aket-ten. "What kind of visitors?" he asked. "What did they say? And what did Lord Ya-tiren do?" He wondered if the Magi had sent someone else to do their dirty work—or if it had been some high-ranking noble acting on their behalf.

"The Magi came themselves," she replied, and shuddered. "The same ones that came for me that day you rescued me. That was when Father was frightened; I don't know what he said, but it was probably what I told him to tell them, that I was ill. The next day, they came again. They wanted to know if I was there, and when Father told them I was still ill, they wanted to know *how* ill, and when I would be well, and what exactly was wrong with me." She flushed. "I have the Far-Seeing Gaze, and—ah—I'm afraid I used it when I knew they were in the house the second time. I wanted to know what *they* wanted."

He shrugged. "That's only wise," he told her. "Lord Ya-tiren probably meant well, trying to protect you from knowing what they said to him, but I don't think he was doing you any favors. It was much better for you to know just how bad things were. So, go on. What did Lord Ya-tiren say to them?"

She rubbed her eyes again; despite his ministrations, they still looked very red and sore. "I think he asked one of his Healer-friends for some advice on what to say. He said that it was woman's troubles, the kind of thing that got Afre-tatef sent home a few moons ago. They wanted to know why I'd never shown any signs of it before, he got irritated and said, 'How am I to know? I am only a father, not a Healer or a Winged One!' Then he told them he had sent me to my aunt on her husband's estate outside the Seventh Canal for a rest. That maybe I would be back, and maybe I wouldn't, and it all depended on how the gods dealt with my troubles. Then he tried to ask them why *they* were so interested in a Winged One when I wasn't training to be a Magus, and that was when they got very nasty." She shuddered again. "It wasn't anything that they said, it was the way that they said it. That Father must be sure to take good care of me, because Fledglings like me were important to the protection of Alta, and the Great Ones took the protection of Alta very seriously, and that I wasn't just his daughter, I was a resource that he was holding in trust for all of Alta and—well, more things like that."

"I can imagine," Kiron said grimly and, in fact, he could. Although he had never been on the receiving end of such treatment, in no small part because anyone who wanted to intimidate him was usually perfectly free to beat him bloody, he had seen that sort of thing at work. "Lovely pots you have. It would be a shame if they were to all be smashed because you didn't have someone around to keep an eye on them for you." "The Headman of the village would really like this favor. You wouldn't want to disappoint him." "You know that people have gotten into trouble over less." "Such a problem your son is—all it would take is one more complaint and who knows what would happen to him—" Oh, yes, he knew the silky tone, the innocent stare, the knife hidden beneath the cloth, the threat that was never implied in such a way that it was obvious to anyone except the one who was threatened.

"Anyway, *you* had warned Father already, and I was already hiding in the servants' quarters. And as soon as he was sure that they were gone, his friend smuggled me here." She sniffed. "I'm supposed to be learning how to Heal dragons. Actually, I am. I thought as long as I was here, I might just as well do it."

He smiled at her, feeling that a pat on the head or her back would not be accepted well at the moment, and anything—well—warmer—might lead somewhere he wasn't yet sure he wanted to go. "Good for you! And that gives me every excuse to come visit you!"

She brightened at that. "It does, doesn't it! That's been the worst of it, it's so *lonely*—"

"We'll just wait until the Magi have given up on you ever coming back," he told her soothingly. "Then maybe we can bring you back as you and we can say that your Gifts have all gone. Could the Magi tell if your Gifts were gone?"

She frowned. "Probably not. The other Winged Ones could, but—but maybe I could hide them." Then she looked as if she was going to burst into tears again. "Oh, this isn't *fair!* I've trained so hard to develop my Gifts, and now—"

"I didn't say not to use them" he pointed out. "Just don't let the Magi know you still have them." He scratched his head in thought. "You know, you could say that your aunt taught you to Heal animals, and we can bring you in to help with the dragons. The Magi almost never come around the dragons; I don't think they like them, much. How does that strike you?"

She sighed. "I suppose this must be my ordeal," she said, sadly. "It certainly feels like an ordeal. And the gods send every Winged One a different sort."

"Then there you are, that's probably exactly what it is," he agreed, deciding that patting her hands would probably be all right. "Uh—do you think the Magi had any idea that your father was lying?"

To his relief, she shook her head. "They haven't got that sort of power," she said firmly. "I'd *know.* I think that's one reason why they need us. And when he wants to be, Father is very good at lying."

For her sake, he hoped so.

He stayed with her as long as he could without interfering with his own duties, and when he left, she was more of her old animated self, determined to make the best of her "ordeal" by learning all she could about dragons and the things that could hurt them or make them sick. She had admitted to him that at this point, there really wasn't anything that any of the senior Winged Ones could teach her about the Gifts that the gods had given her; she had been told in confidence that she was not only the strongest Animal Speaker there was, but was likely to be the most accurate Far-Seeing Eye of her generation, and that what she needed more than anything was practice.

"I can practice here as well as anywhere else," she said after a while. "Maybe better. I can always help those who Heal animals by finding out what the animals are feeling."

He had encouraged her to follow that path; the more she had

to occupy her mind, the less lonely she would be. Aket-ten didn't have the same knack for making friends that Orest did, but she was always willing and eager to help, and he didn't think it would be very long before the Healers were protecting her for her own self and not as a favor to her father.

But there were a great many uncomfortable thoughts that occurred to him as he trudged through the rain, going back across the bridge to the Jousters' Compound on the Third Ring.

If, as he thought, the Magi were burning out the Fledglings' Gifts with their ruthless exploitation of their powers, that explained in part why they were so interested in getting Aket-ten back into their hands. First, she probably represented a great deal of raw strength for their spells. Second, and this might be the most important of the two reasons, they had every reason to *want* to burn her out.

He had, perforce, been learning more about the political structure of Alta lately. It would have been difficult not to, with a prince and the most likely successor to the current Great Ones as one of his trainees. Things just came out in conversation, and the one thing that had struck him more than anything else was that the Magi had become very, very powerful in this land. All but one of the advisory positions that had once been held by Priests were now held by Magi.

It seemed likely to him that the last thing they wanted was for someone who had been Gifted with reliable visions of the future to become a full Winged One—for that someone would be able to advise the Great Ones with no consideration for anything other than what he—or she—Saw. That would take a fair chunk of power out of their hands, and leave them vulnerable to contradiction in Council whenever there were things they wanted done, actions they wanted taken, that might be contrary to what was really best for Alta. Nor was it particularly in their interest to have someone who could See what was going on in Tia and on the border reporting directly to the Great Ones—not when the Magi wanted reports of how their spells were decimating the enemy where it hurt him most, whether or not those reports were true. The very last thing they wanted was someone who could say, definitively, that what the Magi were doing was mostly affecting the lot of poor farmers who had very little to do with the war.

No, that was not something that would make them very happy. He wished that he had someone he could confide in and ask advice of. . . .

Frankly, he wished that Ari was around.

*But that's not possible,* he reminded himself. *It's time to start thinking on your own.*

Well, there was one thing that he could do. He could start educating himself thoroughly on the intricate details of how things were run in Alta—how much power the Magi had, say, and how much the Great Ones were likely to let them get away with.

And he had just the person to help him with that—

Prince Toreth.

Provided, of course, he could do so without betraying his feelings on the subject. But then again, he had a lot of practice in hiding his feelings. With luck, all that practice would stand him in good stead now.

*On the other hand, Toreth has never shown any sign of being fond of the Magi,* he reminded himself. *I wonder if it's possible that I'll find an ally there?*

"The Magi—" Kiron began, in as casual a tone as he could manage.

Toreth was in the middle of turning his egg; Kiron was in the pen with him on the pretense of overseeing him.

"Just what are they, anyway?" he continued, as Toreth finished the quarter turn. "Besides the people who created the Eye, I mean?"

Toreth settled his egg back into the sand, covered all but the very top with hot sand, and gave him an opaque look. "Why are you so curious about the Magi?"

"Because they don't exist in Tia, and that's where I lived most of my life," Kiron replied, trying to look as innocent as possible. "All of the magicians there are in the priesthoods of several temples. Then I come here, and there the Magi are, in their fortress right next to the Great Ones' Palace, and—" he shrugged. "And there's the Eye, of course."

"Oh, yes. The Eye." The sour tone of Toreth's voice made Kiron blink. "The Eye—which, as we are told, is our protection. As the Magi have shown us so carefully, it can strike anywhere outside the First Canal, so we need never fear invasion."

"I must admit, that bothers me," Kiron replied, feeling his way very slowly. "Isn't the point to stop invaders at the Seventh Canal? What's the point of letting everyone know that it can do the same damage closer in?"

Toreth looked at a point over Kiron's shoulder. Kiron knew what was there—the Central Island. And even if Toreth couldn't see the Palace and the Tower of Wisdom peeking over the walls because the awnings had been drawn against the rain, they both knew what was there.

"Oh, yes," Toreth breathed softly. "And my cousins are so dependent on the Magi and their wise counsel—the counsel that has caused us to lose more land to Tia every year. The counsel that tells us to close our doors to outside trade because trade brings change, and the Magi want things in Alta City to remain the same. The Magi, who demand so much, and give so little in return. . . ."

"But the Eye," Kiron ventured.

Toreth laughed harshly. "They have never used it to defend the city. They have never succeeded in creating a second one. They claim the old one can't be moved. And yet—" his voice dropped to a growl, "—and yet half the city's taxes goes into the coffers of the Magi."

That was a shock. Kiron stared at him, not quite believing what he had just heard. "Surely not—"

"Surely," Toreth contradicted him. "And whenever someone sues for peace, or an adviser suggests that it might be time for the

Magi to have a little less of city's revenue, the Magi are in the Great Ones' ears, whispering, reminding them of past wrongs, persuading them of future glory, egging them into a patriotic fever. Oh, yes. I have been there and heard it for myself."

"But they do work for the good of Alta—" Kiron ventured.

Toreth stood straight up and looked directly into Kiron's eyes. "Do they? I have seen no evidence of that. These storms they send down into Tia—are they actually weakening the Tian forces? Or are they merely making people miserable and increasing their determination to crush us? Others have suggested that it would be more effective for the Magi to accompany our army— never have I seen a single Magus in the ranks. Oh, the Magi *do* strive most vigorously—for the good of the Magi. And of late, I have heard uncomfortable tales of visits to the Temple of the Twins." He lifted an eyebrow. "But perhaps *you* know more about that than I?"

"Come to Avatre's pen," Kiron said, making up his mind on the instant. "I would like to discuss some things with you."

Toreth smiled. "I rather hoped you would."

# NINE

KIRON moved the brazier closer to their corner; he did not light a lamp, however. "The Great Ones do not rule in Alta," said Toreth bluntly, when he and Kiron had settled into the corner of Kiron's room off Avatre's pen, a corner where it would not be apparent that the room was even occupied. "The Magi do."

They had each taken a cushion and had settled with their backs to the wall. Rain drummed on the roof, and far-off thunder rumbled; inside, Toreth had dropped easily into the scribe's erect, kneeling posture, while Kiron crossed his legs under him and put his back against the wall, the better to look the prince in the face. There wasn't much light coming from the door and the ceiling-height air slits, but it would have to do. While this statement did not come as a complete surprise to Kiron, the knowledge had a bitter edge to it. "I think I had begun to see the shape of this," he admitted. "Nevertheless, it is ill hearing. How long, do you think?"

Toreth grimaced, and shrugged. "It is hard to say when; rot never sets in all at once. The tree in your garden looks a bit seedy, but you think, 'oh, it is just this or that,' and it does not really concern you until the storm comes and it smashes the roof of your house, and you see that it was all hollow inside, eaten away. It probably began before my great-grandfather was born. I will tell you something that you, who are new-come to Alta, did not know. The Great Ones that currently sit in the Twin Thrones are well over seventy Floods in age."

"That old?" Kiron exclaimed, shocked. In his village, the oldest person was no more than fifty when he died. Most were fortunate to attain forty. Wedded at fourteen or fifteen, they would certainly see the first of their grandchildren born, and what more did anyone need?

Toreth nodded. "And the Great Ones before them were near eighty when they died. And the ones before *them* were ninety."

"But—" Kiron's brow wrinkled as he tried to recall dim memories of adults talking about other adults—marking the generations—saying, "and Old Man so-and-so must have been—" "The oldest man *I* ever heard of was no more than sixty, and—"

The prince leaned forward intently. "And what would you say if you were a ruler, and a Magus came to you and said, 'I can make you live to see your great-great-grandchildren.' What would you grant a man who could offer you that? A position as adviser? A council seat? The post of Vizier? Positions for his friends? And if these people were the same who created a weapon that absolutely meant that this city could *never* be taken by enemies? What would you give him then? If all he wanted was to take some of the burden of rule from you, and leave you to deal with only the pleasant aspects of the Twin Thrones?"

Kiron blinked. "Is that the way of it, then?" he asked softly, feeling dread steal over him.

Toreth pinched the bridge of his nose as if his head pained him. "I have no proof," he admitted. "I have not even a rumor. But at some point three hundred years ago, the Magi began to live to see eighty, ninety, or even a hundred Floods. And about a generation later, the Great Ones of Alta did the same. Kaleth has searched the records, and from the time that the Great Ones began to see such long years, the Magi have had greater and greater say in things, until now—" He shrugged. "What does any man want, if you ask him and he answers without thought? Wealth, power, and a long life. The Great Ones have always had the first two. Now, for the last three reigns, they have the second. And all they had to give up," his voice turned mocking, "was a little *responsibility*."

Kiron tried to reckon up the years in his head. "Toreth—does it seem to you that the war between Alta and Tia began about that time?"

Toreth's eyes narrowed. "As a matter of fact," he said slowly, "It does. There is a thought in your head. What is it?"

"The Magi can take heat from one place where it is not wanted, and put it in the sands of our pens," he said, feeling his way to the heart of the thought. "But where does one get extra years of life? Except that in war. . . ."

Toreth rocked back on his heels, eyes wide. "I like that thought not at all!" he said, and though it was a whisper, the shock in his tone made it as "loud" as a shout.

"No more do I," Kiron replied grimly. "But it is one way to 'profit' from a war."

"There are others," Toreth said, after a long silence. "Yet were I to examine things closely, I doubt not that I should find the Magi's hands outstretched there, too. They are wealthy men; wealthy enough to be above such things as mere noble blood. And when one has the ears of the Great Ones, there are many ways of obtaining more wealth. Theirs is shadow power, but the shadows can hold many things."

Kiron thought silently of all the ways that one could profit from war. The making of weapons, certainly. The supply of tents, of food for the army, of horses, of other gear, from cooking pots to the linen for bandages. And he wondered; certainly the Great One of Tia was a man of no more than middle years, and there were no Magi as such in Tia. But had he not heard of a certain adviser, a little man, a crafty man, a man to whom the Great One listened more often than to others, who had remarkably served in the same capacity to *his* father, and his father's father? How long before that adviser whispered in the Tian's ear, and was heeded and believed—being, in fact, his own best evidence?

He could not be sure. The thought made him ill.

It also had a terrible logic. How else to explain something as senseless as this war, unless someone profited by it?

"I wonder who began it." A peal of thunder punctuated the question.

He did not realize he had said the words aloud until he saw Toreth shrug.

"I do not think that it matters now," Toreth replied. "The question is, how to stop it?"

The words hit Kiron like a hard brick, and stunned him nearly as thoroughly. Once again, he spoke without thinking, as his mind put handfuls of bits of disparate thoughts together. "So long as the Tians have more Jousters than we, there is nothing *Altans* can do to stop it. If the war were fought man to man—"

"Then they could advance no farther, and might be driven back." Toreth nodded approvingly. "Kaleth thinks that if the Tian Jouster advantage could be nullified, so that we could say to our people 'there is no more to fear from the Jousters of Tia, let us have a truce,' then no matter what was whispered in whose ear, the Altans, common and noble alike, would support a truce. The Priests would support a truce; no few of them have lost brothers, fathers, and children to the armies. If the Priests were united, and the Great Ones fostering it, even the Magi would not dare to oppose it. And he believes that if the Tian Jousters no longer ruled the skies, that they could no longer descend upon a village and terrorize it, then the Tians would begin to think on the possibility that it might soon be one of their villages that is served the self-same dish, and support a truce."

"But what of those who poison wells and burn fields by night?" Kiron asked reluctantly.

Toreth sighed. "We had not thought that far," he admitted.

"But we have a start. And the Great Ones are old. They grow no younger, and stolen years are not healthy years, they only prolong life, not turn back the sands of time. Eventually, Kaleth and I will take their places, and then—" his eyes gleamed. "—then the Magi had best look to themselves. We will not be gulled by promises of stolen years. We are not greedy. We will content ourselves with power and wealth, and let the gods send as long a life as they may."

"And in the meantime?" Kiron asked.

The prince tilted his head to the side and shrugged. "We think. We plan. We gather friends to support us when the time comes. Friends of *all* sorts," he added meaningfully.

Once again, Kiron felt as if he had been stunned, as the pieces came together. "Like a wing of a new sort of Jouster?" he asked dryly. "Am I the last?"

Toreth laughed, although it was a laugh with a great deal of irony in it. "No, not quite. Is Orest to be trusted, do you think?"

"With my life, yes," he replied honestly. "With my secret—I am not so sure."

Toreth shook his head with mock-sadness. "Gossips worse than a girl, that one. Perhaps raising a dragonet will steady him. Right now, I would sooner trust his sister. And I wish that she were one of us; she has sense, that Aket-ten, and she is as good a scholar as my brother. And if she grows into the promise of her powers—I could do far worse than have a Far-Sighted Winged One who is not afraid to speak the truth as an adviser. I hope she recovers from her illness and returns to the city soon."

It was on the tip of Kiron's tongue to tell the prince the truth about Aket-ten, but he bit it back. This would be a bad time to spill someone else's secret. Nevertheless— "I might find someone as useful," he said instead. "A Healer, perhaps. I have a friend in the Temple of All Gods."

"'Trust your wife with your household, your brother with your purse, and a Healer with all,'" Toreth quoted the old proverb. "A Healer would be a good addition to our cadre."

"Well, I will wait and speak with her, and perhaps bring her to you." Kiron decided to commit to no more than that.

"Oh, a *she* is it? You sly young jackal!" Toreth grinned and winked. Kiron blushed, which only made it worse. Fortunately, Toreth was not the sort to pursue it any further, except to say, "Well, if she has a sister or a pretty friend, think on me."

"And you a betrothed man!" Kiron chided.

Toreth shrugged and grinned further. "I do not prevent my betrothed from seeking things she finds pleasurable, and she makes no demands upon me. Which is just as well, since I would pay no heed anyway. It was our parents made the arrangement, not us."

That seemed to be the end of the dangerous revelations, but Kiron was perfectly satisfied to leave many more questions unspoken and unanswered. He had more than enough to think on as it was.

Looking back on that conversation a few days later, he could point to it as the moment when his life took another unexpected direction. He seemed to have passed some sort of test, and been accepted into a fellowship that he had not, until that moment, known even existed, a fellowship of which Toreth and Kaleth were the tacit leaders. Nevertheless, when it came to the dragons, *he* was still the trainer and the leader, and if anything, the others tendered him even more respect.

Perhaps that was because he was earning it. Knowing that he would have to show them what to do, even in the midst of the rains, he was training with Avatre. She did not like it, not in the least, but he insisted that she fly in the rain, and learn to handle the tricky currents of the storms. He would not fly her when there was lightning, or up into or above the clouds, but otherwise they were going up once a day at least.

With Toreth's plan already in his mind, he was looking for all the advantages he could find. The Tian Jousters did not fly in the rain; therefore, Altan Jousters would learn how to, beginning with himself and Avatre, for every tiny advantage was something to be snatched. He knew, beyond a shadow of a doubt, that no one could force even the most heavily drugged wild-caught desert dragon into the sky in the rain, but the tame ones—well, that was another story. And in this, at least, the Altans were better equipped, for the *swamp* dragons found it no hardship.

He had figured that he could coax Avatre into it, for certainly even the desert dragons living in the wild had to fly and hunt no matter what the weather, so the thing was possible. And Avatre complained, but cooperated.

He did make sure to reward and praise her lavishly whenever the task was done.

Lord Khumun was astonished—but a handful of the riders of swamp dragons watched them with speculation, and soon began taking *their* mounts up for short practice flights as well. Rain flight was dangerous; everything was slippery, leather straps stretched and loosened, and the wind was hard to read. Sudden downpours could leave you blinded at a critical moment, and the really important thing was to make sure to get the dragon back down before she was chilled, or she would start to weaken. And a chilled dragon could sicken, even die.

Rain flight was miserable, too; it was not possible to wear a rain cape, of course. It wasn't hard to remember to get the dragon out of the sky before she chilled, when the rider was getting numb in the fingers and toes long before that point.

Still, it *was* an advantage, and the riders of swamp dragons were able to go out on patrol and even thwart some Tian raids by being "where they shouldn't be." Lord Khumun was pleased. The swamp dragon riders were more than pleased; finally they were getting their own blows in, and though the victories were small, the effect on morale was enormous.

Kiron was now getting the respect of the older Jousters that he had not gotten before. First, his training (or in some cases, retraining) suggestions, using falconry techniques, had made intractable dragons a bit easier to handle. Now, it was clear that his tame dragon was not "spoiled" since she was doing for him what no other desert dragon was willing to do. He had, with his experiments, given them victories at last. And he was taking the punishment of riding in this miserable wet weather, learning how to do it all the hard way, since there were no other examples. He sensed this new respect in the changed ways that the older men looked at him at first—then the demonstrations went from covert to overt. Someone would have their dragon boy waiting in the landing court with a flask of hot wine when he came down. The best table—the one nearest the kitchen—was left open for him and whoever cared to sit down with him at meals. Greetings went from a cool nod to a slap on the back and a hearty "Saw you up today, good flying, boy." These *were*, after all, veterans, and men as much as ten or fifteen years his senior. They were hardly going to socialize with him, and he didn't expect it—nor particularly *want* it. But the respect, after all those years of being kicked and beaten and regarded as low as the lowly weed he'd been named for—that was victory for him, and it tasted as sweet as the victories over the Tians.

And by extension, the boys of his new wing got some of that respect, too. If they didn't have the background required to savor it as much as he did, they still appreciated it. He had proved that they were not some crazed experiment doomed to fail. And some of those older Jousters who had come to see him and Avatre when they were recovering in Lord Ya-tiren's villa were now speculating enthusiastically about the day when there would be enough of the "youngsters" up and flying that these old veterans could afford the time to raise a tame dragon of their own.

*Well,* he thought, when he first overheard one of those conversations at mealtime, *I will make a point of seeing you get a fine egg on that day.*

He watched the prince watching these scarred veterans, and now that he knew Toreth and Kaleth's long-term plans, he could see Toreth weighing the men in his mind. At some point, the prince's cadre would have to expand beyond the dozen or so of his peers that he had taken into his confidence, and the logical place to start was here, among the Jousters. Of all of the inhabi-tants of Alta, these men were the ones who had the least fear of the Magi, and possibly the most (though carefully veiled) con-tempt—though Kiron suspected that if one was to investigate, probably most soldiers felt the same. And of all of the fighters of Alta, these were the men who saw the most combat. Front-line troops would face Tian troops for short periods in pitched battles; Altan Jousters faced Tian Jousters *every day* outside the season of Rains. And this had been going on for generations—while the Magi sat safely in their tower and did—what? They *said* they were working their spells against the Tians, and protecting Altans, but how could you tell? Until recently, that is—there was no doubt with the new storms that they were sending that they had hit upon something that obviously worked.

But still. They were safe in their tower while they did it. There were probably few fighting men who could view that with less than contempt.

So the prince's plans would probably meet with a great deal of approval here.

"But not now," Toreth said calmly, as he, Gan, Kalen, Oset-re and Kiron gathered one night in Gan's pen. It was no kind of for-mal planning session, but whenever any of the cadre got together, talk tended to drift toward the future, and often a good idea or two came out of it. It was Gan, not Kiron, who suggested seeking support among the older Jousters, and Toreth met the idea with approval. "But not now," he repeated. "First, we have to prove ourselves. All we are this moment is mother hens, sitting on our eggs. *Kiron* hasn't even proved himself yet, except as a flyer and someone who knows his dragons. Until I am a fighting Jouster, and can talk to them as an equal, I won't have respect that I have I've earned for myself."

"But you have the rank," countered Gan, with the unconscious air of superiority of the noble-born. Kiron wondered when he would see how much that rankled those who were of more humble birth. That he would, eventually, Kiron was sure; that languid manner covered a keen mind. "That demands respect!"

"You cannot demand the respect of the common man, Gan," said Kalen, from where he sat in the pool of light cast by Gan's lamp, stitching a giant version of a falcon's hood, for use with new-caught wild dragons. "You can demand obedience and get it, and deference, surely, but you can't demand respect, you have to earn it. Actually, that's exactly how Toreth earned my respect." He looked up with a lazy smile. "At the age of eleven, he and Kaleth had already figured *that* out, and came to where the hawks were mewed, working side by side with me, learning how to care for, tame, and train young falcons exactly as I had. Thus earning my respect. Clever lads."

"Say rather, observant," Toreth replied. "Having a father who is a Commander of Hundreds with a low level of patience makes you observant rather quickly." He pitched his voice to a growl. *"Boys! Princes you may be, but until you are Great Ones, I can whip you from here to the Seventh Canal if you don't care for that hound properly!"*

"Oh, I recall another bellow altogether," said Gan, and put his voice into the same truculent tone. *"I will drown you in the First Canal with my own hands if you do not return my seal ring!"*

"And just what were you doing with your father's seal ring?" asked Oset-re, amused.

"Trying to forge letters making us Captains of Tens, of course!" Toreth replied. "With chariots of our own, plumed helmets, and honey cakes in perpetuity."

Gan choked on his beer, laughing, and Kalen had to pound on his back until he stopped coughing.

Sometimes Kiron could only marvel at the prince's patience, working out plans that could not possibly come to pass in less than a decade. First, he would become a Jouster, while his brother insinuated himself into an administrative position where he would have access to the kinds of documents that would, in Toreth's words, "map out the rot and tell us how far we have to burn."

Then he would make sure that no matter what else happened, the Jousters were built up until their numbers equaled or bettered those of the Tians, so that when he and Kaleth rose to the Thrones, they could call for that truce without sacrificing the safety of their people. Meanwhile, Kaleth would be collecting information, finding who among the powerful and the noble could be counted upon to back Toreth against the Magi, and slowly revealing to them some of their plans. Not the end of the war, however. That was to remain a carefully guarded secret within the inner circle until Toreth and Kaleth were securely in the Twin Thrones. Then would come the overthrow of the Magi, and the signing of a truce with Tia. The farther into the future, of course, the vaguer the plans became, until they were goals rather than plans—but for the near-term, Toreth and his twin had a great deal already mapped out.

Perhaps, especially given their suspicions about the long lives of the Great Ones, other young men would have been plotting the overthrow of the current Great Ones, not a peaceful transition. Not Toreth and Kaleth. "That would undermine everything—and probably get us caught and strangled," Toreth confided to Kiron later that evening. "No. We will have the thrones legitimately, in our time. The only thing that anyone will *ever* be able to prove, even if someone betrays us, is that we wish to restore some of the power that the Magi took back to the priesthood. There is naught wrong with that—and much that would be considered pious."

"Have the Magi tried to cultivate you?" Kiron asked, curiously. He could not imagine the Magi not trying so obvious a ploy with the next in line to the throne.

Toreth laughed aloud, and the others glanced up from the game of hounds and jackals they were playing. "What?" asked Gan.

"Have the Magi tried to cultivate my brother and me?" Toreth asked aloud.

Oset-re snorted. "Like experienced old whores sidling up to drunken sailors!" he replied. Once again, he exercised his talent for imitation, somehow making himself look both haughty and oily at the same time. "Has my Lord Toreth any need for my humble services?" he oozed. "A spell to catch a young lady's attention, perhaps? A talisman for gambling luck, or one against drunkenness?" He flared his nostrils delicately. "Or perhaps you, my Lord Kaleth—I have some scrolls you might find of—interest." He pretended to unfurl a scroll.

Toreth mock-gagged. "I tried to play the cocky—and none too bright—spoiled brat, who is so certain of himself that he mocks the very idea of needing any arcane help. I hope I didn't overplay it. Kaleth simply looked myopic and horrified. He *was* horrified, and properly so—as erotic scrolls go, that one was singularly awful."

Kiron managed to find time to visit Aket-ten twice more during the next half moon. He actually wanted to visit her more than that, but he was afraid that if he went too often, he would draw unwelcome attention to her.

As it was, he took care to pick a time when the rains were particularly heavy—heavy enough that he had the bridge *and* the streets to himself. Furthermore, he took the precaution of stopping in a very popular food and beer shop on the way. If anyone was following him, they'd be hard-put to distinguish which of the patrons of the place he was when he came out. As a Jouster, he was paid just like any other soldier, even if he hadn't actually fought yet, so he had some money in his pouch. That allowed him to stay just long enough to have some duck sausage and hot wine, and when he left, it was at the same time as two other men.

Once again he presented himself at the door of the Temple of All Gods, but this time the slave took him into another part of the private quarters.

A library, of course.

Niches lined the walls, scrolls piled in them, and characters written on the wall beneath each niche told the category. Care for these precious objects was a constant battle between damp and fire, so there were no open windows or open flames here. All the lamps were carefully shielded, but the lack of windows meant that there had to be a great many of them.

The girl who was seated at a distant table, bent over a scroll, looked a lot more like the Aket-ten he knew, though the woolen gown was enough like the one she'd been wearing the last time to be its charcoal-colored sister, and it clung to her young body in a very interesting fashion. Again, as he watched her before she became aware of his presence, he had to think that she was not Orest's "little" sister anymore.

The slave went to her and whispered in her ear; she looked up, and this time, both to his relief and his disappointment, she did not leap up and fling herself at him.

She took the weights off the scroll and let it roll itself back up, stored it in its niche, and only then did she rise to greet him.

She did hurry toward him, though, her face alight with pleasure at seeing him. And she seized both his hands and squeezed them as soon as she was in reach.

"Where's the disguise?" he asked. She was wearing more makeup than usual, but not as much as the last time. He thought she looked very pretty this way.

"One of the Akkadian Healers, my friend Heklatis, is also a Magus," she said. "He didn't tell anyone about it until I arrived, though, because he didn't like what our Magi were doing and he didn't want to have to put up with them trying to get him to join them. He gave me an amulet that he says will make their spells slide off me, and he says that as long as I don't leave the temple without a physical disguise, they won't find me." She made a face. "I don't understand all of it; magic works differently from what a Winged One does. Father gave the Temple money to buy me a body slave and a fan bearer, so when I go out, I'm all wigged and painted and escorted. It's such a bother that I only did it once." She sighed. "Still, it's not a loss. Kephru does wonderful massages, and Takit is useful running errands, so most of the time they're working for the Healers."

"Are you able to practice your skills?" he asked, knowing how strongly she felt about her abilities. The panic in her voice when she had described being temporarily without them made him think that not being able to use them would be very like being cut off from some essential part of her, or having her soul cut in half. "Is it safe?"

"Heklatis says it is," she replied, and shrugged. "Certainly no one has come running here looking for me after I've used them—though I haven't dared to try to See what the Magi are doing or to See the Temple of the Twins. I'm afraid that—" she bit her lip. "—I'm afraid that if another Winged One feels me Watching, the Magi will be told."

Would the Winged Ones actually betray one of their own to the Magi? "You think it's that bad?" he asked soberly.

"I don't know," she replied, looking profoundly unhappy. "I just don't know. *Someone* is allowing them to take the Fledglings every day, and as far as I can tell, no one is objecting to it." Her brows came together and she looked as if she was holding back tears. "And even if the reason they're letting this happen is not that they're on the Magis' side but that they're afraid of the Magi and what they can do, it doesn't make much difference in the long run. People who are afraid would tell on me, too."

Now it was his turn to squeeze her hands, as comfortingly as he could manage. There was hurt in her eyes as well as unhappiness and that lurking fear. *She's been betrayed by the people she thought she could trust the most, and now she is not entirely sure what the truth is, or who she can trust.* And a little thought followed that. *But she trusts me . . . oh, gods, my thanks, she trusts me!*

"I wish there was something I could say or do to help," he said aloud. "I wish I could visit you more often—but Aket-ten, not only have I work I can't neglect, but if I come here too often when I never did before, someone might take notice."

She nodded, and smiled wanly. "And I haven't sent for you for the same reason. I'm keeping busy. The library is where I spend a lot of time. I've mostly been helping the animal Healers though, and just trying to See that Father is all right. He *seems* all right. I don't think they've done anything to him."

"I'll check on him myself on the way back," he promised, and tried to move the conversation to a more cheerful note. "Well, this looks like a place after your own heart! You don't seem so— unhappy as you were last time."

She brightened, and looked more like her old self. "I'm not. The library here is wonderful; I haven't run across more than a handful of scrolls that I've seen before. When I think of something I can do to help, I try to do it, and the rest of the time I stay out of the way. I'm learning what I can about the dragons." Then her jaw jutted a little, stubbornly. "I still think I could be a Jouster. Think of how easily I talk to Avatre! I wish you and Father would have let me hide with Orest."

He suppressed a snicker to avoid hurting her feelings. "Let's find somewhere warm where I can dry off. I want to tell you something. Do you remember Prince Toreth?"

"I think so," she said, leading him out of the library and back to her room. Someone had put up tightly woven reed screens up on the window, which darkened the room and cut off the view of the garden, but which also cut off the draft. Her brazier had made the place comfortably warm; she lit a splinter at it, then went around lighting all the lamps until the room was filled with a warm, golden glow. He hung up his rain cape to dry, then both of them took stools on either side of the brazier.

And he told her all about Prince Toreth and his plans. "And he spoke about you, actually," he finished. "He said that he would much rather have you in his cadre than Orest, because Orest's tongue is a bit too loose, but that you are sensible and intelligent, and he thinks it would be no bad thing to have a Far-Sighted Winged One who is not afraid to speak the truth to advise him."

"Oh!" she exclaimed, putting one hand to her lips in surprise. "I—I am not certain what to say!"

"At the moment, you're supposed to be on a farm beyond the Seventh Canal, so you don't *need* to say anything," he reminded her. "There is no way you could know this if you were where you were supposed to be."

"That's true," she admitted. "I want to think about this." She paused. "Did you mean that—about my becoming a Healer for the dragons and going to the Jousters' Compound once the Magi stop being interested in me?"

"As long as Lord Khumun and your father agree," he replied. "We don't need a Healer for the dragons much, but it would be very useful to have a Far-Sighted Winged One about. And it would be *very* useful to have someone who could talk to the dragons. You might get somewhere in soothing the wild-caught ones, now that we've got them to where they can actually be handled safely, and you can help us train the little ones."

She frowned in thought. "I need to think about this," she repeated.

He decided it was time to drop the subject, and instead went on to tell her about flying in the rain, and the sorties that the swamp dragon riders were doing.

"Their dragons are smaller than the desert dragons, and I think it's the first time some of them have gotten a taste of victory," he concluded. "If there were more of them, it would be all right, because two of them could take a rider on a desert dragon. But being outnumbered and riding smaller beasts makes things hard for them."

"You're making a real difference, then!" she exclaimed with pleasure. "Oh, how wonderful! I wish I was doing half as much."

"And what is it you always told Orest when he started fretting about not being a soldier?" he asked her, with a raised eyebrow.

"'The job of a student is to be a student,'" she sighed. "I suppose I'm a student all over again, then."

"You might as well be," he agreed. "But why don't you tell me why it is that the Healers do not care for the Magi? Because, obviously, they don't or you wouldn't be safe here."

She pursed her lips, and rested her chin on her fist. "I don't know," she admitted. "I never thought to ask."

"Then why don't you ask?" he suggested. "I'd start with that Akkadian you talked about."

"All right," she agreed. "I will."

The remainder of the visit was confined to inconsequential things, and he left her feeling much better about her situation than he had when he had seen her the first time. As he had promised, he looked in on her father on the way back, and with a few carefully chosen words and glances, Lord Ya-tiren indicated that he thought there was still a spy in his household, but that no further pressure had been brought to bear on him to produce his daughter.

The second time he went to visit Aket-ten, he had no news other than that, but she had enough information to make up for it.

"I've asked about," she told him, "though I have tried to be—um—circumspect. And all I've gotten were hints as to the quarrel the Healers have with the Magi. Very mysterious hints, too, with a lot of anger in them. I did find out one thing, though. Partly it's because the Magi are at least half responsible for the war with Tia, and you know how Healers feel about war."

Actually, he didn't know, but he could well guess. You could not be a Healer without feeling a desire to cure the sick and repair the injured so deep it often ran counter to self-preservation. So war must be entirely offensive to a Healer, at the same deep level.

Especially this war, which, the more he learned about it, seemed less understandable. As far as he could tell, it did not serve a purpose now for either side. The Tians could easily expand to the south, going up the Great Mother River instead of down, and the Altans did not seem to have any real interest in the land outside of that needed to support their city.

"How did you find that out?" he asked.

"I've been reading some of the personal commentaries and diaries that got stored in the library," she replied. "I mean, at least they were more interesting than recipes for curing impotence and spots! I found an entire rack of them rolled up in jars at the back of the library, and it turned out that each jar held the personal accounts of each Chief Healer here for—oh, hundreds of years. And right in the middle of one of them was a long tirade against the Magi, because the Magi had managed to persuade the Great Ones to use some trivial border incident as an excuse for war!"

So—there it was. Part of the speculation that he and Toreth had made had been borne out. "Who was in the wrong?" he asked.

She shrugged. "There was no telling. It was in a border village, and by the time it was over, anybody who might have known was either dead or too frightened to talk. The Magi blew it up into a treacherous attack on one of our patrols, unprovoked of course, and the irony is that *they* must have been looking for an excuse, too, because their declaration of war was delivered to us about the same time as ours was to them. But it was quite clear from the tone of the scroll that the Chief Healer was *certain* that if the Magi hadn't been egging on the Great Ones, it could all have been smoothed over."

He rubbed his ear thoughtfully. "Are there other reasons?"

"I think there are," she told him. "But no one will tell me. They hint at it—and it has something to do with something that the Magi are doing either with or for the Great Ones, but they won't tell me. They act as if—well, partly I think it's that they aren't entirely sure that what they think is happening is what is really going on. And partly it's that if what they think is happening is the truth, it's so horrifying to them that they don't want to think about it. If I'm making any sense."

"Oh, you are," he said, and paused. *Should I tell her?*

He stopped, tried to clear his mind of all of his notions of what Aket-ten was, and tried to look at her objectively. It didn't take more than a moment to come to a resolution; he wasn't going to help her by protecting her from things he "thought" she shouldn't know. She had been growing fast in the time he had known her, and that had been accelerated by her recent experiences.

"Toreth and I have been talking about this," he said, slowly, and outlined the whole nauseating scenario. The war, as an excuse to cut lives short—the stolen years from those who had died—

Aket-ten's eyes got bigger and bigger as he went along, and her face grew paler and paler. When at last he finished, she was as white as a lily.

"That's worse than necromancy," she whispered. "But it makes a horrible kind of sense—"

"And if *that* is what the Healers suspect?" he persisted.

"It would explain a lot." She blinked, as though her eyes were stinging, and now he knew she was trying not to cry. "This is really horrible, you know. I don't think you have any idea how horrible this would be to a Winged One."

"Or a Healer," he agreed. "No, I don't." And really, he didn't, perhaps because so much of his own life had been stolen from him that—well, stolen years, a stolen childhood, a life spent in bondage—they all seemed equally wretched. Men died in fighting all the time, whether it was in war, or in a fight over a woman. That someone would plan for so many deaths was sickening, but so were poisoned wells, burned fields, and jars of scorpions tipped into granaries.

"I suppose you couldn't," she said, swallowing. "It—well, it's hard to describe. But—to someone like me, it seems like the most horrible and vicious sort of rape."

He nodded. That made sense. To her it would be much worse than "theft," he could see that. "There's even more to it than that; I think there's something else being stolen by the Magi. I think that they are getting the—the—whatever it is they put into their magic to send the storms against Tia, I think they're stealing from the Fledglings. I think that is why the Fledglings come back drained and exhausted. I think that is why they wanted you so much—because whatever it is, you have a lot of it."

Now she looked angry as well as sick. "Heklatis—the Akkadian —hinted as much," she admitted. "Though he wouldn't come out and say so. But why don't they just *ask?*" That last came out of

her in a kind of wail. "However the war began, we're loyal Altans, if they'd just *ask,* we'd do whatever was needed!"

"Probably because they aren't the sort of people who ask.
They're too used to taking," he said bitterly. *Oh, yes. I know that
type.* "Anyway, taking is easier. Asking requires that you admit
that you need something; taking means you're the strong one and
you can have whatever it is that you want."

But this was getting him angry, and that was counterproductive
at this moment. He forced himself to calm down. "Anyway, now
you know. Or at least, you know the best guesses. You might
want to see if you can't get something more out of the Healers;
letting them know that *you* have some idea of what's going on
might loosen their tongues. If the Healers have some proof that
this is what's going on—well, as the next in line to the Twin
Thrones, *I* think Toreth has a right to know."

"I intend to," she said grimly. "'It is better to have a scorpion
out in the open than under the bed,'" she quoted one of the prov-
erbs that he remembered his mother using.

"True," he agreed. "But it's better still to have it dead beneath
your sandal."

# TEN

"**K**IRON! *Kiron!*" The frantic shout from the pen next to his startled Kiron out of a sound sleep, and it was only thanks to his "training" at the hands of Khefti-the-Fat that he came awake all at once. "Kiron!" the shout came again, and this time, amid the startled replies and complaints all around him, he knew where it had come from and who it was that had called him.

And he grinned, in spite of the panicked tone of Menet-ka's voice. There was only one reason for that level of panic at this particular time, coming from Menet-ka.

The first egg was hatching.

Kiron had actually been expecting this for the past couple of days, and had advised Menet-ka to move a pallet down into the sand next to the egg so that if it began to move, he would know immediately. Not that this would make a great deal of difference to the hatching egg, but it would to Menet-ka, whose hair had begun to stand on end from the shy boy's new habit of constantly and nervously running his fingers through it. So, like Avatre, these babies would be born amid thunder and rain. He considered that a good omen.

And another good thing—though not an omen—was that Menet-ka had begun to come out of his shell since the hatching was so near, to ask questions of Kiron without whispering or mumbling them.

He pulled on a wrap and kilt, ducked under the curtain of water pouring off his awning, went out into the corridor, and poked his head through the door to Menet-ka's pen.

"So the youngsters will be born amid lightning, just like Avatre! That is a fine omen!" he said heartily

Menet-ka just stared at him, as if he hadn't any idea of what Kiron was talking about.

With a sigh, Kiron ducked through a second curtain of water and waded out into the sand to see Menet-ka hovering over the rocking egg, looking very much as if he was going to start pulling his hair out in handfuls next. It might be the middle of the night, but there was no problem seeing him or the egg; Menet-ka had surrounded the pit with lamps nestled into the sand.

"Besides being a good omen," he added helpfully, when the other boy looked at him in doubt, "the one big problem with any kind of hatching egg is drying out in the middle of the process. And it certainly isn't going to dry out in *this* weather!" He waved a hand at the water cascading down off the awning into the deep channels cut especially to drain it away from the hot sands. The sheeting rain glinted like fabric made from glass in the flickering lamplight. In fact, it looked almost as if he and Menet-ka and the egg were entirely enclosed in a room hedged in by water.

*Why is it, I wonder, that babies of all sorts always choose to arrive in the middle of the night, in the middle of the worst weather possible?*

This time, he had a hammer—something he had not had when Avatre hatched. He listened carefully to the egg, putting his ear down against the rocking shell, until he found the spot where the tapping was coming from inside.

"Here," he said, handing the little stone hammer to Menet-ka, and tapping the spot with his index finger. "Use that here. Just tap, don't hit. Remember what I told you, and how we practiced on ostrich eggs. You want to help him crack the shell; he's trying to make an air hole."

"But—!" Menet-ka wailed—but he took the hammer in a hand that shook like reeds in the wind, and he gave the shell a tap. Not too hard, and not too gently. Kiron was proud of him.

The tapping from inside stopped for a moment, then began again, with renewed vigor.

This was the problem with something as big as a dragon egg. In order to protect the dragonet growing inside, it had to be thick and hard. But when the time came for hatching, it was *too* thick and hard for the baby to break out unassisted. Dragon mothers helped their eggs to hatch, though no one had ever seen exactly how. They didn't have beaks to hammer at the shell with, nor did they have hands that could hold a rock. But when Ari had spied on the nests of the wild ones, he had heard them working at the outside of the hatching eggs, so he had known that he would have to help Kashet when the time came.

Ari had in turn told the story any number of times to anyone who would listen. Foremost among the listeners had, of course, been his dragon boy—then called "Vetch," now called by his proper name.

The moment when the egg actually cracked all the way through was marked by a sudden change in the tone of the hammer strike. "Stop!" Kiron said, holding up a hand, but Menet-ka had already stopped, and was watching the "soft" spot breathlessly.

A moment, and then the egg rocked violently, a little triangle of shell popped up, and the end of a snout poked out.

The lamplight was too dim to make out the color, but it was dark, so the dragonet was probably going to be dark, too. "Is he all right? Is he breathing?" Menet-ka asked, on fire with anxiety.

"He's fine; he's got his air hole now, he'll take a rest for a little. Won't you, my lad?" Kiron crooned. In the lamplight, the tiny nostrils flared and relaxed, flared and relaxed, as the dragonet took in his first lungfuls of air.

While the last of the night ebbed, and the sky gradually lightened to gray, Kiron directed Menet-ka in the hatching of his egg. Once the others were awake, they gathered around to watch, each of them knowing that when the time came, it would be he who hovered over the rocking egg with a hammer, listening intently to discover where the dragonet within was chipping now, and adding carefully measured hammer blows to the outside.

And at last, as Kiron had known it would, the egg rocked violently one last time, and broke into two uneven halves, and the new dragonet sprawled out of it and into the sand. Menet-ka gave a cry of joy, and Kiron plucked the hammer out of his hand as he flung himself at his new charge.

"Right," he told the others, who were crowding closer for a look. "Out, all of you. This baby needs one mother, not nine, and he—" he took a look back over his shoulder and corrected himself, "—she won't know who it is if you're all shoving your faces at her. Don't worry," he added, as he herded them out before him. "You'll get your chances soon enough. In fact—Gan, your egg isn't that much younger than Menet-ka's and I'd be surprised if yours didn't start to hatch by tomorrow morning."

That at least sent Gan scrambling back to his pen, and the rest of them realized that in the excitement they had all forgotten about breakfast.

The baby would be fine for a bit without food, and so would Menet-ka, even though the latter didn't have a yolk sac to absorb. Kiron had his own leisurely breakfast, and went to check on Avatre, who was trying with all her might to find out what was going on in the next pen without shoving aside the awning and getting her head wet. He remembered how she had looked when she first hatched, like a heap of wet rubies and topaz. He had known then that she was going to be beautiful, and she was certainly fulfilling his every expectation.

She whined at Kiron as soon as she saw him. He grinned. "All right, my love. Come along, I'll show you." He put a hand on her shoulder—it was so ingrained in her never to leave the pen without him that he didn't need to chain her—and led her to the pen next door. She didn't like going through the dripping water—but then again, she wanted to see what was going next door so badly she put up with it.

Cautiously, she craned her head and neck around the door, and snorted with surprise at the sight of the baby. Menet-ka was oblivious; he had the dragonet's head in his lap, and its wings spread out on either side of it atop the sand to dry, utterly absorbed in his new charge.

"So," Kiron asked his own charge. "What do you think?"

He had been right; this baby was going to be one of the dark ones, an indigo-blue shading to purple on the extremities and in the wing webs. Avatre stretched her neck out a little farther, without going one step more into the pen, and snorted again, then turned her head to look at him.

"Oh, no!" he told her, smothering a laugh at the sight of her widened eyes. "That's Menet-ka's baby, not mine!"

She snorted a third time; then, evidently content and having seen enough, she pulled her head back and nuzzled his hair, relaxing all over. He patted her shoulder, and was momentarily nonplussed to realize just how much higher it seemed than the last time he'd patted it. *Great good gods, she's putting on another growth spurt! At this rate, she'll be big enough to fly combat within a few moons!* He didn't recall the Tian wild-caught dragonets growing that fast. Perhaps *tala* did slow their growth.

But he put that thought aside, and led her back to her pen. "No fear, my love," he told her, making a caress of his voice. "No one could ever take your place."

She gave him a look of renewed confidence with a touch of arrogance, as if to say, "Well, of course not!" and flung herself back into the hot sand of her pen. He laughed, and went to get a bucket of finely chopped meat and bone for the baby's first meal.

They all had dragon boys, of course—not that Kiron ever called on his very much—and the first order of the day was to show Menet-ka's boy exactly how small to chop up the baby's meal.

"And make sure to get plenty of bone into it," he advised, "and some hide and hair. Do you know why?"

The dragon boy shook his head, but looked attentive; that was a good sign, evidently Lord Khumun had made a point of picking out boys who were actually interested in the dragons, and not just taking this as another job.

"The baby needs bone to make bone of his own," Kiron explained, "And the hide and hair help keep his insides clean."

"Oh—like a falcon!" the dragon boy said, brightening. "And like the hunting cats eat grass."

"Exactly." Kiron beamed at him, and the boy flushed with pride at getting the correct answer. "You should also add clean organ meat, too. I know it's a nasty job, but it has to be done. Avatre likes hearts especially," he added as an afterthought.

"Falcons need organ meat too," the boy said, nodding as he chopped the meat into the right-sized bits. "I used to take care of falcons. That is, I did the cleaning and feeding, I never got to handle them—"

"Well, *I* was a dragon boy, and my master was a dragon boy, so do your work well and one day there may be an egg for you, too," Kiron said, and the boy's face lit up. He carried the bucket of bloody bits off to Menet-ka with the air of one carrying a holy relic, and Kiron had to repress a smile.

"Lan-telek!" he called, gesturing to his dragon boy, who was waiting hesitantly just beside the door of the butchery. "Avatre's putting on a growth spurt. I think we'll need two barrows each today if she is. Chores don't stop because there's a new dragonet in the pens."

"Yes, sir, Jouster Kiron, sir," said the dragon boy, bobbing his head awkwardly, and trundled a barrow up to the butcher.

No, chores didn't stop. Dragons were whining for their breakfast. And today there was one more than there had been yesterday.

A good omen.

\* \* \*

Just before the rains ended, there were eight new dragonets in the pens. All of the eggs had hatched successfully. Menet-ka's female was the indigo-purple, Orest ended up with a brilliant blue male the color of a beetle's wings. Kalen got a brown-and-gold female, Pe-atep a scarlet-and-sand male. Gan found himself with a solid green male, Oset-re with a coppery female shading to red. Huras the baker's son got the biggest and most striking dragonet of all, a blue-to-purple-to-scarlet female that weighed almost twice as much on hatching as the others—Jousters were still coming to have a look at her, for she was a real beauty, and no Altan had ever seen such a dragonet before. And Toreth got the quietest, another female, a blue-black shading to silver-blue, who, if she was not the largest or the most brightly colored, already showed a striking level of intelligence.

All of them were demanding. All of them were constantly hungry. Kiron was getting a good idea of how lucky he had been to get Avatre, who had been quiet and good compared to this lot. They certainly kept their "mothers" on the run.

Now the boys were finding out exactly how much work it was going to be to raise a dragonet.

There was not one complaint out of the lot of them. Not even a whisper of a complaint. Not even from Orest, who was now so busy that all of his "outside" friends never saw him anymore, unless they came to the compound—and even then, they found themselves playing a poor second to Orest's beloved Wastet. Orest was as utterly besotted as Kiron had been, and it was his friends who were doing the complaining that Orest was "not amusing anymore" and "had no time for gossip."

Toreth might have missed this new maturity, but his twin Kaleth—without the preoccupation of a dragonet—did not. So after the first moon, with no sign of lapsing on Orest's part, not even when he was so tired by the time the sun went down that he was staggering, Orest became the last of Kiron's Wing to be taken in and made privy to Toreth's plans for the future.

For by then, the first growth spurt was over; with Avatre's

history in mind, and comparing all the dragonets, Kiron had the notion that this was the point where the first "failures" generally occurred in the wild. If parents couldn't manage to bring enough to satisfy all of the dragonets during the point where they were the most vulnerable and needed one parent with them constantly, it would be the smallest and the youngest who failed to compete for food and died. That was perhaps why there had been so much whining and begging in the first moon—although they were not sharing the same nest, they *could* hear each other, and every time one started begging, it would set the rest off. It was competition to live, competition for the next mouthful, because things might thin out at any moment, and the dragonet that got the most food now was that much closer to making it to fledging.

Now, though, they all had put on enough weight that they had a small reserve, and the constant begging eased off, much to the relief of their riders and all those who had to come anywhere near the pens.

All nine human members of the wing gathered in Avatre's pen—Avatre regarded them with a sleepy, indulgent gaze, too old now to be disturbed by voices and lamplight if she chose to sleep. They had discovered that although the rains were over, it was still necessary to keep the awnings up over the pens after dark, for every night, a great storm would sweep across the city, coming from the sea, speeding southward and growing in strength as it moved. These, Kiron had to presume, were the out-of-season storms that had so crippled the Tian Jousters; the Magi had, predictably, not troubled themselves to warn the Jousters of the little fact that the storms would be continuing after dark. It was just a good thing that everyone had felt the storms building and had rushed out to cover the pens before much rain came down. They were, however, relatively minor, coming as they did in the night, without the added energy that the heat of the day generated farther south. The Altan Jousters were hardly affected at all, except for needing to draw the awnings over the sand pits. Not so the

Tians; Altan patrols found the storms raging over Tian territory vicious enough that they had to turn back at the border.

And not so the poor Fledglings. They were still being taken, but now it was under cover of darkness, rather than just after dawn. Kiron tried not to think about their plight too much. There wasn't anything he could do for them—though Toreth had told him in confidence that Kaleth was going to try to find out, if not what was being done to them, at least how they were faring. But he couldn't help thinking about them, even tonight when he was enjoying the company of the others, when the storms rolled overhead, moving for the south.

"Kiron," said Gan, recapturing his attention, "when do you think the dragonets will fledge?"

He shoved his concerns to the back of his mind. "I think, given how fast the babies are growing, that you'll be riding them when the *kamiseen* starts," Kiron told them all. "They seem to be growing faster than Avatre did. I think it's the amount of food they're putting away."

"They're certainly doing that," Huras said ruefully; his little one was eating half again as much as the others, and growing proportionately faster.

"Now, brother, you had better be glad of that," Pe-atep said jovially, slapping him on the back. "You are no lightweight! It is a good thing that your little lady is going to be the biggest of the lot!"

"I may well *be* a lightweight before this is over and she is fully grown," groaned Huras. "It seems all I do is run back and forth with her food!"

"Well," Menet-ka said in his quiet voice, "according to Kiron, they'll be doing more sleeping and be less demanding now. Since they're bigger, they'll be able to hold more food and can go longer between meals, I suppose." He looked at Kiron, who nodded. "So we'll have some freer time to read and plan what's coming next?"

"More to the point, I think we need to begin Jousting training on the ground," Kiron told them. "That was why I asked you to come here tonight. If the dragonets are up to flying by the time of the *kamiseen*, then once they get their skills, we must be ready to train them. You, Huras—there is something in particular I want you and Tathulan to train in—or to be more precise, there is a particular task I want you to train for."

They way he said that got all of their attention. "Oh?" said Huras.

"You're thinking of your mentor, Jouster Ari, and his Kashet, aren't you," said Toreth shrewdly. "You know we're going to have to face him and I have the feeling that you don't want him hurt."

Kiron nodded. "Ari is honorable, and he has a conscience, and I know for a fact he has never harmed anyone who was not fighting him," he replied. "And he is my friend. In fact—he is more than my friend." He looked around the little group. "It is time that I told the true tale of my escape from Tia."

As all of them hung upon his words, he softly related how Avatre had unexpectedly fledged, and how he had been pursued by Tian Jousters—how they managed to outdistance all but Ari— and how, seeing Ari, he had tried to fall to his death rather than be captured and see Avatre taken from him. It had been long enough now that all of them were as besotted with their dragonets as he was; he could see it in their faces that they understood when he told them that he would rather have died than lose her, and rather die than see her torn from him and given over into the care of someone who saw her only as another weapon of war.

He told them how Ari and Kashet caught and saved him—and then how Ari became the co-conspirator in his escape, even to giving his own Gold of Honor to the Bedu to pay for their help.

When he was done, he saw a change in their faces. Until today, even Jouster Ari had been just another faceless Tian enemy. Now, though they did not know Ari as he did, they *did* know that none of them could kill him.

"There was not a dragon alive that could best Kashet, until now," he continued. "But Huras, when she's full grown, your

Tathulan can. She'll outweigh Kashet for certain. I want to work out some way that we can drive Kashet to the ground and take Ari out of the combat without killing him."

"All well and good," said Toreth, "But *then* what?"

"If he's grounded, it won't matter," Kiron said firmly. "And if, every time he flies to combat, he finds himself grounded, either he will stop flying combats and start doing something else, or the Captain of Jousters will find another job for him." He shrugged. "The point is, he's the equivalent of three Jousters; take him out, and we take out a third of a wing."

Toreth nodded slowly. "I'd like to capture him, actually. If he's as honorable as you say, we might be able to get him to swear to take himself and Kashet out of Tia altogether until the war is over."

Kiron heaved a sigh of relief. "I was hoping you would suggest that," he said. "I don't want either of them to suffer."

"Honestly, neither do I," Toreth admitted with a smile. "I had much rather meet him, and one day learn from him. The first man to raise a tame dragon! I want to hear his story from his own lips."

Kiron thought of Ari—how very lonely he had seemed to be, and how well he would fit in with this group. If only fate had not placed them on opposite sides of the conflict. It wasn't fair.

Well, now, at least, he had the wing on his side. It would not be hard to persuade Lord Khumun that Huras should devote himself to taking the infamous Jouster Ari out of the sky. And after that—well, he very much doubted that the Lord of the Jousters would care what happened, so long as Ari and Kashet were no longer a factor in the fighting.

"The rest of us need to learn some new techniques, too," he continued. "It seems to me that we ought to be able to outfly the Tians; I'm not entirely sure that we need to engage in close combat with them if we can find some other way of dealing with them. And it ought to be possible to train our dragons to put up with missiles going past their ears, too—Avatre has certainly learned."

"You're thinking of using bows?" Orest said, looking nervous.

He shook his head. "No. I was thinking of slings and clay pellets. Dragons have an instinct to snap at things going by their heads, and they tend to catch arrows in mid-flight—and the truth is, I would rather not interfere with that instinct. It might save our lives. But Avatre ignores clay pellets. You wouldn't have to hit a man hard enough in the head to knock him out or kill him—all it would take would be a hit; he'd be distracted, or you might get a good hit on the arm and he'd lose his lance. Avatre learned to tolerate the sling whirling around quite quickly out in the desert. New techniques are going to make us ten times more effective than the Jousters who are not going to be ready for them."

"For a while, at least," Gan said thoughtfully. "A Jouster being pelted could start to carry a shield. . . ."

"So you sting his dragon's rump!" countered Oset-re. "No wild-caught dragon, no matter how much *tala* is in her, is going to react well to that!"

"As tough as their hide is, it would have to be a stone rather than a clay pellet," mused Menet-ka. "Still. It's a good idea, and it will nullify their numerical advantage faster than just getting equal numbers out there. Without the dragons giving the Tians the advantage, our casualty rate is going to drop, on the ground as well as in the sky."

Toreth raised an eyebrow, and exchanged a significant look with Kiron. Kiron thought he knew what Toreth was thinking.

*If the casualty rate drops, what happens to the Magi who are counting on a certain number of deaths to prolong their lives? Who will they allow to run short first? Themselves? Ha!*

If the Great Ones were depending on magic to keep them going, and the magic ran out—well, they could very well die. And that could mean that Toreth and Kaleth would be on the Twin Thrones—and in a position to stop the war altogether—a lot faster than they had thought.

"That can only be good," was all he said, and Toreth nodded.

The talk might have gone on long into the night if they had no one to think about but themselves—

—but of course, they didn't.

"I have a hungry dragonet to feed in the morning," Orest said, getting to his feet and stretching.

"As if the rest of us didn't?" retorted Gan. "You're right, though; morning is going to come far too quickly."

The rest of them said their good nights and went back to their pens. All but Toreth, who lingered for a moment.

"Were you thinking about the Magi?" he asked, coming straight to the point.

Kiron nodded. "But don't forget, they aren't to be trusted," he warned. "They could find some other means of gathering years. They haven't resorted to outright, cold-blooded murder yet—"

"—that we know of—" corrected Toreth.

Kiron shivered involuntarily. "That we know of," he agreed. "Still. If they were desperate—"

"Then we have to deal with them before they realize they *are* that desperate," Toreth replied grimly. "Just so you know."

And with that, he returned to his pen as well, leaving Kiron to put out his lamps and climb into his own cot.

His mind played host to some very disturbing thoughts before sleep finally claimed him.


"Father says they've taken the spy out of the household," Aketten announced happily, the next time he came to visit her. "And the priest in charge of all of the Far-Sighted Winged Ones came to visit him right after."

"Really?" he said. "I'll tell you what, let's take this into your garden. Just to be on the safe side."

With the coming of good weather, it was possible to actually enjoy that courtyard with its *latas* pool that lay just outside her room. It was his considered opinion that she spent far too much time in the library, or otherwise indoors.

She nodded, and opened the door into the green space. It was a distinct improvement over being inside, especially on such a warm, pleasant day, with the scent of blooming *latas* in the air. The courtyard was covered in grass, not pavement, and the two of them were able to sprawl at their ease in the sunlight. Aket-ten brought a bread loaf out with her; it wasn't long before she was breaking off crumbs to feed the fat carp that lazed in the pool.

"Now. This important priest came to see your father. Is that good or bad news?" Kiron asked warily.

"Good news," she assured him with a laugh. "He told Father that none of the Winged Ones had sensed anything from me, and they were sure that if I still had my powers, I would have made every effort to Speak from afar with my teachers." She giggled; he sensed it was because she was a little giddy with relief, rather than that she actually thought it was funny.

"So they don't know that *you* don't trust them anymore. Good," he replied.

She nodded, and dusted the last of the crumbs from her hands. "He offered Father his condolences; Father said it made for an interesting conversation. It seemed as if—Father said—that he was disappointed and relieved, all at the same time."

"Maybe he was," Kiron said, thinking aloud. "If he's really unhappy about the way that the Magi are using the Fledglings, he could be relieved that they aren't going to be able to use you anymore. But on the other hand, since everyone thought you were going to be so strong in your powers, and now they think that you aren't, he's disappointed."

"Well, he can just go on being disappointed," she replied tartly—and resentfully. Not that he blamed her. He'd have been resentful and holding a grudge if he had been in her place. "And if he's upset about the way the Fledglings are being used, why doesn't he stop them? Anyway, Father thinks it's safe for me to go back."

Kiron sucked on his lower lip a moment. "It could be. But let's think about how. I wouldn't bet that the Magi are going to take the word of the Winged Ones as true. I don't think the Magi trust anyone. I think that as soon as you are back in your home, they'll send someone to have a look at you."

"So?" she asked, hesitation creeping into her voice.

"So I think you ought to be ready to give them a show," he told her, and he pushed himself up out of the grass. "Let's go find that crafty Akkadian Healer of yours, and see what he thinks."

The Akkadian—who was a short, bandy-legged fellow with a knowing look to him and a full, bushy head of silver-streaked, curly black hair—had plenty of ideas and was just as suspicious of the Magi as Kiron was.

"You'll keep those amulets, of course," he told Aket-ten, brusquely. "I don't care how good those Magi are, my amulets will make them think you are a perfectly ordinary girl."

It took them a little while to put the "show" together, but when they were through, even the suspicious Akkadian was satisfied that it was going to hold up to scrutiny. Furthermore, he agreed to be there the next time that Lord Ya-tiren came to visit, in order to add his weight of authority and experience to Aket-ten's pleas for caution. Kiron went back to the compound feeling that Aket-ten's safety was in capable hands.

Kiron was not there at Lord Ya-tiren's villa when the cart from the country brought Aket-ten "back home" again, but as it happened, by purest chance he was visiting Aket-ten a day later, sitting with her in her courtyard, when a servant came and requested her presence in her father's chamber. "My Lord said to tell you that there is a distinguished visitor to see you."

Kiron and Aket-ten exchanged a glance; they both knew that "distinguished visitor" meant that one of the Magi had, as Kiron had predicted, decided to come to see for himself if Aket-ten really had lost her powers. "Tell my father that I will be there shortly," she said.

"I'd like to come along," said Kiron when they were alone in the courtyard again. "I've never seen a Magus. And Lord Ya-tiren didn't say that you were to come alone."

"No," she admitted thoughtfully. "He didn't. And he knows

you're here. I think that's a good idea, and I have the feeling that he would like you to be there."

So when a rather different version of Aket-ten emerged from her chamber, he got a chance to see what his suggestions and the Akkadian's looked like in practice.

If he hadn't known what was going on, he'd have been shocked to his toes by how wretched she looked.

Firstly, Aket-ten looked shrunken and unnaturally thin—which was the effect of wearing a gown that was two sizes too big for her, with a belt to match. That had been the Akkadian's idea, to make it appear that she had lost an enormous amount of weight and might still be weak and sickly. Her hair was dull, lank and stringy (a bit of oil combed through it and dirt dusted in afterward). There were dark shadows under her eyes (a touch of kohl smudged beneath them) and her skin looked sallow (effective use of a very expensive bit of saffron rubbed into the skin to make it yellowed). The Akkadian had coached her on how to move; Kiron hadn't seen that part of the preparations, but the clever Healer had evidently done a fine job of teaching her, for she looked timid, uncertain, and lacking in all self-confidence. He escorted her to her father's private audience chamber, and had the satisfaction of seeing a startled look on the face of the stranger who was waiting there.

As he had said, he had never seen one of the Magi before; somehow he had gotten the image of a wizened, oily, unpleasant little sneak.

The stranger was indeed unpleasant, but it was because he oozed arrogance. Some might have considered him a handsome man, save for that. He was neither oily nor wizened, and gave no impression of being a sneak. Rather, he was out of the same mold as the most obnoxiously proud and self-assured Tian Jousters that Kiron had known.

*He thinks that whether or not we know it, he knows that he is the master here. He knows that he can take whatever he wants, whenever he wants it, and there is nothing that we can do about it.*

The man's attitude put his back up, but Kiron controlled his reactions and his temper. The last thing he wanted the Magus to know was that *he* had the measure of the man.

*He assumes I'm just a foolish boy, like Orest used to be. I want him to go on assuming that!*

Aket-ten stood before the visitor with her head bowed, her shoulders hunched. The Magus looked down at her with a dissatisfied expression, but his words were pleasant enough.

"I am told that your powers have faded, young Fledgling?" he said, in a voice that would have sounded kindly if you hadn't been aware of the anger beneath it.

"Yes, my Lord," Aket-ten whispered. "I am sorry. All that I have left is the Speech of Beasts. I tried and tried, but—after that morning when—when the Magi came—to test us, they said—it was gone, all gone—" she shook her head, and her shoulders shook. The Magus hopefully took that for silent sobs, but Kiron had a feeling that she was shaking with rage. "I was so sick, after. . . ."

"I hope," the Magus said, accusation in his voice, "that you are not implying that the Magus who came to test you somehow stole your powers from you."

"Oh, no!" she whimpered. "No, I never intended that! No, it was something else—woman's troubles—my own weakness—"

"A pity," the man said, and his lip curled with contempt. It was just a momentary lapse, but Lord Ya-tiren saw it as well as Kiron, and although his lordship kept his face impassive, Kiron saw one hand curl involuntarily into a fist before Lord Ya-tiren relaxed it. "A pity indeed. Those who flower early often fade quickly, it is said. Too bad." His voice held not only contempt, but anger, and perhaps a hint of irritation. "Well, the Speech of Beasts is hardly going to be of much use to your people and your country, girl. I suggest you get yourself a husband, then. This boy, perhaps, would do, if he is a friend of yours." His eyes flickered over to Kiron, passing over him with no interest. "Pass your powers on to your children, and if the gods favor you, they'll have more staying power than you did."

Kiron found his jaw dropping at such cold, calculated rudeness, and even Lord Ya-tiren gasped with anger. But the Magus was turning away. "My thanks, and my condolences, my Lord," he called over his shoulder. "I can find my own way out."

Kiron held his breath; Aket-ten remained with her head bowed for a very long time—then, finally, raised it with a face full of mischief. "It's all right," she said, with some of her old merriness. "He's gone, the arrogant pig!"

"For half a *debek* I would follow after him and beat him like a thieving slave!" Lord Ya-tiren snarled. "The nerve! To so insult my own daughter. In front of me, and in my own house!"

"You have your revenge in that you've successfully stolen what he wanted right from under his nose, my Lord," Kiron reminded him. "And in fact, he has given you and your daughter every excuse you need to send her to the Jousters' Compound. No one will think twice that she seeks to use the last of her Gifts there, and most will believe it is because she wishes also to have my company, and that you are not opposed to this."

The moment the words were out of his mouth, he flushed. Not that he would have taken them back—

But Aket-ten gave him a significant look, and her father a speculative one, and when Aket-ten murmured, "And who is to say that I do not?" her father's look of speculation turned to a sly smile. Kiron felt a wave of heat pass over his entire body, and the fact that he knew he was blushing only made him flush the more.

"That is a good plan," was all that Lord Ya-tiren said, however—for which he was very grateful. "It takes her far from the Temple of the Twin Gods, so that there is little chance our ruse will be detected as she hones her powers in secret. The Magi visit the Jousters' Compound so seldom that it is unlikely she will ever be forced to endure the company of one again. And she will be with her brother and her—friends. I will call upon Lord Khumun this very afternoon and arrange it."

"Her help will be very much appreciated, I promise you, my Lord," Kiron said hastily. "And with that in mind, perhaps I should return—tell the others—make preparations—" He knew he was babbling, but he couldn't seem to stop his mouth from spouting nonsense. "She'll be—we'll be—good morning, then, to you both—I'll take my leave—"

And with that, he turned and fled, and was only grateful *not* to hear Aket-ten's giggles joining her father's amused laughter.

When he got back to the compound, he found it in an uproar, but since virtually everyone was smiling, or even laughing, any alarm he had felt at the noise faded to nothing. And, eventually, he found out what the cause was.

Menet-ka's imperious little indigo-purple dragon, living up to her royal colors, was not inclined to wait patiently for anything she felt she was entitled to. And when Menet-ka had not appeared the moment she bleated for her afternoon meal, she had elected to go and find it—and him—for herself. She had wandered the whole of the compound before she was through, sticking her nose into pens and demanding her "mother" and her food of whoever or whatever was in there. The wild-caught dragons all knew what a baby was, and even the swamp dragons began bellowing on her behalf for her mother, for although no dragon would tend the offspring of another unless its own young had died, all dragons protected and defended any dragonet. This in turn brought the dragon boys and anyone else within hearing, but since not one of them was "mother," Bethlan ignored them. And they all wanted to see what she would do next. So Bethlan toddled up and down the pens, leaving noise and confusion in her wake, until, at long last, she found her "mother" Menet-ka in the butchery, helping his dragon boy chop up her meal. By this time she was so tired that Menet-ka and the boy had to load her up into a barrow and trundle her back to her pen. She was very tired, and a little cold, but no worse for wear, fortunately.

"If she'd gotten too cold, I think she would have joined an adult dragon in its pen," Menet-ka told Kiron, still scarlet with chagrin.

"I think you're probably right. She had the wit to come looking for you, I think she would have had the wit to go lie down some-where warm," Kiron agreed, covering his mirth. "I'm not sure I want to go putting barriers across the doors, though, just yet. Let's wait and see if she does it again, before we think about doing that."

"She won't," Menet-ka said firmly, ears still red. "I won't let her get hungry again."

In stark contrast to imperious little Bethulan, Pe-atep's scarlet-and-sand Deoth was the shyest dragon Kiron had ever seen. When all the fuss had died down, and he checked on *all* the little ones to make sure they were in their pens, he found Pe-atep in the farthest corner of his, crooning over Deoth, who was shivering with fear and hiding his head in Pe-atep's tunic.

"What's wrong with him?" Kiron asked, but very, very quietly; he didn't want to upset the little one more than he already was.

"Nothing really," Pe-atep said, with far more calm than Kiron would have felt, it this had been Avatre. "He's high-strung and sensitive, and I am glad it's me that has him and not Menet-ka."

"Why?" Kiron asked. Pe-atep raised his eyebrows.

"Well, the shyest rider with the shyest dragon? Think about it! We'd never get them off the ground!" Pe-atep ran his hands down the baby's sides. "Poor little fellow. This happens in cats, sometimes; lions mostly, but sometimes cheetahs. One is born that just jumps at everything. You just have to coax them, and make sure that they never fail badly enough at anything to frighten them off it." He chuckled, as the dragonet relaxed and stopped shivering. "There now, you see? It's all right. Nothing bad hap-pened, little one. I'll want you lot to start coming into the pen at odd times, and bring a nice little tidbit with you every time you do. He has to start learning that new things can be nice things. It's the only way to get him through this stage. But once we do, he'll be as brave as a lioness, won't you, my handsome fellow?"

"I'll pass the word," Kiron promised, and walked out softly but confidently.

As he told the others what Pe-atep had requested, he reflected that here, if he wanted it, was another omen. So far, it seemed that the dragonet was matched perfectly to the boy who had gotten it. Menet-ka had the boldest—who was pulling him into the center of attention, which was good for the boy. And Pe-atep, experienced handler of big hunting cats, had the shyest—he who was best equipped to handle such a problem baby out of his own vast experience.

*So Toreth has the quietest but the smartest, I've seen that, too, already. And for someone who doesn't particularly want to draw attention to himself right now, that is the ideal combination. I wonder if that means that Oset-re's Apetma is going to shred his best tunics and kilts so that he loses some of that vanity?* He already knew what Gan's dragon meant to *him*—Gan, who had never taken anything seriously before his dragon hatched, was utterly, completely, wholeheartedly besotted. He was just as in love with the gentle Khaleph as Khaleph was with him. And as for Orest—well, Orest's Wastet was, next to Bethulan, the most demanding of the lot. *Everything* had to be just so for Wastet—his meat chopped to a certain size, his pen cleaned *at once,* his water absolutely pure and fresh. There was no longer room in Orest's world for "close enough."

As for Huras—that was a perfect match, too. The huge Tathulen was so good-natured that the perfectionist was learning to slow down and relax a little. Huras was coming to understand that sometimes "close enough" was good enough.

Wiry little Kalen had brought all of *his* experience as a falconer to taking care of Se-atmen, who repaid his impeccable care with an outpouring of single-hearted love—which you just did not get from a bird of prey. So even Kalen, who Kiron had thought was probably the perfect candidate for taking care of a tame dragon without having to be taught anything, was learning something. . . .

*And I am learning something from all of them,* he thought, as he stood in the doorway of Avatre's pen, and listened to the little sounds coming from all of the pens. *Indeed I am. Now as long as I can keep a little ahead of all of them, we'll be all right!*

# ELEVEN

THREE days later, Aket-ten made her first appearance in the Jousters' Compound. She was accompanied by Lord Khumun, who told Kiron's wing that he wished to see how she would fare in communicating with the dragons for himself.

The boys had been singularly uninterested in "Orest's little sister" and had not been enthusiastic about leaving their precious charges to greet her. That all changed the moment they set eyes on her.

"By the gods!" Gan whispered to Kiron, as all of the boys of Kiron's wing gathered to greet her. "What happened to Orest's 'little' sister?"

"She grew up," Kiron replied shortly, a little dismayed at Gan's words, and surprised to feel a surge of jealousy. Aket-ten looked—well, wonderful. She had somehow achieved a compromise between the hoyden she had been and that elegant, slightly over-painted "lady" he had first seen in the Temple of All Gods. She looked quite comfortable in her skin, and yet there was no doubt whatsoever that she had, in very fact, grown up. Even Toreth was giving her an interested and intrigued look.

Yes, every one of the boys was eyeing her with varying degrees of speculation and interest except Orest himself. Orest was apparently oblivious to the change. He still looked bored, and clearly wished himself elsewhere.

"I have work to do," he whispered irritably to Kiron. "You'd think they'd leave me out of this welcoming-party!" He shook his head. "She's bad enough now as a know-it-all; this is just going to swell her pride like a toad in the rain!"

That his wingmates did not share his impatience didn't seem to register with him at all.

Aket-ten didn't look like someone whose pride was going to swell over all the attention. She looked like someone who knew she had a job to do and was determined to do it well. The encounter with the Magi had changed her profoundly, Kiron decided at last. It had dispelled some cherished illusions, and had forced her to look at the world around her with a high degree of skepticism. He felt sorry for her; the confident child he had rescued back in the swamp was gone.

On the other hand, the cautious girl who had taken the child's place would be a bit easier to live with.

"Do you think you are prepared to attempt a wild-caught dragon?" Lord Khumun asked Aket-ten. "You need not fear them now—I am sure that your brother must have told you that we have been working intensely with them, and that though one must be cautious around them, you need not fear them."

*Where did that come from? I must have been woolgathering.* Kiron shook his head; he had been so busy staring that he had completely lost track of the conversation.

Aket-ten hesitated, then answered carefully. "My Lord, the problem is not that I am afraid of the wild-caught dragons, it is the *tala*. It makes their thoughts so sluggish that I cannot effectively reach them. So while I can easily tell Avatre what it is that Kiron would like her to do, with a wild-caught dragon, I do not believe that I could get past the *tala* and its own natural resistance to captivity. I fear that the best I could manage would be to read it, to tell you how it is feeling at that moment."

"Annoying," the Lord of the Jousters sighed. "Ah, well, that is better than nothing. You can tell us when they are over-drugged, or under-drugged, and if they are injured, ill, or in season. That is something, at least."

She shrugged. "There are many things I can tell you that may help. Animals can suddenly conceive of a dislike for a person or an object, and I can tell you if that happens. I can exert some calming influence on them, provided they have not been provoked into rage. And I can certainly help with the training of the tame ones," she said firmly. "It will be of no difficulty whatsoever to explain to them what is wanted. If they all grow up like Avatre, they will be eager to please, and need only to be told what to do in order to make a try at it."

"Well then, there is a swamp dragon that has been looking a bit seedy of late," Lord Khumun said briskly. "That would be Pa-alet, ridden by Hotef-ba. Let us see what you can make of him."

With Aket-ten at Lord Khumun's side, and the dragon boys trailing along behind, they all paraded over to the part of the compound where Kiron seldom ventured—the pens of the swamp dragons. He had not had much to do with the swamp dragons since advising Lord Khumun on ways to retrain them—though Menet-ka's Bethlan had wandered in twice more, looking for her "mother." As they all moved along the corridor, heads rose on long necks, craning over the walls to peer at the interlopers—slightly smaller heads on slimmer necks than Kiron was used to in an adult dragon. The forehead was broader than that of a desert dragon, though, and the nasal area smaller, and he wondered if they had all been a bit hasty in thinking of the swamp dragons as less intelligent than their desert cousins.

Their colors were more muted and less metallic than those of the desert dragons, and instead of having colors that shaded on all the extremities to a different color, or something lighter or darker, only the bellies shaded to a lighter version of their base color. But what they lacked in brightness of color, they made up for in subtle patterning; with few exceptions, virtually all of them sported diamond-in-diamond patterns down their backs in subtle variations of their base colors. He could see how this would be valuable in the swamp; if they were lying in a hot mud pool, they would look much like the surface of the pool. And if they chose to swim in clearer water, that lighter belly would disguise them from below both from the enormous carp that formed part of their diet and from the crocodiles that lurked on the bottom. Even a dragon had reason to fear a really big crocodile.

They came to the pen of the ailing dragon, who looked up and grunted at their entrance. He was a brown, and he lolled in his pool of hot water with more lethargy than Kiron was used to seeing in a dragon that wasn't trying to sleep through the rains.

"Do you need to touch him?" Lord Khumun asked. "If so, I will send for his dragon boy—"

"No, that will not be necessary, my Lord," Aket-ten replied, with a faint frown of concentration. She stretched out her right hand as if she meant to touch the dragon, but she remained in the doorway, well out of reach. "Ah. Too much *tala*, not enough food, my Lord," she said after a moment, her voice sounding distant and preoccupied. Her eyes stared off into space somewhere, looking distinctly unfocussed. "Something put him off his food at some point recently, a stomach ailment perhaps, but his dragon boy was trying to make sure still he got his full dose. Except that as he lost weight, it was a larger dose than he needed, and the overdose of *tala* has made him lethargic and put him further off his food. Which of course, will make him lose more weight."

She dropped her hand, blinked, and looked up at the Lord of the Jousters, who himself looked impressed. "Can you afford to take him off the fighting roster and put him on a half ration of *tala* until he returns to fighting weight?" she asked. "That would be the surest way to get him to recover, and the fastest."

Lord Khumun visibly weighed the options. "I believe I will have to," he said at last. "He's really not effective now. How long do you think it will take?"

She shrugged. "Half a moon?" she guessed. "For all that I have been studying them, this is the first dragon I have had any contact with besides Avatre."

"Half a moon on half rations of *tala* and all he can eat," said Lord Khumun to the dragon boy in question, who looked very nervous indeed. Half rations of *tala* for a dragon meant a great deal less control over him.

"I think, my Lord," said Kiron, as an idea occurred to him, "that during this period, if it can be managed, you should let his food walk to him on its own four legs. Or perhaps two—it might be easier to send in chickens, or ducks and geese."

"Eh?" Khumun turned to stare at him.

"I mean, we should force-feed the *tala* ration to a sheep or several live fowl and then drive them into the pen," Kiron elaborated. "He's wild-caught; he's *used* to catching and killing his own food. Let him have live food while he's recovering his strength. It will taste better to him, which will perk his appetite, and having something to kill might help him with aggression."

"And the boy will not have to wheel a barrowful of meat close to a testy dragon," Lord Khumun mused. "I think that is a good compromise. Can you manage it?" he asked the dragon boy.

"My lord, if it will keep me out of range of his teeth, I can manage nearly anything," the boy said fervently. Kiron could only reflect how fortunate it was that this was a swamp dragon; the pen was cleaned daily by flushing the pool, which was done from outside. If it had been a desert dragon on half rations—well, he was not sure even leaving it chained short would be protection enough for a boy to clean the pen.

"I will continue to watch his progress," Aket-ten added. "And as soon as I think he is ready, we can put him on his full *tala* ration the same day."

"Already you prove your worth," Khumun said warmly, looking as if he was going to pat her on the head, but stopping before acting on the impulse. "Aket-ten, I am pleased to have your services; our gain is the Winged Ones' loss. Now, I come to a question—will quarters among the female servants of our compound offend you? Your father specifically asked that you be housed here, but I have no better place to put you. I can arrange for a suite of several rooms with a bathing room to yourself, however. I can simply give you all four of the rooms around a courtyard. The quarters are plain and small, but they are clean and private."

She grinned, and for a fleeting moment, Kiron saw the "old" Aket-ten. "Such an arrangement will not displease me at all, my Lord! I can send to my father for things to make such rooms more comfortable, if you could show me now."

"So I shall." Khumun looked at the boys of Kiron's wing as if he had only just realized they were there. "Well—have you nothing to do?" he growled.

"Ah—yes, my Lord," came a ragged chorus of voices, and they scattered before his glare like a covey of quail.

But not before several of them had cast Aket-ten a final appreciative glance; Kiron might have thought that she was oblivious to these attentions, but *he* caught her watching them under half-lowered eyelids, and saw the little smile of satisfaction she wore as she turned to follow Lord Khumun to her new quarters.

He groaned. That was hardly fair! Now he was going to have to compete with all the others—Oset-re with his handsome face, Gan with his glib tongue, Toreth with—with all of his advantages! No, that was not fair at all! How in the name of all the gods was he to compete with all of that?

Well, he could still do one thing that the others couldn't, yet. He and Avatre could fly. And the servants' quarters were just off the practice field. If she was in her courtyard and looked up, she would not be able to avoid seeing the two of them flying.

Avatre was only just big and heavy enough now to begin practicing that maneuver of Ari's that had saved Kiron's life, and of all of the tricks that he planned for his wing, that was the one he wanted them to master first. Yes, they practiced over the net—

but so had the Tian Jousters, and an accident had happened anyway that would have ended in a death had Ari and Kashet not been there. If anyone from *his* wing fell from the back of his dragon, Kiron wanted everyone else to know how to catch him.

They were in the first stages of the trick at the moment. They were using a bag of barley half the weight of a man. One of the other Jousters carried it over his saddle, and let it slip off at a prearranged signal. Kiron had Avatre stationed at hover immediately below, so that the bag didn't fall far or build up much momentum before she caught it, ducking her head under and sliding it along her neck to where he grabbed it. Even so, they missed about half the time, which might have been discouraging if Kiron hadn't known how long it had taken Ari and Kashet to master the exercise. And unlike Ari, who had faced the scorn and amusement of his fellow Jousters right up until the moment when he actually saved someone, the Altan Jousters, who were knocked from their saddles far too often by the Tians with their bigger dragons, were well aware of the value of this "trick." They only wished that their dragons would be willing to learn it. The fact that eventually there would be at least nine fighting Altan dragons who knew how to pluck a falling man out of the air provided a great deal of comfort to them.

So Kiron had full cooperation and help from the rest of the Jousters in the compound. It didn't matter what they were doing at the time; when the one that was currently practicing with him had trouble with his swamp dragon growing restive over the unwelcome proximity of a desert dragon, another rider was willing to take the place of the first.

He and Avatre also practiced Jousting, of course, but he had more of a mind to take to the sky with a sling rather than a lance. Avatre would have to be full-sized before he could Joust, but he could use a sling now. The greatest limitation was that at the moment, she was not strong or fast enough to fly to the combat zones and return on the same day.

They practiced until both dragon and rider were tired; Kiron got in a little target practice while on the wing, just to keep Avatre used to the idea, then brought her in for a much-anticipated grooming and feeding.

He was not at all unhappy to see Aket-ten waiting for him in the landing courtyard when they came in. Now that Growing season had begun, and with it, warmer weather, she was wearing linen gowns instead of wool. And although it wasn't the semi-transparent mist linen favored by the Priestess of Tia, her current gown certainly left even less to the imagination than the woolen gowns she'd been wearing during the rains. The wind kicked up by Avatre's wings as she landed molded the front of the gown as tight to Aket-ten's form as if it had been wet. He felt his ears grow hot.

"You two look very good," Aket-ten said as he dismounted. She held out a hand for Avatre, who was perfectly happy to slide her head under it for a rub. "I would have expected her to be as clumsy as a puppy, trying anything that complicated."

"It isn't the first time," he admitted, then added awkwardly, "You look very nice."

The compliment sounded very flat to him, even as he spoke it, but what else was he to say? *You are prettier than any of the women who chased Ari* was not better! And *You don't look like a little girl anymore* was even worse.

She dimpled at him. "My Akkadian friend Heklatis had some very good ideas about how I should dress and act, and made sure to help me make these things into habits, as well as rebuilding my wardrobe," she said, with some amusement. "For a man who does not find women attractive, he has excellent taste and sound notions. I miss my tunics—but I might as well keep my child lock as stick to the things I used to wear." She sighed. "I wish it was not the case, but he convinced me that how I will dress for the next several years will profoundly affect how people treat me. If I am to be taken seriously, and not dismissed as a hysterical child when I accuse the Magi of wrongdoing, then I must sacrifice some of my freedom and dress the part of a woman. I am quite indebted to him, actually. Even people who knew me in my cradle have been treating me as if they had just realized that I do know what I am doing, and I am not having childish tantrums."

"They are treating you as an adult, because you look like one as well as act like one," Kiron agreed. "Even your father was affected." Then added, "Oh, except Orest, of course."

"Of course." She laughed. "When has a brother ever treated a younger sister as if she had grown up?"

*Possibly when he realizes that Gan, Oset-re, and Toreth are flirting with her,* Kiron thought—and the thought gave him a feeling of gloom for a moment. After all, how could he even hope to compete with the likes of them? Wealth, power, the highest breeding—

*But I'm the wing leader and trainer,* he reminded himself. *They don't have that. And they're still tending babies, not flying combat training.*

"Have you gone to see the dragonets yet?" he asked.

She laughed. "If I hadn't, the others of your wing would have had seizures by now," she said merrily. "Yes, I've seen all of them. And I would never, ever say this to their faces, but the poor little things look terribly unfinished compared with Avatre. However, I've Spoken to all of them, and I can tell you that they are all amazingly healthy and thriving. My only recommendation is to get them all toys *now* and get them interested in playing. They may be clumsy, and they may not be able to do more than mouth pretty colored things, but their minds need stimulation as much as their bodies do." She pursed her lips a moment. "In fact, you had better get Bethulan and Re-eth-katen twice as many toys as the rest, and more interesting ones, because they will get bored the soonest. Perhaps systrums that they can rattle, or soft things that they can carry about and worry like puppies."

He made a mental note to see to it. "Avatre needs a grooming," he told her. "And I know she likes your company. Would you like to come along?"

"No, by now, the servants are back with my things," she told him, and he bit back disappointment. "If I don't direct them, they'll put my bedroom where I'll be hearing chatter and clatter all night long, and my study in the darkest room of the lot. I promise though, I will wait for you at supper."

His spirits rose again. "I'll hold you to that promise," he said, and led Avatre off to the grooming pens feeling very much better.

At supper, however, despite his attempt to sit with Aket-ten in an unobtrusive corner of the enclosure, the others spotted them and settled themselves at the table, completely ignoring some fairly fierce glares on his part.

This eating area could have been the duplicate of the one in the Tian compound; there were the identical wooden tables and benches, the plain stone walls, and nearly the same cooking smells. The only real difference was that besides the movable awnings on lines overhead, the four walls supported permanent awnings as well, held up on posts, so that the area open to the sky was considerably smaller. And beneath the cooking smells, the scent of the compound was much different—with so many swamp dragons here, and with the canal so near, the air was always humid and full of water scent.

*No wonder the Tians are envious of us. We have so much water we have to find ways to getting rid of it, but once you move from the Great Mother River, there is nothing worth having in Tia.*

He wondered what Aket-ten would think of that observation. If they had been alone, he probably would have asked her opinion. But with the others around—well, they'd probably think he was an idiot.

He sat there, tongue-tied, while Gan kept Aket-ten laughing with his imitations and his cleverness. He couldn't help but notice her admiring glances at Oset-re's handsome profile—and neither could Oset-re.

Huras, however, seemed to be on Kiron's side. He had no more advantage than Kiron did in flirting—his father the baker surely did not move in court circles! And, in fact, he probably had a bit less of an advantage, for although he was frighteningly intelligent, he was not much inclined to speak unless he was spoken to, and his large frame and stolid expression often made people think he was stupid. While Kiron didn't think that Aket-ten had made that mistake, Huras also seemed far more interested in what Aket-ten could tell him about Tathulan than about herself.

Since Huras was at the outer end of the table, he got the serving dishes first—and he kept spearing the choicest bits and passing them directly to Kiron with a nod toward Aket-ten and a conspiratorial wink. Kiron was good at taking hints; he passed the bounty on to Aket-ten, and at least got the reward of a nod of thanks and a smile.

And Toreth also seemed, obliquely at least, to be helping Kiron. When Gan was being a little too clever, Toreth deflated him with a barbed bit of wit of his own. And when Oset-re started moving to put that handsome face of his in the best possible light, he asked, innocent as a child, "Are you posing for a statue, Oset-re? I should wait until I had earned my first Gold of Honor if I were you."

Aket-ten had the grace not to laugh at these stabs at the others' vanity, but she hid a smile behind the cover of her jar of beer.

"Aket-ten," asked Orest, suddenly, quite out of nowhere. "What was going on when you left? Did you *really* lose your other powers?"

The group around the table went very quiet, although the chatter from the rest of the eating-court covered the silence.

"Why do you ask?" she said, in so low a voice that they could hardly hear it. Then— "Never mind," she continued. "I will tell you all about it, if you all will come to my courtyard later tonight." She looked around at all of them. "Kiron and Toreth trust you with their secrets; I can do no less."

Toreth started a bit at that, but said nothing. Kiron held his tongue as well. But the rest of the meal was eaten in a peculiar silence—not uncomfortable, but awkward. The boys were not sure what they were going to hear, but they were fairly sure it wasn't something that went well with mild flirtation. Which,

Kiron thought, was surprisingly perceptive of them. But it seemed as though when they were prevented from flirting, they—or Oset-re and Gan at least—didn't know what else to say to her.

In a way, Kiron could sympathize. The things they normally chattered about—the dragonets, the plans for training—didn't fit in with the usual definition of "polite conversation around a young lady." They had no way of knowing that such things would be as interesting to Aket-ten as any of the boys around the table.

Not that Kiron had any experience with "polite conversation around a young lady." He hadn't the breeding or the family background, so he decided that he wasn't even going to try coming up with witty repartee. He'd just talk to Aket-ten, like he would talk to anyone else, like the two of them had talked when she was still with the Healers.

So he and Toreth filled the void. Toreth passed on news from outside, and he reported what he had learned from the older Jousters about how the fighting was going. There actually wasn't much Jousting going on, not with those storms continuing to keep Tian dragons out of the sky. So instead of Jousting, the Altan dragon riders were acting as scouts, and disrupting the Tian camps by means of a number of clever attacks. For instance, setting fire to the wagonloads of fodder for the chariot horses not only frightened the horses and even ran some off the picket lines, but made it necessary to send for more fodder or try and find grazing. And dropping jars full of deadly black scorpions and poisonous adders into the camps was more than just a disruption. For the first time in years, in fact, the Tian lines had been pushed back. Several small villages had been retaken, and the Tians who had arrogantly moved in had fled in confusion. Kiron's only complaint was that at least half the credit for the recent string of victories had to go to the Magi, who kept Tian dragons grounded. Eventually, Aket-ten—looking as if she wished to stay—excused herself, saying she had to supervise the servants setting up her things.

Between them, Toreth and Kiron probably could have kept that particular conversation going all night. But there were, of course, chores to be done, dragonets to be settled into sleep, before they could gather in Aket-ten's new quarters. Of all of them, Kiron had perhaps the lightest duty; the babies needed a last extra feeding to sustain them in their sleep, and they were growing so fast that they all had to have their sensitive skin rubbed with oily cloths before they went to sleep, or they might scratch too hard and damage themselves. Avatre needed nothing more than a little extra grooming, and to be told what a glorious dragon she was and that Kiron would be back soon. She settled into her sand with a sigh of pure pleasure, and was fast asleep in moments as the moon rose over the walls of the compound.

So he was the first to present himself at the door to Aket-ten's courtyard. It hardly merited the title; it couldn't have been more than fifteen paces in length or width, and boasted a tiny, square pool with a few *latas*, a single fish, and a square stone box in which a small acacia tree grew, scenting the night air with its blossoms. There was only one bench; Aket-ten was setting out pillows even as he arrived, and lighting lamps and torches around the walls. Somehow he felt relieved that she was not bringing them into any of those rooms. He helped her with the latter, allowing her to go back into one of the rooms for more cushions.

There were no mosaics adorning the pool, only the plainest of white tiles; there were no paintings on the walls. It had, after all, been a courtyard shared by a dozen servants, all crammed on pallets into three of the four rooms around it—the fourth room being the bathing room, of course. But Aket-ten seemed completely pleased with her new domain.

"Are you all right here?" he asked doubtfully.

"I feel safer here than at home," she replied, "And I wouldn't trust living with the Fledglings now no matter what the senior Winged Ones promised me." She sighed, and sat down on a cushion at the edge of the pool, trailing her fingers in the water. "I don't trust them anymore; I can't. I think they would give me over to the Magi in a heartbeat. I couldn't stay with the Healers either;

I was in the way. They were quite polite about it, but I was an inconvenience at best, and I didn't have a great deal in common with them. Healers are—very *passionate* about what they do, and I just didn't share that passion. Here I'm at least useful."

"I believe you would find a way to be useful no matter where you were," said Toreth, coming in on the end of the statement. "I should warn you, though, Lord Khumun will have our heads if we stay too long here, tonight or any other night."

"I'll chase you out before you get yourselves into trouble," she replied, as the rest straggled in. "I have duties of my own, too—ones I might as well tell you now, because it answers my brother's question." She looked around at everyone but Kiron. "No, I did *not* lose my powers—which were Animal Speech, the Silent Speech with a fellow Winged One, and the Far-Seeing Eye. I did not have the Seer's Eye, which imparts a view of the future; I did *seem* to have it at first, but it was the Far-Seeing eye, not the ability to look into the future. I disappointed my teachers in that regard. Frankly—given how things have turned out—I think I am just as glad."

"Why?" Gan asked, choosing a flat cushion of woven reeds for himself.

"Because I think if I had possessed the Seer's Eye—no matter how far I went, the Magi would have come looking for me." She shivered. "I am far less of a threat to them without it—"

"A threat?" her brother gaped at her.

"I'll get to that in a moment." She took a deep breath, and closed her eyes for a moment. "First, you should all know that one of my agreed-upon duties here is that I will be employing the Far-Seeing Eye privately for the benefit of Lord Khumun and the Jousters, and I will do so around dawn, because the Winged Ones are occupied with the Dawn Rites then. Which is why I will be getting up just as early as all of you. They do not know that I never lost my powers. I do not wish them to know this, for they would tell the Magi. Lord Khumun knows because Kiron and my father trust him, and he has no love at all for the Magi."

Gan rubbed the bridge of his nose; he had completely lost his usual air of languid boredom. "So Lord Khumun knows the truth about you. Who else, besides your father and Kiron?"

"The Healers at the Temple of All Gods, which is where I was hiding, rather than going to my aunt," she said immediately, as Orest continued to gape at her. "You know about the Magi and why I fled, then?"

Toreth nodded. "I think half of us do. My brother is trying to find out exactly what they're doing with the Fledglings—" he began. She held up her hand.

"Wait a moment, and let me explain to the rest." Briefly she outlined what had happened to her, and what the Magi had been doing with the rest of the Fledglings. Kiron volunteered what he had witnessed—the Fledglings being taken away looking like sleepwalkers, and returning looking utterly exhausted. "But as for finding out what is going on inside the Tower of Wisdom, don't bother—I can tell you. The Magi are stealing some form of power from us—from the Fledglings—to fuel the spell that sends the storms down on Tia." She smiled grimly at their nods; by this time none of them was surprised, and she didn't look as if she had expected any of them to be so. "Here is what you don't yet know; when the last chance of sending rain is over, they do not intend to stop."

Toreth's head came up, like a hound on a scent. "For the purpose of—?" he asked delicately.

"That, I cannot tell you. But I learned this, not from watching with my power, because I will not dare that, but from the memories that an Akkadian Healer coaxed out of my mind." She grimaced. "The Magi believe that the Fledglings are made blind and deaf to what goes on around them as they are being drained of their strength. They are *not*. But there is a spell of forgetfulness placed upon them before they are allowed to leave. The Akkadian knew it of old, and knew the counter. I remember everything that happened that single time I was taken, and everything that was said and done. This is how I know that, had I the Seer's Eye, the

Magi would have pursued me to the ends of the earth. They cannot permit someone with the Seer's Eye in any strength to mature into his power. He might reveal the future to the Great Ones—and if he did, the Great Ones and their advisers would soon know that the Magi intend to be the ones to rule in Alta, making those who sit upon the Twin Thrones little more than figureheads."

"I should like to speak with that Akkadian one day soon," said Toreth, as if to himself.

Aket-ten said nothing for a moment. Then she looked up. "Kiron told me that you have—a path you wish to travel, when the gods call the Great Ones?"

"But not before their time," Toreth said swiftly. "Yes. I believe it is time that the Magi began to practice their craft with—supervision. And with a great many conditions that they must follow. And I believe that it is time to end this foolish war, which eats blood and lives, and gives nothing in return."

"Then I am with you," Aket-ten said simply. "Though I fear that there is little I can offer you."

"You can offer your testimony when the time comes," Toreth replied, grimly. "Other things, too, maybe. Perhaps you can persuade this Akkadian friend of yours to share some of his time with me. I should like to learn how it is that the Magi do their work, and what constraints can be placed upon their excesses."

"Perhaps you could hire more Akkadians?" Gan suggested brightly, making them all laugh.

As if that had somehow released unspoken tension, talk drifted into lighter topics. Having discovered that yes, Aket-ten *was* as fascinated and enthralled by the dragons as they all were—if, perhaps, not quite as obsessed—the little gathering turned into something very like an ordinary evening. Aket-ten sent a servant for food and jars of beer, brought out the Hounds and Jackals box, and responded to flirtations with clever retorts.

For a while, Kiron was afraid that she did so only because she wished to keep the way clear for Toreth, but when she delivered a set-down to the prince as well, he relaxed.

For his part, he did not even want to attempt a flirtation, and kept a sharp watch on his words. If Gan and Oset-re, who were so clever at such things, were left nursing their egos, what hope had he of getting anything other than the same response?

Aket-ten might look like an "ordinary" well-born girl, but it was clear to Kiron that she was not in the least interested in the sorts of things that the other boys believed "ordinary" girls concerned themselves with. Not that he was terribly familiar with that sort of thing; he was far more familiar with the way that the older Jousters jibed with the girls who served them their beer. But what passed for a witty innuendo with a slave or a serving girl was probably going to earn him a slap.

He wanted some of her attention all for himself. So he challenged her to a game of Hounds and Jackals, and had the satisfaction of not only holding his own against her, but of presenting her with something that she did find pleasurable.

Eventually, the others drifted off to their respective pens until only he and Toreth were left. Orest had been the first to go, wearing a puzzled, even bewildered look, as if his sister had suddenly turned into a stranger before his very eyes. Toreth was watching the game with every evidence of interest, and Kiron was determined to fight it out to the last piece. Finally, with only one Hound left, she took out both of his remaining Jackals.

"Well fought!" Toreth exclaimed, as Kiron congratulated her. "My Lady, I should like to request a match tomorrow night."

"You can have your match, provided you always call me Aket-ten, and nothing more," she replied, flushed with victory, and putting up the pieces. "I have taken a dislike to being called 'my Lady.'"

"Gladly. And seeing you play—both of you—I note that you both use unconventional strategy." He looked keenly from Kiron to Aket-ten and back again. "Now, the one thing that the Magi can do—at a cost that none of us wish to continue paying—is to negate the superiority of the Tian Jousters, if only temporarily."

Kiron nodded, though he wondered fleetingly if the prince *ever* thought of anything other than the war. Or—*wars*. For there was no doubt in his mind that he considered himself to be at war now with the Magi. Aket-ten tilted her head to the side, and regarded him thoughtfully.

"This is true," she admitted. "But there is no other option, short of fielding equal or superior numbers ourselves. Is there?"

"That, Aket-ten and Kiron, is what I would like you to think on," he told them. "Because *you*, both of you, may see something that Kaleth and I have not."

Kiron blinked. "I suppose that is possible," he replied, but dubiously. "Perhaps. In time—"

"And what have we *but* time?" the prince retorted, spreading his hands wide. "We have one solution—the tame dragons. One of them is better than four Jousters on *tala*-drugged beasts. We are not desperate for a solution, I merely want you to see if you can devise more than one. No archer goes into battle with a single bow string."

Aket-ten nodded briskly. "That is only reasonable," she said. "Now, as for my Akkadian, it may be several days before I can speak with him, and more before I can persuade him to speak with you. He is reluctant to admit his training."

"And what have I but time?" the prince repeated. "If you can persuade him, well and good. If not, perhaps on the day when my brother and I sit on the Twin Thrones, he will be willing to come forward. Until then, anything he might tell us is nothing we can put into immediate use."

"There is that," Kiron agreed, and stifled a yawn. "Dawn comes early—"

"Earlier every morning until Midsummer," Aket-ten agreed cheerfully. "So, I fear, my guests, you must consider yourselves to be invited to leave!"

"And we will take the invitation in the spirit with which it was given," said the prince, standing up and giving her a slavish bow that made her laugh. He offered a hand to Kiron, who took it to pull himself to his feet. "Until tomorrow, Aket-ten! I look forward to our match!"

"Until tomorrow," she replied, her voice a little muffled as she bent to blow out a lamp.

"Well fought," Toreth repeated, slapping Kiron on the back as they left.

But he said it in a tone that left Kiron wondering. Was he talking about their game of Hounds and Jackals or some other contest altogether?

Kiron had thought that beautiful Tathulan, Huras' enormous female dragonet, would probably lose some of her relative size as the others caught up with her. But as the days passed, that didn't happen. She continued to grow at the same rate as all the others—which meant she was still half again as large as the nearest in size.

"She'll be fledging long before Bethlan," Kiron observed, watching as she tossed her current favorite plaything, a bag loosely stuffed with straw, into the air with a flip of her head. It was a singularly beautiful head; dark blue along the neck ridge and in a blaze down her forehead, fading to a glorious purple, which in turn faded to scarlet on the underside of her jaw and on her muzzle.

"You think?" Huras asked doubtfully. "She doesn't act any differently from the others. She's just bigger. I thought that you told us that the biggest and the strongest were the firstborn."

"That's what Ari told me, but now I wonder. He couldn't see the wild ones' nests all that well when he spied on them, and the only dragon he really ever had any experience with was Kashet." Kiron rubbed the side of his face with the back of his hand. "When it comes right down to it, at this point, we all have eight times the experience with dragonets that he did."

"Well, in that case, I think she'll fledge right in order," Huras said firmly. "I think it's more to do with when they're ready, not how big they are."

He might have said more, but a steady bleating had just started from their right and was approaching. They exchanged a look.

"That doesn't sound like Bethlan," said Huras.

"No, it doesn't," Kiron replied, already on his way to the doorway.

He was just in time to intercept, not Bethlan, but Gan's Khaleph. "Oh, no, baby!" he said, laughing, barring the way with his arms outstretched. "Not two wanderers! Back you go—"

But Khaleph wasn't going to be turned back quite so easily. Instead, he ducked past Kiron and—unexpectedly—into Tathulan's pen.

Both dragonets stopped what they were doing with snorts, and stared at one another.

"Do you think we should chase him out?" Huras asked, in a worried whisper, as Khaleph edged forward a little, neck stretched out so far toward Tathulan that he seemed twice his usual length.

"No—no, let's see how they react to each other, first," Kiron said cautiously. "They've never seen another dragon—and Bethlan gets along fine with that swamp dragon she keeps visiting."

Now Tathulan had her neck stretched out nearly as far. The two touched noses, snorting in surprise, and jumped back.

Kiron stifled his laughter. Huras still looked worried—though why *he* should be worried, when Tathulan was far more likely to injure Khaleph than the other way around, made no sense to Kiron.

The little emerald-green male stretched out his head again, and this time, when he touched noses with the bigger female, he didn't snort and jump back. Instead, he carefully eased himself down into the sand pit with Tathulan.

Now the two of them began a careful circling of each other, rather like two strange dogs—though unlike dogs, neither made any attempt to nip. Then they stopped, and both of them looked at Huras and Kiron.

"What do they want?" Huras asked urgently.

"It's all right," Kiron told the two dragonets—he was, after all, the one they both knew. "It's fine, little ones."

They looked at each other. And then Khaleph stretched out his neck and head again, one eye on Tathulan, only this time it was toward Tathulan's stuffed sack.

She immediately figured out what he was after, and snatched it away from under his nose.

Clumsily, he gave chase. They romped all over the pen, while Kiron and Huras scrambled out of their way, and the moment he seemed to lose interest in the chase, she stopped, and dropped the sack, pretending to ignore it until he snatched it up and she bumbled joyfully after him.

"Kiron! They're playing!" Huras said in astonishment. "I never heard of anything like that!"

"Nobody's ever had tame dragons growing up in front of their eyes either," Kiron pointed out, as Khaleph lost the sack and Tathulan snatched it away again. "For all we know, they play like this in the nest."

Just then, Gan came bursting in, hearing their voices and in a panic because Khaleph was not in his pen. He stopped dead at the sight of the two dragonets romping together.

"Kiron!" he burst out, when he could finally make his mouth work. "They're playing!"

"And I think we ought to let them all play together," Kiron replied. "They'll have to work together, let's let them get used to each other early."

So the next time little Bethlan went looking for Menet-ka, Kalen steered her into the pen of his female Se-atmen, and soon there was a whirling ball of indigo-blue and brown-gold play-wrestling in Se-atmen's pen. Toreth deliberately led his Re-eth-katen into Apetma's pen; clever little Re-eth-katen was soon poking her nose into *every* pen to find a playmate, much to Avatre's disgust. Orest's Wastet and Pe-atep's Deoth met in the corridor, and in the surprise of the moment, went tumbling into the tenth, empty pen, where they made a fine mess of the oddments that had been stored there. At Kiron's request, a gate was built across the end of their corridor so that the babies did not get themselves into trouble by assuming that the adult dragons would be as ready to play as their fellow dragonets, and then they were permitted full freedom of the entire set of pens. This had the happy side effect of freeing half the boys while the other half took it in turn to watch over all the babies, and all the babies got used to obeying someone besides "mother." It had another happy side effect; they grew stronger and much more coordinated with every day spent in play, and as for nights, they were so tired by the time darkness fell that you could not have awakened them with a trumpet.

However, all the boys soon learned that you either found a way to secure your belongings or you found them being used as playthings. Curtains across the doors stopped some of the dragonets, but not all. Finally, the carpenters were brought in to build actual *doors* after Lord Khumun tired of replacing bed coverings.

"What's next, the furniture?" he grumbled to Kiron. "No, don't answer that. *I* can see how fast they're growing." And he gave the orders for doors.

The dragonets found the carpenters to be even more fascinating than the furniture, and followed the poor men from pen to pen, crowding around to watch, tasting the wooden planks, trying to steal the tools. It made for an interesting day for everyone, as the boys tried to keep the dragonets away from the carpenters, and the dragonets tried to get at the carpenters, and the carpenters worked probably a great deal faster than they ever had in their lives, sure that the dragonets would go from tasting the wood to tasting them.

Avatre had never acted like this—but then, Avatre had been raised in isolation from every other dragon but Kashet. Kashet had been an adult, not at all interested in playing; it gave Kiron a pang to think of how lonely she must have been.

And yet, he had spent every free moment of time with her. And he had played with her. So perhaps she had been all right.

The one thing he found himself wishing, though, was impossible.

He could not help but think how entranced Ari would have been to see all of this, and wish that his mentor could have been there.

It might even have made him laugh again. And that would have been worth more to Kiron than all the Gold of Honor in Alta.

# TWELVE

**KIRON** stood before the single most important man in the compound, and asked for the moon, the sun, and the stars.

"I want to teach the boys how to fly a dragon *now,*" said Kiron to Lord Khumun. "I think that putting an inexperienced rider on a fledgling dragon is going to get someone hurt or killed, and there are people who have the ears of the Great Ones who would be pleased if that happened."

He did not come out and say that the Magi would be just as glad if the Jousters began having a bout of trouble, but they both knew who he was talking about. For once, the Magi were not getting the credit for victory. Their storms might be keeping the Tian Jousters on the ground, but it was the Altan Jousters, not some storms too far away to be seen, that were being lauded as the force that was turning the tide in this war.

So Kiron had intercepted Lord Khumun just after his daily inspection of the dragon pens, for Lord Khumun did not leave the running of the compound up to his Overseer—or rather, Lord Khumun *was* the Overseer, in the sense that he personally inspected everything, every day, and knew the names of every inhabitant of the compound right down to the dragon boys.

The Lord of the Jousters regarded him steadily, arms crossed over his chest. "All right. I can see where that might be true enough. And it is true that the failure of one of us reflects badly on all of us. What did you have in mind, bearing in mind that all of the dragons we have are out fighting or flying patrols every day?"

Kiron cleared his throat, and began his carefully prepared argument, reminding himself that the worst that could happen would be that Lord Khumun would say "no." "Simply flying—taking off, doing simple maneuvers over the compound, and landing—isn't going to task a dragon at all, especially not if it's only enough to get their muscles warmed up. I want my boys to start taking the beasts up and warming them up before their assigned rider takes them out, and that is how they will learn to fly before their own dragonets fledge. To start with, I want to use only the two desert dragons that laid our eggs. They're both Tian dragons, so they were caught in Tia as fledglings rather than adults and they're tamer. And frankly, they're lazier. A lazy dragon is what I want for a new rider."

Lord Khumun nodded thoughtfully, and pursed his lips. "And I can also see where having your boys warm up a lazy dragon might actually be to our advantage. I've noticed that those two lose some of their lethargy once they've been moving for a while. Go on."

Yes indeed, Lord Khumun knew everything having to do with the Jousters and their beasts. There could be no equivalent to "Vetch and Avatre" here; had anyone hidden an egg or a growing dragonet in an empty pen, Lord Khumun would have known within the day. Not that Kiron could fault Haraket, the Overseer of the Tian Compound—the Altan Compound was less than half the size of the Tian equivalent. It wasn't that Haraket was careless; no, it was that Lord Khumun was an absolute fanatic about all things having to do with his Jousters.

On the other hand, there would be no equivalent to the dreadful accident that allowed Avatre to be hatched either.

"I'll go up on Avatre at the same time, keeping the height advantage above them, so that if the dragon tries any tricks, we can
herd them down again. Two dragons doing two runs each day
means that my boys will each get a practice ride every other day."
Now he made a face. "I'd put them up on Avatre, too, but there'd
be no one up there with them as a safeguard."

"That assumes she could be gotten into the air with you still on
the ground," Lord Khumun pointed out. "I think it unlikely that at
this stage she would accept another rider. Perhaps when she is
older, but not now."

*He's talking as if he is in favor of this already. Actually, I suppose
if he wasn't he would have said no from the beginning. And he's not
going to ask me to put the others on Avatre to teach them either.
Thanks be to the gods!* Kiron relaxed a little at passing one hurdle—
and the truth was, though he could think of other excuses why he
didn't want his friends to train on Avatre's back, the real reason
was that he didn't want to share her. The mere thought of someone else in her saddle made him acutely unhappy. "With the training I've been giving them on the mock dragon, I think they'll be
comfortable in the air pretty quickly." He waited to see what
Lord Khumun would have to say about this, for Lord Khumun
had been remarkably silent on the subject of Kiron's unorthodox
training methods. But what was he to do? Traditionally, the
Jousters of Alta had been presented with fully-grown, trained,
*tala*-drugged dragons, and taught to fly on them from the beginning. The dragonets were nowhere near big enough to ride.

The mock dragon had been an idea of his own. He had racked
his brain for weeks to come up with a way to simulate flying, and
finally, watching a new awning being put up over a pen gave him
the idea. Some training was done by putting a saddle at one end
of a lever with a weight at the other, but that only gave the rider
up-and-down motion. And it wasn't very far off the ground.

The training of the Tian dragons, with the dragons tethered
within their pens, would be part of the training, but it wouldn't
bring the boys along nearly as fast as Kiron wanted—and what

was more, both rider and dragonet would be beginners. As he had said, putting two beginning flyers into the air at once was trouble waiting to happen.

Look what had happened to him, and he had some experience at flying by then!

Then, somehow, watching that awning being restrung, combined with the tethered fledgling, cascaded in his mind into the mock dragon.

A tightly-packed bundle of reeds the size of a dragon's chest had been put in the center of a courtyard. Ropes had been strung through enormous eye bolts driven into the stone in each corner of the yard at the top of the wall. The ropes were then brought to the center of the yard and tied to the bundle. A dragon saddle was put on it, one of the boys strapped himself into the saddle, and then eight muscular slaves pulled on the ropes to heave the whole contraption into the air until it was suspended above the court, and the boy with it. A thick pile of loose straw with straw-filled mattresses atop that was positioned beneath the bundle.

And then the games began.

The object of the boy in the saddle was to remain in the saddle and relatively in control of the situation, which translated as keeping his balance no matter what happened. The object of the slaves was to unseat him. At first, this had been limited to imitating the sorts of movements that a dragon would make while flying—the swooping up and down of wing-beat flying, pitches to the right or left. Once those were mastered, though, all bets were off, and the slaves were given leave to make the mock dragon do anything they could manage, whether or not a real dragon would be capable of the motion. And although Kiron had done his best to make sure the mock dragon wouldn't actually flip upside down, the slaves had managed to find a way to make it do what it wasn't supposed to.

The boys came off at first, of course, restraining straps or no restraining straps. They had plenty of bruises to show for it. And they got sick at first. Not anymore.

As a consequence, he was reasonably certain that the two desert dragons would not be able to do anything to rid themselves of their brand-new riders.

"I think that's a reasonable idea," said Lord Khumun. "It doesn't tax the dragons, you've got safeguards in mind. And then what will you follow this with, once your wing is comfortable with the two desert dragons?"

"I want them to all take the same sort of warm-up flights on the swamp dragons, so that all of them go up, twice a day, every day." This wasn't as dangerous as it might have been before the swamp dragons had been retrained. And there was a big advantage that the swamp dragons had over the desert dragons in this case; they were smaller, so they were less inclined to try violent maneuvers to rid themselves of an unwanted rider.

Once again, Lord Khumun nodded. "I like that. If anything, the swamp dragons need warming up more than the desert dragons do, especially in the morning. Do you think that once your riders have mastered the swamp dragons, their own will be near fledging?"

"I don't know, my Lord," Kiron said honestly. "But if they are not, I propose sending one or two out with a senior Jouster on border-patrol flights, once a day. Not fighting, but simply patrolling. If you choose to replace injured or exhausted Jousters in this way—well, just because the rider is injured or exhausted, that doesn't mean the dragon is, and there is no reason to let the dragon laze about his pen and get out of condition."

"I see your point, and although I would like to consult with the senior Jousters on that idea, even this last phase of your plan has its merits," Lord Khumun acknowledged. "Very well. You can put the first stage of your plan into action, and the second as well. We will then see if we actually need to proceed to the third stage when the time comes."

Kiron bowed deeply out of overwhelming gratitude. "Thank you, my Lord. I do not believe you will be less than happy with the results."

When he rose again, Lord Khumun was smiling. "I can see why you made a poor serf," he said softly. "It was the same reason why you make an excellent leader. Go on with you. I'm sure your wing is waiting to hear the results of your request to me."

Kiron bowed again, and—well, he didn't run, but he wanted to. He satisfied dignity with a very brisk walk to the area the senior Jousters had begun to call "the Nursery." Not that anyone really minded the name—the place was full of baby dragons, after all, and though the senior Jousters might have looked on Kiron's wing with a certain level of patronization, it was paternal patronization. And all they had to do was to look at Avatre and the things she could do to know what the future held for the rest of the babies in the Nursery.

The others all knew what he was going to ask, of course. They'd all been talking about the idea for the last several days. They were too wise to wait for him anywhere near Lord Khumun's quarters, but they pounced on him as a group the moment he entered the corridor nearest the Nursery.

Before they could start chattering at him, he held up his hands in the victory sign, and the corridor echoed with their cheers. He had to smile at that. Oh, they were so eager to get into the sky, even the ones who'd been sick on the mock dragon. How easily they forgot!

"Oh, don't start cheering until after you've had a taste of what those two beasts I'm going to start you on can think up in the way of torment for a new flyer!" he warned them, laughing. "Don't forget for a moment that these are mean old cows who would much rather be in their sand wallows being treated like princesses than have to work for their meat. It's going to be especially bad for the first two to ride them, in the morning. They *hate* getting up, and they'll take it out on you!"

"But you and Avatre will be there to teach them better manners," said Gan gaily. "There's nothing to worry about, is there, lads?"

Kiron sighed. Enough enthusiasm to build a palace and not a

brick of common sense among them. Well, they would see soon enough for themselves that he hadn't been joking. The first few days were going to be—interesting.

*No wonder Haraket was bald. He must have torn his own hair out long before I ever came to the compound.*

He had to wonder, though. Were all young riders such over-confident idiots?

Sut-ke-re, rider of Jatel, laughed when he asked that question aloud. "Ah, Kiron," he said, with a twinkle in his eye, "Are not most young men in general overconfident idiots? I think that is the essence of a young man."

"Well—" he said, and flushed when he thought of what he had done to win Avatre for himself. It had been insane. He should never have been able to pull it off. At least he hadn't been over-confident—he'd been terrified every moment of every day that he would be caught—but he'd been a fool to even try it in the first place. "I suppose so. If not overconfident, then—at least, we are all foolhardy. And as for idiots—well, I suppose we are that, too."

"I think it is in the nature of young men," Sut-ke-re said, pulling off his short wig and rubbing his shaved head as he squinted up at the sun. "Young men are willing to take risks that older men would not even think of trying. Young men believe they are immortal, I do think. I know that they are impatient with tradition. If they were not, they would never attempt the half of what they do, and no new thing would ever be tried."

"Such as growing dragons from the egg?" Kiron hazarded.

"Such as growing dragons from the egg," Sut-ke-re confirmed. "Now, here is my dilemma. On the one hand, I would rather that your wing did traditional training. On the other hand, there are no dragons to spare for traditional training, and even if there were, there are young men two or three years older than your boys are, who have had other sorts of military training, who are waiting for a dragon. There are always more trained warriors wanting to be Jousters than there are dragons. And I agree with you that putting two fledgling flyers into the air at the same time is foolhardy. So I agreed, and so did Ke-shuth."

"Jouster," said Kiron, trying to put as much gratitude as he could muster into his voice, "Thank you."

Sut-ke-re shrugged. "I can see no reason to object to your borrowing Jatel before I am ready to ride out, for she is a lazy cow and could surely stand to be ridden far more in a day than I ride her. And Ke-shuth will be pleased to have his slug Orthele warmed up and more inclined to move when he comes to take her out as well."

So, he had gotten past the second hurdle with not so much as a single objection! "Thank you, Jouster Sut-ke-re," Kiron said again, with relief as well as gratitude. He bowed slightly, and turned to go give the boys the good news.

"Just you keep them out of trouble!" Sut-ke-re called after him, though there was amusement in his voice. "If ever I turn up and there's a sprained foot or a strained wing, a broken strap or an exhausted dragon, there will be a reckoning!"

This made for a change in the babies' routine. The dragonets were no longer clamoring for food constantly; they were content with several large meals every day now, which made it possible for the boys to get away long enough to train in between feedings. But for the two on the morning flights of the new stage of training, the dragonets had to be fed by someone else, otherwise the two boys in question would not have time to fly before the wings went up.

That "someone" was Aket-ten.

She had, in fact, volunteered for the duty, and Kiron had been concerned that she would not be up to it. Feeding the babies was still a messy, bloody job, and he would not have blamed her for taking one look and deciding it was not for her.

In fact, she took to it without a flinch or a word of complaint, and by the time Toreth and Huras were ready for their first real flights, she had fed every one of the babies, under the supervision of its "mother," at least twice.

As for the babies, once they got over the surprise of seeing someone different from their "mother" with food in hand, they accepted her without question or pause. In fact, they began to obey her nearly as well as they obeyed their "mothers," which meant that she could take a turn at the baby minding when they played together.

"If I'm going to be Speaking with them, and possibly helping them when they're sick or hurt, I'd better be prepared to feed them, now, hadn't I?" she replied, when Kiron had suggested that she might find it unpleasant. "If I have to help hand feed a very sick or injured dragon, it's not going to be much different from what I'm doing now except in terms of scale." Since she was exactly right, there hadn't been anything he could do except to thank her and turn her over to the boys to be shown what to do.

By this point, the dragonets were bonded strongly enough with their riders that having someone else feed them once every couple of days wasn't going to make a difference. And Aket-ten was right; better to have them associate her with a very pleasant experience now, so that when she had to help them under *un*pleasant conditions, they would trust her.

On the first morning of the new training, Kiron had the dragon boys bring Jatel and Orthele to the landing courtyard after they had been saddled. There was no other way to get both boys up into the air under supervision at the same time. Both dragons were heartily displeased with this change in routine, and hissed and whined at each other when they were led into the courtyard. But Kiron had strong slaves standing by to help the dragon boys if needed, and though the two dragons grumbled, they didn't actually do anything, thus being true to their essentially lazy natures.

Kiron and Avatre took off as soon as Toreth and Huras were in their saddles. Avatre watched the two dragons below her with great interest as he put her into a little circle above the court. As soon as he thought their position was good, he waved to the dragon boys below; they unhitched the chains, and the two riders gave their dragons the signal to fly.

And nothing happened.

Now this was not entirely unexpected. Their regular riders knew what to do, but both of the desert dragons had probably assessed these inexperienced boys within moments as being riders that they could afford to ignore, and they were not going to move unless they were forced. It was hard to force a dragon to do something it didn't want to do—and they held grudges when you did.

So Kiron did the forcing.

He had considered stinging them with clay pellets from his sling and had thought better of the idea. He didn't want these dragons to associate his boys with being "bitten" by a clay pellet. So instead, he had laid another plan to get the dragons to fly.

He gave a second signal—and on the other side of the wall, one of the local pigeon keepers flung open his portable coop, and several dozen rock doves burst into the air with a whirring explosion of wings.

As Kiron very well knew, when one winged thing suddenly explodes into the sky, virtually every other winged thing nearby will do the same. The instinct to flee the unexpected is a powerful one, and in general, winged creatures are uniquely vulnerable when grounded, so when the eyes and ears took in the signal *Fly!*, it was likely that they would do so without hesitation.

The dragons were no exception.

Even Avatre started at the explosion of wings; Jatel and Orthele *leaped* for the sky, their muscles and wings moving before their heads had a chance to interfere. Toreth and Huras hung on for dear life as the dragons climbed, each surging wingbeat throwing them back, then forward, in their saddles.

Avatre got a little more height; Aket-ten had done her best to convey what the dragon's duties were going to be this morning, and apparently Avatre had understood. As Toreth and Huras gradually, and successfully, exerted more and more control over their mounts, Avatre kept watchful vigil just above them. Whenever either of the two looked as if she was going to take command of the situation to do what she wanted, Avatre followed Kiron's directions and made a feint at her. Avatre might not be fully grown yet, but she had the superior position, and the other two hated physical confrontation with another dragon. Historically, they closed for combat with great reluctance, and never tried to lay into an enemy dragon with tooth or claw the way the swamp dragons sometimes did.

Finally they were answering the simple commands that the boys gave them with a minimum of objection, and Kiron got a little more height to let the boys put the two dragons through their paces. Up here, with the sun beating down on them, it was hot already, though the first hints that the *kamiseen* would start soon were definitely in the wind. All three dragons were soon moving easily and freely, and the little grunts and hisses of complaint from below stopped coming. Kiron was enjoying himself completely, and so was Avatre, when he looked down to the landing courtyard and saw someone waving a bit of white linen in the signal that the proper riders were ready to go out.

There was a moment of confusion for the two adult dragons, who were not used to landing so soon after taking off; Avatre had to come down very near to them in order to persuade them to land. And they hissed a bit in complaint when they saw their proper riders and realized that the first flight had been nothing more then a warm-up.

But though they hissed, they took to the sky again with no sign of reluctance, and joined up with the rest of the wing. Only when he was sure that they were not going to give their riders any trouble—and thus a reason to object to this training scheme—did Kiron turn toward the boys of his own wing.

Huras looked a little pale. Toreth, however, was gazing after the departed dragons with a look of longing.

"It will be too long until the day after tomorrow," said Toreth.

Huras snorted. "For you, maybe," was all he said.

Kiron recalled his own first experience with real flight, and sympathized. But he didn't offer that sympathy to Huras, who would only learn that one got used to flying by actually getting used to it. And he wanted to be a Jouster—Jousters didn't ride their dragons on the ground.

By the end of the fourth day, Jatel and Orthele were resigned to the new schedule, and if they were not happy about it, they had at least stopped being so uncooperative. There had been two instances of trying to dump their riders, neither of which had been anything like as violent as some of the convulsions the mock dragon could produce. There were three attempts to refuse to take off, all three of which had been overcome by a release of pigeons. And once, Jatel had tried to snap at Huras, who had shocked her by punching her on the nose. He hadn't hurt her, but he certainly got her attention, and her respect, for after that, she was as good with him as she was with her regular rider.

As for Aket-ten—

Kiron soon learned that she had a scheme of her own in mind to help them all.

The air was hot, humid, and far too still. Virtually everyone was taking a rest from the heat. Kiron, however, could not find Aket-ten anywhere. She was not in her quarters, not with the wing's dragonets, and she had not left word with her servants that she was leaving the compound. She never left the compound without telling them where she was going, for she still did not trust the Magi, and feared that if any of them even suspected she still had her powers, they would try to carry her off.

She was probably right to fear that. Though Kiron no longer spied on the Magi when they came to take the Fledglings in the evening, he had heard from Kaleth that the young Fledglings were not looking good. Whatever the Magi were taking from them was beginning to run out. If they thought Aket-ten—fresh, rested, and full of energy—was still able to be drained, they would be on her like a falcon on a dove.

Finally, after questioning every person whose path he crossed, he found someone who had seen her, and the direction surprised him.

*What can she possibly want in the swamp dragon pens?* he wondered, as he crossed over into the section where the pens held water instead of sand. He followed the directions he had been given until he found her—at the pen of the same swamp dragon that had been placed on half-rations of *tala*.

She was sitting well out of reach of the chained dragon, staring at him. He was immersed in his hot water with only his head and neck sticking out of the water, his chain slack enough that it was lying on the bottom of the pool, staring back at her.

The place smelled like a bath; odd, he would have thought there might be an unpleasant tang to it. Evidently the swamp dragons were as clean and fastidious as their larger cousins. This dragon was a very dark reddish brown, his patterning laid out in a slightly paler and more golden brown. He looked like a weather-aged statue, he lay so still, his golden-brown eyes staring intently at Aket-ten. There was a tension in the air, however, that told him that their relaxed poses were entirely a deception.

"They are smarter than we thought they were," she said quietly, without looking around at Kiron. "Mind, they aren't as intelligent as an ape, and I am not certain I would even put them at the same level as a truly smart dog, but this fellow is definitely as smart as any of the desert dragons. Whoever decided that they were not as bright because they weren't as big or as pretty made a fundamental error."

"Huh." He squatted down where he was, resting on his heels, and stared at the dragon himself. He wondered what she was getting from the beast's thoughts. This was as close as she was ever going to get to a wild dragon's mind.

"Partly it's the *tala*," she continued absently, rubbing the palms of her hands up and down her bare upper arms in a completely unconscious gesture. "I think they're a little more sensitive to it than the desert dragons."

"Well, it's a desert plant," he reminded her. "And if we don't find the wild *tala* and harvest it, there are a lot of animals that eat it. Desert dragons are probably used to getting some of it in their prey, so they've gotten used to the effect of it."

"That could be," she agreed. She and the dragon continued to match unblinking stares. "You know, falcons hate this. Being stared at, I mean. It's a challenge; that's one way they challenge each other. Cats, too. In cats, the first one that looks away loses, and is going to get attacked. He sees my staring at him as something else. Some kind of contact. I wonder if they have a very primitive kind of Speaking? Something that requires eye contact?" She never once dropped her gaze. "It doesn't seem to bother him at all that I can put thoughts into his head—and what's more, he *knows* that they're mine and not his own." She tilted her head to the side. "I thought I might have been sensing something like that from the dragonets, too."

"Haven't you ever felt that from any of the other adult dragons?" he asked curiously.

She shrugged. "If they do have some form of Speaking, the *tala* blocks it. I can't look away right now, by the way. If I do, I'll be saying he's the stronger of the two of us."

"I'd gotten that idea," said Kiron. "Did you have something in mind by coming here?"

"I did." She continued to stare; was the dragon beginning to look a little uneasy beneath that unrelenting gaze? "I wanted to see if these swamp fellows were just as smart as their desert cousins. I wanted to have a look into the head of one that wasn't completely foggy with *tala*. I never intended to get into a staring contest, but I don't dare back down now. It's either predator or prey, and I must prove which one I am, for he only respects the former."

At just that moment, the dragon gave up, dropping his eyes and his head in a gesture of submission.

Aket-ten stood up, slowly and carefully, her eyes still never leaving the dragon's. She moved toward the pool.

As Kiron held his breath and got ready to pull her to safety, the dragon slid his way through the water toward her.

She held out her hand, fearlessly—but palm down, not up.

With infinite care, the dragon moved forward until the chain was stretched tight—and pushed the tip of his nose beneath her hand.

He closed his eyes and sighed. And waited.

*What does that mean to a dragon?* he wondered. The nose was the most sensitive part. You couldn't kill a dragon by slashing at its nose, but—

*But—they're like crocodiles,* he realized at that moment. He'd seen the dragonets immobilize each other briefly in play by grabbing the muzzle. You could make it impossible for him to attack you by holding his mouth closed. *And if you were a dragon, and you seized your rival by the nose, and you clamped down on it and closed off the nostrils as well—your rival would be dead. You'd smother him.*

So that was what it meant to a dragon! Total, complete surrender. . . .

*For the moment, anyway.* Like all wild things, the hierarchy within a flight of dragons was always changing. One was always challenging another. Mostly staring contests though, and perhaps Aket-ten was right, perhaps they did some shoving about, invisibly, will-to-will as well.

She rubbed the sensitive skin around the dragon's nostrils. "Give me a brush," she demanded, without looking away.

"What?" he asked.

"A brush," she said patiently. "I'm getting into the pool with him to give him a scrub. It's the equivalent of a sand rubbing. This is what *they* do—the one who wins grooms the one who lost."

Kiron looked around and saw that, sure enough, there were several brushes with heavy, stiff bristles hanging on the wall. He got one and brought it to Aket-ten. She held out her hand without looking at him, and he put the brush into it. Only then did she wade into the dragon's pool, handsome yellow sheath dress and all, hissing a little at the heat as she got in.

Had this been anyone other than Aket-ten, he never would have allowed it. In the same pool, as a dragon on a half-ration of *tala*, well within his grabbing distance?

But it was Aket-ten, and if there was anyone who knew what she was doing at this moment, it was Aket-ten.

She didn't give the swamp dragon a full grooming; that would have taken all afternoon. But she did get some of the worst, and apparently itchiest, spots. The dragon moaned and sighed and leaned into her strokes until she patted him on the shoulder and climbed out, her dress streaming—and leaving nothing at all to the imagination.

He flushed; she didn't seem to notice. Then again, she was being very careful around an unsedated dragon; a little thing like having a dress that was now so transparent you might as well be wearing nothing at all was not going to trouble her.

Whatever she was putting into the dragon's mind worked. He didn't even snap at her. When she was out of reach, Kiron wordlessly handed her a towel.

"Now is the point when I ask you what you thought you were accomplishing when you started this, rather than what you were doing," he said, after a moment, as she dried herself off as best she could. "Since you seem to have worked out how to be the king dragon in a flight. Or queen," he added, as an afterthought. "I think Ari said the dominant dragon can be male *or* female."

She shrugged. "Finding things out. And I have; we need to drop the dose of *tala* that the swamp dragons get by about a double handful. Mostly though, I found out how we can get swamp dragon eggs without getting the collectors killed. So when your wing has proven itself, we can also raise swamp dragons from the egg for the next lot to fly." She raised an eyebrow at him. "Think about a wing of dragons who are tame like Avatre who not only can fly in the rain, but like it."

"Huh." There was no doubt that it would be an incredible advantage. "So, how do we get eggs without someone getting killed?" he asked.

"The same way we've been dosing him." She stared at him now, waiting. And he could have hit himself for not thinking of it himself.

"Ducks and geese, I suppose?" he hazarded. She nodded. "And when whichever dragon is watching the nest is drugged enough, we move in. I assume you'd be watching the dragon's mind to make sure the nest watcher wasn't going to wake up."

"Don't take more than two of the four eggs, though," she warned. "That's reasonable. Only one in four is going to get past its first year anyway, but you'd better give them two chances at it, or you'll start depleting the population."

She went off to her quarters then, to change into something drier. He went to find Lord Khumun to report on what she had learned—though he did *not* tell Lord Khumun that she had gotten into the pool to groom her subject. He left that part out, saying only that she had established herself as that particular dragon's superior, using her powers. Then he described how swamp dragon nests could be raided for eggs.

The Lord of the Jousters looked at him askance. "That would be useful knowledge if we wanted swamp dragons," he said reluctantly. "But—*swamp* dragons?"

"Which can be flown in the storms?" he countered. "My Lord, look at your current riders! Every day during the magic-made rains they have flown out, and every day have brought back one form of victory or another! And consider that tame swamp dragons could probably be persuaded to fly even during the whole season of Rains!" He surprised himself with his passion. Compared with Avatre, the swamp-dragons were so—

—*hmm. Maybe they aren't.* He thought about the intent gaze, the feeling of challenge. Aket-ten was right. It was the *tala* that made them seem so dull. He said as much.

"What is more, my Lord, though the swamp dragons are smaller, a Jouster on a desert dragon is going to have some difficulty in defending against *two* attackers." He saw the puzzlement in Lord Khumun's eyes, and elaborated. "What if we got enough swamp dragons to outnumber them?"

The gleam in Lord Khumun's eyes told him that he had won.

When they met at dinner, he told the rest of the boys what had happened, and how Aket-ten had discovered the means to get swamp dragon eggs to augment the desert dragon eggs that they could get from mating Jatel and Orthele. And initially they all had the same reaction as Lord Khumun at the suggestion. But Gan said suddenly, "You know, I believe I have seen some old wall texts in a temple somewhere, all about the first dragon Jousters. I do believe that they used *swamp* dragons, not desert dragons. So Aket-ten is right; they must be just as smart as the desert ones, they're just smaller."

"And if the odds are two-to-one in our favor, it won't matter how small the dragons are," Toreth put in quietly.

"No," said Kiron into the silence. "It won't, will it?"

"So that's the way the wind blows. . . ." Huras nodded. "Clever little Aket-ten! Do you suppose she figured that out?"

"Yes she did, and all by herself, thank you very much," said Aket-ten tartly from the doorway. "It will be up to you layabouts to work out how to train yourselves, so we can prove to every doubter in Alta that the tame dragons are superior, and that we can train Jousters to go with the tame dragons."

She strolled into the kitchen courtyard and took her usual place at their table. "There are some things you'll just have to do for yourselves," she continued, with deceptive sweetness. "Now that I've done the hard part."

"The hard part?" Orest said, and Kiron winced to himself, seeing exactly how Aket-ten's brother had set himself up for a clever retort on her part. And there was nothing he could do about it because—

"Of course," she replied, with a disarming smile. "I've done all the thinking."

—*too late.* Kiron sighed and intervened. "She's just teasing you, Orest."

But the explosion he had expected didn't come. Orest just shrugged. "I'm not much good at thinking," he said with complete candor. "She can do all the thinking for both of us, if she wants. I like the swampie idea, though. Be one in *their* eye if just as they think they have us outnumbered, *we* show up with a two-to-one advantage and dragons that can fly rings around theirs."

"That it would," said Toreth smoothly, as Aket-ten gaped at her brother. "So, Aket-ten, tell us more about how you approached this dragon today—"

*By the gods,* he thought, listening to the boys question her closely. *Aket-ten isn't the only one growing up. So is her brother.*

Indeed; they were all growing up. And none too soon. Because by the end of the Dry season, if his own calculations were correct, they were all going to face the enemy in the field for the first time. And the advantage, numerically at least, was still with the enemy.

If they weren't grown up by then, it would be too late.

The dragonets were being fitted for their first saddles and harness, using Avatre's outgrown harness as a model. And for once, there were servants here in the dragonet pens who didn't have to be persuaded that the babies were tame.

The old harness maker and his assistant swarmed all over Wastet like a pair of cleaner birds on a river horse. Wastet regarded them with bright curiosity, while Orest stood by.

"And your colors are blue and scarlet, young lord?" asked the assistant, taking notes on a potsherd. "May I ask why you have colors at all?"

"To differentiate us, not only from our fellow Altan Jousters, but more importantly, from the Tian ones," Kiron replied for Orest. "We don't want someone from our own side seeing a desert dragon and thinking it's ridden by a Tian."

"And we want to be able to keep track of the others in our

wing," Orest added. "So we can do things that we've practiced together."

"But why different colors for each of you?" the assistant persisted. "I should think you could make out who is who by the colors of your dragons. No one is going to mistake this beetle-colored beauty for any of the others."

"First of all, we didn't know they would all hatch out different colors," Kiron replied. "Second, from a distance they can still be confused—take Avatre, she's scarlet and gold, which is awfully close to Pe-atep's Deoth, who's red and sand colored. Or Kalen's Se-atmen, brown and gold, who could be taken for Oset-re's copper-red Apetma. And third, we're only the first wing of tame desert dragons. There are two female desert dragons that can provide us with more eggs every two years. Eventually there are going to be Jousters with the same color dragons; we need ways to tell them apart in the air, and we might as well start now and get our eyes used to looking for the combination of dragon colors and rider and harness colors."

"Ah," the assistant said, contented now. "You see, I like to know why one is asked to do something unusual—"

"And thus, you are too damned curious and prying, you young whelp," the old man growled. "If you worked as well as you jabbered, we'd have the harnesses done by now."

"Yes, master," the assistant said, sounding not at all subservient. He turned back to Kiron. "And you are wanting streamers that can be easily torn away in the same colors as well?"

Kiron nodded. "We'll be using them in training, to teach the dragons to get in close for harassment, but I don't want something that is going interfere with flying—"

The assistant dismissed that with a shrug. "Colored grass, loosely woven," he replied. "Fastened to the back of the saddle. Easily done."

"As easily as I am going to beat you if we don't get these dragons measured!" scolded the old man. "Get on with you!"

The two of them moved on to Apetma's pen. Orest and Kiron exchanged grins.

"What were those extra straps you ordered for?" Orest asked when they had gone. "He didn't ask about those."

"Probably because they seem perfectly logical to someone who has never been a Jouster," Kiron replied, sobering. "I don't want any accidents. Avatre and I still haven't mastered the 'falling-man' catch. Maybe the senior Jousters will think this is effete, but I want all of you belted down into your saddles when we begin training."

Orest nodded slowly. "I've no objection," he replied, slowly. "Now that I've been up on dragons—it's a long way down to the ground. I wouldn't like to fall—"

"Oh, I'm not worried about falling. The Tian Jousters used to say that it isn't the fall that kills you," Kiron replied with a straight face.

"Oh? So what is it?" Once again, Orest walked straight into the joke.

"It's the hitting the ground that kills you," Kiron replied, and ran out of Wastet's pen with a brush following him.

He particularly wanted to catch up with the harness makers before they left Oset-re's Apetma. By now, he half suspected that the boys had forgotten that their dragons were to be harnessed up in the riders' colors—but Kiron remembered Oset-re's fuss about having colors that didn't clash with a dragon's colors. He'd gotten black and white; was that sufficiently neutral for him to be content? The last thing he wanted was for Oset-re to be unhappy about a little thing like the colors of his harness when it was so easy to fix—

But he found Oset-re perfectly at ease as the harness makers nattered on about what color should be where to avoid soiling the white parts.

"Are you still all right with black and white?" he asked Oset-re cautiously. "It's not to late to change—"

"Oh, Apetma is going to look amazing," Oset-re said breezily, holding her head and gazing into her coppery eyes. "Aren't you, my love? There won't be another dragon out there as striking as you—" And as he crooned to her, she butted his head gently with her copper-red nose and crooned back at him. And at that moment, Kiron realized that it would not have mattered to the formerly vain Oset-re if Apetma had been dun and his colors green and gray, he would *still* have been sure she was the most beautiful of the lot. He was just as besotted with Apetma as any of them, and nothing was half as important anymore as his dragon.

Kiron left the pen feeling, although he was not sure why, as if he had just won a war.

# THIRTEEN

FROM BELOW, the view was fascinating, as brilliantly colored dragons soared and dove in the cloudless sky. Watching the dragons practice and train had always been a popular pastime for those who could afford to take the time away from their proper jobs—but now people were snatching a few moments just to come and gape.

The boys were now "safe" to be up on their own during some games, thanks to the many days of going up to warm up other Jousters' dragons. When they were paired off in noncombat exercises, Kiron liked to leave Avatre in the pen once in a while and just go out to the practice field to watch as if he was one of the spectators. At the moment, the fledglings were ribbon chasing in sets of two, one with the ribbon, one trying to get it. They were over their "clumsy" stage at last, and now he was allowing all eight of them up in the sky at the same time. Since they weren't very fast at this yet, they were able to avoid collisions that lack of practice and skill would have made inevitable at an adult speed.

The spectators, however, were not aware of the fledglings' imperfections. They were here to watch and wonder, and marvel.

The boys weren't heroes yet—but the next set of Jousters, waiting their turn to go up and go through the same games, were. And if the swamp dragons weren't as pretty up in the sky, they were a lot more exciting; they could double back on their own paths in the blink of an eye, and even literally fly rings around each other. None of them could match Avatre, however. She was able to tumble and wingover in a way that none of the others would, because none of the others were as alert and aware as she was, nor were they anywhere near as cooperative. She would try anything he asked her to, which was why he was very, very careful about what he asked her to do.

There were quite a few brand new game exercises, and new forms of combat being practiced up there—and down near ground level as well—these days. At night, Kiron and his wing thrashed out new ideas, and tried to come up with better plans all the time. Some of the things that they had tried worked, some didn't, and some were useful only as agility training.

Take the ribbon chasing, for instance. One dragon would have a ribbon tied to his harness, and a second dragon would be sent up to take it. It was the job of the first rider to keep the second from snatching that ribbon. It had no application to combat whatsoever, but it certainly trained the dragons and riders in evasive maneuvering.

It was hot and very humid down here on the ground with the green, rank scent of the canals everywhere; in Alta, the Dry season wasn't actually *dry*, not with all of the canals around. Kiron felt sweat tricking down the back of his neck and making his scalp prickle, and wished he was up there. The layer of humid air stopped about halfway to where the dragons were playing now and that was where the dry *kamiseen* wind began. He listened to the spectators with half of his attention; they found the ribbon chasing to be absolutely enthralling. He couldn't blame them; the game was fun to watch, and even more fun to participate in.

On the other hand, one of the near-ground tactics *was* a combat-trick, and was going to be extremely useful. One of the things that Tian dragons did was to dive down on an Altan army and snatch a commander right out of the midst of his men, rising in the air to drop him to his death. The swamp dragons weren't big enough to pull that off.

Neither were the fledglings, nor would they be for at least another year. But they would try to do anything that their riders asked them to, once Aket-ten put it into their heads. And one of those things was a new, and potentially deadlier equivalent to what the Tians did. It, too, was intended to serve the purpose of eliminating important enemy commanders.

The fledglings took to it immediately, for it fit in so well with their natural hunting skills that they hardly had anything to learn.

They would rise to the top of a thermal, and their rider would pick a target and signal the general area where it was. Since Tian commanders wore blue war helmets, the fledglings themselves were able to tell exactly who the target was now. They would fix their eyes on the target, then fold their wings and dive. At the last possible moment, they would snap their wings open and turn the dive into a blindingly fast aerial dash at just out of spear reach from the ground. If they had been hunting, that would have ended in them smashing into their prey, knocking it over, and soaring up again to come down a second time on the now-unconscious prey to kill it.

Since this was a combat maneuver, they would aim straight for the target, and at the last possible moment, the rider would launch a javelin at it. What with being thrown from the back of a speeding dragon, when the javelins hit, they usually went all the way through the straw targets, out the other side, and buried themselves a good hand-length into the dirt. How often they *did* hit depended on the skill of the rider. Orest was the most accurate of the boys, hitting his targets well over three quarters of the time, Huras the least, a little better than three out of ten. Kiron himself was somewhere in the middle, and as a consequence, preferred to use the weapon he was most familiar with, the sling. Using a lead pellet instead of a clay one, he was usually able to knock the target's "head" clean off with an accuracy comparable to Orest with a javelin.

This was very popular with the spectators on the ground, who actually got to see something besides pretty patterns in the sky. It was heartening for them, too; it was one thing to hear about distant victories, it was quite another to see your fighters actually doing something that looked effective and aggressive.

Even the older Jousters had gotten inspired by the successes of the youngsters to try as much of what was being done in fledgling practice as they could command their own dragons to cooperate with. And there, unfortunately, Aket-ten could do only so much. While she could dominate every fighting dragon in the compound now, that only meant that they would obey *her*, not their own riders. And in order to be alert enough to respond the complicated commands, they would have to be on half rations of *tala*, which made them arguably dangerous. Still there were a handful of the older Jousters experimenting with slings, though not one of them had managed to get his mount to tolerate a javelin whizzing past its head. They usually turned and snapped it out of the air, and no one wanted to discourage that behavior, since it meant that the dragons were also catching arrows that had been sent in the Jouster's direction.

The older Jousters had swiftly worked out for themselves that they needed to learn such things, and quickly, too. Now that the Magi-sent storms had ended with the onset of the Dry season, and the *kamiseen* winds had begun to blow, the Jousters of Tia were back in the air and in support of troops who were angry that they had been lately driven back.

Still, on the ground, the Altans could match them man for man, and for now they were holding the land that they had regained.

And with the help of the new tactics that Kiron was working out, the Altan Jousters were succeeding in avoiding the Tians, forcing them to work much harder to go after them, and keeping them from attacking Altan commanders.

Kiron could well imagine the level of frustration that must have been building in the Tian Jousters. Always, *always*, the Altans had stayed and fought, man to man, dragon to dragon—and of course, since the desert dragons outweighed the swamp dragons, most of the time the victory in a conventional Joust went to the Tian and he was then free to wreak whatever havoc he cared to on the troops below. If the Altan was lucky, he was just driven off. If he wasn't, someone would be building a funerary shrine for him by nightfall, as his dragon flew off without him, freeing itself of harness and saddle, and reverting to the wild.

Now, though, the Altans weren't staying and fighting; in fact, there was precious little Jousting going on at all. The Tians found their dragons—and themselves—stung with clay pellets. Or they found their opponents luring them into tail chases that they could not possibly win, which left them far from the scene of battle and too exhausted to accomplish anything when they got back. And when the slingers switched from clay pellets to lead, their hits on either Tian Jousters or Tian commanders on the ground could be devastating.

Now, Kiron knew the Tians, and knew what their ultimate answer would be to the change in situation: put more Jousters in the air so that one could pursue and one attack ground troops. Because they still outnumbered their Altan counterparts, and once every Altan Jouster was fully engaged, whether in combat or in a tail chase, there would still be Tian Jousters to conduct their devastating campaigns on the troops below.

But they hadn't yet done that and, for now, the lines were holding steady at the regained border.

As a consequence, Lord Khumun's star was rising. According to Kaleth, he was getting more of a hearing in Council meetings with the Great Ones, although he was being very cautious about what he said. This was enormously satisfying for Kaleth and Toreth, who could have discussed every little nuance and rumor and political implication for hours if the others hadn't been patently bored with all the political dancing.

But there was one thing that *was* important; the more power

that Lord Khumun had, the safer Aket-ten would be. He had
made it very clear that Aket-ten's presence was very important
to the Jousters' Compound, and even if the Magi took every
Fledgling of even mediocre ability and drained them all to the point
where their power was not returning, at the moment, they could
not touch Aket-ten.

Two of the ribbon chases ended simultaneously; the other two
looked as if they would go on until all four dragonets were tired.
Kiron put his fingers into the corners of his mouth and whistled
shrilly.

In answer, the "combatants" broke off and returned to the
ground, leaving the sky free for the older Jousters.

"Kiron!" called Toreth, as they all led their dragonets toward
the compound. Kiron left the crowd of spectators and joined
them.

"Good matches," he said, approvingly. Toreth nodded his head.

"They're getting stronger. I think we need more practice
time," the prince said. "And I know how you feel about practicing
over a net—but what about practicing over water?"

"Not the canals, surely," Kiron replied with skepticism. He
couldn't imagine using the canals instead of a net. Their movements would be even more restricted than over the net.

"No—I thought the ocean," the Prince replied, looking eager
to try the experiment.

But Kiron shook his head. He hadn't yet actually seen the ocean
and the port of Alta City, but he was not exactly eager to do so
either. Water, stretching as far as the eye could see? All right, he
knew how to swim—but not that well. And neither did the others,
he suspected. "If someone goes off, there's no easy rescue," he
pointed out. "It's one thing to go off the back of your dragon to
rescue someone when you know the water's no deeper than your
neck, but it's quite another to go plunging into water deeper than
you can even imagine. And what about waves? I've heard there
are waves big enough to swamp huge boats! What would happen
if one of those hit you?"

The prince's face fell.

"I'll tell you what, though," Kiron continued, making up his mind about something else. "I think we can find some empty property somewhere, and set up a place with straw men for more targeting practice."

Toreth's face brightened again. "As far away from here as possible," he suggested.

"Oh?" asked Gan, coming up to join them, his dragonet whuffling at his hair. "Why? Not that I mind; I have quite enough admirers as it is, and I weary of women flinging themselves at me." He fanned his face with a languid hand, and got the laugh he was looking for.

"Because I want *them*—" Toreth jerked his chin at the Jousters practicing in the sky above them "—to get the attention. Not us. I want *them* to be the heroes all the time. Let them come watch us if they want, and try some of what we do if they can, but I don't think they should have to share the attention and the glory with a wing of boys who've never flown in battle. It's not fair, and it's not right."

Orest tossed his head to get his hair back over his shoulders. "Rumblings of discontent?" he suggested.

"Not yet," said Toreth. "I want to prevent them."

Pe-atep nodded. "They're good men, and right now, they're grateful to you for coming up with ways to counter the Tians, but I've already heard some jokes about us being the 'pretty ones' that everyone wants to watch. Once the jokes start, there's the possibility the joking will be covering resentment." Pe-atep tended to spend more time around the senior Jousters than anyone other than Kalen, since his experience with training lions and cheetahs for hunting made him very useful in training the wild-caught dragons.

Kalen seconded that. "I've heard the same." The falconer shrugged. "Better safe than sorry, I always say. We make it clear that we don't care about having an audience, that we're serious about our training, they'll be more inclined to take us seriously, too."

He was right. Kiron wouldn't have thought of any of that for himself, but Toreth was right, and so were Kalen and Pe-atep. At the moment, the wing had the respect of the older Jousters, but if fighting men thought that a group of boys just coming into their beards was trying to "steal" what they had actually fought to gain, there would be resentment and anger. Kiron nodded. "Frankly, I think we ought to concentrate on targeting anyway. It makes no sense for us to even think about traditional Jousting until our dragons are bigger. I think we will be able to fight soon, but it will have to be our way."

"One day," Orest said, looking at him comically, "you will say something that is less than practical and sensible, something that is driven by no forethought and nothing but passion, and I will probably collapse with shock."

The bottom dropped out of the world. The universe jolted. Kiron sat straight up in bed with a yell of fear.

His mind was blank, but his gut was a-roil, and inside he was nothing but a chaos storm of sheer terror. He was *so* terrified, in fact, that for one mind-numbing moment, he didn't realize that every dragon in the compound was keening with a fear that at least equaled his.

Including Avatre.

And the ground was moving, in rolling waves.

How could that be? The *ground* was moving!

But it didn't matter that the ground was shaking—and it didn't matter that he was frightened out of his wits. Hearing Avatre cry out for him shook him back into his wits, and he fell off his cot and flung himself at the door. Avatre needed him! That was more important than anything else, including his own terror.

It was exactly like trying to move in a nightmare.

The shaking floor seemed to pitch itself out from under his feet, and he tumbled over sideways in the thick, hot darkness, bruising himself all over when the floor he'd thought was farther away hit him. The groaning of the stones around him made him sure he was going to be buried at any moment, and when he fell, he hit his elbow wrong, startling another yelp out of him. But Avatre needed him, and he crawled across the floor on hands and knees, felt his way past the door. The ground heaved again, and he was tossed into the sand of her pit. There was dust everywhere— where was it coming from? He couldn't see it, of course, but he could *feel* it in his eyes, taste it in the oven-heat of the air. And the sand seemed unnaturally slick, and it kept trying to suck him down—fortunately, he knew it was no more than waist-deep, but the way it kept pulling at his limbs was as terrifying as everything else, as if it was alive and wanted to devour him. Following Avatre's cries, he got to her side, where he got both his arms around her neck and hung on for dear life, closing his eyes and trying to soothe her when he himself was certain that the end of the world had come.

And then—it was over. Just like that. A strange silence filled the humid darkness, where a moment before there had been nothing but the cries of frightened humans and dragons, and the roaring of the earth.

"By the Great Ram's horns!" said a shaking voice just on the other side of the wall, "That was a nasty one! Bethlan's fine—is everyone all right?"

It was Menet-ka. So at least one of his wing was fine.

The dragon keening began again, starting with one of the babies—not Bethlan, it was farther away than that. A ragged chorus answered him. Kiron tried to speak but found he couldn't. His throat seemed paralyzed. All of his fear seemed to have filled his throat and choked it.

"Kiron?" Menet-ka called, then, more urgently, *"Kiron?"*

"Kiron!" Toreth shouted. "Wingleader! Are you all right?"

*It's over. It's over,* he told himself. He uttered a strangled croak, coughed, and managed, "Here—*here*—"

Then he got a little better control of himself. He was the

wingleader—the trainer—as he cradled Avatre's head against his chest, he managed to suck enough air into his lungs—air still strangely full of dust—to call out, "Dragons all right? No one hurt? No one trapped?"

This time the ragged chorus answered him instead of Toreth, all in the affirmative. He tried to think of what they should do next—except that there was nothing they could do, because they must all be as disoriented as he was. "All right," he said. "Don't move. Not until there's light and we can see—" because all of the lanterns were gone, smashed, he supposed, and without the moon it was as dark as a cave. "Don't crawl around; there's no telling what's fallen over and what's broken, and if you slash yourself open on a broken jar, nobody's going to be able to come to help you."

The keening from the Nursery eased, then stopped, as the boys got their dragonets quieted. Outside the Nursery, dragons were still complaining; he could only hope that darkness and *tala* would keep them calmer than they might have been were they not drugged.

"Well," said Toreth's voice, sounding far more philosophical than he was feeling, "I suppose you're right. The sand is soft enough."

The others agreed. "I'm going back to sleep," said Huras, his voice sounding muffled in the distance. "It's not as if I haven't slept in the pit before this."

He heard nothing more than whines and murmurs then, as the rest of them soothed their dragonets. He stroke Avatre's snout, and wondered—though it was hard describe a thought so fearful as his as mere "wondering"—just what had happened. Had it been some evil spirit that had attacked them? Was it the anger of a god? How could the ground move like that? Had it only been the Jouster's Compound, or had the whole city been rattled like this? If so—he'd heard the stones groaning, how could any building stand under something like that? The soldiery here on Third Ring were probably all right; they lived most of the time in tents anyway. But what about the temples? What about the manors and palaces?

What about all the mud-brick buildings on Fourth and Fifth rings? The mud-brick farmhouses on Sixth and beyond? He began feeling sick; mud brick was only stacked with more mud between in lieu of mortar. It surely couldn't have held. And at night, in the dark—if he'd had trouble getting out of a single room, how hard would it be to get out of a house?

Avatre whimpered and shook, and he held her, talking soothingly until she stopped shaking, then stopped whimpering, then, impossibly, fell asleep again. And he felt the heat of the sand soaking into him, so at least whatever had happened hadn't broken the magic on the sand pit. Her head was in his lap, but she was big enough now that he could lean over sideways and rest against her chest and just shut his gritty eyes for a moment and let the heat soothe his bruises.

He woke for the second time with a yell—

And blinked in the soft, monochrome light of predawn at Aketten, who was crouched in the sand beside him, one hand on his shoulder. It hadn't been the earth moving that had awakened him this time, it had been her, shaking him.

"Are you all right?" she asked. "Nothing worse than bruises?" She looked disheveled; hadn't bothered with even eye makeup, and looked as if she had just thrown on the first shift that came to her hand.

"I'm fine," he managed, willing his heart to stop racing. "What—*was* that?" He didn't specify what "that" was, but he didn't exactly have to.

"Earthshake," she said matter-of-factly. "We get them all the time, though usually not as bad as the one last night. But, of course—you were born and raised far enough down the Great Mother River that even when your family was still part of Alta, you never felt them, did you? Some people claim it is the anger of Seft that does it, but the Winged Ones know it isn't." She hesitated a moment. "Or at least, if it is, no Winged One has ever seen the actual hand of the God doing it. Besides that, we've always been able to warn people well in advance of when one was going to happen, so if it was the anger of a God, you'd think He would have stopped us from telling people."

"What went wrong this time?" he asked thickly. His eyes were still sore from all of the grit, and he rubbed at his gluey lashes to try and unstick them. "Why wasn't there a warning?"

It was light enough that he could see her frown. "I don't know, not for certain," she replied flatly. "But I can guess. The Fledglings weren't enough to satisfy the need for whatever it is that the Magi were draining from them, or maybe they've started to drain some of them so dry that their powers really are gone for good, and the Magi have started to come for the Winged Ones themselves. That's the only reason *I* can think of why the ones with the Fore-Visions didn't see this earthshake and warn everyone it was coming. They should have. They've always known when a shake was coming, even a little one that barely rattles the pots, and they've always sent out warnings."

Maybe later he would be as angry as she clearly was; now all he could think of was the welfare of the rest of the compound. "Is anyone in the compound hurt? Are the rest of the dragons all right?" He couldn't hear any more whimpering or keening; in fact, all he heard was the usual groans and complaints of dragons who hated to be roused in the morning.

"A few people were hurt by falling stone, all but one of them servants," she said, "but not badly. This compound is built to handle shakes. The dragons are all fine. One of the pools cracked and drained, and the poor dragon in it spent a miserable and cold night so far as he was concerned, but there are spare pens, and we've already moved the dragon there. It'll be worse in the city," she added with resignation. "There will be people killed, I'm sure, several hundred, if not several thousand. And a lot more will be hurt and probably half of those will die, too, eventually."

"Um—why?" he asked.

"Because they weren't warned!" she snapped. "I told you, we

know what to do when there is going to be a big shake! With warning, we all move out to sleep in our gardens! Even if you don't have a garden, when there's a shake warning, people sleep in the temple gardens, beside the canals, anywhere that there's no walls to fall on them. Without warning—people are inside, their walls come down, their roofs collapse—" He heard the mounting anger in her voice, and she must have realized it too. She stopped for a moment, and closed her eyes. He could hear her breathing carefully, taking several slow, deep breaths before opening her eyes again, and continuing in a more controlled voice. She was still angry, though; he knew her well enough to understand that her stony expression meant that she was just controlling herself. He had first seen it when she was trying not to show how afraid she was of the Magi; now he doubted that she was hiding fear. "That's the thing, you see. If we have warning, an earthshake doesn't hurt anything but buildings, and buildings can be mended. It will be bad in the Second and Third Ring, but in the Fourth and Fifth—it will be horrible. The poorer the district is, the worse it will be. The wealthy have homes built to account for shaking, but the poor build of mud brick, on land that becomes like quicksand when there's a shake. That's why there *must* be a warning—"

Her voice trembled with rage, and her jaw was clenched. "The Magi," she said, her facade cracking again. "The Magi did this."

"If the Magi are to blame," he ventured, "then surely the Great Ones will act?" He couldn't imagine the Great Ones not acting. They were the guardians of their people. How could they ignore something as egregious as this?

"One hopes," she replied, all the anger suddenly draining from her, as the water had drained from that cracked pool. "I'd better go. I'm the only one that can soothe the wild-caught dragons, and every time there is a little shake, or they even think there is a little shake, they are becoming hysterical. If we aren't to have to drug them to sleep with *tala*, I'd better do that."

She got up off her knees, brushed the sand off her sleeveless robe, and left. He stared after her. He had never seen her look so hopeless before. What did she know about the Winged Ones and the Magi that he didn't?

Whatever it was, she was evidently certain that the Magi would never be taken to task for draining the power from those who were supposed to protect Alta from catastrophes such as this one. What was it that made her so certain?

Maybe it was nothing worse than her own fears speaking. After all, the Winged Ones had failed to protect her from the Magi; now she probably mistrusted everyone. And he couldn't blame her either.

As the light strengthened, he looked around Avatre's pen and assessed the damages. All the lanterns were smashed, fallen out of their niches or off their shelves, lying in broken pieces on the floor. There was a crack running up one wall of the pen, and there was another at the corner of his room. Gan and Toreth's quarters hadn't fared so well. In fact, had Toreth been in his cot, he probably would have been dead, because a huge block of stone had dislodged itself from his ceiling and flattened his cot. But in fact, Toreth had been sleeping outside his room since the Dry season began because of the heat, and that liking for fresh air had probably saved his life. It turned out that he was not the only one who had been sleeping outside; most of the wing had been doing so. This was incomprehensible to Kiron, who had been forced to sleep under the stars for most of his life, and found the presence of a roof equated to a feeling of—well, of luxury. Free people slept in houses; only serfs and slaves slept in the open.

As for Gan, one whole corner of the outer wall of his dragon's pen was gone, collapsed, and Gan was swearing that he was going to find the stonemason who was responsible and make him fix it with nothing more than his bare hands. Kiron was a little worried; there was so much more to worry about than the collapse of a wall—

"Huh," said Kalen, when Gan went back to his pen, still ranting. "Don't worry about it, Kiron. This is just his way of exhausting his fear. We're all scared—if we can't rely on the Winged Ones to warn us anymore, what are we going to do?"

Kiron realized that the falconer was right. With one exception—himself—it wasn't what had happened that was the disaster, it was that they hadn't been warned.

In the end, the reports that came from the rest of the city were not as disastrous as Aket-ten had feared. Many people (in fact, virtually anyone who had a garden) *were* sleeping in their gardens for the sake of coolness, and so were safe when the shaking began. There were deaths, though, and many, many injuries, and people all over the city were asking why there had been no warning.

Aket-ten would have taken up her very rudimentary Healing kit and gone out to help the Healers, except that both her father and Lord Khumun forbade her to do any such thing. Lord Khumun told her so first, when she came to him to ask permission to leave; a note from her father (who evidently knew his daughter well) came a little later.

Kiron had gone with her, after failing to dissuade her from her fixed purpose himself. He hung back as Lord Khumun gave her a very stony glare. "The dragons are a hair's breadth from going mad with fear," Lord Khumun told her sternly. "Every time there is an after-shaking, they bellow worse than after the first shake. Who is there to soothe them if you go running off in the city? And just what do you think several dozen terrified, loose dragons would do, if they broke loose from their chains, and escaped the compound?"

Aket-ten looked as if she had eaten something very sour. Then she took another deep breath, and bowed her head in obedience to Lord Khumun's orders.

And he was right, of course, excepting only that several dozen newly freed and terrified dragons would probably do nothing worse than fly off. Still, there was always the chance that one would decide to get a bit of his own back, as it were. And Aket-ten was the only person in the compound that could soothe the dragons. By now, some of them were so upset that they didn't want to eat, which meant until she got them quieted, it wouldn't be possible to get *tala* into them either.

Kiron didn't want her out there for reasons of his own. If she was right, and the Magi were taking up the Winged Ones as well as the Fledglings, then the moment she stepped outside the compound walls, she was in danger.

He didn't tell her that, though. He had the feeling, looking at her strained, angry face all day, that any little thing might cause her to lose all self-control. Maybe that had already occurred to her. And maybe she was using anger as a bulwark against fear. If so, if he pressed her with more warnings, she might break down into hysterics—certainly there were plenty of other people right in the compound who had lost their heads today; more than one senior Jouster, as a matter of fact. There were several people who had been taken off and plied with palm wine or qat until they felt calm or just too drunk to care. He wouldn't blame her if she blew up—but right now, they couldn't afford to be without her.

Because earthshake or no, they had to get at least one wing into the sky. And the only way they could do that was for her to get enough dragons calmed down to form a wing. The troops in the south needed dragons and Jousters to distract the Jousters of Tia; the disaster in the city could be compounded by a disastrous loss of men and territory if no dragons could get to the combat.

The ground continued to shake a little, all that day and into the night. None of the dragonets wanted to fly, and Kiron didn't blame them. Finally by the following morning, he told the boys to stuff the little ones with as much food as they would eat.

"If they're full, they'll sleep, and if they sleep, they'll get over their fear," he said reasonably. And when Lord Khumun heard what he had ordered, he ordered the same for every dragon that was not flying the working wing that day.

Kiron even got Avatre stuffed as full as she could hold, and eventually she, too, slept fitfully in the hot sand of her pen.

That left him with time on his hands, and seeing Aket-ten still vibrating between fear and anger and nearly bursting with the need to do something, he finally took her aside.

"Look," he said, "You can't go out, but I can. I'll go out into the city for you, and help. Will that make you feel any better?"

"Just what do you think *you* can do?" she responded waspishly, then clapped her hand over her mouth, her eyes filling with tears. "I'm sorry! I didn't mean that—"

He had held back a retort of his own; seeing two tears spill over and run down her cheeks made him glad of that momentary restraint. "I can do something you can't," he pointed out gently. "I'm bigger and stronger than you, and I am quite, quite used to hard physical labor. I can help dig people out. And if you stay here and keep an eye on Avatre and the little ones, I can do that without needing to worry about them."

She bowed her head. "Then, thank you," she said quietly—and went back to her work of calming the agitated dragons.

The other boys decided that going into the city would be a good idea. Pe-atep wanted to look in on his successor anyway; he was worried about the cats. And Kalen wanted to check on the health of his former charges, the falcons. Huras was dying to find out how his father and neighbors were, and perhaps, if there was heavy damage, help get some of the ovens going again. "People need to eat," he pointed out. "If they can't bake their own bread, we can do it for them." Menet-ka, Orest, Gan, and Oset-re volunteered to stay to mind the dragonets so that the others could go out; Toreth promised to check on all of the families of the nobly-born and pass on word to both sides.

After telling Lord Khumun of their intentions, Kiron did go out, dressed in an old kilt, and not to the Second Ring either. Assuming that the military could take care of themselves, and the nobles and wealthy could purchase whatever help they needed, he went across the causeways to the Fifth Ring, where most of the poorer sections of Alta were. There, as he had promised her, he labored for the rest of the day in a gang of other common folk, digging out houses where there might have been injured folk still trapped.

By the end of the day they were only finding bodies, and he reckoned it was time to go home. Not to be crude about it—but it would not matter one day, or two, if a body was recovered. The spirit would be satisfied by the proper prayers and rites whenever it was found.

He trudged back across the causeways, feeling tired enough to lie down in Avatre's hot sand and bake all night to get the aches out. It had been a hard, hard day. He hadn't labored this much since he'd worked for Khefti. But every time they'd gotten someone out still alive, still able to go to the hands of the Healers that had swarmed down to the Fifth Ring, it had felt as if he had won a prize.

Because of detours, of causeways and bridges being closed or blocked, he actually had to go to the Second Ring to get down to the Third again. His path took him past the Temple of the Twins just at dusk. He hadn't planned it that way, but just as he got close enough to see the front portico, he realized that the nightly procession of Fledglings to the Tower of Wisdom had just begun.

He stopped, and stared. What were they thinking? The city lay disorganized and, in places, in ruins! Surely they could put off their regular magics for a few nights!

Then he realized that by gawping at them, he was making himself conspicuous, and put his head down, walking onward, trusting to his coating of dust to make him anonymous.

And as he drew nearer, he also realized that a good half of the people trudging slack-faced at the orders of the Magi in charge were far too old to be Fledglings.

Nor was he the only one to have noted this.

"Hoi!" shouted an old man, face contorted with anger, and so covered in dust from stone and brick it was impossible to see what color his complexion really was. "Where are you a-goin' with them Winged Ones?"

He planted himself firmly in the path of the Magi, and stood there with his hands on his hips, staring defiantly at them.

The Magus in the lead drew himself up in affront. "Just who—" the man began.

The commoner interrupted him. "They was supposed to *warn* us!" he shouted, growing more angry by the moment. "They was supposed to *tell* us so none got hurt! And how come they didn't, eh? Eh?"

By now, the shouting had attracted a crowd—angry people, most of them, who were surrounding the Magi and their charges, looking daggers at them. No—not at the Winged Ones, who were oblivious to all of this. All the anger was directed straight at the Magi.

"I don't—" said the Magus in charge haughtily, but what he *"didn't,"* Kiron would never know, for he was shouted down again by a different commoner.

*"We* know why!" the man cried out. "We seen you, comin' here every night! First ye drag off the young 'uns, and they come back looking like ye sucked 'em up dry and threw back the husk. *Then* that's not good enough for ye, and ye start a-takin' the Winged Ones, them as is supposed to be our protection, and *they* come back a-lookin' the same! Ye think we be blind? Ye think we be stupid?"

Since this was probably precisely what the Magi had thought, they exchanged bewildered and alarmed gazes.

"Well, we ain't!" shouted the first man. "We know what's what! 'Tis *your* fault my sister's boys are dead! 'Tis *your* fault innkeeper's girl's lost a leg! Without your meddlin' we'd have *had* our warning', as is proper! 'Tis *your* fault, all of it!"

The crowd began to shout, and just as the Magi belatedly realized their danger, the crowd became a mob.

At that point, the Winged Ones seemed to come out of their stupor, and with looks of alarm, scuttled back to their temple. They needn't have worried; they weren't the targets of the mob's anger. The Magi, however, were.

Not just anger either. People at the rear were picking up stones and pieces of wood, and there just happened to be quite a bit of that sort of thing lying around at the moment.

And at that point, Kiron decided that the smart thing would be to leave.

He doubled back on his path and took the long way back to the compound, leaving the shouting behind him as he dropped any pretense of dignity and ran. A mob of a few dozen people wasn't going to win against the Magi, of course. But he didn't want to get caught in the middle of it.

And besides, he needed to get back to Toreth, and tell him that their surmise was correct. If anyone could get the ear of the Great Ones with the truth now, it would be him.

# FOURTEEN

TORETH went white. "No—" he said, aghast. "Surely not—"
But Kiron saw by his expression that he really didn't need
to repeat his assertion; Toreth's reply was not an indication that
he didn't believe his wingleader, it was more that the very idea of
leaving the city defenseless against its worst threat was so un-
thinkable and appalling.

"I—" Toreth said, staring blankly into space for a moment.
"This is evil hearing," he said at last. "I would not have thought
any creature of this city, be he never so base, would have put his
own desires ahead of the safety of all."

Kiron had had plenty of time to think about this before he took
Toreth aside after dinner and told him what he'd seen. Several
things had occurred to him.

Now, although he had been perfectly willing to accept as a
given that the Magi were stealing the years of soldiers slain in
battle to prolong their own lives, it had occurred to him that to
the others, this was just idle speculation, a kind of ghost story. It
was horrible to contemplate, and deep down inside, they didn't
truly believe it. And he could hardly blame them for their skepti-

cism, for none of them had seen the blank-faced Fledglings being led away, nor the look of stark terror on Aket-ten's face when she fled the Magi.

But if it was really true, then the victories of the Altan troops must have been maddening to them. Victorious armies do not take as many casualties as those that are losing. If they had come to depend on those stolen years, they must have been growing desperate. Desperate enough to take away a primary protection for the city and steal its power?

Desperate enough to take that protection away in the hopes of making up the falling number of available deaths?

Kiron thought it more than likely.

"Consider that our thought was right: they may have been battening on the deaths of Altan soldiers to prolong their own lives," Kiron said bluntly. "Is it so short a step from stealing the years of dead soldiers to stealing the years of children crushed beneath a falling wall?"

"May the gods save us, if that be so," Toreth said softly. "I find it hard to countenance—"

*He doesn't know how ruthless the very ruthless can be.*

It made him sick, it made him angry. Here he had faced down Tian tyranny only to find it in the place where he had thought to find his sanctuary. He had thought that only the Tians were the evil ones in this war. He had been wrong. Evil flourished on both sides.

Active evil, and passive, in the shape of the Great Ones, who were supposed to protect their people and guard them, and who were happy to leave the real responsibility in the hands of others that they might have only the pleasure of the office, and not the duty. . . .

"Here is another prediction, then," Kiron retorted, who had seen the fear on the faces of the Magi facing the mob. Men like that did not like being made to feel fear. When they got to safety, their first thought would be of revenge. "And if it comes to pass, then you may take it that the Magi are capable of every bit of that and more. The Eye of Light—"

"What of it?" Toreth replied, absently, still contemplating with horror the idea that anyone in authority could deliberately choose something that would cause so much death and devastation, purely so that he and his could profit from it.

"I believe the Magi will demonstrate it tomorrow," said Kiron, his voice hard with anger. "Or the next day. Soon, at any rate. When they were set upon by common folk, it would hardly have pleased them, and they are going to want both revenge and a way to make the commoners fear them too much to interfere with them ever again. I believe that they will find some excuse—that there is a plague of rats there, or some other specious reason—to destroy the ruins in the neighborhood of the beer shop across the avenue from the Temple of the Twins. And I shouldn't be at all surprised if perfectly repairable homes and businesses are turned to glass in the process."

Toreth looked up sharply. *"Why?"* he demanded.

Kiron shrugged. "The Magi are men to whom little matters but their own good," he said. "Like my old master Khefti. When anything bad happened to Khefti, as soon as he was over his first fright, he looked for revenge. I believe they will, too. If they have grown so great in their own minds as to place their power above the welfare of the folk of the city, they will have grown great enough to believe that whatever they want is also right and proper."

"Ah, gods." Toreth buried his face in his hands. "The rot goes deep," he said, his voice muffled.

Kiron thought it best to leave him alone at that point. He had a lot to think about. In some ways, Toreth and Kaleth, raised amid the endless political infighting among the royal families, had been anything but sheltered. Still, there were other ways in which they had been very sheltered indeed. They had never seen evil, amoral men under conditions in which their evil was recognizable. They were so used to petty evil that they had a great deal of difficulty in believing in great evil. And they had not made the intuitive leap that those who practiced petty evil were perfectly capable of undertaking great evil, and lacked only the perceived need and the opportunity to do so. Kiron felt oddly sorry for him. He had once been certain that there were things in his world he could be certain of. Not anymore.

He stood in the corridor—still only partly cleaned up, and with fewer than a third of the lamps replaced—and debated telling Aket-ten what he had seen and heard. On the one hand, it could make her more angry, more fearful, or both. On the other—it might serve to warn her.

*Not tonight,* he decided at last. *Not until things are closer to normal. Unless, of course, she insists on going where the Magi can find her.*

As he turned into his own door, something struck him so forcibly that he stopped dead in his tracks. When he had first come here, he had only been afraid that he would not be accepted. It had never occurred to him that he would find Khefti's form of evil writ larger among his own people. The rot went deep. Just *how* deep? Could it be cut out, or was it too deep to cut out without killing the tree? He had once told Ari and the Bedu that if he did not like Alta, or was mistreated there, he and Avatre would just leave. That was still an option—

*But not before I make a stab at standing and fighting.*

There was no such rot among the Jousters; he was fairly sure of that. Yet the Jousters were a tool, and the weakness of any tool is that it may be used all unwittingly. And there was the war to consider—the Tians would not cease from pressing their attack, no matter what was going on in Alta, nor would they stop committing atrocities on Altan villagers. Toreth's plan called for negating the Tian advantage so that a real truce could be pressed for, by drastically increasing the number of Jousters.

But what if the Jousters could be eliminated altogether, from both sides?

*The armies will have to square off man-to-man, and there will be very little that the Magi can do that will make any appreciable differ-ence.* Would that mean a change in their status?

*Probably not.* He sighed, and went straight to Avatre who was sitting up in her sand. Waiting for him, patient as a statue made of rubies and gold, but far warmer and infinitely more desirable.

He went to her and sat down in the sand beside her. No matter how bad things got, at least he had Avatre, and she had him.

He only hoped that Toreth got the same measure of comfort from Re-eth-katen, because tonight, he sorely needed it.

By morning there were rumors of the confrontation with the Magi "somewhere" on the Second Ring, but nothing was confirmed. Kiron kept his mouth shut, even around the boys, but Toreth looked very unhappy to hear Kiron's story confirmed.

There were more rumors flying when he went out for the second day in a row to help on the Fourth and Fifth Rings. And this time, Menet-ka, Orest, and Oset-re took a turn in going to see their families. They let Huras go out for the second day in a row, because he was, indeed, helping his father to bake for the entire area—but he was not going to be restricted to walking. He was flying Tathulan; the heat from the ovens would keep her happy.

Kiron, however, was walking. He decided to make a detour across the Second Ring—considerably out of his way, but he wanted to see if there was any sign of yesterday's near-riot. When he passed the Temple of the Twins, he saw that it was shut up tight, which was a very new thing indeed. There was some damage around the Second Ring, as he had seen yesterday, but with the exception of a few places like beer shops and markets, it was minimal. There was no sign of yesterday's disturbance.

To say that things were in a state of chaos was a profound understatement, and the contrast between the Second and Third Rings, where rescue, cleanup, and even rebuilding were organized and well underway, was profound. No one was rebuilding in the Fourth and Fifth Rings. In fact, no one was really cleaning up. There was no organization, except as people organized the members of their own families into work parties. And if there was only one survivor left—well, that one person worked alone, moving the rubble, usually with bare hands.

The shake did not seem to have struck everywhere in the Rings with the same force. In some places, damage was minimal; in others, shocked and bewildered people sat outside the piles of broken bricks and cracked timbers that had been their homes, unable to comprehend what had happened to them, or were slowly and methodically moving over the piles, removing them brick by brick, hoping to find something to save—or some*one*. You could easily tell the latter. They were the ones working with tears cutting channels through the caked dirt and dust on their faces. They were the ones Kiron tried to help first.

Even when all he could do was to help move bricks. "Where did you see him last?" he would ask. "Where was she sleeping?" And the survivor, so choked with grief that he or she was unable to speak, would point instead. And Kiron would start, trying to pick a "safe" spot to pitch the rubble to, because he did not want to discover that the survivor had been wrong, and he had, all unwittingly, been piling more debris atop someone already buried. Yesterday had been bad after the first rescues were done, because the people he found were sometimes still alive, but one look told him that not even the finest Healer could save them. Today, at least as he worked, he knew that he was only going to recover the bodies so that the ghosts would not wander. Once he uncovered a hand, and once, a foot, and the survivor shoved him aside, weeping, to do the rest of the work. That was when he left, with his part over.

He was in the middle of what had been someone's sleeping-chamber, when the cries and shouting began.

He'd had his back to the Central Island, so he didn't see what everyone was shouting about directly—but suddenly, he had a shadow stretching out stark and black in front of him. Filled with a sense of dread, he turned.

Before he had half-completed the turn, he had to squint against the brightness. The slender reed of light cutting down from the Tower of Wisdom was too bright to look at, brighter than lightning, a painful blue-white rod that began at the tip of the Tower, and ended somewhere down in the Second Ring. He thought it was moving, although at the angle he was, it was difficult to tell. But there was no doubt at all that it was touching, and torching, something in the Second Ring.

Just as he had predicted.

Then, with no warning, it was gone, leaving behind an after-image that crossed his field of vision in a dazzle of purple, and a burning, acrid scent in the air. Then as the after-image faded, he saw that there were fires in the Second Ring where there had been none before.

All around him, work had stopped as people stared, slack-jawed, at the fires and the place where the Eye of Light had cut across the Second Ring. There was absolute silence for a very long time, a silence heavy, and appalled, as if no one could quite believe what they had seen.

Then, into the ponderous silence, the sound of a single brick falling.

That broke the spell, and hesitantly, fearfully, people went back to work.

The rumors began to fly almost immediately. Most absurd, of course, was that the Magi had discovered a nest of subversive Tian priests—ones that had actually caused the earthshake—and had used the Eye to burn them out. Most prevalent, and most accurate, was that the only things that had been burned belonged to those folk on Second Ring who had confronted the Magi the night before. No one really bought into the first rumor, but there was no doubt that, whatever people might say, deep down inside the one that they believed was the second.

Kiron kept his mouth shut, volunteering nothing. Knowing the Magi, he would not doubt that there were spies about—or at least, people who would report what was said back to the Tower of Wisdom for a reward. Fortunately, no one knew he had actually *been* there when the confrontation took place, so no one asked him any questions. Once in a while, some of those he was helping asked him what he was and where he belonged, and he answered, truthfully, that he was one of the new young Jousters with the baby dragons. And for a moment, tragic gazes would soften, and perhaps, someone would say, "Ah. The pretty ones . . . but why are you here?"

"Because you need help," he would tell them.

Shortly before noon, an official-looking fellow in an absurdly clean kilt showed up, took up a stance in the middle of what had been the street, and began shouting.

"All hear!" he cried. "All hear! Hear the words of the Great Ones to the people of Alta!"

Some folk dropped what they were doing to gather around him, but most simply went on with their work, keeping an ear and half of their attention on him. If this bothered him, it didn't show. He looked bored with the entire proceedings, and a bit impatient, as if he wanted to get this business over with and get back to something important.

He was thin and energetic, with the look of a scribe and the lungs of a military commander. He wore a yellow-and-white sash running from his right shoulder to his left hip, and a matching striped headcloth.

"Who is that?" Kiron muttered to the man he was helping, in an undertone.

"Royal Herald," the man muttered back, without taking his attention off the pile of rubble they were moving.

The man continued to shout his summoning call until he either grew tired of it, or figured he had gathered around all the people he was going to get.

"The Gods have unfolded to the Great Ones that the mighty earthshake was caused by the false Tian Priests!" the Herald proclaimed. "So subtle their work, and so wrapped in dark magic, that there was no foretelling that it would strike."

"Bollocks," the man with Kiron muttered. "If they were that good, they'd have flattened the Central Island."

"When the damage to the First, Second, and Third Rings has been cleared, the army will send men and tools here."

The man snorted. "By that time, we'll have cleared it with our hands alone." The back of his neck was red with anger as he turned away from Kiron, and he flung the piece of beam he had picked up with great force onto the pile of trash.

"The hiding places of foul spies of the false Tian Priests, the stores where they have secreted poisons and weapons, have been discovered on the Second Ring. In their wisdom, the Magi of the Tower have sent forth the Eye of Light to cleanse these places." Kiron risked a glance at the Herald, and saw that the man was watching him and the house owner with narrowed gaze. "As more such hiding places are discovered, they will be cleansed, so fear not to see the Eye Opened, but rejoice that the Magi watch over all of Alta."

Having delivered his message to this part of the Ring, the Herald did not wait for questioning, but strode on and outward.

The man with Kiron spat. "Bastards. 'Poisons and weapons and spies,' my ass! Places where people are asking questions is more like! Pockets of people wanting to know why the Winged Ones didn't warn us!"

Another man in what was left of the next house over straightened and looked warningly at him. "I'd be careful about what I say, Atef-ka," the neighbor said. "I'm not saying you aren't right—but if you are, well—you saw their answer."

Atef-ka looked bleakly at his neighbor. "Too right," was all he replied, but both of them looked sick.

Well, for all that he had predicted just this action, Kiron felt sick, too. Sick, and angry.

He had to return to the compound to feed and exercise Avatre, and to do so, because once again bridges were closed except for certain "privileged" folk, he had to go to the Second Ring to get to the Third, and pass right by the site where the Eye had touched.

There was nothing there but a slab of glasslike, fused earth, still hot. Fires smoldered around the perimeter. And the silent, white faces of those whose duties kept them here said it all.

But when he got back to the compound, there was someone waiting for him, in his chamber, along with Aket-ten. Someone he had not expected to see there.

"Healer Heklatis!" he said in surprise. "But what—"

"The Temple of All Gods is no longer a safe haven for me," the Akkadian said grimly. There was no smile in his eyes at all. "Or at least for my magic. I suspect a spy has been planted in the Temple of All Gods, and since the Magi are looking very, very hard for a mythical Tian Priest-Mage on the Second Ring, I deemed it wise to come assign myself to the military on Third Ring."

"That is an ugly thought, Healer," Kiron replied. "Though— maybe a wise one."

"There is an uglier scar on the Second Ring, provoked by no more than a demand for truth, Jouster," said Heklatis grimly. "And truth and trust are the means by which civilization holds off barbarism. When those in power intend to abuse that power, they look to an outside enemy in order to trick their people into pressing the means to their own abuse into the hands of the abusers. If an enemy does not exist, it will be manufactured, and all manner of horrors attributed to it, so that anyone who demands truth and accountability is set upon as being unpatriotic. And so that, when someone said to be an enemy is found, there will be few questions asked about guilt or innocence, and many faces averted when he is taken away."

Kiron thought about his own experience in the Fourth Ring, and nodded.

"Now," continued Heklatis, "I could remain in the Temple of All Gods and take my chances on being discovered as a clandestine Magus—and knowing that the Magi of the Tower are bent on finding a foreign enemy Magus, I think we can both see where that would take me. Since I do not desire to be cast into a dungeon to rot, or killed, or tormented to reveal what I allegedly

know, I have come to offer my services to the military—the Jousters, to be specific, because I also have no wish to see the war
from close at hand."

"You have not come to me, I hope!" Kiron replied. "I have no
power to engage you—"

"No, to Lord Khumun, of course, who has accepted me and
my skills with thanks," Heklatis responded. "Although he has told
me to assign myself to the welfare of those on the Fourth and
Fifth Ring during the current crisis. I confess that I am pleasantly
surprised. I had not expected to find someone with a title who
understands the responsibilities that should come with that title."

"And does he know that you are a Magus?" Kiron asked
sharply.

Heklatis shrugged. "I told him nothing but the truth; that Healers learn their trade differently in Akkad, which he already knew,
and I feared that, being a foreigner, I might become a target for
ill-will, which he quickly understood. If he asks, I will admit to him
that I am also a Magus. If he does not, my silence is his best defense should I be traced here by your Magi."

Kiron, who had been about to open his mouth to rebuke the
Healer for not telling the whole truth, shut it again. Heklatis was
right. "I hope you are going to be discreet, then," he said.

Heklatis snorted, and favored him with a look of withering
scorn. "I believe," he replied, "that I am aware of the dangers.
Especially as I was close enough to the lash of the Eye today to
have cooked my dinner in its fires."

"They gave no warning?" Kiron said, aghast. He had assumed
that the Magi would at least have warned people that the punishment was coming! Even a moment or two would have been
enough!

"None. And while I have not heard of any that died there, well,
the question is, would I?" Heklatis asked. "After claiming first
that they had found a plague spot, and when that was not believed, that they had uncovered a nest of traitors, would anyone

come forward and say, 'You incinerated my poor, innocent cousin without warning'? I think it unlikely."

Aket-ten had been silent throughout this conversation. Finally, she said, in a very small voice, "How can the Great Ones be unaware of this?"

"If they are unaware," Heklatis said bitterly, "they must be complete idiots, and I had never heard that of them. Oh, they know. They just do not care—so long as what they wish is done. The Magi are too useful to them, for some reason, and they count the lives of mere Altan citizens of no account, I suspect. But they will never admit that they know what the Magi are doing, because then people would say that they did not care about untruth and injustice. And they will not welcome anyone who tries to enlighten them as to true conditions."

"Oh—oh, no—" Aket-ten said in dismay.

"*What?*" both Heklatis and Kiron said sharply.

"Toreth—Toreth has gone to the Palace, to demand audience of the Great Ones by right of being the Heir," she said, and clapped her hand over her mouth. "When the Eye was opened, he said that you had predicted this, and that the Great Ones must be told what the Magi have done!"

"The poor fool." Heklatis slumped where he sat. "I only pray he has not signed his own death warrant."

"But you fear he has," Kiron said heavily. The Healer nodded, as Aket-ten looked from one to the other in horror.

"Surely not," stammered Aket-ten. "He and Kaleth are the Heirs!"

*But there are other Heirs,* Kiron thought, and saw the same thought in Heklatis' eyes.

"Well," the Healer said, too heartily. "He and his brother are favored of the gods. Surely."

"Surely," said Kiron, who did not believe it at all.

Toreth did not return in time to feed his dragonet; they could not leave the poor thing alone, so Aket-ten did it for him, then brought in Wastet to play with her until they were both tired. At that point, Kiron decided that he had to tell the other boys of the wing just where Toreth had gone, and why.

Gan and Orest were the only ones who were truly concerned. The rest of them looked anxious for a moment, then Oset-re said, "Ah, he's God-watched, that one! He can fall in the marsh and come up clean, with *latas* in either hand!" And the rest of the laughed, and each recounted some tale of how Toreth had always had the luck of ten men, and for most of them, their concern melted away.

Not for Kiron—and not for Gan and Orest either. He saw it in their faces and, no doubt, they saw it in his.

But Toreth did not return in time for dinner, and by that time, Kiron decided to go to Lord Khumun.

He did not tell Lord Khumun about their speculation—that the Magi were prolonging their own lives, and possibly the lives of the Great Ones, at the expense of others. He did tell Lord Khumun what he had seen—first the Fledglings, then the Winged Ones, being taken off by the Magi and returned looking drained. He spoke of the confrontation, the accusations, of telling Toreth about it, and his own prediction that the Magi would take revenge for the affront by using the Eye on those who had insulted them so gravely. And he repeated what Aket-ten had told him about Toreth. His Lordship heard him out, his face a mask, then shook his head. "The Magi are high in the councils of the Great Ones. I do not think you or Toreth truly understand their power. You should know I can do nothing against them," he said heavily, with the sound of defeat in his words. "The Great Ones will hear no word against them."

"And there are other possible Heirs," Kiron replied, voice flat and dead, nausea rising in the back of his throat. His worst fears were confirmed—and despite what Lord Khumun thought, he understood only too well that the Magi were far more powerful than Toreth had believed.

Lord Khumun nodded, then mustered a smile. "But Toreth is a

young man, a boy, even, and the hot words of boys are without meaning. I cannot imagine the Great Ones taking him seriously. They are probably administering a lecture to him about meddling in things he does not understand at this very moment." His own words seemed to hearten the Lord of the Jousters, and he sounded more sure of himself. "He will be in disgrace for a time— but they cannot take him from the Jousters, and they cannot take his companions from him, and the gods know his heart is true. Go wait in his quarters for him, for he will probably be in need of his friends."

Kiron bowed, and left, feeling himself divided by his emotions. On the one hand, he was very angry with Lord Khumun for not standing up for Toreth. On the other—he understood, only too well, that Lord Khumun's hands were tied. And surely Lord Khumun was right; if anyone should know the way of things, Lord Khumun would. His fears must be unfounded. The Magi couldn't take the words of even a young prince as a threat.

*But*— he thought, his mind darkening. *Think how long they live, how far in advance they must plan. He is only a prince now, but even with magic, one day the Great Ones must die. And now they know that Toreth will never be won over.*

So he did as he had been told; he went back to the pens, and waited, but as the time crept on, he felt his heart sinking. And his hope faded of ever seeing Toreth again. Little Re-eth-katen was unwontedly silent, and curled into her sands like a blue-and-silver shadow, ignoring him.

*They will imprison him. They will have him exiled. No. No, he knows too much, and while he lives, he and Kaleth are still the Heirs. They dare not leave him alive. . . .* He remained in Toreth's pen, but with no hope.

So when the prince himself stumbled into the pen, near to dawn, Kiron at first thought he was a ghost.

He certainly could have been. He was as pale as if he had been drained completely of blood, his eyes were bloodshot and swollen, as red as the eyes of demons. And he stared at Kiron with no sign of recognition.

"Toreth?" Kiron gasped, "Prince?"

Toreth shook himself all over, like a dog. "They would not listen," he said dully. "I never got past the first words. They told me not to meddle in things I could not understand. They treated me like a boy who has come to complain that a war chariot on the way to battle has broken his toy."

"So—" Kiron dared to hope. "The Magi don't know that you know what they are doing?"

Toreth shook his head. "No. Yes. I don't know," he said, finally. "*I* didn't tell them. I hardly got more than a word or two in. I am disgraced, you see. They brought in my father, and lectured me in front of him. Then they brought in my betrothed, Nofret, and did the same. They cannot take my dragon, or my place in the Jousters, but they have made it clear that a dog in the street will have more chance for advancement from the ranks than I. I am not—*quite*—being declared a traitor. But I am being held up as an example of how dissension aids the enemy. They cannot cut me from the succession, but—oh, Kiron!—I had not seen them, close up, in more than two years, and now they looked no older than thirty! And the Magi are the same! I did not see a single gray hair among them all!"

*So. They have another way to solve this. They can, and will, outlive us.*

"At this rate, you will die of old age, and they will still be sitting on the Twin Thrones," Kiron replied, a cold numbness spreading over him.

Toreth's head sagged. "We are defeated," he said. "And I am disgraced and friendless."

"Ah," said Gan, putting his head around the doorway, his hair all tousled from sleeping. "So I am no friend, then?"

Toreth started; clearly, he had been so sunk in his misery that he had not heard Gan come behind him. "No!" he protested.

"But—surely your parents will not wish you to associate yourself with a known traitor—"

"My parents can take themselves off on a scenic tour of hell before they tell me who my friends will be," Gan said pleasantly. "And I suspect every lad in the wing will say the same."

"Besides, most of them won't have to defy their parents," Kiron pointed out. "Certainly Lord Ya-tiren has no love for the Magi. Enough of us are commoners that their parents will not care. We followed you before; nothing has changed that *I* can see."

Toreth looked like a man who has suddenly been reprieved. "Do you mean that?" he pleaded.

"Of course he means it," said Oset-re with irritation. "Didn't we all stay up most of the night to greet you when you returned? Kiron is right, nothing has changed, except the opinions of a few stupid people whose parties you wouldn't have wanted to attend anyway! Now go to bed, Toreth. We'll discuss all of this later."

He withdrew; Gan did the same. Toreth stared at Kiron as if he could not believe what had just happened.

"Go to sleep, Toreth," Kiron said. "Oset-re is right."

"But—" Toreth began.

*"Go to sleep."*

Toreth stumbled into his chamber at the back of the pen, but at least now he looked less like a walking corpse. Kiron went back to his own pen, tiptoed around Avatre, and settled back into his cot for a little more precious time before he *had* to get up.

But he had trouble finding sleep again. Too many thoughts were buzzing in his head. Finally he got up, and went to see if Aket-ten might be awake at this early hour. She had always been used to going to the Temple for Dawn Rites—was she still waking that early anyway?

She was.

He found her in the courtyard of her chambers, and with her, Heklatis.

"Toreth came back," he said as they looked up, and gave them the gist what the prince had said. Heklatis heaved a sigh of relief. "They looked at him and saw a handsome, muscle-bound fool," the Healer replied. "Good!"

Aket-ten looked almost faint with relief.

Kiron felt a stab of that same emotion he'd gotten at the thought of anyone else riding Avatre. This time he knew it for what it was.

Jealousy. He was jealous that Aket-ten should be that concerned for Toreth. It shocked and surprised him to the core.

He covered it by going in and sitting down. "I don't think he's safe—" he began.

"Neither do I!" Heklatis said firmly. "I will be doing what work I can to safeguard him. This is not over; the Great Ones could still die. There are always accidents, illnesses. Now that they know that he knows—he is not safe. Fortunately, it only takes a little magic, properly used, to defeat greater magic." He grinned mirthlessly, showing a great many teeth. "And I have the advantage over them. I know how they are schooled; they do not know how *I* am."

Kiron took a deep breath. "I came here to ask if the two of you can do something. I want to find a way to remove the Jousters from both armies."

They both looked at him, as if wondering where in the world that idea came from, and why he would ask them to help with it.

"Both armies? That is no small task you set us," Heklatis admitted reluctantly, "But I believe I see what your point is. Remove the Jousters, and it is army against army, in which we are equal. Remove the Jousters, and you remove the reason to send storms—which, unless they can concoct some better spell to use against the Tians, also removes the overt reason for the support of the Magi."

*Leaving only the stolen years, which even the Great Ones dare not admit to. If that is not forbidden magic, it is perilous close.*

"It was Toreth's idea that, eventually *we* could negate the Tian

Jousters," said Kiron. "But I fear that we may not have the time, now. If the Magi dare to use the Eye against dissenters—"

"Then they have grown too powerful, and we should look for other ways to take some of that power from them." Heklatis nodded. "Well, we can do that. We can also look for ways to armor the Winged Ones against being used. And we can look for allies." He raised one eyebrow. "The Bedu, do you think?"

Kiron had to shrug. "I do not know. I do not know that anyone knows the Bedu well enough to guess what they will think or do."

"But they have a use for gold, and they might well feel threatened by our Magi," Heklatis persisted. "Yes?"

Kiron nodded after a moment. "Yes to both, I think. They have their own magics, and the Magi cannot help but see that as a rivalry, if not a danger."

"Then Aket-ten and I will pursue the first path together, and I—and eventually you—will pursue the second. Agreed?" asked Heklatis.

*Oh, yes, the Magi should be shivering in their beds,* Kiron thought cynically. *A half-trained Jouster, a Winged Fledgling, and a foreign Healer. We shall defeat them and send them packing and still have time for breakfast!*

But, "Agreed," he said anyway. Because it was that—or despair. And he was not yet ready for despair.

# FIFTEEN

K IRON was not ready for despair, but despair followed its own laws, and arrived on tattered wings.

It came on the wind, spreading in a sound that no one in all of Alta had ever heard before, a keening wail of a cry that broke the heart before anyone even knew the cause. It engulfed them, took them, shook them.

The sound struck all three of them like blows of a lance; all three of them gasped as one. Kiron rose, but it was Aket-ten who was halfway to the door before he was halfway to his feet.

The wail led him to the source, hard on her heels, with Heklatis not far behind, to the dragonets' pens—to Toreth's pen—

—to where Toreth's dragon Re-eth-katen stood, blue-black head pointed skyward, silver-blue neck outstretched, wailing her unbearable loss to an uncaring sky.

—to where Toreth lay, sprawled half out of his cot, eyes wide with fear and fixed in death.

"Toreth!" Kiron wailed himself, and started for his friend.

"Wait!" Heklatis barked, throwing out an arm to stop him, halting him in his tracks. Just in time, as the head of the largest cobra that Kiron had ever seen rose up out of the blanket half covering Toreth's body. It hissed, and flared its hood, daring all of them—because by now, the doorway was crowded with people—to come any closer.

The dragon went silent. In the silence, the cobra rose farther above Toreth's body and swayed back and forth.

There was a murmur of fear, and as the cobra bent forward, they all moved involuntarily back.

"The sign of the gods—" someone muttered at the back of the crowd. "Don't touch it!" cried someone else. "It is sacred to the gods!"

"Not *my* gods," said Heklatis impatiently. He looked around swiftly, seized a sling and a handful of pellets from the weapon rack against the wall, and before anyone could stop him, let fly.

It was either the best, or the luckiest shot that Kiron had ever seen in his life, for it hit the cobra right in the head. The snake tumbled off Toreth's body, and Heklatis made sure of the beast a moment later. He dashed across the intervening space, and crushed what was left of the head and hood beneath his sandal.

No one else moved. Not even Kiron, who felt as if he was paralyzed and could not have moved to save his own life. It was Heklatis who tenderly draped the blanket over Toreth's face, then picked up the body of the prince, blanket and all, and carried it out. Kiron had no idea that the bandy-legged little Healer was so strong; he carried the burden as if it was nothing. The crowd parted before him, and closed up behind him, but still, no one moved except to get out of the Healer's way.

"The sign of the gods—" someone else murmured. But all Kiron could think was—*I was in that chamber before he came back. There was no snake there, and there is no way for a snake to get past his dragon. Snakes can't abide dragons, and dragons eat snakes. How did it get there?*

*Had* the gods sent their sacred serpent to punish Toreth? *Were* the gods truly favoring the Magi against all the rest of their people?

The dragon began her keening again, and a wave of chill passed over him. A shadow seemed to pass over them all, and the wings of despair enveloped them.

*The gods. The sign of the gods. How can you go against the gods?*

He started to shake, and he was not the only one. He put one hand against the wall, fear welling up inside him in a bleak, black tide.

It came between him and everything else, and he felt it weaken him until he could not stand. Slowly he sank down into the sand pit, as the dragon wailed her heartbreak, and people began to back away carefully, as if this place and everything that was in it held some dreadful curse.

He lost himself in despair and grief. His eyes burned, and yet he could not weep. His throat felt choked with a lump of tears that would not leave him. His eyes burned, and he closed them, but the images in his mind kept playing over and over—Toreth, alive but a few moments ago, and now dead, with that look of terror on his face—

"This foul creature was sent."

He looked up, startled to find that he was no longer alone. Heklatis stood there, face set in a mask of rage, toeing what was left of the cobra.

"What?" he asked, somehow getting the word past the lump in his throat.

"This was no accident, and no act of the gods," the Healer said flatly. "This snake was *sent*. It is a Fetch, a thing called into a place by magic, and commanded to act by its master. Someone brought it here specifically to attack and kill the prince. I can taste the magic, smell it, a vile odor—" He shook his head, the gray-streaked curls of his hair bouncing. "They must not have known there would be a Magus here, or they would have covered their tracks." He glanced over at Kiron, who was staring at him in bewilderment. "You don't understand what I'm saying, do you? Let me put it simply. The Magi murdered Toreth, and did it in a way that would look like either an accident, or a god-sent curse, depending on how the murder was interpreted. And they did it before anyone outside the court learned what it was that brought Toreth before the Great Ones. They did it while his disgrace was still vivid in everyone's mind, and before anyone got a chance to think about what he said and wonder how much truth was in it."

"Murder?"

The word was an echo of the same one in Kiron's mind, but it came from Lord Khumun's lips.

Heklatis looked up, toward the door to the pen. Kiron turned as well. Lord Khumun stood there with an expression as stony as the Healer's was full of anger.

"Yes, my Lord," said the Healer. "Murder. There are many ways of covering the truth, and that is one of them—to silence the truth teller, permanently."

Lord Khumun did not look surprised. "I feared this," he said heavily, "But I hoped—he was only a boy—"

"He was Prince and Heir," replied Heklatis flatly, as the dragon continued to keen. "They could not afford to let him live. And look to yourself, my Lord. *Your* star has been rising of late, and the Magi, I fear, will brook no rivals now. And they are clearly no longer content with simple opposition; they have chosen annihilation for those who would stand in their path."

Kiron would never have imagined Lord Khumun blanching, but he saw that very thing now. And if Lord Khumun was afraid—

The Lord of the Jousters swallowed, and then seemed to notice that Kiron was still sitting there. "Go to your quarters, Wingleader," he said, but it was not with the bark of an order. "This changes nothing except the size of your wing."

The lump of grief rose again within him. "Yes, my Lord," he managed to choke out, and then, at last, the tears began, and he stumbled out of the pen, blindly, feeling his way back to his own pen and the comforting presence of Avatre.

Except that Avatre was as agitated as he was, and whimpered deep in her throat. The keening wail of the grieving dragonet was cutting across the entire Compound, and as the dragons awoke to it, they began to add their chorus of agitation to her howl of mourning. As he threw his arms around Avatre's neck, she curled it down around his shoulders and whimpered into his ear while he wept against the soft, slick surface of her chest.

And wept. And wept. Whenever he thought he had himself under control, his control broke again; it was the dragon that did it, her lamenting filled the whole compound and still there was no end to it, and all he could do, all anyone could do, was to mourn with her, until he had cried himself into a mummy, into dust, and blew away on the wind.

And then—it stopped.

For a moment longer, the other dragons still whined or moaned, but after a moment or two, their own plaints died away, leaving a strange and uncomfortable silence.

Slowly, he pulled himself together. Avatre stopped whimpering, stopped trying to curl herself around him. He raised his head, she raised hers. Then she nosed his wet cheek, and made a tentative, sad little echo of her hunger call.

"I know," he said, and patted her jaw. "I know, my love."

He levered himself up out of the sand, stiffly; he rubbed the tear stains from his cheeks with the back of one hand, the sand grating across the hot lines etched there by his weeping. Then he went to look for Avatre's breakfast.

He roused Avatre's dragon boy from *his* bewildered grief, and together they fetched Avatre's meat. Then he sent the boy to bring food to the other dragonets of the wing, while he tended to Avatre himself.

She ate—not swiftly, not with her usual exuberance and appetite, but she ate. And when she was done, he apologized to her for leaving, and with dread in his heart, went to the bereft dragon's pen.

And found Aket-ten there, feeding Re-eth-katen tiny bits of meat, as if she was a baby again, crooning to her. She looked up at him. Her eyes were swollen and red, her cheeks tear-streaked, and yet somehow she had battled through her own bereavement to come to soothe and comfort the little dragon. Where she had gotten the strength, he could not even guess.

"As soon as she can move, I'm taking her to the empty pen at the end," she said, in a voice that brooked no argument. "And then I'm moving my things there. She needs me."

She glared defiance at him, but he was not about to argue with her. Not in this mood. He just nodded, and backed his way out. At this point, he didn't care what she did, as long as she got that terrible wailing to stop, and kept the dragonet from starving herself to death. Another rider could be found eventually, and then he would argue that it was not appropriate for a young lady to be housed among so many young men.

Later. Not now.

Besides, somehow he had to get the others going, to establish a semblance of normality. More than ever, they had to get on their feet, get going, get back to business, and prove themselves. The Magi would be watching them now, sure that Toreth had cultivated a hotbed of dissent here, and waiting for the chance to make them fail. Therefore, they had to succeed, and yet at the same time, they had to deceive the Magi into thinking that they were insignificant, harmless. Toreth would have wanted that.

Throughout the sixty days of mourning, as the prince's body was prepared for burial with all the care due a Prince and Heir, that phrase kept coming up among the boys that were left. Spoken, or unspoken, it was always there. *Toreth would have wanted this.*

The wing got back into the air, back into practice, pushing themselves and their dragons as never before, because Toreth would have wanted that. Heklatis worked feverishly, making their own personal amulets into magic sinks, imbued with every sort of protection that his imagination and the powers of his own mind and body could muster, because Toreth would have wanted his wingmates protected against the evil that the Magi could summon. Aket-ten devoted herself to the welfare of the dragon that she renamed "Re-eth-ke"—"the shining sun-spirit"—because

Toreth would not have wanted his dragon to pine herself to death. And within twenty days, Aket-ten was garbed in a kilt and a breast wrap, flying that dragon, first in simple exercise, then in support of the training games, then in the training games and combat practice again. She was not much good at the targeting, except with the sling, but no one could outfly her. And somehow, Lord Khumun never brought forth another boy for Re-eth-ke, and it never seemed terribly urgent to Kiron that he find a substitute—

Truth to tell, he didn't think he could bear to look at Re-eth-ke and see another boy in her saddle. Seeing Aket-ten there didn't hurt; in a way, it was only right that after nursing the dragon back from its depression, she have the same freedom of the skies as the rest of them. He could see it in her face—when she was on the ground, there were anxiety lines there, the haunting flicker of fear that never left her, and the constant nag of worry that at any moment, the Magi might come for her. Up in the sky, all that left her. How could he take that from her? There might have been problems with a young woman in the midst of so many young men, but she never acted like a young "woman." She might have flirted mildly with them before—she did nothing of the sort now. She acted like one of the wing, with the same earnest determination as any of them, and a complete lack of anything that could be considered flirtation.

So, by the time that Toreth's funerary shrine was done, and his mummified body placed in it, and his spirit released to cross the Star-Bridge, Aket-ten had become a part of the wing, and never a murmur against her.

Not even from the senior Jousters. The Dry season aged toward winter, but everything seemed disjointed and wrong, somehow. The senior Jousters went out; some came back, some did not. Lord Khumun never ordered Kiron's wing out at all. In a way, that was a relief; in a way, it felt as if the Lord of the Jousters had abandoned them.

At last the body was mummified, the shrine was complete, and with a shock, Kiron realized with a shock that it was time to say a final farewell. They all went to the funeral rites—and it was only at that moment that the anger he had felt before Toreth's death finally awoke again. Because the rites were—perfunctory.

In fact, it felt like an extension of Toreth's disgrace, as if his own parents believed that the cobra had really been a sign of the gods' displeasure. When they all arrived at the dock to take the funeral barge to the City of the Dead, Kiron had to look twice to recognize that they did have the right barge, and not one for some insignificant shopkeeper. The barge was small, the decoration sparse, the flowers—well, the only flowers were those brought by the wing. The offerings for the gods were the only things that were there in profusion, in overabundance, in fact, as if Toreth's parents were trying desperately to bribe the gods into a good humor.

There was no escort of professional mourners. Toreth's own parents did not attend. There was only Kaleth, looking like five kinds of death himself, to represent the family, and the wing, to represent his friends.

The voyage took place in utter silence. There were no chants, no dirges. When they all disembarked at the City of the Dead, there was only a decorated cart hauled by a single ox to greet them, with the mason and the painter. Kiron half-expected the shrine to have been shorted as well, but there, at least, the job had been done handsomely. . . .

Then again, perhaps Toreth's parents feared that he would haunt them otherwise.

The shrine, a masonry construction about the size of a room, was carved and painted all over with the prayers for the dead. Inside it should have already been stocked with *abshati* figures and offerings and everything that Toreth would need in the afterlife, sealed in several chambers. Only one chamber remained unsealed; the one for his coffin, before which further offerings could be made over time.

If any were—

*We will,* he thought fiercely. *And I don't care who knows that we're doing so.*

The Priest and Priestess of Enefis, the God of the Dead, hurried through the rites until Kaleth stepped forward, forcibly took the regalia from the priest, and a moment later, Aket-ten confronted the priestess who gave hers over without a murmur. And instead of the Priest and Priestess, they finished the rites, properly, and only when all was complete to the last detail, did they return the sacred implements to their rightful wielders. Everyone knew the rites, of course, and anyone could perform them—

—but to have to step in to do the job properly when there was a Priest and Priestess there was a sign that something was badly out of kilter.

The body bearers installed the mummy in its niche with what seemed to Kiron to be unseemly haste. Only the mason, who sealed the body in, and the painter, who painted Toreth's likeness on the freshly plastered wall, did their jobs with dignity and grace. And only the wing and Kaleth stayed to watch it done.

When even the painter and the mason were gone, Kaleth turned to stumble away—and Kiron, moved by only *Toreth would have wanted this* put out a hand and caught Kaleth's shoulder.

"Come back with us," he said, to Kaleth's frozen face. "Don't go—to your parents' house. Come home with us."

"What?" the young man—prince no longer—asked harshly. "And try to take his place? Pretend I'm not afraid of heights, pretend that I am fit to be a warrior when I know I'm not, try to get *his* dragon to accept me, and try to—"

"No," Kiron said simply. "Come back with us, be yourself, and make a home with us. Do you not think we like you for yourself, and wish your company? Aket-ten tends to Re-eth-ke. She saved Re-eth-ke's life by comforting her, she trains Re-eth-ke now, and I would not let you take the dragon from her now, even if you wanted her. We don't want a replacement for Toreth, we want *Kaleth,* our friend, who needs someone to share his grief with, just as we do. Come and be yourself, with us, who are *your* friends."

He didn't know where those words had come from, but they must have been the right ones, for something within Kaleth visibly broke. His face crumpled, and he began to weep, as if for the last sixty days he had kept his own grief pent behind a dam.

Gan took one side of him, and Orest the other, and they helped him along. Kiron hurried his steps and went on ahead, to make certain that all of Toreth's things had been taken from the empty pen, and it was bare of everything but the essentials. Kaleth had seldom come here; mostly they had met in Kiron's pen. There would be no memories in that place for him, and likely he would never know that it had been Toreth's unless someone told him.

The pen was empty, the sand clean and smooth, the room held only the cot and some linen. Even Toreth's colors had been painted over on the door outside the room. Re-eth-ke had new colors now, scarlet and white, chosen by Aket-ten.

Kiron found an unoccupied slave and sent him in search of the things that Kaleth would need for his comfort.

Then he went in search of Heklatis, and told him what was toward.

"I don't know what his parents think they're doing," he said bleakly, "But something tells me that if we *don't* get him away from them, he'll—do something drastic."

The Healer nodded.

"Good. This is the best place for him. I will make a potion so he can sleep when he is wept out; I suspect he has done as little of that as of sleeping."

Kiron sent a message to Lord Ya-tiren; three slaves returned laden with cushions and lamps, scrolls and papyrus and all the things a scribe needed, including a comfortable chair, a clever little table. In short, all the things needed to make the little chamber into a place of welcome and refuge for a scholar.

It was an unexpected and amazingly kind and thoughtful act that brought tears to Kiron's eyes again. He could not help but contrast *this* with Kaleth's own parents and their actions.

But then, Lord Ya-tiren was a scholar, and he understood another such. Lord Ya-tiren *knew* the truth and believed it; apparently Kaleth's parents were not even willing to listen to it. Or they were too afraid to acknowledge that it was the truth. Kiron blessed his benefactor's name, vowed to find a way to make it up to him, and got the chamber in readiness. And when the wing brought Kaleth back with them, Heklatis, too, was waiting there.

Kiron had expected Aket-ten to be foremost of those offering Kaleth comfort, but to his surprise, she was nowhere to be found. It was only when he heard the sound of light sandals on the stone, and looked out into the corridor, that he saw her. And she was not alone; there was a young woman with her—a woman several years Kiron's senior, dressed in the kind of expensive linen gown and jewels, the elaborate wig and face paint, that a court lady would wear.

For one wild moment, he wondered if this was Kaleth's mother—but a better look told him that if she had given birth to the twin princes, she would have had to do so as a toddler. And it was only when Aket-ten shoved the boys aside so that the young woman could get to Kaleth's side, when he watched Kaleth's face transform when he saw her, and saw him seek her embrace as a refuge from the world, that he realized that this wasn't a sister either.

Aket-ten, with a look on her face that said that she was very satisfied with her work, shoved past the boys again to get to Kiron. She cleared her throat significantly; the boys started, and looked at her, and when she took Kiron's elbow and steered him out into the corridor, they followed suit.

"Aket-ten," said Gan incredulously, "Is that Marit-te-en?"

She nodded. "Toreth might have been indifferent to his betrothed, but Kaleth is not Toreth." She sighed. "All things considered, maybe that wasn't so bad. Anyway, I had the feeling when Marit didn't turn up at the rites that either Kaleth was avoiding her, or that her people were keeping her from him. I went to her parents' house to find out which; they couldn't stop me from seeking her out, so when I found out that she was frantic with worry for him, I got her and brought her here."

"Couldn't stop. . . ." Gan snorted. "Now that's an understatement. They wouldn't dare snub the daughter of Lord Ya-tiren."

Aket-ten shrugged. "If she says she's visiting me, and it isn't common knowledge that Kaleth is here, then I see no reason to enlighten anyone as to who she's really seeing."

"You did exactly the right thing," Kiron told her warmly, and she flushed, and smiled a little, for the first time in sixty days.

"And so did you," she replied. "I think he should stay here from now on and never go home. His parents are being horrid to him; they believe everything the Magi have been saying about Toreth, and they're taking it out on Kaleth. The rest of the court is afraid to go anywhere near him; even if they don't believe the Magi, they're afraid to risk their anger."

Kiron looked around at the others, who nodded or shrugged. "He's our friend, too," said Gan defiantly. "He should not only stay here as long as he wants, I think we ought to figure out something he can do to be part of the wing."

"He can help me," said Heklatis, coming out of the door with the empty potion cup in one hand. He hesitated a moment, the continued, "It is well known among the Magi of the Akkadians that great stress and turmoil can awaken things that slumbered within us and might otherwise not have been awakened." He licked his lips. "And—there is another thought among my people, that in some ways twins are not only bound in mystical ways, but that in a sense they are one extraordinary person, and that if one dies, the other is given all that the other had. The two of them might not have individually had much in the way of magic, but now that his twin is gone—" Heklatis shook his head. "To make the story short, I sense that he might be a newly awakened Magus or Winged One. And of all things, I do *not* want the Magi to learn this. I can protect him until he knows enough to protect himself, but not if he is living elsewhere, out of my immediate reach."

"It's settled, then." Kiron nodded. "And—" He hesitated; but there was something prompting the next words, which came out of his mouth without any notion of *his* that he was going to say them. "—we all know that he didn't look much like his brother? Well, I say he should be someone else while he's here."

"Kaleth's a common enough name," offered Oset-re. "Or call him Kaleth-ke, which is even commoner."

"Kaleth-ke, my apprentice Healer." Heklatis nodded. "I'll set this straight with Lord Khumun, and make this offer to Kaleth after he awakens. I do not believe that he will argue with the plan."

"Me either," Kiron said quietly, remembering the look that had been on Kaleth's face before he made his offer of sanctuary. "Not in the least."

From the very moment when Kaleth joined the wing, although conditions outside their little group grew harder and bleaker with every passing day, within the group, something had changed for the better. Within the group, there was a sense that they had become more than a team; that they had become something of a family—with Heklatis standing in as "father," perhaps, and a family in which there was little quarreling. It was just as well that this was so, because outside the compound, things were not going so well.

As the winter progressed, the physical damage done by the earthshake was finally all repaired—but the mental and emotional damage only worsened. Kiron felt it every moment he was outside the compound, and he wasn't even a Winged One. He could hardly imagine how difficult it must be for those who were sensitive to such things.

The people of Alta were afraid.

They were afraid that the next earthshake would also come without warning, and they were right to be afraid, because the Magi were still raiding the Temple of the Twins and the Winged Ones for their victims, and even (so the rumor went) casting speculative eyes on the Temple of All Gods and the Healers. All over the city, people were trying to concoct ways to protect them-selves when the next shake came. Some solutions were better, some worse, but all of them had one thing in common. They were expensive.

So, the choice was, far too often, between protecting your family from earthshake, or eating. And even if you had made the choice for the former, there was no telling if your solution would work until the next shake came. So the fear never really left any-one. It was worse at night, when children cried as they were put to bed, for fear that the walls would come down on them in the darkness. Even adults stayed wakeful, with the result that a good proportion of the population went about their daily business look-ing tired, with dark-circled eyes.

They were afraid of the Magi, though the Eye of Light (thank the gods!) did not open a second time on the Rings. Still, the les-son had been clear and was still visible—challenge the Magi and pay, obstruct the Magi and pay, threaten the Magi and pay. There were plenty of rumors about how many people had been inciner-ated by the Eye; that only increased the fear. So far as Kiron was aware, no one had actually confirmed any deaths—but as Heklatis had said, would anyone dare?

They were afraid of each other. Though no laws were decreed making dissent and expression of dissent into an actual crime, enough people were accused of being traitors and, if not hauled up before a magistrate and jailed, certainly set upon by their fellow citizens, that no one dared speak out. It was bad enough to be accused of being "unpatriotic," but if you weren't careful, you could also be accused of being an agent of Tia, sent to foment discontent and discord. And that *was* a crime. There was a note of hysteria in much patriotic fervor now, as if the "patriot" was trying much too hard to keep from being added to someone's list. The only sure way to be safe was to be among the Great Ones' chosen friends or others of rank and privilege. Thus far, no one had dared to accuse any of the nobles.

Yet.

Lord Ya-tiren kept away from the court; this did not excite any suspicion, for he had until now been in the habit of devoting himself to the two pursuits of managing his estate and his scholarship. He had eyes and ears in the court, though, and that was how Kiron knew that if nerves were on edge in the city, they were grated raw in the court. If people were uneasy around their neighbors in the city, then they eyed each other with the brittle certainty that they were going to betray each other at the first opportunity in the court.

The ordinary citizens were sure that the nobles were safe from accusations. The nobles were just as certain that accusations within the court were just a matter of time. If the Heir could be rebuked and disgraced, no one was safe.

Toreth's name was never spoken, and if Kaleth's parents missed him, they were making no show of it. He did send one message that he was staying with friends elsewhere, though he did not specify where. He did make arrangements for messages to be sent back to him. No message ever came, nor did his parents send anyone to search for him.

"I am useless to them now," Kaleth noted dully. "When we were the Heirs, it was different; they were the parents of the Princes, and basked in the reflected glory, I suppose. Now, I am nothing but a spare son, and a tainted one at that."

Kiron ground his teeth in anger when he heard that. He could not imagine parents using and discarding their children so callously. It only made him the more determined to give Kaleth a kind of second family here.

But Marit-te-en was at the compound nearly every other day, and she was their second, and much closer source for what was going on in the halls of the Great Ones. Unlike Kaleth and Toreth, she and her sister were identical, had the habit of always dressing alike, and thus it was a trivial thing for Marit to slip away, leaving her sister to play the roles of both twins.

Frankly, as he came to know Marit, Kiron was coming to sense that there had been one flaw in Toreth's personality at least. How could someone as intelligent as Toreth not have warmed up to his betrothed? Everyone agreed that Nofret-te-en was as personable as Marit, and Marit was brave, warm-hearted, and if not as clever and quick as Aket-ten, she had her own sort of wisdom. According to Gan and Oset-re, as well as both Marit and Kaleth, the girls were as alike in personality as they were in appearance. Granted, they were nearer to Ari's age than they were to Kaleth's, but still—

*If I had never met Aket-ten,* Kiron thought, and more than once, *I would be coaxing Marit to bring her sister here. . . .*

It was Marit who opened to them the state of things at court, for Marit and her sister were ladies-in-waiting to the (to Kiron) heretofore unknown half of the Great Ones, the twin wives.

"There are two councils now," Marit said one evening, as they all huddled around braziers in Kaleth's room, on one of the coldest and longest nights of the year. "Though we do not think the original council is aware of the—" she wrinkled her brow in thought, "—I suppose I could call it the 'shadow council,' for it works in the shadows. The Great Ladies joke about it, actually. They seem to think it very funny that the council that everyone sees is the one without power, and all decisions are being made by the council no one knows about except for those who are on it."

Kaleth's mouth twisted as if he were tasting something very sour. "Let me guess. The shadow council is all Magi."

Marit nodded. "Still," she said, sounding less dismayed than Kiron would have expected, "It is not all bad."

"I cannot imagine how—" Gan began.

"Ah," Marit interrupted, with a wan smile, "You see, the Great Ladies, not trusting servants, call upon their own ladies-in-waiting to serve at these meetings. I have seen them, as has Nofret. They may show one face in public, but the Magi hate each other as much as they hate rivals outside the Tower of Wisdom. More so, perhaps, in some ways. They are constantly seeking to topple one another. That is probably the only thing that keeps them from becoming all-powerful."

"Well, that's something, at least," Gan said, scratching his head. "But are you sure of that?"

Marit smiled mirthlessly. "They are not only at each others' throats, they are making real efforts to slay one another. Just today, Nofret told me, someone attempted to poison Magus Kephru with the wine served at the shadow council meeting. If he had not taken the precaution of testing it first, whoever it was would have succeeded. And no one but another Magus could place poison in a single cup when all were served from the same jar."

"Oh," Gan replied, rather nonplussed. "That is—interesting."

"But not useful, at least, not to us," Heklatis opined. "I would not trust any of them as an ally, and that is the only possible use any of them could be to us."

"Oh, I don't know," Kiron said thoughtfully. "Anything bad that happens to any of them is likely to be placed first at the doorstep of the nearest rival, and then every other Magus, and only third at an outsider."

"You have a point." Oset-re sucked on his lower lip. "The problem is, they each have a half century or more of experience in active deceit and treachery to call upon, whereas we—" he shrugged. "Experience and treachery will overcome youth and idealism with no effort whatsoever."

Kiron shook his head. "But we have some of that experience available to us."

"Not unless you are far older than you look!" said Gan.

Kiron sighed. "Perhaps, having grown up with education available to you, you think too lightly of it. I do not. Scrolls, Gan. Volumes of wisdom available to all of us at any time. You have studied more of them than I. What do our texts, the words of our great generals, say to do when an enemy has superior resources?"

"Run away?" Gan suggested brightly.

"Move to a theater where he no longer commands those resources," Kaleth said immediately. "Find ways to deny him those resources."

Kiron turned to Aket-ten and Heklatis. "This is where I ask you if you have an answer to that question I asked you some time ago."

He didn't actually expect an answer; he really just wanted them to say "no," or that they were still working on it, so that he could explain to the rest what his idea was—an idea even more urgent now that Toreth was no longer with them.

But to his shock and amazement, the two looked at each other for a long moment. And then Aket-ten answered, soberly, "I believe that we do."

# SIXTEEN

G AN looked from Kiron to Aket-ten and back again. "I don't suppose you would care to explain that? I don't mean to be rude, but—well, I'm not completely sure just how a girl and a Healer could fit into this situation, no matter *what* you asked them to find."

Kiron ignored Aket-ten's glare. He knew she'd have a few words later—with him, or with Gan, or both—but she would just have to control her annoyance for now.

"Toreth's long-term plan was to put enough Jousters into the field that we could negate the Tian Jousters *without* needing the storms that the Magi were sending," he reminded them.

Kaleth swallowed at the sound of Toreth's name, but nodded. "I recall that," he said. "We both thought that once the Magi were no longer necessary to the war, their influence would wane somewhat. That was before we realized what *else* they were doing, of course. Still, even then, it was a good plan. If nothing else, they would stop draining the Winged Ones in order to send the storms."

That made them all silent, and Marit shuddered. "When Kaleth told me—I could hardly believe it. But then Nofret and I saw the Great Ladies growing ever so slightly younger looking, not older, day by day—now they appear to be perhaps half their actual age." She shook her head. "I cannot fathom why no one else notices, unless it is sheer willfulness *not* to see. Everyone does speak of how well-preserved they are, or how they have lost weight and become more fit, but they say nothing about looking so— unnaturally young. The great blessing is 'May you live a thousand years,' but to think that this is what they might be trying to do—it is monstrous—"

"But only the Magi know what is truly happening, and I think that none but us suspect, because as you say, people do not *want* to know," Kiron reminded her. "And there is only one way to stop them. Someone who is revered by all Altans must speak out. Someone who is trusted by all Altans must tell the truth. And someone whom all Altans know is able to part the curtains of Time must say what lies on the other side of them. In short, the plan is still good, for we need the Winged Ones to be freed, willing to tell what was done to them, and perhaps, willing to say what will happen in the days to come if the Magi are not stopped. Now that they *know* what the Magi will do to them, once they are in their powers again, I think they will fight to keep from being further abused, and I believe that they will speak out."

He looked over to Aket-ten, who nodded, slowly. "They were foolish in allowing the Magi access to them before, but I think that they will rebel once they are no longer controlled and drained," she said. "At least, I hope they will." Her voice faltered. "But they are only human, and they can still be compelled by fear. I do not know what would be the greater for them, the fear of the Magi or the fear that they will be accused of aiding the enemy by refusing to be used by the Magi. I—"

"They will," Kaleth said, in an odd, flat tone of voice—a voice which nevertheless had a strange sort of echo to it, as if he spoke from within a cave. It was so odd, in fact, that all of them looked at him in sudden concern.

He was sitting straight up, forearms lying flat along his thighs, eyes staring into nothing. His back was completely ridged, his head up, his feet and legs exactly parallel. It was an oddly familiar pose; Kiron knew he had seen it a hundred times, but where?

The look in Kaleth's eyes, though—it sent a shiver up his spine. His eyes might be staring into nothing, or apparently into nothing, but they weren't blank or glazed. Oh, no—Kaleth saw something, something none of the rest of them could see.

"He's—" Gan began, looking awe-struck.

"Shh!" Aket-ten reached over and clapped her hand over his mouth. "Don't disturb him!" she whispered urgently. "We must hear all of it!"

"End the need for storms, and the Magi will drain the Winged Ones no longer. In their arrogance, they believe that the Winged Ones are cowed, and will continue to bend their necks to the yoke, but they are wrong. The Winged Ones already are in rebellion; they merely lack the strength to take their rebellion further. When they recover their strength, they will fight. They will bar the door of the temple to the Magi, they will muster their protections, and they will resist all attempts to take them again. And then—and—then—" his voice began to fade, "—then—the paths divide—"

Suddenly, Kaleth blinked, and his entire posture changed; he shook his head slightly, raised one hand to his forehead, and blinked again. "Why are you all staring at me?" he asked, looking puzzled.

Aket-ten let out her breath in a sigh. "Well," she said, with a nod. "Let me put it this way. You were sitting in the Python's Pose."

At first Kaleth looked at her with a smile, as if he thought she was joking. But a moment later, the smile disappeared. "I was?" he asked, incredulously.

She nodded—and so did the rest of them, even Kiron. Now that she had named that posture for what it was, he knew where he had seen that rigid, statuelike pose that Kaleth had taken. In statues, of course, statues of the Winged Ones about to prophesy. So Heklatis had been right! Kaleth had, either through shock or some other means, become a channel for the power to see into the future!

Aket-ten elaborated, while all this went through Kiron's mind. "Your eyes looked into the depths of time, and your voice told what you saw. We all saw it, we all heard it. You told us that if we can stop the Magi from draining the Winged Ones, then the Winged Ones will fight to keep from being so misused ever again."

"The—" Kaleth looked at her as if she was mad. And there was, perhaps, a tinge of fear in his voice. He knew exactly what Aket-ten was saying, and it frightened him. "No. But—I never— but I—"

"Yes, you are, and I should know," Aket-ten said firmly. "I have spent years in the Temple of the Twins, and for many of those years, it was thought that I would have the power that you just displayed."

Kaleth shook his head dumbly, as Marit took his hand, but Aket-ten was pitiless. "You might as well accept it, for the gods will have their way, whether you are willing or not. You are a Winged One now, Kaleth, and you have the Seer's Eye. It is a pity you have never been trained, and even more that I do not know how to train you."

"Why?" Kiron asked, "What difference would training make?"

Aket-ten sighed. "Those who are trained can, with proper preparation, part the Veils at will. It is a fearsome task, and does not often give a clear path, for the future is rooted in the present and changes with each thing that we do now. The Sighted cannot always see all of the possible paths either. But at least they can hold the Sight as long as they have the strength. For Kaleth, untrained, the Sight will come and go without any warning."

"But—but—" Kaleth looked from one to another of them, as if seeking for someone to tell him that Aket-ten was wrong. "This is not—but I—" He looked for a moment as if he was about to weep. "I can't—I can't possibly—"

It was Marit who took both his hands in hers then, put her head close to his, and murmured something that none of them could make out. It seemed to be what he needed to hear, though, for after a moment, he relaxed, just a little, and lost that stricken look. "As the gods will it, then," he said. "It is not for me to fight them. Perhaps I will be of some use. I am of little other use, so far as I can tell."

Kiron coughed. "More than *some* use," he said, as the attention turned back to him. "You have confirmed what I had only hoped, which means that my plan—and Toreth's plan—is sound. If there is a path in the future that frees the Winged Ones from the clutches of the Magi, then it can only be by one means that I know of."

"It would be useful," Gan complained, "if we could but *hear* this plan! So far, there has been nothing but mystery from you! It is hard to judge any plan when there has not even been a hint of what you intend to do!"

Kiron took a deep breath, and looked around at them all before beginning. "If we cannot negate the Tian Jousters with our own numbers, then the only other answer is to remove the Jousters altogether. On both sides, if need be, and to be honest, I think that this may be required. I asked Heklatis and Aket-ten to find a way, thinking perhaps that in magic and the powers of a Winged One combined there might be an answer."

"And we have one, we think," she said slowly. "Though it is not what you might have been thinking. If Heklatis were not a Magus *and* a Healer, I do not think that we would have found it, but—well, it is simple. The Jousters are nothing without their dragons. The Magi have dealt with them by keeping them grounded with storms, but we realized that if we could keep the dragons out of the sky by some other means, that would be the end of the Tian Jousters."

"We didn't want to poison them," Heklatis said. "For one

thing, it would be very hard to do, and for another, it would just be *wrong*. For the same reason we didn't want to give them a disease."

Aket-ten nodded. "That was when we realized that without the *tala*, there are no Jousters, because without the *tala*, the dragons who are not tame cannot be controlled. And if we found a way to keep *tala* out of the dragons, eventually the effects would wear off—and you know better than I what that would mean."

"And?" Kiron prompted, as the others made various noises indicating surprise or agreement.

"We looked for something that would kill the *tala* plant," she said. "We didn't find it—but instead, we found something better." She held up her hand to keep him from interrupting. "You know, if we started to kill the plants, the Tians would surely notice, and perhaps find something to take the place of *tala*. What we found is better, because it does not kill the *tala*, it makes the power of the berries weaken once they are harvested. The strength is gone in days. In less than a moon, they are no longer good for anything. And the Tians will never suspect until it is too late. How long a stockpile do you think the Tians have, Kiron?"

He thought. "Once the new crop is being harvested, a month perhaps. Certainly not more."

Aket-ten nodded. "So when the Dry starts, the berries begin to ripen, and they begin harvesting; once last year's berries are used up and they start to use the tainted berries, within two or three days, their dragons will be uncontrollable. There is just one problem; once we spread this disease, we cannot confine it to Tia. It will come to Alta as well."

Kiron winced. "Ah. That is a difficulty—"

"Not so much as you think," said Lord Khumun from behind him.

They all jumped. Kiron leaped to his feet and turned. The light from the lamps on either side of the door fell on Lord Khumun's

ALTA 305

face illuminating features that were unwontedly bleak with weariness. "My Lord—what have you heard—"

"From the time that young Kaleth began to prophesy," Lord Khumun said heavily. "And you have awakened both my fears and my hopes. Something *must* change in Alta, or Alta as we know it will cease to be, and soon—and I should not like to live in the society that will take its place. When the power is in the hands of those who stand in the shadows, shadows come to fall over everything. Young Toreth's murder was only the first, I fear, of many. And to tell the truth, I am not altogether certain it was even the *first*. Too many of those who have been taken up as 'agents of the enemy' have never been heard of again. And no one knows exactly who might have fallen under the Eye."

Kiron shivered to hear the words spoken aloud. *Young Toreth's murder.* So Lord Khumun knew the death for what it was.

*At least we aren't alone. . . .*

"You may have wondered why I have kept you of Kiron's wing from being sent to the fighting," Lord Khumun continued in what seemed to be an abrupt change of subject. "It is because since Toreth's death, the Jousters are being flung to the enemy like tidbits to jackals. You have not seen it; I have kept the knowledge from you, deliberately, for I was not sure what you would make of it."

He looked at them gravely.

"My Lord, I think we are not surprised," said Orest after a moment. "Toreth's death taught us that the Magi will not tolerate rivals, and in their way, the Jousters are rivals for power."

Lord Khumun nodded. "So I believe. What they did not anticipate, I think, is that these new war games and tactics of yours are keeping my Jousters alive."

He looked straight at Kiron, who felt himself flush with pleasure.

"And there, the subject comes back to you lot. I have kept the knowledge of the true situation from you, lest you feel you must fling yourselves into the fray." The Lord of the Jousters smiled kindly upon them, and somehow managed to keep from looking patronizing. "I knew that if you felt strongly enough, you would disobey even my orders. Now, not even the Magi truly believe that you lot are ready for war, and they know that ordering mere boys to the fighting will make even their supporters look askance at them, so as long as you were not volunteering, and so long as we were having fewer casualties than before, I could keep you safe."

"But the senior Jousters—" Huras said worriedly.

"Exactly. Meanwhile—we go out, day after day, and we are becoming exhausted. At some point, not even your clever new tactics will save us." Lord Khumun grimaced. "There is no doubt that you are right; the Magi will permit no rival for their power to exist. They have been trying very hard to eliminate us. And I had rather see the dragons gone than watch my men die for no good reason."

Kiron let out the breath he had been holding. "Then, my Lord, the best thing for you is this. If you can, if you have thieves that can get into the Tian Jousters' Compound, send men to seize as much *tala* as you can. It is better for us to have it than the Tians, and the more of the old, untainted *tala* we have, the better for us. And then, let us do this thing that we have spoken of without your knowledge, for what we do without your knowledge you cannot be held accountable for."

Lord Khumun looked as if he was about to protest, then stopped. "From the mouths of babes comes wisdom," he muttered, then turned and vanished into the darkness.

"So, tell us," Kiron continued, turning to Aket-ten.

"It is a disease, which puts no outward sign upon the plant, save only a bit of bloom upon the berry when it is still unripe, which is gone when it is dried. Heklatis used his magic to find it, and his knowledge of Healing and herbs swiftly told him what it did. The disease spreads by a dust made from the bloom itself, and we can use magic to make much, much more of it from the bit that we have." She looked rather pleased with herself. Kiron didn't blame her. "What is more, I thought of a way to spread it, quickly. When the rains begin, a dragon or two can climb above the clouds with baskets of the dust, and let them loose upon the winds. The dust will be carried into Tia, and brought down to earth with the rains."

"And the Magi, who have made the winds to be so much greater than they used to be, will be the ones to carry the blight!" Gan slapped his leg with glee. "By all the gods, Aket-ten, this is choice!"

She smiled with grim pleasure. "We, who have truly tame dragons, will be the only ones whose dragons still behave, and I will leave it to you to think how that can be useful. But I believe that the wild-caught dragons will actually obey for some time out of habit—and at any rate, if we successfully take a stockpile of undiseased Tian *tala*, we will be able to keep our dragons under control longer."

"We should reckon on not getting any," Kiron warned. "Unless we can seize raw berries before they get to the Tian compound, I doubt that we will be able to get any. If Lord Khumun has agents who are also thieves, maybe—it is not at all guarded—but the odds are long."

"Then our *tala* and theirs will run out about the same time." She sighed. "Still. Our Jousters will know that their dragons are going to go wild, but the Tians will not, and they may miss the signs. So perhaps *our* task should be to sting the Tian dragons into their own rebellion on the very day when the last of the *tala* is gone from their bodies. And with foreknowledge that it will happen, our Jousters can release their dragons, or allow them to slip their chains, or something of the sort. Or even take them out, and when they begin to get restive, land them behind our lines and turn them loose." She shrugged. "The Magi will contribute nothing to the war once the Jousters are gone, unless they create another Eye of Light that can be taken to the enemy."

"I do not think they can," Heklatis said broodingly. "Which is just as well for all of us, of course."

Recalling the carnage that the Eye had caused, Kiron shuddered. "More than just as well," he replied. "I am not so sure but that it would not be better for Alta if the thing were destroyed."

"There are those on the Second Ring who would agree with you," said Heklatis, and left it at that.

There really was not much else to be said after that. Heklatis and Aket-ten reckoned that it would take until the start of the rains to produce a sufficiency of the dust to infect the *tala* plants.

And then Aket-ten produced another little surprise for them. "I will borrow a swamp dragon and take her up to release the dust in the clouds above the storms—" she began, casually.

"Hoi!" he said sharply. "What do you mean, *you* will borrow a swamp dragon? You've never flown any dragon but Re-eth-ke!"

"I can control any dragon in the compound," she retorted. "Re-eth-ke is too young to take into a storm, and at any rate, she would hate flying in rain and storm, but there isn't a dragon in this compound who won't fly for me. I'll take one of the oldest and canniest."

"You'll do nothing of the sort!" he replied hotly. "If anybody goes flying with that dust of yours, it will be *me.*"

"On what dragon?" she shot back. "Not even Avatre will fly in the kind of hell the Magi have been creating on the first day of the rains, and rightly. The swamp dragons know storms. They can read them the way desert dragons read thermals! But they won't fly for you, not into a storm they won't. On a day of ordinary rains, yes, but not into a Magus-bred storm."

"She has you there," Heklatis said, with what Kiron considered to be an annoying level of calm detachment.

"And just what would Lord Ya-tiren have to say to me if I allowed you—" he began, and the moment the words were out of his mouth, he knew that they were a mistake, but it was too late to call them back.

"If you *allowed?*" she snarled, getting to her feet, her eyes blazing fury at him. "If you *allowed?* Just who and what are you,

Wingleader Kiron, to say what I shall and shall not be *allowed* to do? I am responsible to no one but *myself* for my actions and—"

"And Lord Ya-tiren would certainly hold Kiron responsible should any accident take place, regardless of that, Aket-ten," Heklatis said reasonably. "And while it is true that Avatre would balk at carrying him above the heart of the storm, and that none of the swamp dragons would carry him on their own either, if you were to talk to one of them, you could persuade it to accompany you and your mount. Couldn't you?"

The Healer looked into both their angry faces and smiled. "I suggest a compromise. Two swamp dragons, to carry you, Aket-ten, and you, Kiron. I should not approve myself of either of you going up alone in any case. It will be dangerous, flying under those conditions. It would be better to have a partner. Don't you both agree?"

Even though the very idea of Aket-ten flying under those very conditions appalled him, Kiron swallowed, and nodded. Reluctantly, Aket-ten did the same.

"Good," Heklatis said. "I thought you would both be sensible. Now, we need to think of an excuse to send you both up under those conditions. People might well ask, you know. It will do no one any good for you to excite curiosity. The Magi may notice. Others will notice. So why would two Jousters be flying at the height of a storm?"

They all exchanged a look, and Aket-ten reluctantly sat down again. "I can't think of anything," Kiron admitted.

"Nor I," said Oset-re, usually so quick-witted.

"Well, we needn't think of one immediately," Aket-ten pointed out. "We have some few days yet. But we had better find one before then, and make sure it's sound."

"And on that note, I will take my leave," said Heklatis, and smiled, but this time grimly. "Lord Khumun is right about one thing; his Jousters are being flung into the fray without any regard for how exhausted they are becoming. I've been seeing injuries, and I expect to see more, and worse, tomorrow and each succeeding day. Good night, young friends, and remember that the worst thing that the enemy can do to us is set us at each others' throats."

He sauntered off into the darkness, as they stared after him. Finally it was Marit that broke the silence.

"I wonder which enemy he meant?" she mused aloud. "The Tians—or the Magi?"

Aket-ten still had not forgiven him by the next day; she glared at him every time he saw her, and it made him half crazy. He had agreed that she should go up, so what more did she want from him? It was horribly unfair, too, when all he had been trying to do was to protect her!

He said as much, crossly, to her brother, as they both unharnessed their dragons in the landing courtyard after a long, hard practice. With cooperative dragons it was easier to do it *here*, where their dragon boys could take the gear to a room just off the court for cleaning and mending. Having tame dragons was making for a lot of changes, most of which made the dragon boys' jobs easier. Orest looked at him as if he really was crazy. "Honestly, I thought you were smarter than that," he retorted, handing the neck reins to the boy to be taken away. "The last thing my sister wants is someone to protect her!"

Kiron blinked, and paused while he handed over his own kit. "But—" he said, finally, bewildered, "That day in the temple, when she came running at me—"

"Oh, yes, you would take the one time she was out of her depth and scared to death as the measure of how she is normally," Orest replied, with a laugh. "No, really, *think*, would you? When, other than that, has she ever run out of danger looking for someone to protect her from it? Not her! Oh, no, she runs straight *into* danger, every time! If she wanted someone to protect her, do you think she'd have come *here?* Think about it, think of the options available to the daughter of Lord Ya-tiren!"

Kiron did, pausing with one hand on Avatre's shoulder, and

swiftly realized that if Aket-ten had wanted a protector, she could have found one virtually anywhere. She could have married some powerful lord; she could have gone to that aunt who lived past the Sixth Canal. She could have gotten herself made into a priest-ess of some temple other than that of the Twins. Hamun or Aby-desus, for instance, or Hathen. The temples to those gods were all far from Alta City, out in the delta.

For that matter, she could have gotten herself married to some merchant prince, an Akkadian, or a tin merchant from Thyres, and taken far away from Alta. An Akkadian would have treated her with awe, as a Winged One, and a husband from Thyres, while not understanding in the least what a Winged One was, would have made her his full partner in his business, as was the Thyresian way. She would have been taken to a life of luxury or adventure—or, in the case of a Thyresian, perhaps both.

No, her brother was right. She didn't want protecting. And under most circumstances she wouldn't need protecting either.

"Not that I'm faulting you," Orest continued. "Nothing like. Aket-ten was an idiot to think she could ride a dragon up into a storm without having someone along in case something went wrong. And honestly, if you think you dare risk Avatre in all those down- and updrafts, I think you ought to take *her*, not some swamp dragon. That trick of yours of catching a falling rider— well, that would make *me* feel better about her going up there in that sort of a tempest." He shook his head. "I have to tell you, she's like to drive me mad, sometimes. Give me a proper girl like Marit. One that knows her limits!"

"I'm not going to apologize for wanting to protect her!" Kiron protested hotly.

"I'm not saying you should. Just don't make the same mistake in the future," Orest replied. "Or if you do, don't be surprised when she bites your head off."

He patted Wastet's bright blue shoulder, and led him off to the pens, leaving Kiron staring after him. Finally Kiron shook his head and went back to his own work—in this case, taking Avatre for her sand bath.

He thought about what Orest had said while he worked the sand over his beloved until she gleamed, every gold scale burnished like the Gold of Honor, every scarlet scale gleaming like a sacred jewel. And he couldn't help but notice that she was a *lot* bigger. Nearly full grown, in fact. If anyone got a good look at her, not just glimpsed from the ground, they could be forgiven for wondering why the two of them weren't out fighting with the rest of the Jousters, and never mind that *he* didn't think they were more than half trained.

Well, that was another good reason for practicing so far away from the usual practice grounds.

So Orest thought that his sister believed that she'd had her independence and self-reliance questioned? On one level, it made sense, for other than that one time, she'd never looked for help from him, or from anyone else as far as he knew. Well, look at how he'd met her in the first place! Any other girl who'd been told to go look for a fish in the marshes where the river horses and crocodiles were would have gone straight to her father or one of her teachers to complain! But not Aket-ten, no, she had gone right out into the swamp with only a servant, and if her brother hadn't intercepted her and gone along, she would have been completely alone out there.

Which, of course, on another level made no sense at all, since she was a lot older than that girl who'd gone to the marshes, she'd had a lot of experience in where her bull-headed stubbornness would take her, and you would have thought she'd have learned better by now. She *had* been flying, she *knew* how tricky the winds and thermals could get even without any weather to complicate them, so how could she possibly think she was capable of flying a strange dragon into the teeth of the storm? That wasn't being brave and capable, that was being foolhardy!

*Yes, well, you* set off across the desert alone on a barely fledged *dragon,* part of him whispered. *So you're hardly one to talk about being foolhardy, are you?*

But I had guides! he protested.

*Fat lot of good those little pebbles were going to do if you got caught up in a sandstorm, or were ambushed by predators,* that part of him retorted. *And let's not even mention that you were supposed to be hunting for Avatre and yourself, and when was the last time you had hunted before that trip? You'd slung pebbles at lizards and the odd bird, hoping to bring something down to add to the scraps Khefti-the-Fat gave you. You're two of a kind, you are. You see something that you want, really want, and you don't let anything stand in the way of getting it, do you?*

He decided to ignore that little voice, as he rubbed Avatre down with sweet-scented oil-soaked polishing cloths. Let her be offended; she'd just have to get over it on her own. Besides, there were other things concerning him right now.

Resolutely, he shoved Aket-ten out of his thoughts.

With Avatre clean and oiled, he led her to the pen, where her dragon boy was waiting with her meal. She crooned with pleasure and set to, while the boy laughed at her eagerness. The boys assigned to the tame wing had long since learned what their charges were like, and most of them were hoping for tame dragons of their own one day.

*Well, it still might happen,* he thought, as the boy moved fearlessly about the pen, casting fond glances at Avatre. *There are swamp dragon eggs to steal, and one day, ours might well mate.* That was far more likely since the babies had been playing together before they fledged. He had noticed an interesting difference in Avatre's behavior, compared to any of the youngsters. She held herself aloof from the youngsters, as if she wasn't aware that she was a dragon—whereas they were in and out of each other's pens as soon as they were allowed to wander. They had learned the command to stay, once they were old enough to learn any commands at all, and they obeyed pretty well—but there was a great deal of fraternization among the eight over the course of a day, whereas Avatre greeted any interloper in her pen with a distinctly aloof and offended gaze.

He left Avatre to her dinner, for there was something else he wanted to know.

Two somethings, actually. And he didn't have to go to Aketten to find out either of them.

Heklatis spent most of the morning making the disease dust, and most of the afternoon and evening resting afterward. So he was resting in the courtyard just off his rooms when Kiron went looking for him. He was lying on a cot in the middle of the tiny courtyard, basking in the sun like a lizard on a rock, and he greeted Kiron's footsteps with a raised head and an ironically lifted eyebrow.

"I hope you are not seeking my aid in reconciling you with Aket-ten," the Healer drawled. "I am not particularly interested in mending the quarrels of young lovers."

Kiron flushed. He thought about protesting that he wasn't Aket-ten's lover, and thought better of it. If he did protest, Heklatis would only be more certain that he was. And probably tease him about it. The Healer had an acid wit, and was not reticent about exercising it.

"I wanted to ask you about the dust you're making, and about some other things," he said, sitting down on a stone bench in the shade. "But first, I want to know about the dust. Is it safe around people? I mean, could I get the disease by breathing it or something? And how are you making it, exactly?"

"Well! Sensible questions! I stand amazed." Heklatis raised both eyebrows in an exaggerated look of surprise, turned on his side to face Kiron, and propped his head on his hand. "You cannot get the disease; it is a disease of plants. However, because the dust is poisonous in large quantities, you could become ill if you stuck your nose in a bag and inhaled, so I advise against doing anything of the sort. Doing so would also make you liable to lung sickness, which would also make you extremely ill and might kill you."

So. That meant that to release the dust, they would not want to be in its path or below it until most of it had been carried off. "In that case, the best option would be to carry it in leather bags, cut the bottom of the bag when we get above the storm, and keep climbing, zigzagging back and forth, until the bags are empty." He nodded. "How are you making it?"

"Ah, now that is a truly interesting question!" Heklatis' eyes finally lit up with enthusiasm. "We had a small quantity to begin with, and we proved what it did without using more than half of that store. It is related to a fungus very common in the swamp, and what I am doing is this: I have sent slaves to gather the common stuff, and when I have extracted as large a batch as I can manipulate, I magically prepare the batch, then take a pinch of the disease dust and drop it in. And by what we Akkadians refer to as the 'Law of Contamination,' the pile of fungus dust is converted to disease dust. Not," he added, "without great effort, however. The Magi in the Tower have the Winged Ones to draw upon for their storm-magic, for instance; I have only myself, Aket-ten, and now Kaleth. And I refuse to drain my young assistants as the Magi drain the Winged Ones."

Kiron stared at him in fascination. "Can you make anything into anything else that way?" he asked.

"In theory, yes," the Healer replied, and sighed heavily. "In practice, however, the nearer that what you want is to what you are transforming, the easier it is. As I said, the fungus is a very near relative to the disease. Gold, for instance, is nothing near as like to lead as the alchymists would prefer to believe. I could make fresh water out of marsh water, for instance, about as easily, but turning spelt into barley would be nearly as difficult as changing lead to gold. This is why an Akkadian Magus, no matter how skilled he is, is unlikely to be a wealthy man."

"I see," said Kiron, who didn't see at all. He decided that it didn't matter.

"This is why Akkadian Magi have as many apprentices as they can afford," Heklatis went on wistfully. "The young have so much more energy than an adult, and they simply squander it. It does them little good, for they don't have the skills to use it properly . . . ah, I digress."

Kiron nodded. He hadn't come here to learn about Akkadian Magi, but about Altan Magi. "What about the Eye, then? Do you have any idea how that works? Better still, have you any idea how to make it *stop* working?"

"Ah, the Eye—" Heklatis' whole face lit up. "Before I saw it, I would have had to tell you that I had no idea what it was or how it worked. Now however, I do have some notion. Wait a moment, and I will get something to show you."

The Healer got up—slowly, Kiron noticed, and as if he was as weak as someone recovering from a long disease—and went into his rooms. He came out again with a piece of polished glass. "Watch," he said, as he put a bit of dried leaf and some bits of bark in a little pile on the ground. He held up the glass between the sun and the pile, and moved it back and forth until a tiny, very intensely bright spot appeared on the top of the pile. Then he held the glass quite still.

In a few moments, a wisp of smoke wreathed up from the bright spot, and the leaf began to blacken. Then, suddenly, a flame leaped up from the black spot! Kiron jumped back, startled.

"Remind you of anything?" Heklatis asked slyly, standing up and crushing out the tiny fire with his sandal.

"The Eye!" Kiron exclaimed. Although he had seen no beam of light, the bright spot on the ground, and the way the fire sprang up under it, were strongly reminiscent of how the Eye had worked.

Heklatis nodded. "I have looked back into the records and I can find no accounts of the Eye being used at night, or even on a cloudy day. No, it is always bright sunshine, and usually on or around noon. I think that the main part of the Eye is a lens, and the rest is perhaps some magical or mechanical way of gathering and concentrating a great deal more sunlight than just a simple lens could account for. A simple lens would not be able to reach very far, for instance. But I expect it would be as much a mechanical contraption as it is magical."

"Which explains why they have not made a smaller Eye?" Kiron hazarded. "A smaller Eye would not be nearly as powerful?"

Heklatis nodded. "Such an apparatus would not be very portable either—and I suspect that there is some source of power there, in or under the Tower, and only there. That would account for the beam of light."

"So if we were to go and try to wreck the Eye at night, or on a cloudy day, they would not be able to use it against us?" Kiron said, in sudden speculation.

"So I believe." Heklatis nodded. "And the best way to get to it would be to come at it from above."

They exchanged a look. "Dragons," breathed Kiron. "And *that* is why the Magi dislike the Jousters!"

"Dislike? I would have said that they fear the Jousters, as they would any force that can take that special weapon from them. It seems logical," agreed Heklatis. "And I would go further than that. I believe that the stronger they grow in their power, the more they come to hate and fear the Jousters rather than less, and the more they wish to destroy them if they can."

"You know," Kiron said, after a long pause, "That is not the most comforting thing you have ever said to me."

Heklatis did not smile.

# SEVENTEEN

$\mathcal{S}$OMETIMES Kiron had thought there would not be enough time before the rains began; others that the awaited day could not come quickly enough.

Meanwhile, the dragonets—swiftly and daily growing so large that they really needed to be called "dragons" now—continued to grow in more ways than just size.

Take little Re-eth-ke, for instance; she might be small, but she was as quick as a thought, and exquisitely sensitive to emotions. It wasn't hard to tell how Aket-ten was feeling; all you had to do was look at Re-eth-ke. When Aket-ten was happy, the blue-and-silver dragon would bounce everywhere, and flirt through the sky like a bit of thistledown. When she was depressed, Re-eth-ke became a shadow. And when Aket-ten was angry—well, it was best not to get in Re-eth-ke's way.

Tathulan, the huge and striking female belonging to Huras, was, like Huras, quiet and serious. When she was in the air, she was all business, and very single-minded about everything Huras asked her to do.

And then there was Wastet, Orest's beetle-blue male. Now,

given how much like their riders both Re-eth-ke and Tathulan were, one might think that all dragons were like the ones who had raised them. Wastet could not have been more *unlike* Orest. Kiron considered Orest to be his first and best friend next to his sister Aket-ten, but he was not blind to Orest's faults. Orest was still careless and forgetful, and now and then inclined to puff himself up. But Wastet was steady, just a little slower than the rest, and if a dragon could be "modest," Wastet was every bit of that. Some of Wastet's steadiness was rubbing off on Orest, and to Kiron's mind, that was a very good thing. Of all of the dragons, Wastet was the one most likely to be right where he was supposed to be, no matter what was happening.

Se-atmen was fiery and temperamental. She was the one most likely to lose her temper in practice, and it was a good thing that Kalen was so experienced in handling touchy falcons, because he had his hands full with her. Oset-re's Apetma could also be as fiery in temper as her copper red color.

Pe-atep's Deoth was still shy—shy on the ground, anyway. He was a little lion in the air. He had been the last to fledge, and it had taken all of the persuasion Aket-ten could muster to get him more than a few feet off the ground. But once he discovered flight, it was hard to stop him; given the chance, he would have flown everywhere.

Gan's Khaleph was as relaxed as Se-atmen and Apetma were fiery. Nothing ever flustered him; not mistakes, not accidents. He was the first to recover from the earthshake, and with Wastet, was the one who could always be counted upon to do exactly what he was asked.

Then there was Bethlan. First-born of all the clutches, she was another Kashet; clever, strong, agile, and possessed of a wicked sense of humor. Like Kashet, she was a blue, but an indigo-blue shading to purple. Like Kashet, she was gregarious and outgoing. Of all of them, she was the most likely to be in someone else's pen. Some of her gregariousness was rubbing off on shy Menet-ka, and that was no bad thing.

So waiting for the rains was hardly boring, seeing all these emerging personalities working together. And when the announcement did come, it placed a new burden of worry and responsibility on his shoulders, yet relieved a burden of waiting.

The word had come, not from the Temple of the Twins, but from the Tower of Wisdom. *Tomorrow, the rains begin.*

Kiron wondered just how ominous other folk in Alta City found it that it had been the Magi, and not the Winged Ones, who had announced the start of the rains this year. And why had it come from the Magi? Oh, certainly, they were the ones who would trigger the rains, but why had they elected to announce the fact? Was it that there were no Winged Ones fit to tell when the rains would start? Or were the Magi trying to supplant the Winged Ones, to take their place in the minds of the people?

*If so, they had better start thinking of a way to predict earthshakes,* Kiron thought grimly, looking up at the Tower when his dragon boy brought him the word. *Because telling someone what you plan to do, and predicting what the elements are going to do, are two very different things. And while people might get annoyed by having their property spoiled by an unpredicted rainstorm, they are flatly terrified of unpredicted earthshakes. And rightly so since a rainstorm is only an annoyance; it is the earthshakes that can kill them.*

Nevertheless, he went about taking care of the usual preparations for the start of the rains without any outward show that this announcement had set his heart racing. He and his dragon boy pulled the awning over Avatre's pen, and over the pen that was currently Kaleth's home as well. Anything that might be blown away was secured, anything that might be ruined by rain taken away and put in storage or under awnings. All over the compound, the same precautions and preparations for the rains were taking place, just as if this year was like last year, or the year before, or a hundred years ago.

But when Kiron came out of the vacant pen, he saw Aket-ten struggling with the heavy awning of Re-eth-ke's pen, and he went to help her. She gave him a look of gratitude as he reached up with a rake and poked the place where it had stuck until it was freed, then helped her pull the canvas all the way across and secure it.

"I forgot you'd never done this before," he said casually, and gave her a *look*.

*Tomorrow we go up,* that look said wordlessly. And she must have understood it, because her eyes narrowed, and she nodded.

"We ought to see if Vash and Letoth will fly in the worst of it," she replied. "They're the heaviest of the swamp dragons, the best-suited to storm riding, and it would be useful to know if we could put them up no matter what the conditions."

*Why, bless her, she thought of an excuse!* He had come up a blank, no matter how hard he had tried. It was a good excuse, too, because she was right. They knew that the swamp dragons would fly in rain, but would they fly in *storm?*

"They won't fly for their Jousters," he said doubtfully, for the benefit of anyone who might be spying on them. "I'm fairly sure of that."

There might not be anyone there, but there was no point in taking a chance. Heklatis had told them of a kind of magical spying that could be done, that not even his amulets could completely foil, using birds as the Magis' eyes and ears. Since that time, during the day, under the open sky, they had been careful not to divulge anything that they didn't *want* the Magi to know.

And there were a couple of rock doves perched up on the wall of Re-eth-ke's pen. They'd fluttered up when the awning went by, but came right back down again. Spies? Or just birds who knew there was always some sort of food around the compound?

"They might not fly for their Jousters, but they will for me," she said confidently. "I may not be good as a Winged Fledgling anymore, but I can still talk to beasts, and I can persuade even the dragons to do almost anything for me."

"I'd rather you didn't go up alone," he said.

She gave him a fearsome glare, but replied, "I could fly Letoth, if you're willing to try Vash. If you fly close, I'll be able to speak to both of them and convince Vash to carry you."

"I've flown Vash before," he replied—an untruth, but the Magi wouldn't know that. "She's a lazy pig, but not so bad other than that; if you can get her up in the sky, I can control her. All right, we can try first thing in the morning. But if you aren't ready to go when I am, you can forget it; I'll tell Letoth's boy, and Vash's, too, you aren't to go up alone."

She made a rude face at him, which he ignored. "I'll be up before you are," she said, with just a touch of sharpness in her tone. "You just go get us permission to borrow them."

*If anyone was listening, they heard only that we're going to try flying dragons in the storm. That can't possibly be of any interest.* With that set up, he left her to ready Re-eth-ke's pen for the rains on her own, and went off to report to Lord Khumun, to get permission for the borrowing from the two senior Jousters—and, as he had threatened, to tell Letoth and Vash's dragon boys that they were not to allow Aket-ten to take a dragon out in the storm by herself. Aket-ten, for all of her bravado, would not dare to borrow a dragon without permission, for the senior Jousters might well take it into their heads to reward such impertinence with a thrashing. And it would not matter to them whose daughter she was; they had thrashed boys of higher rank than she was. They were technically her father's equal in rank.

And they also knew that Lord Ya-tiren would punish his daughter himself for taking a dragon without permission. And so did Aket-ten. Indulged she might be, but she was not spoiled. Kiron had the distinct impression that Lord Ya-tiren had raised all of his children with a very clear set of rules, and the knowledge of what happened when you broke those rules.

She knew, of course, that she would get short shrift herself from the senior Jousters if she asked them—which was why she had told *him* to get the permission. They were still of the mind-set that a girl of any rank was best employed in housekeeping and child rearing—or, if she happened to be a Winged One or a priestess or Healer, properly doing her job in the appropriate temple. Girls did not belong in the Jousters' Compound, except as servants and entertainers. She had pushed the line by being a Healer for the dragons, but although that *pushed* the line, she had not quite crossed it.

But this business of flying a dragon had them looking at her narrowly. While they were grateful that she had stopped Re-eth-ke's keening, and they grudgingly accepted that she had to fly the dragonet to keep it healthy and exercised, they were one and all adamant that a girl had no business thinking of herself as a Jouster. And only the carefully fostered illusion that Kiron and Heklatis were "in control of her" kept her from being snubbed, or worse.

So, it was Kiron, wingleader of his own wing, respected trainer and the boy who had worked out ways of making the smaller, lighter dragons able to challenge the larger desert dragons, who approached to ask permission to borrow Vash and Letoth. Kiron, the senior Jousters felt, had *earned* their respect. He was, if not quite one of them, certainly their equal.

"It would be damned useful to find out if we can get *anything* to fly in the worst of the muck," said Vash's rider thoughtfully, when Kiron approached him. "We might have an emergency where a dragon would be the fastest messenger, or need to fly a hit-and-run attack."

Letoth's Jouster said much the same, and added, "If you can get above the clouds, I'd bet you can teach that old sow it's not so bad up there. You'll have to go pretty high, though, and the winds will probably be fierce. *She* won't mind, not while she's working, but you might want to wrap up."

"I'd thought about that," Kiron replied, grateful beyond words that the Jouster had already outlined *exactly* what he planned to do. It made him feel better that someone with far more experience was warning him about things he'd thought of. Should anyone ask, in fact, he could say that he'd gotten advice from both senior Jousters. "I had one of the slaves copy the wool leg coverings and shirts that those amber-trading barbarians wear, and I got some sheepskins to wrap up in, too."

The Jouster shuddered with the look of someone who did not care to find himself wrapped up in wool *at all*. "Better you than me, boy. Deflea yourself after, the gods only know where those sheepskins have been, or what they've collected."

Kiron laughed, and promised, and went off to Lord Khumun to report what he and Aket-ten were going to do. And Lord Khumun gave him a look that asked, *Is this expedition concerning something I don't want to know about?*

Kiron gave a terse little nod, and went on with his explanation of what he and Aket-ten were going to wear to keep from turning blue with cold.

Lord Khumun gave his permission readily enough, and so the path was clear.

He could hardly sleep at all that night. He lay in the darkness, tossing and turning, trying to relax, and trying *not* to fly the whole plan in his mind, over and over and over—and especially trying not to think of all of the things that could go wrong.

Finally he managed to wear himself out so badly, that he fell asleep in spite of himself. Not that his dreams were any more tranquil, but at least they were dreams.

He woke, as he had last rain season, to the sound of thunder. The scent of rain pervaded everything, and over it, the odd, sharp smell that came when lightning struck nearby. Once again, he rolled out of his cot with the canvas of the awning over the pen glowing with continuous lightning.

This time, however, he pulled on a long-sleeved woolen tunic and a set of one-piece woolen leggings, and tied over them a couple of foot-shaped woolen bags to keep his feet warm. Wool, he had been told, stayed warm even when it was wet; if they managed to get above the storm, it would be freezing cold up there, and by the time they got there, they would be soaked. As it was, it was uncomfortably cold now, and the odd woolen clothing, heavy and clumsy as it made him feel, was rather comfortable.

He picked up a cape made of sheepskin, and padded past Ava-tre, awkward in the woolen foot bags. In the corridor outside, itself covered with an awning, there was no sign of life. That was odd; he would have expected to find Aket-ten dancing from foot to foot with impatience.

He went to Re-eth-ke's pen and eased past the dragon to peek into Aket-ten's sleeping chamber. The long lump under her blanket told him that she was still asleep. Very odd. He didn't think she was faking it either.

He was dreadfully tempted then to leave her there and try to take up Vash alone—

*But I told her it was too dangerous to go up alone under conditions like this,* he reminded himself. *She'll never believe my cautions again if I turn around and go up by myself. Besides, without her, Vash probably won't move.*

He eased into the chamber, reached out a cautious hand and shook what he thought was her shoulder. It was hard to tell for certain; it was very dark in here, and apparently Aket-ten was one of those people who slept with the blanket pulled up over her head. There was a faint scent of flowers in the air; he thought it might be from the perfume cones she kept around. She seldom actually wore them on her hair or wigs as most noble ladies did; instead, she left them where the sun would shine on them, or where gentle heat from a brazier would release the perfume into the room.

As it happened, the thing he shook was her shoulder. And a grunt was her only response. He shook her again, harder this time. It was like trying to shake a rock outcropping.

*"Mmph!"* she complained, without really moving much. "Wha—?" The blanket stirred a little.

"Aket-ten!" he said sharply, speaking loudly to be heard above the thunder, giving her a really hard shake. "Get up! The rains are beginning, and we need to take the dragons up in it!"

"Go 'way—" she mumbled, and pulled the blanket tighter around herself. She didn't even react to his presence in her room.

He stood there, confused. She had been twice as eager as he to take on this task! What was her problem? He knew she couldn't be sick. Had she changed her mind about going up? Surely not—

No, there had to be some other reason, and once again, he wondered why no one else seemed to find the terrible lightning storm overhead in the least disturbing.

*It is thundering so hard I can scarcely hear myself think, yet everyone* but *me is sleeping through it, just like last time. I wonder—*

It was beginning to look to him that the Magi had spread some sort of spell across the city to keep the sleepers in their beds until the rains were triggered by their magic. Could it be that the reason he was not still asleep was that he had not been born in Alta City? It was the only explanation that he could think of, though it was just as possible that he was unusually resistant to whatever magic they were doing. Some people were harder to drug than others; he supposed that some people were harder to cast spells upon.

It could well be, then, that the Magi were to blame for Aket-ten's apparent sloth—but such idle speculations were not getting Aket-ten up.

He tried shaking her so hard he rattled the cot, with just about the same result. The harder he shook her, the tighter she curled up. Short of bringing a wall down on her, he didn't think merely shaking her was going to do any good.

So with a sigh, he finally decided that he would have to resort to the unthinkably rude. Even serfs who had been worked to exhaustion and were more dead than asleep responded to what he was about to do.

He went out, got a pot full of cold water, came back to her chamber, pulled back the covers over her head, and dumped the contents of the pot over her face.

Then he jumped back and a good thing, too, because she came

up with a yell, swinging wildly at the darkness around her. She was awake now, all right, angry, and spitting fury. And it was a good thing that she was still tangled up in her blanket, because she probably would have given him a bloody nose for his little trick.

But she was tangled up in her blanket, and the time it took her to struggle free was enough for him to protest and try to explain, with all the sincerity he could muster and from the other side of the chamber, "Aket-ten! I'm sorry! I swear I am sorry, and I will make it up to you! It was the only way I could wake you up, I swear to you, and I tried, I really tried!"

She stood there in the semidarkness, kicking free of the blanket, and he was terribly glad that it *was* semidarkness that filled the chamber because she wasn't wearing anything at all beneath that blanket. All that wool suddenly felt very hot, and very prickly, as he flushed. Not that what she usually wore was much less revealing, but still—

She stood panting with anger, but it was anger that was cooling as she listened to him babble out his explanation. Finally, she tossed her wet hair over her shoulder and said, with great suspicion, "You swear on your father's ghost? You swear that my brother didn't put you up to this?"

"I swear!" he said immediately. "And there's something very odd going on. There's not a single other person awake, and I bet if you were to lie down, you'd be asleep in a moment. What's more, I bet if we tried to go wake any of the others up, they'd be as hard to stir as you were. It was just like this at the start of the rains last year. I was the only one awake. It was—" he shook his head "—it was disturbing."

"The Magi," she said instantly, confirming his suspicion. "There must be something that they don't want anyone to see about the start of the rains." He couldn't see her face, but he could hear the frown in her voice. "I'm not sure I want to know what it is, or why."

He swallowed. He wasn't either, now that he came to think about it. If the Magi were not at all reticent about people knowing they were interfering with the Winged Ones, what was it they felt they had to hide—and felt it so strongly they had to put the entire city to sleep?

His mouth tasted sour. *I can't do everything,* he reminded himself. *All I can do is try to follow Toreth's plan, and hope that once we take the Jousters out of the mix—it will weaken the Magi. Only then can we try to come up with the next plan.*

"Whatever it is, it's nothing we can do anything about," she said flatly, echoing his own thoughts. "We take the Jousters out of the war and free the Winged Ones. They have more authority than we."

She moved over to the wall, into the complete darkness, and he heard her fumbling about, then the sounds of someone putting on unfamiliar garments. Then she came back into the dim light from the doorway, pausing only to tie her wool foot bags in place. "If there's something that the Magi don't want people to watch, I want to see it. Come on!"

Together, carrying their sheepskin capes, they padded down the corridor to the landing courtyard. And there, just as last year, they watched the spectacular lighting and thunder show that centered on the Tower of Wisdom. Kiron was not altogether certain, but it seemed to him that it was more violent than it had been last year. Then again, the Magi were using the Winged Ones now, and not the Fledglings. He felt sick, wondering just what it was that was happening inside that tower.

Aket-ten frowned with concentration as she watched it, braiding up her hair as she did. "I wish I knew what to look for," she mumbled, staring fixedly at the point in the sky that was just above the tower, around which all of the storm clouds seemed to be rotating. "Gods take them! What could be so important that they need to keep the whole city asleep? I wish I had thought to ask Heklatis to watch this. Is it too late to try and wake him, do you think?"

"Maybe. If everything happens the way it did last year, the

whole storm is going to break soon. How long has *that* been going on?" he asked.

She shook her head, and tossed the end of her braid over her shoulder. "I don't know. I mean, everyone always sleeps on the first day of the rains, it's a holiday even for slaves. There's not a lot of point in getting up early, the downpour is too heavy, and it's too dark to do anything until later in the day. I always looked forward to it and never thought about it, not really, and I suppose that's how everyone else feels. It's been this way for years, anyway."

Finally the show ended in that tremendous *crack* of lightning and peal of thunder that he remembered from the previous year, and the skies opened up. They stood there, staring at the water-falls of rain pouring from the sky, then finally she shook her head.

"Let's go get the dust," she said. "Heklatis said he was fixing rainproof bags for us last night."

They made their way to Heklatis' quarters. Aket-ten pulled her cape over her head and made a dash across his courtyard to the first door, which led into a room Heklatis used as a workshop. She came back a moment later with four bulging, heavy-looking bags, made of leather, shiny with beeswax rubbed on the outside.

"Here they are," she said, putting two of them down at his feet. "And he rigged that way to release the dust for us, like he promised! He must have found a way to make it work."

Kiron picked up one of the bags to examine it with interest. Heklatis had pledged that he was going to try to find a way for them to trickle the dust out gradually without having to cut a hole in the bottom of the bag while flying. He couldn't test it without losing the dust, of course, but it looked as if the clever Akkadian had been as good as his word. There was a sturdy wooden handle attached to a stout leather cord, which in turn was attached to a patch on the bottom of the bag that looked as if it was meant to rip free with a good hard tug. He put the bag down again.

"I hope you brought a knife anyway," he said. Aket-ten fumbled at the front of her tunic and pulled up a cord, which was attached to a small knife in a leather sheath hung around her neck. Kiron's was strapped over his woolen leg coverings on his right calf. He nodded.

"The day isn't getting longer," he said, and led the way to Vash's pen.

It took some doing to get the swamp dragon up out of her wallow. It was cold out of the water, and dark, and she didn't want to leave. He didn't blame her; if he'd had any choice, he would be in bed at this moment himself. Aket-ten spent a great deal of time nose-to-nose with the dull green dragon before she emerged from the water with a groan, and grumbled her way over to the saddle stand so that he could put her rig on her.

Once Aket-ten judged it was safe to leave the two of them alone, she went back out into the corridor to deal with Letoth herself.

Either Letoth was more cooperative, or Vash was much more stubborn—in either case, by the time Kiron finished harnessing Vash, fastening the bags behind her saddle, and leading her out into the corridor, Aket-ten and Letoth were waiting for them. The rain drumming on the canvas awning and pouring down the sides into the drainage channel was a reminder that they were in for a miserable ride.

Both dragons balked at the entrance to the landing courtyard, and once again, Aket-ten had to stand nose-to-nose with both of them for some time before they heaved huge, hot sighs that that smelled of iron and blood, and allowed themselves to be led out into the rain.

And once in the rain, it was impossible to speak except in a shout.

The dragons snorted their distaste, and tossed their heads unhappily, while Kiron and Aket-ten found themselves wrapped in sodden, heavy cloth. And if the wet wool wasn't cold, it also wasn't particularly pleasant; it was heavy, it clung and made it hard to move, and it stank of soggy sheep. They made their way into the center of the court, Aket-ten got both beasts to lie down, and the two of them clambered up into their saddles.

Vash got to her feet first, groaning. Letoth followed suit. It was Aket-ten who gave the signal to fly; Letoth rose first, flying heavily, and Vash followed her a moment later. With the rain pouring down on them, they wallowed into the sky. Kiron and Aket-ten were just baggage at that point; for his part, Kiron couldn't see anything beyond the curtain of rain, and certainly couldn't hear. He just hung on and let the dragon pick her course, so long as it was up. Her wings pounded through the sodden air, as she labored upward with all her might. Kiron was just glad that he and Aket-ten were much smaller than the Jousters who usually rode these beasts, or they never would have gotten into the air at all.

It took forever. There was no way to keep track of time, as Vash's lungs heaved under his legs, and he felt her muscles straining to drive her upward, while his muscles ached from the strain of being in the saddle of a dragon in a steep climb. Occasionally, there was a flash of lightning, followed by a distant roar of thunder, but somehow the dragons were staying out of the area around the tower.

Then came the winds.

It must have been right beneath the clouds, or perhaps just inside them; the rain slackened a little, and then—

Vash bucked sideways as a gust of wind hit her wings and flung her over. She fought for control, Kiron balancing in his saddle to help her, and kept from being tumbled through the air by a small miracle. Then, before they could fully recover, another gust hit them, driving them in a different direction. Now they were inside the cloud, some rain, but mostly inky-black, tempest-driven mist that stung when it hit like a sandstorm, and winds that tossed poor Vash around like a leaf.

Vash spread her wings as the third gust hit her, and with a strangled cry, drove upward with all her might. She surged underneath him, throwing him back in the saddle with powerful wingbeats, and he fought for balance, then flung himself forward over her neck and clinging to avoid overbalancing her. The lightning stink was in his nostrils; it was all he could smell, and he wondered with horrified fascination what would happen if lightning struck the two of them.

He could see in the set of her head and neck, and in the spread of her wings, that she was angry. Angry enough, it seemed, to be determined to fight her way up through this cloud and into the blue sky above. He doubted that she was even thinking of him now. All of her concentration was on *up*—she knew the sun was up there, and she could, she *would*, get up there with it!

And then, just when he thought the darkness inside the cloud would never end, just when he wondered if he and Vash had died back there, and this was the limbo of an unhappy ghost, she drove through the top of the cloud and up into the sunlight.

He barely had time to look around before Aket-ten and Letoth came surging up beside them like a leaping fish, trailing wisps of cloud stuff behind them.

Aket-ten recovered first. She shook back her woolen sheepskin cape as Letoth spread her wings and let the strong wind carry her, panting with exertion. With a nudge of his knee and a pull on the reins, Kiron sent Vash after her.

It was a different world. He had been high before, but never this high. Together they soared in a strange world, floored with white fleeces, roofed with the blue sky, and empty but for swift, strong winds. Cold—it was as cold as he had ever remembered being, and he dared not think how high they must be. And it was silent, but for the high, thin whistle of the wind in his ears, and the beating of the dragons' wings. Surely this was far, far higher than he had ever flown, even on Avatre.

It was wonderful beyond words. He took a deep breath of the clean, clear air, and felt as intoxicated as if he had drunk three jars of palm wine. This was freedom such as he had never tasted before. It was as if he and Aket-ten were the only two humans alive in the world, a world made solely for their pleasure.

Aket-ten cast him a wild glance, full of delight, and despite the gravity of their task, he grinned back at her.

Even the dragons seemed to enjoy this place of white and blue and intense light. They soared and tacked back and forth on the wind, staying just above the cloud tops, as he and Aket-ten whooped and laughed with the sheer pleasure of the flight. The air might be cold, but it was also as dry as that over the desert; in no time their clothing and even their cloaks were no more than damp, and the wool was doing its proper job of keeping them warm. Only his nose, his hands, and his ears were cold, and he solved the last by hunching his head down into the fleece of his cloak.

Finally, with a sigh, Kiron recalled himself to duty. He waved a hand at Aket-ten—not wanting to take more than one hand off the saddle hold—and pointed at the bags. She nodded, and pulled the wooden handle on the one nearest him so he could signal her if it had ripped loose properly.

The patch on the bottom ripped off, exposing an open gash in the thick leather—and a thin, gray dust began to drift out, to be caught up on the wind and whipped away in moments.

Satisfied that Heklatis' creation was working as it should, Kiron signaled to Aket-ten that all was well, and ripped loose the patch from the first of his bags. She nodded vigorously after a moment—

And then, with the best possible combination of business and pleasure, they sent Vash and Letoth in great swooping curves and shallow climbs followed by long dives, kiting their way all over the sky. He had been afraid, given Heklatis' warnings, that the dust would be so thick it would be dangerous to breathe, but in fact, the wind was carrying it away so fast that he couldn't even see it except as a bit of misty gray right under the bag. So that meant they didn't need to try to avoid it, and they just flew where they wanted to, until the first two bags were empty and flapping loose against the dragons' sides, causing them no end of annoyance. Vash even bent to bite at it, and since Kiron saw no reason to take it back down again, he simply cut it loose and let it fall away into the clouds. When Aket-ten saw what he had done, she did the same, and then they pulled the patches on their second bags and began the procedure all over again.

By this time their clothing was dry and they were actually warm. Or at least, Kiron was, and he thought by the pink of Aket-ten's cheeks that she was, too. The release of the second lot of dust was no more difficult than the first, and when they had cut their second bags loose, Kiron felt an extreme reluctance to fight their way back down through the clouds again.

*All right,* he decided, *There's no reason to be down there until we have to. Why don't we just fly until the dragons are hungry? We'll let them decide when they want to go home.*

Out of the corner of his eye, he caught Aket-ten waving at him; she mimed diving down. He pointed at Vash's head, tried to mime being hungry, and pointed at Vash's head again. She frowned—then smiled, and nodded.

For the rest of the morning, they circled and rode the winds together, and the only way in Kiron's mind that it could have been more perfect would have been if they were on the same dragon. As it was, they only way they could share their pleasure was by signs and smiles.

Still, he absorbed every moment, cramming it into his memory along with the precious memories of Avatre's first flight above the desert into freedom, of her first good hunt, of the long flight above the swamps of Alta. He would hold these memories, storing them to take out and savor, as an antidote to fear and grief and pain to come. There would be bad times; just as surely as there were good times, there would be bad ones, and he would need memories like this when they came. If ever there had been a perfect moment in his life, it was this, and he gave in to the intoxication of pure flight.

But eventually, as he had known it must, it had to end. He felt Vash tugging in one particular direction, and she made a huge turn, then went from soaring to real flying, beating her way against the wind with powerful wing thrusts. For a moment, he was puzzled—but then he realized that he had forgotten a little detail.

Up here in the clouds, *he* had no idea where he was. But Vash knew. Just as the birds knew where "home" was, even when they could not see it, Vash and Letoth knew where the compound was. They were hungry, and the compound meant "food"—they might have soared leagues away from it, but they were used to flying enormous distances to get to the battlefield or on patrol. The wind was strong, but the *kamiseen* was stronger, and they flew against it as a matter of routine; it was no match for their powerful muscles.

Letoth, with the lighter burden of Aket-ten, swiftly overtook Vash and then went into the lead. This spurred Vash on to better efforts, and the two of them labored across the sky as Kiron marveled that they clearly knew exactly where they were going despite the fact that there was nothing visible but clouds that looked exactly like all other clouds beneath them.

Then, without any warning at all, ahead of him, Letoth suddenly folded her wings and *dove*. Surprised into a scream, Aket-ten grabbed the saddle with both hands as her mount vanished into the clouds.

Kiron had only that much warning to grab the saddle himself, as Vash did the same.

His stomach got left somewhere far behind him. It might be a controlled dive, but it felt exactly like plummeting, and his body reacted with terror. A scream ripped out of his own throat, and his hands clenched onto the front of the saddle so hard that they ached.

*Trust Vash. She knows what she's doing. She won't crash. She was wild-caught as an adult, she must have done this before. Trust Vash!*

They were through the clouds and the turbulence inside them in two heartbeats, falling like a pair of stones out and into the rain. And as they fell through the bottom of the clouds, he saw Letoth and Aket-ten beside him, her hair streaming behind her, her sheepskin cape flapping loose, her mouth still open in a scream—

—and then the rain curtains parted for a moment, and he saw a canal—a bridge—the compound! The rain closed in, then parted again beneath another gust of wind, and the compound was rushing at them, fast—*too* fast—

Then Vash snapped her wings open, slowing their fall. The rain and the wind slowed it further, and she began to backwing, pulling her hindquarters under him, making her body into an enormous secondary "wing" to slow them still further—

And then, with three thunderous wingbeats, they were down, and Letoth beside them, down in the landing courtyard, skidding to a halt on the rain-slick earth. A slip, and a skid, and Vash folded her wings.

And there they were, safe again, with rain pouring down over them, soaked to the skin, and frightened out of their bodies, almost, and yet, at the same time, full of triumph.

And there were four people running toward them, shouting welcome over the drum of the rain—two Jousters, two dragon boys. And Kiron realized in that moment that—bless them!— Vash and Letoth's riders had figured out from their long absence that when they came back, he and Aket-ten would be in no shape to tend to the dragons themselves.

He managed, somehow, to get his leg over Vash's saddle, and slid down to splash into the courtyard to land on legs that shook with fatigue. Vash's rider steadied him, then slapped him on the back.

"Great landing!" the Jouster shouted into his ear over the rain. "Didn't think the old cow had it in her! How did she fly?"

"Wonderful! Fantastic! It can be done!" he shouted back. "In fact, once we were over the storm, she liked it! She didn't want to come back until she got hungry!"

"Well, she'll get her reward for certain!" the Jouster laughed. "You go get dry and warm. Well done, both of you!"

The Jousters and their dragon boys led the two dragons off to their meal and their warm wallows; Aket-ten waited for Vash to get out of the way, then half staggered through the rain to his side. He put a steadying arm around her, and to his joy, she not only did not object, but leaned into him.

"I want heat!" she croaked over the rain, "And I want to be dry again—"

He laughed. "Me, too!" he agreed, and with heads bent against the downpour as the skies opened up again, they plodded back to their wing. Now there was nothing for it but to wait.

Wait, and see how far a plan could take them.

# EIGHTEEN

RAIN drummed on the awnings overhead, and dripped down between the gaps onto the stone paving of the kitchen courtyard. Kiron was exhausted, and so were the rest of his wing; Kiron felt as if he could scarcely hold his head up. They sat around their customary table, staring at their dinner, so tired they could hardly eat. They weren't the only ones; the senior Jousters were just as exhausted if not more so, and there wasn't a man without some sort of minor injury among them, bruises, wrenched muscles, sprains. The main difference, really, was that the senior Jousters had been flying fighting missions, and the boys had only been practicing.

Heklatis was going from table to table, peering into eyes here, demanding to see throats there, and pouring an occasional dose from a steaming jug he carried, demanding it be drunk down on the spot. No one really minded; Heklatis' potions were always drinkable, and sometimes they were even tasty. He had more than made himself useful here, he had made himself indispensable. This was just as well for someone who was trying to keep the Magi from discovering he, too, was a Magus. Should anyone come looking for a Magus hereabouts, he would have the entire compound swearing he was so good a Healer he could not possibly have any time for anything else.

Practice had been difficult as usual. The desert dragons had protested every moment they had to spend in the rain, and Kiron couldn't blame them one bit. They weren't meant for this muck, and if it hadn't been for Kaleth's premonitions, he wouldn't have forced them out into the weather at all. The rains had always been a time for rest and recovery for the Jousters of Tia, and it would have been nice if it could have been the same for the Jousters of Alta.

Each of the tame dragons had reacted differently to the rain. Apetma sulked and had temper tantrums. Se-atmen was lethargic, as if she could not muster any energy. Re-eth-ke was nervous, and made mistakes. Khaleph was clumsy; perhaps he was affected more by the cold. Bethlan slept and slept and slept when she wasn't practicing or eating. Deoth whined the entire time he was in the air. Wastet growled at everyone except Orest, and Tathulan just gazed at everyone with the saddest eyes. As for poor Avatre, she hung her head with depression that didn't ease until she was back in her sand wallow. He hated asking this of them— but he felt as if he had no choice. The Magi were watching them all, he knew it, he felt it, and Heklatis confirmed it. If they didn't put on a good show of doing their best to get themselves into combat-ready shape, it wouldn't be long before the veiled accusations started. And then, perhaps, the open ones. They had been Toreth's friends, and Kaleth lived among them. It would be so easy to point the finger of accusation at them all.

Kaleth's premonitions were coming more often now—actually, they looked more like fits when it came down to it; the boy would sit bolt upright in that peculiarly rigid pose, stare into something only he could see, his mouth would open, and that hollow voice would say things. Kiron just considered that they were lucky that Kaleth's pronouncements were clear and unambiguous. According to Aket-ten, most of the current practitioners of the Seer's

Eye among the Winged Ones were so cryptic that they required interpreters.

The Magi were watching them all, according to Kaleth as well as Heklatis, and would take any pretext to accuse Toreth's friends of treason. The warnings had been timely, coming right after the start of the rains. It wasn't just the ten of them, of course; Marit later confirmed that any of Toreth's friends inside or outside the compound were under intense scrutiny. For that matter, it wasn't only Toreth's friends and acquaintances. Outside of that circle, it seemed there were rumors of people being hauled off and imprisoned every other day on suspicion of disloyalty. Tempers were always a little raw during the rains, but this year nerves were being stretched to the breaking point. The word "treason" was being made to apply to anything that the Magi didn't like— "traitors" were those who dared to differ with anything that they wanted.

Nevertheless, the boys were determined to give the Magi no excuse to voice their suspicions. So while the senior Jousters went out to fight, Kiron's wing went out to practice, making a show of using even the most miserable weather to train, even if they wouldn't be expected to go to fight for another two seasons at best. Kiron could only remind himself, as he saw the misery in Avatre's eyes, that if she had been in the wild, she would have had to hunt for her food every day regardless of the conditions. The best he could do for her and the others was to make certain that though they did get wet, they never got chilled, and they were always fed the best that the compound had to offer. That, and a great deal of love and attention, was all he could do to try and make up for her daily struggle in the wet.

There wasn't much he could do for the boys other than commandeer the empty pen of one of the swamp dragons (one whose rider had been lost in combat before the rains, and who had not returned) for daily hot soaks for everyone.

The cooks had taken the universal exhaustion of everyone with a dragon into consideration, and were providing meals that were comforting to the spirit and warming to the body. Tonight, dinner was meat-and-lentil soup, thick, hot, and filling—and most of all, extremely tasty, soothing to the stomach and not requiring much chewing—a consideration when several of the Jousters had facial bruises, either from flying accidents, or being cracked across the jaw by missiles from below. Kiron tasted his, judged it cool enough to eat, and spooned some up. It was wonderful, and so flavorful it actually woke up his appetite, and he ate it slowly, with bread so fresh it steamed when he broke it open and so soft it almost melted in his mouth.

Everyone else was eating the same way, heads propped up on one hand, leaning over the table, so weary they were half-asleep and prodded on only by their hunger. If the Magi were spying on them now by what Heklatis called "scrying," they were having a singularly dull time of it, for all that they were seeing was tables full of warriors weary from fulfilling their duty.

Because the senior Jousters weren't using the practice field, and no one was going to play spectator in the rain, at last Kiron's wing was able to practice right at the Compound. And because they were having to fly slowly anyway, and missile weapons were useless, they were practicing real Jousting. Kiron didn't expect them to ever have to use the skill, but it was better to have it than not, and the spies would take it amiss if they weren't trying to learn it.

There was a new modification to the harnesses; Kiron had mandated it for the boys, first, but now even the senior Jousters had asked for the additions. "We can't afford pride," one of them had growled. "There are too few of us."

So now everyone had harness straps holding them to their saddles. The straps could be broken—oh, yes—and if a Jouster was hit hard enough to break the straps, he would certainly fall to his death—but it took a lot more to kill an Altan Jouster now, at least.

So there were bruises and strains among them, as well as the

Jousters, compounded with their simple exhaustion. Orest even had a spectacularly black eye.

Only one person looked alert, for Kaleth ate with them now instead of by himself. He had decided to do this on his own; it had taken him something of an effort, and Kiron was very proud of him for taking that step. Normally he was as silent as the rest of them during a meal, but tonight, after a cautious glance to see that no one was within easy listening range, he leaned over and whispered, "I have to talk to you all after dinner."

Kiron groaned inwardly—Orest, who was clearly in some pain, groaned openly. "Can't it wait?" he asked plaintively.

"No. Come to Heklatis' quarters," Kaleth said shortly, looked around again, and went back to his meal as if he had said nothing at all.

But that certainly got their attention. Heklatis' quarters were securely guarded against every sort of magical spying that the Healer knew of; they had only gone there once or twice, when they wanted to be sure that nothing they said could be overheard. The first time had been when he and Aket-ten reported the successful release of the dust, the second, when Heklatis wanted them to hear that the Temple of the Twins was now tended only by servants, the Winged Ones being in their quarters from the time the Magi brought them back from the tower until the time the Magi came for them again in the morning.

Now, Heklatis had certainly lived up to the reputation of Akkadians as being as clever as five cats and as slippery as a serpent, because he had managed to arrange things so that even if a Magus discovered all of the protections on his quarters, himself, and the boys, he had a perfectly logical explanation that would hold up to the closest scrutiny.

All of the "shields and wards" as he called them had been cast on the images of *his* gods in his quarters, images that had indisputably come with him from Akkad. He could protest in all innocence that he had no idea there was any magic on them, but that they *had* been blessed by the priests of his nation. And as for the protections on himself, the boys, and Aket-ten, well, *those* were all centered in Akkadian amulets, which he could claim had also come with him and been similarly blessed, and to prove it, he still had a chest full of similar amulets, all of which had gotten the same "blessing."

It was unlikely in the extreme that anyone would even guess that he and Kiron had spent the better part of two days making a mold of his amulet, casting dozens of copies, firing them, and stringing them on cords, nor that it had been Heklatis, not some priest, who had put the spells on them. How supremely ironic it had been, that Kiron had used the skills he had picked up in the service of Khefti-the-Fat!

As for why Heklatis would have bestowed those amulets on the boys—the reason was simple. He, and they, would claim truthfully that they had asked for them, seeing the image of a winged solar disk on them, so like the same symbol of the Altan sun god.

Clever, clever Akkadian. How would they have managed without him?

He would have liked to ask Kaleth about a hundred questions, but Kaleth downed the last of his soup, drinking it straight from the bowl, and left the table. The rest of them exchanged glances after he left that varied from resignation to astonishment. Whatever was going on, it was Kaleth, above all of them, who had the most to lose, and knew how careful they must be. He would not have told them to do this unless there was a very, very good reason.

So, how to come up with a good excuse for the whole lot of them to descend on Heklatis. . . .

*It seems as if I spend half my life now trying to come up with innocent reasons to do something in case someone is watching*, he thought wearily. *I am very tired of this.*

He couldn't help but wonder now—if he had known that this was what his life would come to, would he have returned to Alta at all?

Finally Kiron spoke aloud. "You all look like trampled barley," he said. "And I *feel* like trampled barley. Finish your dinner, and as wingleader, I am ordering the entire wing to visit the Healer. I want him to look us over carefully, one and all. Potions at dinner are all very well, but I think we ought to get the Healer to check us completely. The last thing I want is for one or more of us to fall ill. A mistake in the air can be fatal."

"Well," said Gan, after a moment. "Since he mixed the last potion he gave *me* with distilled palm wine, I'm not going to object too strongly. I'm tired, but too nervy to sleep anyway; maybe he can give me something to make me relax and drop off."

The rest nodded. "I want something for this eye," Orest said ruefully—ruefully, because the eye was his own fault. He had actually smacked himself with the Jousting lance.

Kiron didn't hurry them as they finished their meal. That would have looked odd, and the last thing he wanted was for anything to look odd at the moment. Besides, no matter how urgent Kaleth thought the situation was, he was in no great hurry to hear it. Only when they were all through, Aket-ten included, did he nod and climb stiffly over the bench to lead them to Heklatis' rooms.

They were able to walk under awnings most of the way, and only had to dash under the young waterfall pouring down over the awning at the break where the corridor met the entrance to the courtyard. By now it was dark, but the door of the main room was open and warm lantern light shone invitingly out at them.

The room was as inviting as the light had promised, and their host had laid out cushions and stools for all of them. Kaleth was already there, waiting for them and looking as tense as a strung harp, and so was Heklatis, of course. Once they were all inside, Heklatis shut the door after them, and made a peculiar, twisting little gesture on the surface of it.

Kaleth relaxed at once. "Now we can talk," he said with gratitude. "Kiron, I have to leave."

Kiron was more than a little startled. That was not what he had expected to hear! "All right," he said cautiously. "So—"

"It's not what you think," Kaleth interrupted. "It's not that the Magi are coming for me yet, and it's not that I don't feel as if I belong among you, because I do."

"What is it, then?" Orest asked.

"I had a vision today while you were all at afternoon practice," he said. "Heklatis was with me, and what made it different was that this is one I remembered afterward." His expression took on a little of that far-away look it got when he was actually having a vision. "I spoke with one of the Bedu, the Blue People, and he said—I think it was a 'he'—said you would remember him. He said he was the one who guided you to the edge of the delta marshes from the last oasis, and told you that you had to stop being Vetch and start being Kiron."

Kiron blinked. He might have been skeptical about this "vision" —except that right there was the proof that it was a true one. There was no way that Kaleth could have known what that final Mouth of the Bedu had said to him about leaving his serf-self behind, because he had never told anyone. "All right," he repeated. "So what else did you see?"

"It wasn't so much what I saw as what I was shown," Kaleth said, and now he looked at them each in turn, his expression sober and a little frightened. "I have to leave, and meet with this Bedu. He's going to help me find a place where we can make a refuge, a secure hiding place, a *sanctuary*. He—the Bedu—said, and my vision showed me, that we're going to need it. He said he and the other Bedu like him had been having the same vision as me, and he had been appointed to vision-speak me to make me understand, because I hadn't been trained and otherwise I might not understand how important it was that I do this."

"A refuge?" Gan said, skeptically. "For who?"

"You, at least at first," Kaleth replied. "Because once the Jousters are no more because the *tala* fails and the dragons all escape, the Magi won't let you nine live."

Even though Kiron had more than half expected to hear something like this some day, it came as a jolt. He felt cold all over, and it wasn't because of the rain, winds, and chill. It was an ugly thing to hear that someone intended your death.

Kiron turned his gaze on Aket-ten. "You're in that nine. You need to understand that."

"I already did," Aket-ten said bitterly.

Kiron suspected that he wasn't the only person to feel as if a line of ice-laced fire ran down his spine at that moment. But he believed Kaleth. Oh, my, yes. He had seen what the Magi could and would do to those they considered threats, and the last remaining Jousters in Alta would be a threat to their continued aggrandizement of power, if nothing else.

"Me, too, of course—well, I'll already be there. And after us, others will come," Kaleth continued, "Mostly from Alta, though not all. You, too, Heklatis."

"I suspected as much," the Healer said dryly. "For one thing, I'm rather too closely linked with the lot of you, for another, if there are no Jousters, they won't need a Healer now, will they?"

"But the thing is, I have to meet with the Bedu, and pay them to help me in the desert, and find the place. *They* don't even know it exists, the one who spoke to me said that the Bedu think it's only a legend." He looked triumphant. "It's Te-pa-ten-ke, the Lost City, and my visions are going to lead me to it."

*That* held them frozen in their seats for a moment. Everyone knew about the Lost City, how it had been buried by a mammoth sandstorm in a single night. It had supposedly incurred the anger of the god Haras, because the inhabitants had turned into brigands, preying on their neighbors, and after they cast out their own priests for warning them, he had raised his hand against them. But no one had ever seen it, not even the Bedu whose home the desert was.

"I should say," Kaleth continued, "that I'll pay them for passage, and then when I find the city, I know where to find a store of gold to pay them to help me set it up for you. The Bedu with the visions trust me, of course, but they're poor—"

"Exactly," Kiron put in, as the others began to look a bit skeptical at all this talk of payment. "The desert takes everything you have just to survive. The Bedu have nothing to spare to sustain an outsider. They need payment in order to get extra supplies for you."

He nodded. "And then, they'll need more gold to get the supplies to help me make the place livable for the rest of us." He looked a little feverish, but had an air of triumph about him, and a look as if he had at last found meaning for his life and a great goal to pursue.

Well, if that was the case, Kiron couldn't blame him for looking triumphant. In many ways, he had emerged from Toreth's shadow and come into his own kingdom. . . .

"So if you're going to be wandering out in the desert, just how are we supposed to find you and this refuge?" Oset-re asked, with a touch of irony. "I don't fancy flying off across the wastelands trying to find a place that shouldn't exist."

"You won't have to. The Bedu will find you and bring you to me when the time comes. The Mouth will know when and where to find you. That's all I know." He shrugged. "The visions showed me the city, but not how you'll end up there, though I think it's bound to be when the dragons go wild. And it's getting dangerous for me to be here; I'm not sure why, I only know that it is. The Bedu said so, too. I'll leave in the morning, so this is the last time we'll all meet before I see you in Te-pa-ten-ke."

Kiron cast a glance over at Heklatis, who interpreted the look correctly. "I believe him, Kiron," the Healer said. "I think this is a true vision. I told you once that these things come in fragments; we should just be glad that he got enough to know the next part of the plan."

"We essentially destroy the Jousters, then escape into a refuge," Kiron mused aloud. "It could be worse, I suppose."

Kaleth scowled at him. "Yes, it *could*," he said with annoyance verging on anger. "You could come back to the compound after the battle, and the Magi could wipe you all out of the sky with the

Eye. I've seen *that*, too, and I don't want to see it truly happen instead of being a maybe-future!"

That stopped Kiron dead; in fact, they all went as still as stone for a moment, and in the silence, the rain outside was very loud indeed.

"All right," Kiron said into the silence. "In that case, let's all work on making sure that particular maybe-future never has a chance of coming true."

Kiron half expected that no one outside of their little group and Marit and her sister Nofret would even notice that Kaleth was gone, and as far as he was able to tell, that was the case. Lord Khumun did not mention it, there were no rumors from the court, and in fact, Kaleth's absence might well even be a relief for some. Kiron did not even attempt to keep up the fiction that he was still there, though if anyone asked him, he was going to say, truthfully, that Kaleth had left one night leaving no word of where he was going, and then add, "Though he spoke once of trying to find the Lost City."

He figured that such a statement would brand Kaleth as completely mad. Even the Magi would probably not bother to look for him after that.

But no one outside the group ever spoke of him; perhaps, like Toreth, they were all trying to pretend he had never existed. Perhaps they were trying not to draw attention to themselves. Perhaps both.

But within half a moon, and deep into the rains, they all got a rude shock, and Kiron was very, very glad that Kaleth *had* gone. It went down as one of the black moments of his life.

Lord Khumun sent dragon boys around to the entire compound that morning as they all awakened, saying that he wished to address them over breakfast. Kiron fed Avatre without thinking very much about it; though it wasn't usual for Lord Khumun to address them all together, it wasn't unheard of. Perhaps the work of the Jousters in the worst of the rains had gotten noticed and the

Great Ones wanted to send a reward of some sort, or at least, a word of commendation.

*They certainly deserve it,* he thought, with more than a bit of bitterness. *More than the Magi, if you were to ask me.* After all, *they* were having to fly in that magic-befouled weather, and because of their efforts, the border had been pressed back yet again—almost to the place it had been when Kiron's own village had been lost to the Tians so many years ago.

But when Lord Khumun finally appeared to the restless crowd of Jousters waiting for him in the kitchen courtyard, he was not alone.

There was a Magus with him, and at the sight of the man, the muttering men in the courtyard went deathly quiet. It seemed at that moment that every drop of rain on the awnings overhead, and dripping down between the gaps in the cloth, was terribly, terribly loud.

Aket-ten sucked in a breath, and Kiron was very glad that she was sitting at the back of them all, and they were at a table at the back of the wall. There were a lot of taller, older men between them and the Magus, and yet the man's penetrating eyes seemed to sweep the crowd and see all of them. Kiron would very much rather have been in complete shadow at that moment, and he hoped that the Magus had only seen a sort of shape, and not that there was a girl among them. He did *not* want Aket-ten to be noticed.

It was not a comfortable sensation. Those eyes were as cold and as dead as opaque pebbles, and Kiron would have wagered at that moment that he was looking at a man who would bury his own mother alive if it got him something he wanted. But at least his gaze didn't rest on any of them.

"This is Magus Mut-ke-re," said Lord Khumun carefully—too carefully—into the silence. "The Great Ones have decreed that he is to have oversight of the Jousters, in order that the Magi may make the best use of us. Our tactics, so successful now, they say, will become even more successful with a Magus to guide us."

There were worlds of hidden meaning there, and Kiron was under no illusion that he could read more than half of them. It would have taken someone like Toreth or Kaleth, versed in the double-dealing of the court, to decipher all of them. Some were clear enough, though. Lord Khumun was under no illusion that the Magus was there to "help" the Jousters.

*The man is here to spy on us, he means,* Kiron thought instantly, and was passionately grateful that now there was nothing to hide—no dust, no plan to spread it, and no Kaleth with his visions. What would the Magi have done, had they discovered Toreth's brother had become a Winged One, untrained, and of the sort that they dreaded most? At the least he could have expected to be dragged off to the Tower of Wisdom to be used and used up. At the worst—Kiron preferred not to think about what the worst could be. He had the horrible suspicion he couldn't possibly imagine it.

No wonder Kaleth had said that he was in danger. If he'd had any hint from his visions that this was coming, he could only have read it as imperative that he get away.

And how fortunate it was that they had already found ways of explaining everything else that the Magi might take exception to! Everyone had the stories straight, and no one would deviate from them or fumble out contradictory explanations.

The Magus nodded at Lord Khumun's words, but said nothing. He only *looked,* looked at all of them, hunting with his eyes, searching for some sign of rebellion, perhaps. Kiron set his chin, straightened his back, and *looked* right back again. He would not show this man that he was afraid. If he saw anything, let him see defiance and be damned to him. Let him see rebellion, if that was what he was looking for. He could suspect it all he wanted; Kiron's actions would not give him any ammunition for an accusation.

"The Magus' words are to be obeyed as mine," Lord Khumun said tonelessly, making it very clear in that moment just who was the new ruler here—if the Magus' attitude hadn't already made that clear.

It was not an auspicious beginning for the day.

By the time the day was over, it was quite clear that there was no love lost between the Magus and his new charges. Kiron was not the only Jouster to meet the appearances of the Magus with outward—but bare—civility. Mut-ke-re poked his long nose into everything, from the kitchen to the sand-bath pen, and asked abrupt questions wherever he went. The dragons didn't like him, and greeted his appearance with hisses and whines. Even the best-tempered of them made no bones about their dislike of him. He repaid their displays with no visible expression whatsoever.

The Jousters ignored him, except when he addressed one of them directly, and they gave him as little opportunity to do *that* as possible. They kept out of his way until time to fly, then quickly took their dragons to the landing courtyard, knowing he would not venture out into the rain, then mounted as fast as they could, and got their dragons into the air. The dragons didn't even care to linger.

That left him only Kiron's wing to inspect.

He surprised Kiron by appearing soundlessly in the door to Avatre's pen, appearing out of the gloom while Kiron was harnessing her. The first Kiron knew he was there was when he cleared his throat ostentatiously. Kiron might have jumped, but Avatre covered it by swinging her head toward the doorway, eyes wide.

"Well," the Magus said, in an arrogant tone of voice, "So this is the famous Tian Jouster boy and his dragon."

There were many replies that Kiron could have made to that, and most of them would have been rude. He bit his tongue as Avatre stuck out her neck and hissed at him, and confined himself to simply saying, "I am still in training, and I was not aware that I was famous, my Lord."

The Magus grunted. Kiron remained silent, continuing his work, moving slowly and carefully to keep from fumbling anything out of nervousness. Avatre showed her teeth.

"Isn't she big enough to fly to combat?" the Magus said, with growing irritation when his continuing silence could not prod anything more out of Kiron.

"She is not fully trained, my Lord, and neither am I," he replied, deciding that it was more than worth the irritation it would cause the Magus to hear the same answers repeated and rephrased, over and over. "And we are both much younger than even the traditionally trained Jousters and their dragons. Size is no indication of age or skill, my Lord, nor of readiness, much less of trained competence."

This time the reply was a snort. "So what is it that you claim? That you are inept?"

"That I am untrained in traditional Jousting, my Lord," Kiron said, keeping his tone even. "Avatre is a desert dragon, my Lord, and they grow to be much larger than those you are used to seeing. She is no older than three years; the youngest of your fighting dragons is three times that age. And I have been training for little more than one year; the least training that your Jousters receive before they take to the battlefield is two years." He couldn't help it; his voice took on an edge of anger, though he did his best to control it. "Are you suggesting, my Lord, that I should attempt things that are beyond my skill and hers? That we should risk, not only ourselves, but the lives of those who would wrongly depend on us, thinking we *are* skilled and practiced Jousters? That we should engage in the monumental hubris of believing we are ready for things we have no business trying, merely because we are—if indeed we are—famous? That, my Lord, would not only be foolhardy, it would border on—treason, wouldn't you say? To *knowingly* go into a battle, aware that we cannot do what is asked of us when there are others depending on us to do what we cannot? Are you suggesting that this would be a good idea?"

There, he had flung the challenge back in the Magus' face. And now he looked up, to see a most peculiar expression there. Surprise—and perhaps a touch of fear?

*So, even the Magi are not immune to accusations of treason.* It was something unexpected, and something he decided to think about—later. *And they're not used to having their weapons used against them.* That was something else to think about. It suggested a number of ways of dealing with this man.

"Your pardon, my Lord, but you are standing in our path, and I should not like Avatre to strike at you," he said, with poisonous politeness. "I would do my best to prevent it, of course, but that may not be entirely possible, when it is clear that she has taken an intense dislike to you. And if we are to take up our duty, every moment of training, even in these conditions, which she, as a desert dragon, is particularly unsuited to, is precious."

Avatre punctuated his words with a hiss and snap in the Magus' direction. The man actually stepped back a pace.

"In fact, my Lord," Kiron pointed out, unable to resist being able to do so, "these dragons are performing far and away above what their Tian relatives can do. The other desert dragons that we have, the ones that are not tame, are remaining in the pens and cannot be persuaded into the sky by any means during the rains. Nor can the Tian dragons. But *our* dragons will work for us, even under conditions that they hate. No one sane could ask more than that."

The Magus stepped back another two paces, as Kiron led Avatre forward one. A third backward step took him into the corridor, as he clearly searched for something to say, and just as clearly came from his search with no good results.

"I suggest that you get on with it, then," he snarled at last, and—fled.

He fled the entire section where the boys lived, in fact, for as Kiron led Avatre out of her pen, he saw the tail of the man's robe vanishing around the corner into the main corridor.

"Let's get out of here!" he called harshly, as human and draconic noses poked around the doorframes. "We have training to do."

A ragged chorus of assent met his command, and as he led Avatre toward the landing courtyard with the rain drumming down on canvas above him, he heard the slap of leather soles on the stone behind him, and the clatter of dragon claws.

He led the procession with his head held high and without a backward glance. He felt the Magus' glare on the back of his neck from the shelter of one of the other doorways as they passed. Avatre felt it, too, and hissed again, but made no move otherwise as he put a steadying hand on her shoulder.

*Let him look and glare.* All he would see was Kiron, doing his duty despite conditions that would excuse anyone else from fulfilling them. And Kiron's wing, following their leader and their trainer, obedient, and ready to serve Alta as soon as they were able.

Yes, let him look. He would find no treason here.

What they wanted was not treason to Alta. If anything, it would be the saving of their land. And he kept his head high as they went out in the pouring rain, secure in the sure knowledge of that, if of nothing else.

# NINETEEN

T HE MAGUS was wont to appear out of nowhere, drop an acidic remark or an impertinent question, and wait to see how badly he had shaken his prey. He was quite successful at it most of the time. He had Aket-ten so rattled that she fled whenever he was near, and he had even the senior Jousters frowning and growling into their beer.

However, Kiron felt that he had gotten the upper hand on their first—and thus far, only—exchange. Perhaps that was why there had not been a second one. He did not succeed in rattling Heklatis at all, not even when the inevitable confrontation over the magic guarding his quarters came, early in the afternoon of his second day as their overseer.

Kiron was privileged to be there for that incident, and to his mind, it was the one bright moment since the Magus had descended on them.

He was actually seeing Heklatis for a legitimate complaint; a badly bruised forearm. The dragonets were not big enough to do a "falling-man" catch, so he had decided to try a different tactic—he reasoned that if they could at least slow a fall, he might get there in time to save whoever had been knocked from the saddle. So the new maneuver they were trying to perfect was of coming in under the falling "body," holding it for a moment, then letting it slip only to have another dragonet come in from below for a second catch. It was a clever idea in theory; in practice, it only made the falling victim's path less predictable, and had ended up in a lot of bruises.

Fortunately, even the experienced Jousters, who had shunned such things before, had taken to wearing saddle straps around their waists now, and extra-heavy girths on their saddles. Between the violent flying that their dragons were doing to evade projectiles from below, and their own exhaustion, no one wanted to take the chance of being knocked off a dragon in mid-flight.

"Well, that's a bone bruise," said Heklatis, finally, after a long and careful examination. "It is going to take a while to heal. The best I can offer you is a poultice of wormwood for the outside, and suggest a heavier hand than usual on the beer jars for the in—"

*"Healer!"* came a furious shout from the courtyard outside, making them both jump. They stared at the cloth hanging over the door, which let fresh air in while keeping most of the bugs out, and giving some privacy. *"What devilry are you up to in there?"*

They both recognized the voice, of course, after nearly two days of listening to it. "I am seeing a patient, my Lord Magus," said Heklatis, in a thickened version of his Akkadian accent, so that he made the word "Magus" sound like "Maggot" and Kiron had to choke down a laugh. "I beg your pardon if I fail to understand what you mean by 'devilry.'"

"That *magic!*" shouted the Magus, and he sounded nearly beside himself with rage. "That filthy, foreign magic! Your quarters are riddled with it! How *dare* you practice magic here? Get out here and explain yourself, this instant!"

"Why must I come out there?" Heklatis wondered softly. "I would have expected someone like him to simply barge in here."

"I don't think he can come in," whispered Kiron, with ill-concealed glee. "I don't think he can get past your wards!"

"Really now? Hmm." Heklatis' eyes danced with malicious merriment. "What an unexpectedly pleasant side effect! Well, I suppose we had better come out. Wait a moment, though." He took the time to tie the wet poultice he had prepared over the bruise on Kiron's arm. "All right, now we go."

Kiron came out first, followed by the Healer. The Magus glared at him and then in the same instant, dismissed him as unimportant, and transferred the glare to the Healer. "Answer me, rot you! How dare you practice magic here?"

Heklatis' brow wrinkled, and he spread his hands wide. "Forgive me, my Lord, but are you referring to the young dragon rider's poultice? I assure you, there is no magic there. Merely wormwood in vinegar and other herbs."

"No, I am *not* referring to the god-rotted poultice!" the Magus snarled. "I am referring to *magic*. Your room there *reeks* of it! I cannot even pass the door to inspect!"

"Magic, my Lord?" Heklatis repeated ingenuously. "But my Lord, I am a simple Akkadian Healer. Where would I have learned magic?" He widened his eyes and looked as innocent as a child.

"How should I know where you learned it?" countered the Magus. "That—"

"Ah, wait, my Lord," Heklatis interrupted him, with a wild wave of both hands. "Perhaps I know what is the cause of your misapprehension—"

He—well, the only word was *minced*—back into the work-room. Kiron knew, of course, that Heklatis was one of those who preferred his own sex to that of women, but he had never, ever, seen Heklatis behave in a feminine manner before, much less in such an exaggerated fashion. And when he saw the look of disdain mixed with extreme discomfort on the Magus' face, he knew why Heklatis was acting so out of character.

A moment later he—now the word was definitely *flounced*—back out, with one of the statues of his gods in his hands. Specifically chosen to make the Magus as uncomfortable as possible, it was the king of the Akkadian gods, stark nude, accompanied by a slender young man serving as his cup-bearer, and the two of them were in a pose that suggested that it shortly wasn't going to be the *cup* that the young man was bearing. Akkadian art was quite realistic. The Magus actually broke into a sweat.

Though judging from his words, it might not have been the subject of the statue—or at least, not *only* the subject—that was making him sweat. "Yesss," he hissed, pointing a finger at the statue. "That's one source—that—"

Heklatis regarded it fondly. "Well, then, there is your explanation, my lord. It is not *magic* that you sense, but the blessing of my gods! I took all my household images to the appropriate temples to have them blessed before I left to journey here. And I took the precaution of acquiring a large store of specially blessed amulets at the same time. I supposed that some of my patients might seek the blessing of a god when they came to me to be healed, and I was right."

"Heresy!" said the Magus in a strangled voice. Somehow he didn't sound sincere. Not surprising, considering that what the Magi were doing, in raiding the Temple of the Twins for the Winged Ones in order to work their magic, might well actually *be* heresy.

"I beg your pardon?" Heklatis frowned. "There is no law in Alta barring the worship of other gods than those you Altans worship. The contrary, in fact. And I make offerings at both sets of altars, yours and mine, anyway. So where is the heresy in that?"

"It is—" but the Magus could get no further; he simply spluttered and shuffled his feet in impotent rage.

"Are you suggesting that the Great Ones are planning on barring the worship of one's own gods in one's own household?" Heklatis continued, eyes glittering dangerously. "I certainly hope that is not the case. I would not remain in this city for a single moment, if I thought that was true—and neither would any other Akkadian, and of course, I would have to tell my compatriots of the change in the law as soon as I could." He held out his free hand and studied his fingernails carefully. "I think the Great Ones would soon come to regret that before too long. Given the kinds of positions that Akkadians fill all over this city. . . ."

A veiled threat, and they both knew it—and they both knew that Akkadians did serve in key functions all over Alta, and what was more, they would pack up and leave, taking their skills and their accumulated wealth with them, if they were denied the right to have images of their choosing in their household, and worship their own gods. Heklatis wasn't bluffing. And the Magus knew it.

*Point to Heklatis,* Kiron thought.

The Magus seethed with impotent rage.

"But of course, I am sure this is all just a simple misunderstanding," Heklatis continued, turning a shining smile on the Magus. "And now that you realize that what you *thought* was foreign magic is simply the bountiful blessing of my gods, you know that there is nothing to worry about here. Well, at least not *magically* speaking." To Kiron's surprise and delight, Heklatis began to simper at the Magus. "And I wouldn't call it *worry.* But unlike mighty Theus, I find older, not younger, men to be the best cup companions. . . ."

The Magus made a strangled sound in the back of his throat, went dead white, and fled.

Kiron stuffed both hands against his mouth to keep from laughing aloud until the Magus was well out of hearing distance. It was very hard, but fortunately, he was laughing *so* hard that he couldn't get a sound out anyway. By that point, the convulsions that shook him made it impossible to breathe for several moments. Tears streamed down his face, and he had to sink to his knees, rocking back and forth as he clamped his arms to his sides.

Finally, he sucked in air again in an enormous gasp, and looked up. Heklatis' grin very nearly set him off again.

"Oh—dear gods!" he gasped, tears still coursing down his cheeks. "Did—you—see—his—*face?*"

Heklatis made a rude sound. "As if I would touch *him* with a barge pole!" he said cheerfully. "Let me get dear old Theus back to his altar, while you get yourself under control before you do yourself an injury. You can dislocate your own jaw by stretching it too far, you know."

That just set him off again, and Heklatis made an exasperated sigh and went back inside his workroom. Fortunately, he stayed there long enough for Kiron to stop laughing, wipe his eyes, and get back to his feet.

"I think," the Healer said, as he came back into the courtyard again, "that I might just lodge an official protest with the Great Ones about this incident. I very much doubt that it will rid us of the man, but it will put them all on notice that I was serious."

"Well, now we know that not only can he not scry past your wards, he can't even get physically past your wards," Kiron pointed out. "That's useful!"

"Ye-es," Heklatis replied thoughtfully. "The thing is, I wonder why? My magic has never had that effect before. I shall have to look into that very carefully."

"I had better get back to the wing," Kiron replied, with some regret, for it was comforting, knowing he was standing in the middle of the one place in the compound that wretched Magus was never going to go.

"Yes, go," Heklatis said, absently making a shooing motion. "Keep the poultice damp while you wear it, but take it off to fly or do other work. And keep it away from Avatre; I don't think she'll try to eat it, but it could make her ill."

"Thank you, Healer," Kiron said, but Heklatis was already going through the door curtain, mumbling something under his breath.

When they all got together in Kiron's room later that night, there was something waiting for him—and Kiron was unsurprised to see that it was an Akkadian statue. This one he happened to *know* was no goddess, it was a simple artistic piece, but he had no doubt that Heklatis had put the same wards on it as were on his real god images. He decided, if asked, to claim that this was the Akkadian equivalent of We-te-esh, the Goddess of Luck and Love—a rather natural deity for a young man to worship, and doubly so for a Jouster. The fact that it was a fine little figure of an exceptionally lovely, completely unclothed young lady was just incidental. Right?

*Aket-ten isn't going to like it,* he thought, placing the image on the little shrine in the corner. He surveyed it, and smiled. Heklatis certainly knew Kiron's taste very well. *Aket-ten is going to have to get over it.* There was plenty of Altan art—well, perhaps not plenty, but certainly a reasonable amount, including on the walls of the public places in Lord Ya-tiren's villa—that depicted dancing girls wearing little more than a string of beads. There was no logical reason for her to take exception to this piece—which meant, of course, in the contrary nature of girls, that she would.

The others noticed the addition—the boys with sly looks and elbows to each others' ribs, and Aket-ten with a frown, then a disdainful sniff—and he explained what had happened that afternoon with great gusto.

When he got to the part about Heklatis flirting with the Magus, even Aket-ten had to stifle howls of laughter.

"I know I've seen this in Heklatis' rooms," he said, gesturing to the statue, "And I think I'm probably supposed to say it's an Akkadian goddess he gave me. If this does what I think it's going to do, it'll keep that rotted Magus out of here as well."

Aket-ten turned a look on the statue that, had it been wood instead of marble, would have set it afire. "I think it should have been that image of Epialon, then," she said pointedly, her brows furrowing in a frown.

"Now, Aket-ten, you know that you'd never get Heklatis to part with any of his handsome lads," teased Gan. "This was probably the only image he didn't want to keep for himself!"

Aket-ten colored, and opened her mouth to say something, when she was interrupted by noises outside the door. It was Avatre, snorting and rearing up out of her sand like a rising cobra. There was someone shadowed against the light from the corridor in the doorway to the pen. For one moment, Kiron felt a jolt of alarm—

"Avatre!" came a hissing whisper out of the dark. "Hush! It's only me!"

"Marit!" exclaimed Kiron, more quick-witted than the rest in recognizing the voice and realizing that the silhouette was too short to be the Magus. "What are you doing here?"

"Us," corrected Marit, as Avatre also belatedly recognized her voice and settled back into her wallow with a grumble. And indeed, it was two figures, not one, that emerged, blinking, into the light spilling from the doorway.

At first glance, it was hard to tell which of the girls that pulled back the hoods of their rain capes was Marit. They were, literally, as alike as two barley-grains. Or at least, it seemed that way to Kiron, but evidently Aket-ten had some arcane way, unknown to mere males, of telling them apart, for she looked at the left-hand one of the pair and said sharply, "Nofret! What are you doing here?"

The handsome young woman turned grave, faintly shadowed eyes on Aket-ten and said simply, "Escaping."

Both of them put down bundles that had been hidden beneath their capes. "We assumed that the worst had already happened to us," Marit said bitterly. "We were wrong."

"What *worst?*" asked Aket-ten. "You haven't been banished or anything, have you?"

Nofret sighed. "No. But believe me, it is a good thing that Toreth and Kaleth taught us about making many plans, well ahead of time, because we needed them."

Marit nodded, and the two of them pulled off their rain capes and settled down onto cushions that the other boys offered. Kiron noticed that they were dressed—oddly enough—in simple clothing, more like that one of their servants would have worn. "This afternoon the entire court was summoned by the Great Ones after a long morning Council meeting; the first we knew about it was when the Great Ladies sent us to be bathed and dressed by their servants. By the time we got our wits about us, we were already in a procession, and the next thing we knew, a new royal clan had been made, and we were being betrothed to a pair of Magi we'd never seen before."

"And if they're twins," added Nofret, with a lift of her eyebrow, and a toss of her head, "*I* am a dragon."

"What did you do?" asked Gan, looking utterly stunned.

"We went along with it, of course," Nofret replied. "The vows aren't valid. These men aren't in a royal clan, no matter what the Great Ones decree; the laws of the gods say that you can't create a new royal clan unless an old one dies out. And even if both our betrotheds were dead, which they aren't, we can't be wedded to anyone who is not of royal blood without our consent, which we did not give and were not asked for during the ceremony. No matter what words were spoken over us, we are not betrothed in the eyes of the gods, and that is all Marit and I care about."

Marit nodded. "When Toreth died, we knew it was always possible we would be asked to marry others in the royal clans—well, Nofret anyway. When Kaleth went away, we did think it was possible we both might have to, so we started making plans of what to do."

Now Nofret smiled fondly on her sister. "I didn't care—I liked Toreth well enough, he was a good boy, but—" she shrugged. "Marriage to him would have been fine, but marriage to anyone else who was tolerable would also have been fine. But Marit truly loves Kaleth, and *I* won't let her be forced away from him. So we began laying all sorts of plans—we even tried to think of ways of faking our own deaths! I must say, though, it never occurred to us that the Great Ones would have done something like this."

"But we knew if we made a fuss, we would be watched like vials of saffron, but if we acted happy about it—which we did— we'd be allowed to do anything we pleased. So we acted like children given sticks of honey," said Marit. Her nose wrinkled with scorn. "Everyone must think we're brainless, or that we're frantic to get *any* husband. Or else that we're so desperate to get back in the succession that we'd willingly marry the sacred baboons. Nofret made sure of that, by babbling about how honored and thankful she was and hanging all over that repulsive reptile they betrothed her to as if he was a god, and when I figured out what she was doing, I just did the same."

"Oh, yes." Nofret smiled cynically. "I was *full* of questions for the Great Ladies afterward. How quickly could we be married, would we have our places back in the order of precedence, how soon could our husbands be confirmed in the succession, when we were wedded would we get to wear the Lesser Crowns, would we have our own set of ladies and attendants suitable to our station—I think I was being so greedy there at the end that even the Great Ladies were beginning to wonder if this had been a good idea after all."

Marit tilted her head to one side, knowingly. "Serves them right. There were a lot of honors we could have claimed that we didn't because Toreth and Kaleth couldn't be bothered with court functions. I started talking about having a Lesser Court of our own. That made them really nervous."

"And they should be," said Heklatis, slipping into the room be-hind them like a ghost. "I wonder if the Great Ones will ever real-ize that the moment you wed, their days are numbered?"

No one even jumped. They were all so used to Heklatis coming and going silently that they just nodded at him.

"Perhaps the Ladies will," Nofret replied. "We certainly did our best to put the idea in their heads with our questions. Hello, Heklatis. We've run away."

"So I gathered. And since there is no hue and cry being raised across the First Canal, I assume you found a way to do so without raising suspicion?" Heklatis said easily, taking a place next to Kiron, and looking around at them all. "Hello, Kiron, did you like my little gift? I left one for Aket-ten, too, just now. Hermia, God-dess of the Hearth. I never much cared for that image; a little too placid and bovine for my taste. You can claim she's At-thera, your cow goddess; the wet-nurse to the god Haras, if I recall. I'm sure our friend will find that to be a suitably appropriate and pious image for a proper young lady to worship." He sniggered.

Aket-ten scowled, but didn't immediately reply, since Nofret was already talking. "We're officially on religious retreat in the Temple of At-thera, as a matter of fact," Nofret told them. "And it wasn't even our idea! Our original plan was to be such a plague that the Great Ladies would send us to father's country estate, but this was even better."

Marit chuckled. "After we began asking all those questions, the Great Ladies suddenly recalled that when a new royal clan marries into the succession, the brides must spend a moon in religious retreat and instruction in a temple of their choice before the wedding. Of course, *we* have never heard of anything of the sort, but we agreed to it with some pouting, and chose the Goddess At-thera because they haven't got one single priestess of noble blood there. And it's brilliant, it couldn't fit any better with our plans; we were supposed to leave all our attendants behind, be escorted by Royal Guards to whom one lady looks like every other lady, and live as the priestesses do."

"So they won't know that the Nofret and Marit that left the palace in their rain capes and with their escort are not us," said Nofret. "All that they will see is a pair of twins."

"Right, I've got that part," said Kiron. "But where did you find substitutes?"

She sighed heavily. "Do you have any idea how often someone thinks that a clever gift for twins is a pair of twin body slaves? We just looked through our handmaidens until we found the ones we thought stood the best chance of carrying off the deception. We explained the situation to them, and divided our jewels with them—which, after two sets of betrothal gifts in addition to what we already owned, is more than we could carry anyway. They'll be under guard, of course, which will give us at least a few days and possibly a week or two before *they* escape and run away."

Well, that explained the plain linen shifts and horsehair wigs. Marit wrung out the hem of her shift, and added, "Of course,

they won't be in any danger of being caught, because the Great
Ones and the Magi will be looking for Nofret and Marit, not a pair
of escaped slaves."

"And 'Marit and Nofret' ordered the two 'slaves' here as a gift
for Aket-ten, so they won't even be missing from our entourage
at the palace." Nofret smiled in triumph, and Kiron didn't blame
her; the plan was very, very clever.

Except, perhaps for one small detail. "What if they betray
you?" he asked.

Marit made a sour face. "That's the first thing we made sure
of. They're Tian, and they're slaves. We explained to them—in
great detail—just *how* they would be questioned if they betrayed
us. Because no one would ever believe that they didn't know
every detail of our plans, now, would they? And Tian slaves—
well, I reminded them that it would never even occur to anyone
to reward them for betraying us. I pointed out that they would be
the first to be suspected, reminded them of what the Magi did to
Toreth, to the Winged Ones, and to everyone who was in the
way when they opened the Eye. I told them what *I* knew about
how the inquisitors question slaves, which is rather more than I
actually want to know, to tell you the truth, and pointed out that
there are a lot more options open to someone torturing a female."

Heklatis looked at her with awestruck fascination. "You horrible young woman!" he said, admiration in his voice.

"Not horrible," Nofret corrected. "Brutally honest, and realistic. I didn't enjoy telling them, and I wasn't trying to intimidate
them. We gave them the truth, and then a chance to escape with
wealth. We picked the cleverest, because they have the best
chance of escaping quickly, and we picked the temple they have
the best chance of escaping from. On the whole, I think we should
be commended. They certainly didn't seem displeased with the
bargain."

"They didn't have a choice, though," said Kiron doubtfully.

"They didn't have a choice about being made slaves either,"
Nofret retorted. "They were lucky past all reason. They *could*

have been bought by a brothel, and weren't—they *could* have been bought by almost anyone to serve as pleasure slaves, and escaped that fate, too. Instead, they were bought and given to us, and then got a chance to take back their freedom, all for the price of silence, a little play-acting, and some cleverness in escaping. In their position, I would be weeping with gratitude in front of the statue of At-thera tonight, and planning to offer prayers of thanksgiving for the rest of my life once I got away."

*She has a point,* Kiron conceded.

"So now I assume you want us to get you—where?" asked Gan.

"To Kaleth," said Marit immediately. "He's managed to get three messages smuggled to me since he left. The last one said, 'The hawk rises above the storm; the desert finds its own.'"

Kiron, Heklatis, and Aket-ten exchanged looks. It was Heklatis who spoke, slowly, as if he was thinking aloud.

"The boy has the Seer's Eye," he said. "And he's with the Mouths, who presumably have something of the same and can teach him how to call visions instead of waiting to be struck by them. We all know how he feels about you, Marit—" she colored, and Nofret bit her lip, and looked pensive, "—and it is reasonable to assume he has been trying to watch you from a distance. So it is also reasonable that if we can get you to the edge of the desert, he will know, or possibly already knows, where you will be."

Aket-ten shrugged when Marit looked to her for confirmation of this speculation. "I can't think of any other interpretation. The question is how can we get you there quickly, and with as little to track you by as possible?"

"Amulets will take care of the latter," said Heklatis, sucking on his lower lip. "But—"

"We *fly* you out," Kiron said suddenly. "That's what the first part of the message means! Or we fly you as far as Avatre and Re-eth-ke can take you in half a day. Thank the gods this happened during the rains! Aket-ten and I have already gone up above the clouds, and the winds can take us a long way without the dragons tiring, Re-eth-ke can carry double, since two girls are light, Avatre is big enough to carry double *and* baggage—"

"Ha!" said Heklatis, slapping his thigh and startling them all. "Hoist on their own tackle! I can borrow those winds that the Magi are using, or one of them, anyway, to take you straight west in the morning, and straight east in the afternoon! As fast as that air is moving, it will take you all the way to the desert and back with no one the wiser!"

Aket-ten grinned for the first time. "No one is going to miss us for that long, are they?"

Kiron shook his head. "No, they won't. And even if someone were to come out to watch us, they won't stay for long, because there's nothing to see once the dragons are in the air. Look, here's what we'll do—"

Marit and Nofret slept in Aket-ten's room, secure in the knowledge that with Heklatis' guardian goddess there, the Magi would not be able to spy on the chamber. In the morning, everyone behaved absolutely normally. The Magus did not even glare at them more than usual; Kiron suspected that this might be because he was not aware that two of Heklatis' "blessed" statues had come to roost elsewhere. It had occurred to him before he went to sleep that night that the Magus could not seem to sense other magic unless he actively ran into it, either by trying to use his own magic, or by physically crossing it. So, since he would not try to go into a dragon pen anymore, they were safe from discovery for a while. Of the lot of them, if he was searching for pockets of discontent or conspiracies among Toreth and Kaleth's friends, he would be looking at the nobly born boys who had been the twin princes' childhood friends, not Kiron or Aket-ten. Kiron, after all, had no real power and no influential friends except Lord Ya-tiren, who was well known for his retiring nature. And Aket-ten had been playing the part of a frightened mouse.

They went out to practice, as usual. And, as often happened, a couple of dragon boys, muffled in rain capes and carrying heavy bundles, went out to the practice field, ostensibly to assist. But there wasn't anyone in the compound who noticed their departure—as Heklatis was supposed to make very sure—and there wasn't anyone at the practice field to see their arrival—as Kiron and the rest made very sure.

They all landed for equipment checks, and the dragon boys moved in among them. There certainly wasn't anyone to see that when the dragons took off again, Aket-ten had a second rider strapped in behind her, while Kiron had another and both bundles.

Avatre lumbered heavily into the air, taking a good long while to get up to speed with her triple burden. She didn't complain, though, and Kiron didn't feel any faltering in her wingbeats, so he assumed that she was all right with the extra weight. When he gave her the signal to go up farther than she was used to in this weather, though, he sensed her hesitation. He gave it to her again, with a little more force.

She thought about his command for a moment, but before she could make up her mind, Re-eth-ke shot past them, heading straight up into the clouds. Either that decided her, or else Aket-ten had managed to "speak" with her to tell her what they wanted, and that there would be sunlight up there; with a snort, she followed.

The journey was a repetition of the one they had taken on that pair of swamp dragons when he and Aket-ten had gone up to spread the dust—but without quite as much of the buffeting inside the clouds as the last time. As Avatre was hit by contrary winds, by unexpected updrafts and even a downdraft or two that made his stomach plunge and his passenger scream with fear, he thought that the turbulence was perhaps half that of the initial storm. And if that pig of a swamp dragon could handle it. . . .

His steadiness seemed to give Avatre confidence, and she fought her way back after every obstacle. Finally, she lifted her head a little as if she sensed something.

At that moment, it seemed to Kiron that the rain-filled mist above him was marginally brighter.

With a mighty surge of wings, and the added help of another unexpected updraft, they burst out of the clouds and into the sunlight.

Despite their head start, and Re-eth-ke's lighter burden, it was a moment or two after that before Aket-ten and her passenger lumbered up into the light, and they did so a good six furlongs away from Avatre. Following Kiron's signals, Avatre wheeled toward them; he wanted to be closer before they tried the next part of the journey.

It was then that he noticed that his passenger was clutching him around the waist so tightly that, if he had not been wearing the Altan Jouster's broad, thick, leather belt that protected the midsection, he'd have been having trouble breathing.

"Are you all right?" he called back over his shoulder.

"No," said a strangled voice in his ear. "But don't stop."

He spared a brief thought of *poor thing* for her, but had no time for anything more; the next bit would be tricky and required a lot of concentration. As he now knew from experience, the winds up this high were layered; while he had never yet come across one layer going in the completely opposite direction of another, he *had* encountered winds moving at right angles to each other. The Magi probably paid very little attention to their magic once they set it in motion, and as long as the rains went south, that was all they cared about. There was a single channel of wind up here, above the clouds and rain, that Heklatis had "purloined," deflecting it so that instead of going north to south, it curved off to the west. It would be high, Heklatis had told him. Perhaps higher than he had ever flown before, and Avatre, who could read the winds better than he, and who had more experience than Re-eth-ke, would have to find it. He signaled to Aket-ten, who nodded vigorously, then sent Avatre up.

She was not at all averse to this idea; this clear, dry air was much more to her liking than spending the day trying to fly through the pouring rain.

It was cold, and getting colder; he was glad of the extra clothing they were wearing. He and Aket-ten were wearing those woolen garments; Nofret and Marit had to make do with a pair of woolen robes with the skirts cut and bound around their legs. At least they were drying out quickly.

Avatre seemed unhampered by the cold. Up she went, with Kiron consistently giving her the signal that she should go *west*. And she tried, with the strong winds up here carrying them farther south all the time as she tacked against them. And she kept looking, craning her neck around, searching—he had the feeling she knew what he was asking of her.

When they planned this last night, he had wondered if she would understand what she needed to do without Aket-ten being able to give her clear directions. The "up" part was easy, but she had not flown on a long flight since they had arrived in Alta; would she understand that they needed to take one now?

Her bright eyes darted this way and that as she continued to climb, continued to fight the south-flowing winds—and then, just as he had seen her sense the clear air above them, he saw her find something else.

It was nothing that he could see, but she did, and she redoubled her efforts, driving strongly upward toward a place in the sky that seemed no different to him than any other place in the sky—

Until she was in the middle of it.

And then—ah, then she spread her wings wide and suddenly they were *shooting* westward, in the middle of a current that took them at right angles to the flow of the clouds underneath them. This time, with something to compare their speed to, it was clear that they were flying at a dizzying pace, both the highest and the fastest that he had ever flown before.

He glanced around, and caught a glimpse of Aket-ten right behind him. That was all he needed to know; that, and the position of the sun. When it was at its zenith, they would have to go down, no matter where they were, because at that point, this wind would die for a while, and then reverse itself.

They hoped that this would be somewhere that Kaleth was

waiting for them, but Kiron did not believe in counting on hope alone, no more than Nofret and Marit did. The boys had together scraped up enough ordinary currency in bronze and silver to get a cart and donkey. He and Aket-ten should have enough time to find a farm, buy a cart and donkey, and send the young women out to the desert's edge, where they could sell the cart and donkey and have enough money to provision themselves while they took some of their jewels apart and pounded things like rings and delicate ornaments into unrecognizable bits of silver, electrum, and gold. Then, if Kaleth had still not put in an appearance, they could go to one of the places at the desert's edge where the Bedu came to trade and buy their way into one of the encampments and wait there.

Kiron never counted on anything. Especially not luck.

But before the sun reached the appointed spot, the clouds began to thin in front of them. Soon there were gaps below where Kiron could see the green of the farmlands. And then, when he looked ahead, he realized that it was not the white of more clouds that formed the horizon, but the white sands of the desert—

And the farms beneath turned to scrub, the scrub to dry-scape plants, and then, just as the wind dropped away to nothing and Avatre went into a long, slow glide downward, the sparse desert-edge plants turned to true desert.

This was the moment that he realized just how high they were.

His passenger realized it at the same moment that he did; she shrieked in his ear, startling Avatre into a side-slip, and buried her face in his shoulder.

He didn't blame her.

Their woolens had kept them warm, but it had been a bit hard to get his breath. Now he knew why.

Suddenly Re-eth-ke folded her wings and went into a dive; taken by complete surprise, he only had the wit to direct Avatre to follow her. And follow she did.

It was not the sort of heart-thumping, near-vertical stoop that he and Aket-ten had endured on their first such flight, but it was steep enough, and he heard his passenger's muffled wails of pure terror against his shoulder. Re-eth-ke evidently saw something that he couldn't, for she had her eyes fixed on some point in the blank expanse of desert below. This was not so much a dive as a series of steep spirals; the dragons were somehow steering with their tails, and had just enough wing extended to slow their fall a little.

About the time when he made out that the thing that Re-eth-ke had spotted was a group of four beasts and two men, she tucked her hindquarters under and fanned her wings more, slowing the dive even further; a moment later, Avatre did the same. When he made out that the riders were muffled in Bedu robes and veils, and the beasts were camels, they were moving no faster than they usually were when they made landings, and they were spiraling down in a series of shallow, lazy circles, while the men and beasts watched, the men calmly, the camels nervously. The honks and groans of their complaints drifted up to him, and one of the men laughed at something the other said.

Then the wings of both dragons snapped open to the fullest, simultaneously, and they began backwinging furiously. They touched down within a heartbeat of each other.

Kiron's passenger might have been still too terrified to move; that was not the case with the other passenger. *She* had unbuckled her restraining strap and was sliding down Re-eth-ke's back unassisted while the dust they had kicked up was still settling.

One of the men jumped out of his saddle, and began trotting toward them. She hardly seemed to touch the ground as she ran to meet him, cape flying behind her. He caught her up in a tight embrace and held her, while Kiron muttered to the young woman behind him, "You can look up now, Nofret. We're down, Kaleth's here, and something a little easier to ride is with him."

"I'm not a coward. . . ." came the trembling reply.

"You'd be a fool if that ride hadn't terrified you," Kiron replied. "And *you* didn't have anything to take your mind off the end of it. Here, I'll help you." He helped her to detach her icy-cold, fear-rigid fingers from his belt, while the second man took something off the back of one of the camels and beckoned to Aket-ten.

By the time he got Nofret down off the back of Avatre, Aket-ten was dragging a woven palm-leaf cloth full of dead goat over to Re-eth-ke, who had her neck stretched out toward it, nostrils flared. The man was dragging a second such burden right behind her; while Re-eth-ke started hungrily on the first installment of her meal, Aket-ten took the second from him. Kiron caught up with the man at the camels, and they brought both halves of Avatre's meat to her. Kaleth had thought of everything. But then, he should have figured on that. Even before the Wings descended on him, Kaleth tried to think of everything.

Marit and Kaleth were still locked in their embrace, to no one's surprise. Nofret was sitting on their baggage, which she had managed to get down off Avatre's back, her head in her hands, now the very image of patient waiting.

"Well, I see you have left Vetch far behind you, Jouster," said the Bedu, in an amused voice.

"And I see that your clan has prospered enough to afford us four goats this time, Mouth of the Bedu," Kiron replied, with a lopsided grin.

"Oh, they have been paid for, be assured of that, Kiron of Alta," said the Bedu. "We have found your city, and have re-named it Sanctuary. As the young Eyes of Alta foresaw, there was treasure there, enough to provision it and make it ready."

So the Lost City really did exist! He thought longingly of it—it would be so good not to have to go back, to be able to fly on, into the clean desert, and land at the end of the journey in a place where he did not have to fear spying eyes, and the fingers of accusation—

But he still had a great task unfinished. "Let's hope it is indeed a sanctuary for those who need it," he said stoically, as Marit and Kaleth at last broke their embrace, and finally came to help Nofret with the bags. Re-eth-ke had finished the last of her meal; Avatre was on the last mouthful. "Right now, if *we* aren't to need it prematurely, we need to get back. I want our part in this all to be over with as little shed blood as may be, and that will need all nine of us."

"Indeed." The Mouth bowed his head, then raised it again, and looked at Kiron shrewdly. "In the depths of the night we count those whose lives our actions have cost, yet the gods never tell us the numbers of those whose lives were spared because of what we have done. You may choose to think on that, when the night seems long." He blinked owlishly above his veil. "And that is as it is. Your part is yet to come, and after that, it is in the hands of the gods. Fly fast and safe, Jouster. We will meet in Sanctuary."

Aket-ten was already in the saddle again, buckling on her restraining strap. She looked back at him, grinned, but gestured upward. He took the hint, and signaled Avatre to kneel, climbing up in the saddle himself.

"Ride swift and safe, Mouth of the Bedu!" he replied, as he buckled on his strap. "We meet in Sanctuary!"

His last sight of them, as the two dragons clawed for height into the clear sky, was of the four camels plodding back into the desert. He hoped that whatever was to come, Sanctuary would live up to its name.

# TWENTY

I T DIDN'T look like anything at all, really; just a faint, grayish haze on the surface of the three ripe *tala* berries in Kiron's hand. It could have been dust, except that dust didn't rub off. It could have been almost anything, or nothing at all, just an odd color on the hard little berries. Kiron handed them back to Heklatis, who took them with a smile and a raised eyebrow. "The harvest looks good this year," he said.

"Yes," Heklatis replied blandly. "They're all like that, plump and well-colored. From here to the southern border of Tia, or so I'm told by the few who venture there. Whatever else, the rains were good for the *tala*."

Lord Khumun nodded gravely. "So a week to dry, and then we can use them, which is just as well, since I think we have scarcely a week in stockpile." *He* knew, of course. He had frowned at the odd color of the berries, had looked up at Heklatis who had nodded, then both of them smiled, just a little. Kiron contained his glee with an effort, for he knew that the Tians had no more *tala* stockpiled than the Altans did. The Altan agents had not been able to steal any *tala*, but they had done the next best thing; during the rains, they had made holes in the roofs of the storage rooms where it was kept, to deny it to the enemy. The rain and the rot that followed spoiled it, or most of it. Only the *tala* actually stored at the Jousters' Compound had been spared.

Lord Khumun's smile was a weary one; once the rains had ended, his lot had been fraught with difficulty, for the Magus placed in governance over all of them had flexed his muscles and ordered impossible things. A return to traditional Jousting; that had been the first thing, of course—well, he could order all he wanted, but the Magi could not compel obedience on the battlefield, at least, not yet, and the Jousters had bowed their heads and continued with Kiron's tactics. But besides that, he had ordered all of them into the sky, twice a day, every day, with no rest and little recovery for the injured, and that was taking a toll on them. As tired as they had been during the rains, they were bone-weary now. Lord Khumun's sad smile told Kiron that he would be glad to see an end to the situation at last, even though it meant there would be no more Jousters and he would have no more command.

Kiron could not imagine what the Magi were thinking of. Were they trying to be rid of the Jousters themselves? It seemed unlikely—

Or were they only trying to get rid of the old Jousters, seeking to replace them with young men of their choosing?

Kiron decided to ask Heklatis about that, this evening. Right now, he had a practice session to run.

They had gone back to using that distant practice field the day that the rains started to taper off, even though the senior Jousters were so much in the air that they didn't have time, much less the need, to practice. Kiron didn't want an audience where the Magi could see that they had gathered one. He did not want attention drawn to his wing.

They did have an audience, though, for their new exercises, which were quite exciting, even though there wasn't a single person out there other than the wing and Heklatis who knew what they were for.

He got back to the pen in time to find his dragon boy cinching the last strap down on Avatre; he checked them all, as he always did, and smiled. "Good job," he said. "As always."

The lad grinned, as he gave Avatre the command to kneel. No more vaulting into the saddle from the ground for him anymore; Avatre had gotten too big for that. There was absolutely no doubt in his mind now that *tala* slowed the dragons' growth as well as dulling their minds and instincts. Avatre was much bigger than her mother had been, and might even be a hair bigger than Kashet when he last saw Ari's dragon, and she still had another two to four years of growth ahead of her. She was bigger than every other adult desert dragon in the compound.

He gave her the signal to fly, and she leaped straight up from the pen, just as Kashet always had. He took her up over the compound and waited, circling on a thermal, while the rest finished their harnessing and joined him. They lined up in a V-shaped formation, with Avatre at the point, and headed for the practice grounds.

He was the target, since Avatre was the oldest and most experienced flyer. By now she could perform everything he remembered Kashet doing, which meant that she could outperform most, if not all, of the Tian dragons. The exercises they were all running now—which would be crucial very soon—were harassing maneuvers. Kiron had gone to the swamps and watched as the swamp dragons challenged each other and drove each other out of hunting territories. Then he had come home and taught the harassment techniques to the wing. Avatre hated this; what the others were doing spoke to her deepest instincts, and she wanted, badly, to turn on them. That she didn't bespoke her deep bond of trust with Kiron; he only wished he could reward her patience as it deserved.

*Tala*-drugged dragons would respond with irritation, but would continue to obey their riders. Undrugged dragons, or those for whom the *tala* was wearing off, would try to chase the interlopers out of their territory until they realized that the dragon was immature—he'd seen that, too, in the swamp. Then they would realize that there was a sky full of better targets and potential mates, and there were wretched little hairless baboons on their backs that should be gotten rid of before the proper business of draconic life could be taken up.

And that would be the end of the Jousters.

There was still one matter that he had not come up with a plan for—warning the Altan Jousters of what was to come. He wanted to do that; it didn't seem at all fair not to. But there might be one or more among them who would tell the Magus, and he did not know what would happen then. . . .

But that was a week or more away, and he still had time to think of a plan, or so he hoped.

They arrived at the practice field, which was just on the inside of the Seventh Canal. On the other side were the great estates and small, unprotected villages. He was not particularly surprised to see that there was a crowd gathered to watch. At least, this was so far out that it was unlikely there were any Magi here to note that they were *not* practicing traditional Jousting. He set Avatre up; the others went higher; each of them would take it in turn to harass her. She hissed; she knew what was coming, and she hated it.

The wild-caught dragons would hate it even more. And when the battle was over, and all the dragons scattered, Kiron's wing would fly due west until—well, probably until they picked up a guide at the edge of the desert. Kashet had found them once; presumably he would find them again. It was a more tenuous plan than Kiron liked, but it was a lot less fragile than it had been before Marit and Nofret had been forced to flee.

The search for them had begun—discreetly—two weeks after their actual escape, but it had not been kept quiet for long. Too many people knew, and more people were involved all the time as the search spread outward. Nothing had been found; their choice of collaborators had been perfect. Not that this had stopped the Magi's plan; the "twin" Magi had simply been rebetrothed to another set of girl twins—only this was a pair of toddlers. The marriage would not be able to take place for another decade at best, though this was nothing more than a postponement.

Given their recent record, it was entirely possible that the spouses of some other set of royal female twins—including the current Heirs-apparent—might come to an unfortunate end. People would talk, but if nothing could be proved. . . .

Huras and his dragon came down first. Kiron ducked, as they few by close enough that Tathulan's talons brushed his back. Avatre snapped; he didn't bother to stop her reflexive action, because their enemies would do the same, and he wanted the youngsters to learn to avoid the deadly jaws. Tathulan dodged neatly out of the way with a squeal, and Huras side-slipped her out of the way.

It was all horribly depressing, and it made Kiron want to throw himself into a canal and drown sometimes. Only the promise of Kaleth's visions kept him going, these days, for if things in the compound were bad, things in the city were worse.

It seemed as if every time he looked, someone else had been taken up for treason. The Temple of the Twins was actually closed; supposedly, because the Winged Ones were so important to Alta, they were husbanding their strength so that they could answer the Great Ones' needs on the instant. Kiron knew the truth, though, and it was exactly as he and Aket-ten had feared.

The Magi had exhausted the Fledglings completely, leaving many of them without power anymore, and even some feeble-minded or comatose. The Winged Ones, older and stronger and better trained, had resisted being burned out in that way, and now that the rains were over, they might be left alone to recover. But with no new Fledglings left to train to replace those who had failed—and another season of rains ahead—there was no telling what was going to happen. Certainly the people of Alta were now vulnerable to earthshakes in a way that they had not been for generations. And already there had been mutterings about "testing" the Healers to see if they could "aid" the Magi as well as the Winged Ones could.

Heklatis said that there was rebellion among the Healers, though; so much so that no Magi would be allowed to get near the Temple of All Gods, much less inside it. And if anyone tried—well, they would have to bring a force big enough to overpower all the Healers and all their servants, and there were weapons being improvised that would probably break any spells of coercion such as were apparently used on the Winged Ones. Heklatis said such things required the Magi's concentration; they'd be hard put to concentrate after getting facefuls of vinegar or lemon juice—or having leeches drop from the ceiling on them. If the Healers felt savage—

*You shouldn't anger someone who knows as much about pain as a Healer does.*

Re-eth-ke and Menet-ka's Bethlan came in together, one on either side of him, moving fast. Fast enough to knock Avatre down a few feet with the turbulence of their passing. Avatre was too busy trying to recover to notice that Orest's blue Wastet was right behind them; he came in low enough to snatch one of the tear-away streamers from Avatre's saddle with his foreclaws. Avatre was enraged, and gave chase; Kiron was thrilled. They could get an entire wing aroused with a single pass with moves like that!

And just as Avatre started to gain on the fleeing dragonets, they parted, going left, right, and straight up—and there, coming straight at them, was Oset-re and Apetma. Avatre yelped, and folded her wings to drop. Apetma passed right through the spot where she had been.

Poor Avatre had had enough. She went all the way to the ground, and Kiron had to spend a goodly amount of time soothing her hurt feelings while the others chased after each other to catch streamers in a general melee. She might have a ruffled temper, but he was extremely satisfied. The *tala* could run out tomorrow, and they would be ready.

Except for telling their own Jousters what was about to happen.

He still had no answer for that question.

When they got back to the compound, they all landed in the landing courtyard; not even Avatre was quite skilled enough yet to land in her own pen. Once down, he made sure to spend some time walking Avatre around to all the other dragons before they all went back to their pens, to make certain they were all friends again. Aket-ten went with him, "talking" to Avatre about it, and to the others as well.

"Does it do any good?" he asked her anxiously as they walked Avatre and Re-eth-ke back together. "Do they understand?"

"Actually, I think so, more each time we do this. Avatre understands that this is part of training, and I *think* she understands that the others are harassing her because their riders are asking them to, not because this was their idea." She smiled slightly. "I was going to say, 'not because they want to,' but I'm afraid they get a great deal of gleeful pleasure out of harassing her and getting away with it. But it's like good-natured children being given permission to be naughty, not real aggression."

"Good," he said, with a sigh of relief. "The last thing we need is to have them start attacking each other right now."

They parted then, with Aket-ten taking Re-eth-ke on back to her pen, and Kiron turning into Avatre's. He and his dragon boy got her unharnessed and fed; once she had settled, he went to see Heklatis.

He found the Healer with one of the senior Jousters, splinting a broken arm. Kiron was shocked; a broken arm was not the only injury the man had sustained. His face was a mass of bruises, and so was the half of his body that had the broken arm.

"What happened?" he blurted.

The man grunted. "Strap saved my life. Tian had a lance with a wood core and a stone tip inside the papyrus. If I hadn't been belted into the saddle, I'd be dead." It was a little hard to understand him; his lips and jaw were so swollen that his words were slurred and muffled.

"They were following orders," Heklatis said neutrally. "They were Jousting. However, no one told them that the Tians had new lances."

"Bigger dragons to start with, *and* lances like that—we've not got a chance," the Jouster growled. He might have said more, but at that moment, Lord Khumun, and what seemed like all of the senior Jousters in the compound descended on Heklatis' quarters like a storm. All of them were shouting, or at least talking, at once, and all of them were angry. Heklatis shook his head at them; Kiron couldn't make out more than a word or two either. Finally Lord Khumun held up a hand for silence.

Miraculously, he got it.

"What is this all about?" Heklatis asked, aghast.

"The Magus just gave orders that every senior Jouster is to fly *every* flight, no matter what!" shouted someone from the back. "He included everyone on the injured list *by name!* Even you, Ahsheptah!"

*"What?"* The injured man and Heklatis spoke—or rather bellowed—at the same time. The cacophony started again. Lord Khumun held up his hand, and it died.

But it was Kiron who spoke first. "My Lords," he said, enunciating each word with such care that he was sure even the most stupid of them would understand that he meant something far more than he was saying. "I do believe that my wing and I can help you with some new strategy. Will you rouse your mounts and come with me to our practice field? Lord Khumun, I can take you, Heklatis, you should go with Aket-ten, and my Lord Ahsheptah, I believe you ought to ride behind Huras, rather than flying just now. Will you come?"

They stared at him for a moment, as if he was a baboon that had somehow produced human speech. Then Lord Khumun said, "Jousters, I think this is a *very good idea.* We need to *practice* where no one will *interfere* with us—"

There were still looks of total bewilderment, but no one demurred. In fact, after the first few began taking hesitant steps toward their dragon pens, the rest followed. Kiron and Heklatis helped the injured Jouster to his feet, and made their way to the boys' pens. Fortunately, he met them in the corridor just as they were about to go elsewhere.

"Get the dragons harnessed and up," he ordered shortly, to their astonishment. "We need to go to the practice field. Aketten, you have Heklatis, Huras, you take this man. Fast! I want to get there and back before anyone notices!"

The wing understood, at any rate. And to his immense satisfaction, although they were the last to know, they were all the first into the air, even Huras, with the injured Jouster.

They led the way to their field, and landed there. The dragons had all just been fed (and drugged) and were sleepy—and while they were irritated at being forced to fly, they were inclined to lie right down on the warm grass in the sun and bask rather than quarrel or wander. Simply staking their reins down kept them in one place. The Jousters all gathered around Kiron and Lord Khumun, who both looked to Heklatis.

"Give me a moment," the Healer muttered. He closed his eyes, and began to chant under his breath, and shortly he was sweating as if he was trying to shove a heavy stone up a ramp all by himself. He grew paler, too—and just when he began to sway a little with exhaustion, he stopped, opened his eyes—and sat down hard in the grass.

"They won't find us, not for a while," he said heavily. "And if they try to scry, what they'll see is all of you practicing up there—" he pointed at the sky above.

"He's a Magus, as well as a Healer," Kiron explained to the baffled faces. "And—that's where our story begins, I suppose."

He explained everything; Toreth's original plan, and why he had decided to make the Jousters into a force to make the Tians forge a real peace, their long discussions, the change in the plan after Toreth's murder by the Magi, Kaleth's visions—and finally, what they had done to the *tala*. "In a few days, you'll be using the new stuff," he told them. "And so will they. Once the dragons aren't drugged anymore, we thought they would probably obey for a while out of habit, but we planned to go along on one last flight and—goad the Tian dragons into rage, so they'd throw their riders and escape. We were going to warn you so that you could ride your dragons down to the ground and turn them loose."

Silence. Kiron began to sweat. Told out like this, to senior Jousters—it didn't seem like such a good plan anymore.

"The Magi are trying to kill us anyway," growled the injured man. "Isn't that obvious? It's better to be a live dog than a dead lion!"

After a moment, there was some muttering of agreement. "But why?" asked someone else in a bewildered voice. "That's what I don't understand!"

All eyes went back to Kiron, who was still in a cold sweat. "I don't know," he said finally, "but at practice today, I started to wonder something. What if they wanted to replace all of you with their own men? I mean—Heklatis thinks that the Eye can't be used on cloudy days or at night, and it's not really good enough to get one person—but a dragon and rider are. What if he wanted to replace all of you with men who would—follow orders, and if those orders were to use your dragons on Altans, would do it without question?"

Silence again, but this time, utterly stunned. The injured man sat down with a thud.

"Blessed gods," said one.

Heklatis looked as if he had swallowed a sea urchin. "The theory fits," he said, with so much barely-suppressed rage in his voice that those nearest him took a step back. "And what a *fine* way to besiege a place and prevent anyone who might help from coming near it! Such as—the Temple of All Gods?"

A gasp met his words, but no one disagreed with him. That this violated everything every Altan believed in was so obvious that it didn't need saying.

It was Lord Khumun who broke that third silence, by turning to Kiron, removing his sash of office, and offering it to Kiron. "It is your plan, young Lord Kiron," he said, simply. "Lead us."

Kiron stared at the sash, then into Lord Khumun's face. All he could feel was panic; all he could think of was, *I don't want to be a leader!*

But his hands took the sash by themselves, his mouth opened, and words came out.

"I think that this will work—"

Above the wing, nothing but sky. Below the wing—so far below that they looked like fancifully colored little songbirds—were the dragons of Alta.

*"You have ordered all the Jousters into the sky, my Lord Magus. We are not the best, but we are ready."*

For the past two days, the dragons had been restive as the old *tala* wore out of their systems. By now, the larger dragons of Tia must be getting very touchy indeed. Their dragon boys would be giving them higher doses of the false *tala*. It would hold for a while, but not long. Certainly not long enough to get them through what Kiron's wing was about to inflict on them.

*The Magus stared at him, then smiled. He looked exactly like a crocodile. "Well done, Jouster Kiron. I will commend your loyalty and zeal to serve to the Great Ones."*

Somewhere out there in the desert, he hoped, Kaleth was waiting.

Whether they would all survive to reach him was another story. These were not fellow wingmates that they were about to harass. These were full-grown desert dragons, all wild-caught, and now, all of very uncertain temper.

Except, of course, for a single tame dragon that Kiron especially did not want to face.

*What would the Magi think, when none of the Jousters returned, and they found a compound peopled only by slaves and servants?* He hoped they would think that all of them had died, and that Lord

Khumun and Heklatis had deserted, rather than be held responsible for such a massive failure. He really, truly hoped that the Magi would send out trappers to take wild dragons and try the false *tala* on them. That would be—festive.

Somewhere, down there, was a covered ox cart carrying an old peasant man and a quarrelsome old woman, heading east. Hidden in the cart, beneath a false bottom, were a dozen images of Akkadian gods and goddesses—and one statue of a comely woman that was not a goddess—along with all the wealth that Lord Khumun and Heklatis could put together. Heklatis had looked disturbingly comfortable in that linen gown and woman's wig. But the statues ensured that the Magi might look for them, but they would not find them.

*They had all worn Jousting armor and carried lances. The moment that they passed over the Seventh Canal, the armor and lances had come falling out of the sky like a strange rain.*

No one was going to be encumbered today. No one was fighting today. The senior Jousters were going to let the Tians chase them until their own dragons got too restive—then they were going to take them down behind the Altan lines and let them go. That was the plan, anyway.

*No more need for Jousting armor. There would be no more Jousters. There might be dragon riders, but there would be no more Jousters.*

Down there, so far below that they looked like ants, were the Tian and Altan armies—and there—coming up from the south, were the Tian Jousters.

Up here it all seemed so very simple, and Kiron's mind felt strangely detached. Was this how the gods saw things, as tiny figures at a distance? It was impossible to tell individual warriors on the ground, and even the dragons were little more than scraps of color, swirling around each other, as if moved by the wind. If so, no wonder the gods failed to answer prayers. You couldn't see blood from up here; you couldn't see death, or suffering.

*But I'm not a god*, Kiron thought, taking in a sudden deep breath of air as the first of the little bits of color broke off and headed for the ground. *And I may not see it, but I know it's there. It's time to do what I can to stop it.*

He gave Avatre the signal to dive.

He didn't have to see his wing following his lead; he felt it. He didn't want Aket-ten to be here, but—but he needed every dragon, and little Re-eth-ke was the smartest, the swiftest, the most agile of them all. And besides, he couldn't have kept Aket-ten away short of knocking her out, stuffing her in a bag, and putting her in Lord Khumun's cart.

And he knew very well what would happen to him then, if he made it to Sanctuary . . . Aket-ten would finish what the Tian Jousters started.

He picked out a dragon, a big one, a blue-and-green, chasing an Altan brown swamp dragon. He gave Avatre the signal for a raking attack without the claws.

The Tian never even knew he was coming; all he knew was that suddenly something big and red came up from behind, moving twice as fast as he was, and nearly knocked him out of his saddle with the buffeting wake of its passage.

And his dragon, already giving him trouble, went mad.

Kiron glanced back over his shoulder. The Tian had broken off the original chase and was now after him. There was another pair of Tians ahead of him, with just barely enough room between them to fit a third—he decided on the instant to fill that gap, and kept Avatre going straight ahead while she still had the momentum of her dive.

She blew through the two of them; he glanced back. The purple blundered into the gold-and-green, then the blue crashed into both of them. Angry screeches, the first he had ever heard from a dragon, followed him as he sent Avatre into a wingover and headed her back up for more height. She rowed her wings in the air, all business, ignoring the chaos she had left behind.

He looked down. There were dull-colored dragons and a few bright ones flying free, now. The dull ones were streaking back for the marshes of Alta, tearing bits of their harness off as they went. The bright ones seemed confused.

He spotted another good target; a pair of Tian dragons going for the grounded Altan Jousters, although their Jousters seemed to be having some difficulty in getting them to go where they wanted. This time he didn't even have to give Avatre a signal; she seemed to sense where he was looking, as she had when they hunted in the desert together, and plunged downward toward the new target.

This time she chose her own attack; the fisted one. Kiron felt the *thump* as she hit something, though whether it was the dragon or the Jouster, he could not have told for sure. She bounced back up; the dragon she hit blundered into the second, and that was two more Tians out of the melee.

As she clawed for height again, he took a look below. Now the Tian dragons in pursuit were chasing *his* wingmates, and even as he watched, he saw two of them break off, writhing and bucking in the air, deciding suddenly that the irritating nuisances on their backs were worse than the irritating nuisances that were harassing them.

Avatre paused at the top of her climb—

And suddenly Kiron's vision was filled with a blue-and-gold dragon.

Bleak eyes stared through him from within the slits of a Jousting helmet.

*"I told you not to get on the other side of a Joust from me!"* Ari shouted, his voice hollow, his words filled with anger and pain. And he struck for Kiron with his lance.

But Avatre was faster, and she had been learning evasive moves from the moment Kiron entered the Altan compound.

She did a wingover, and Ari's lance swished through empty air. She turned the wingover into a dive, heading for the ground this time. Kiron did not have to look behind to know that Kashet was in hot pursuit.

This was a mistake; Kashet was as good at ground-scorching

dives as Avatre, and he had more practice. He touched Avatre with a signal; she responded instantly, flipping over in a side-slip tumble that put them upside-down for an instant.

Kashet shot past. Kiron sent Avatre up, and back in the opposite direction. It happened to be east.

Time to run.

He gave her the signal she wanted.

For the second time in her life, Kashet pursued Avatre into the desert. This time the odds were better; she was stronger, bigger, and faster, with infinitely more endurance. He hadn't known that Ari was trying to help them the first time, he'd thought that the Jouster, his Master, was trying to catch them to bring them back to a mutual captivity.

Now he didn't know what Ari wanted, but he knew what Ari's devotion to duty would make him try to do, and he didn't want to find out if friendship would win over duty.

He leaned down over Avatre's neck, making himself as small as possible—and then gave her an entirely different signal.

He dropped the reins. She was the best judge of what to do now; he would live or die by her instinct and ability.

She responded at first only by deepening her wingbeats and making her climb a little steeper. Then she turned her head, just a trifle—looked back over her own shoulder—and did a wingover to the left.

Once again, Kashet shot past. This time, though, he fanned his wings furiously to brake—and *she* shot past *him* as she turned her wingover into a shallow dive and continued on eastward. She had tricked him into dumping his speed!

Kiron's heart leaped. Kashet had never fought a dragon that was his equal before, but Avatre had been training with eight other tame dragons. So he might have more Jousting experience, but she knew how to trick another dragon.

Kiron longed to look back, but resisted the temptation. The battlefield was far behind them, but they were still not over the desert yet. Avatre turned her dive into a climb, and glanced back.

And ducked, spilling the wind from her wings. Kashet shot by overhead.

*This isn't good—he's got more speed now and more height than we do—*

And two more dragons shot past, a blue-black and silver-blue blur, and a purple-blue-scarlet beauty; Tathulan, who was nearly the size of Kashet, and Re-eth-ke. The largest *and* the smartest!

Kashet was in the middle of a wingover when Tathulan bulled past, using her own wake to send Kashet into a tumble. But the tumble sent Kashet where he wanted to go, straight into Avatre and the great blue locked claws with her and they began to plummet toward the earth in an obscene echo of a mating fall.

Kiron screamed in terror, seeing his death rushing toward him—

A blue-black-and-silver thunderbolt struck both of them. Re-eth-ke had rammed them with chest and fisted foreclaws. Kiron caught sight of Aket-ten's ashen face for a moment, then Re-eth-ke flapped away. But the blow had startled Kashet so that he let go, and Avatre wrenched free.

She snapped her wings open; with a jar that shook him to his teeth, she backwinged for a moment, then got control again and lumbered upward.

Another indigo dragon scorched past her; Bethlan, cutting between Avatre and Kashet. Another—this time a red-and-sand streak that was Deoth. Kashet wasn't going to be distracted; Kiron could almost feel Kashet's hot breath on the back of his neck. He was going to close again—

Avatre ducked, and tumbled—and Apetma, Se-atmen and Wastet slammed into Kashet from three sides in a copper, brown, and brilliant blue pinwheel.

Kiron had often heard from old fighters that, at a moment of extreme crisis, time seems to slow. He had never believed that until this moment, when he saw Ari's body jounce upward in his saddle—saw the restraining strap snap with a sound like a whip crack, and watched Ari tumble down over Kashet's shoulder with the same graceful, languid motion as a petal dropping from a flower—

His mouth opened. He thought he shouted. He *knew* he gave Avatre a signal she knew better than any other.

She fought out of her tumble; stretched out her neck. Made one desperate wingbeat. A second. And on the third, got under Ari's falling body with that expert flip of her head and neck that tossed him, sliding down the neck to lodge against the saddle—

But not quite right.

Ari slipped, and slid off her right shoulder.

Kiron screamed again, and grabbed for Ari's arm as he fell for the second time. He caught it, and was slammed against Avatre's neck by the sudden weight. She struggled for control; he howled with anguish as his arm seemed to flame with pain. He felt his fingers slipping, looked down into Ari's eyes, and saw bleak despair and resignation.

Slowly, agonizingly, Kiron's grip slipped as Avatre lumbered sideways, pulled over by the weight. She didn't know what to do, and he couldn't tell her to land without letting go of Ari—

The fingers slid—down the forearm.

Wrist.

Gone.

Just as Re-eth-ke slid right underneath.

Ari landed across Re-eth-ke's shoulders. Astride.

He screamed in pain. Kiron didn't blame him. But at least while he was racked with pain, he wasn't fighting anyone; Aket-ten wrapped her arms around him and sent Re-eth-ke to the ground; Re-eth-ke was perfectly happy to go.

The rest followed her down; panting and weak with reaction, Kiron let Avatre drift in a slow spiral behind them. He didn't even think about Kashet—

Until they landed beside Re-eth-ke, and Aket-ten, who had Ari on the ground beside her, and the great blue-and-gold dragon powered out of the sky like a lightning bolt, heading straight for them.

This time it was Avatre who interposed herself between Kashet and his prey, while Kiron howled, his voice cracking, *"Kashet! NO!"*

And Kashet—stopped.

A strange look came into the blue dragon's eyes, and his nostrils dilated as he sniffed in Kiron's direction. "Kashet," he said hoarsely, "You know me. We didn't mean to hurt him. We'll make him better."

The dragon sniffed again, and made a gurgling whine in the back of his throat. Kiron slid down off Avatre's shoulder; his knees were wobbly, but they held him. He stepped toward Kashet, holding out his hand. "Kashet," he said as calmly as he could, "Remember? Remember Vetch?"

Kashet lowered his head down and sniffed his palm—

—and sighed.

And folded his legs underneath himself with a groan, and dropped down into the sand.

Sand?

Kiron looked around. They had reached the edge of the desert, and he hadn't even noticed.

He patted Avatre, who walked over to Kashet and sniffed him with deep suspicion, then stood guard over him. He trudged over to where the others were gathered around Ari—well, all but Aket-ten. *She* was leaning against Re-eth-ke, just out of sight of the others, leaning against her dragon's shoulder. She looked white as fine linen, and he didn't feel much better.

He knelt down next to Ari, who was clearly in pain.

"Let me, young Kiron."

The hand on his shoulder was attached to an arm clothed in Bedu blue; a moment later, the hand had gone to Ari's forehead, and the Bedu was whispering a few unfamiliar words. The agony left Ari's face, but now the pain there was of a very different sort. He looked straight into Kiron's eyes.

"Why didn't you let me die?" he asked bitterly.

"And years ago, why didn't you let me?" Kiron replied without thinking.

"Because there has been enough of death on both sides, fools," the Mouth of the Bedu said roughly. "And enough of wallowing in self-pity. Get up, Jouster, who is a Jouster no more." And he grasped Ari's wrist, and hauled him to his feet, turning him so that he faced into the west.

Dozens of brightly colored dots were speeding overhead, coming toward them. One shot past directly overhead, and a little later a bit of harness fell out of the sky to hit Gan in the head.

"Ow!" Gan shouted, indignantly, and shook his fist at the retreating dragon. "We freed you, ungrateful wretch! Ingrate!"

"There are no more Jousters, Ari, rider of Kashet," said the Bedu. "Neither Tian, nor Altan. There never will be again. You are freed of your oaths."

Ari—blinked. His lips twitched. "You, who speak for your gods, claim *that?*"

"No," said Kaleth, pushing his way between Oset-re and Peatep. "I, who speak for the gods of both Tia *and* Alta, say that."

This was not a Kaleth that Kiron had ever seen before. Leaner, browner, full of fire and energy, and with a look to his eyes as if he had seen all there was of pleasure *and* pain and had come to accept both as part of a greater whole. Now it was Kiron's turn to blink.

And all he could think was, *If only Toreth were here to see this. He would be so happy—and so proud.* For Kaleth, who had always stood in his brother's shadow, had come into his own.

Kaleth had something else new—around his neck was the hawk pectoral of a Priest of Haras, and on both shoulders were tattoos of the symbol of the Winged Ones.

"Priest?" said Ari falteringly.

"And Winged One of Alta," replied Kaleth. He took Ari's upper arm in a firm grasp. "And as both, I say to you—you are freed of your oaths, which had come to strangle you. There are no more Jousters. The dragons will answer to no bond save love.

And so, you have no duty to return to. I give you the wings of the hawk, to choose your fate. You may go anywhere you choose, and leave behind everything that has caused you such pain as made you ask 'Why did you not let me die.'"

"Or?" asked Ari, looking into Kaleth's eyes.

"Or—you may accept that pain, accept the burden of responsibility once again, and help us to do somewhat that may—*may*— bring a cure to the disease that rots both Tia and Alta." Kaleth's gaze was steady. "I promise nothing. The future is in flux, and my visions are not clear. But this I do pledge; those who join us in Sanctuary are vowed with one heart to the goal of ending this wretched war and casting down those who fatten upon it. We have hands, we have plans, and we will *try*."

Ari closed his eyes, and Kiron held his breath. He felt as if he balanced on the edge of a knife blade. He didn't know *why* it was so important to have Ari with them—other than to himself, that is—but he sensed that it was.

And so did Kaleth. But Kaleth was giving him the choice, to stay or to go, of his own will.

Ari opened his eyes, and looked straight at Kiron—then past Kiron, to where Avatre guarded an exhausted Kashet.

And he smiled.

"Take me to this Sanctuary of yours," he said. "I should like to *try*."

# EPILOGUE

S ᴀɴᴄᴛᴜᴀʀʏ—
    Kiron stood on the top of a squat, wind-eroded tower, and looked down at the improvised pens where ten dragons wallowed in sun-heated sand, as contented as ever dragons could be. The Lost City was a very strange place. He had thought it would seem desolate, and haunted by the ghosts of thousands. It actually seemed empty, and waiting, as if it never had held people before this moment. The buildings were familiar, yet unfamiliar, the shapes like those of Alta and Tia, yet unlike. Partly it was the utter lack of paintings, inscriptions, and carvings; there weren't even any statues of gods here. Partly it was the curves of the walls; there wasn't a straight line here anywhere. The dragons liked it, though. Perhaps it reminded them of the wind- and water-cut valleys and caves where their kind made their homes.

    There was water here, the first need of life, an underground source that seemed bottomless. You reached it through the well house in the center of Sanctuary, which covered the stairway down, which in turn led to a cave and a huge spring-fed pool.

    Sanctuary itself provided the shelters, far more than the current population needed, although there were more people trickling in all the time. The first two had been Lord Khumun and Heklatis, the latter having shed his womanly disguise, but after them had come several of the dragon boys of Alta *and* Tia (including Baken!) some of the Healers of Alta, and other folk, common and noble. One of those had been Lord Ya-tiren, who had doubled the population of Sanctuary by bringing with him his entire household. Aket-ten and Orest could not have been more overjoyed.

Kiron could not have been more relieved.

Aket-ten came up through the hole in the roof of the tower to stand beside him. He smiled at her, and made room for her to sit on the sand-scoured parapet. "Look—" she said, pointing straight down below.

Directly below was Kashet's pen. Entering it were Ari—and Nofret.

Their voices drifted up on the hot wind.

"—but of course there can be more dragons, and more dragon riders," Nofret was saying, in a voice that sounded surprised. "It is not so difficult! How do we get young falcons? We take them from the nest, of course—and we can do the same with dragonets. We have ten dragons that can guard us while we take a single youngster, and we can ensure we do no harm by taking the ones that might not otherwise live, just as we do with falcons!"

"That never occurred to me," Ari replied, sounding surprised. "But—by Haras, you are right! We can set a watch on the dragon nests—take the ones that are not prospering—take the ones from parents that are not skilled—"

"And tell me, are there not times when the parents are slain, as happens with falcons?" Nofret asked "Or injured, or killed by a disease? We can save those entire clutches—and of course, since they will have bonded first to their parents, they will eventually breed as well, and then we will have the best of both sorts of dragon, tame *and* wild!"

Her voice was alight with enthusiasm, as Kiron had never heard before. And Ari's when he replied, was warm with pleasure.

"How is it that you know so much about falcons?" he asked, "And care so much about dragons? I have—forgive me, my lady, but I admit my experience with women is rather limited—I never met a woman who—who—"

"Who thought about more than hair and gowns and jewels?" she laughed. "But I was a falconer, Ari! I helped tend and raise my father's birds—Pe-atep was my father's man, and I trained him! As for dragons, well—the first time I met Aket-ten and saw her Re-eth-ke, my thought was not, *that was Toreth's dragon*, it was *I want one like that!* I confess to you, I was raw with envy, and I would have traded every gown, wig, and gem in the world for a dragon of my own."

"Ah, now I understand why you thought so much about how to gain more!" Ari laughed—and his hand inched toward Nofret's.

"Oh, I must also confess that my first flight was utterly terrify-ing," she said, a smile still in her voice, "And for a little while—a *little*—I thought 'perhaps this is not for me'— but I managed to get beyond that fear as I watched Aket-ten and Kiron flying away into the sky."

And her hand inched toward his.

And when they touched, their fingers curled around each oth-er's, interlacing until they seemed that they had never been apart.

"I believe, my Lady," said Ari softly, "that we must needs find you a dragonet of your own. I should not like to find you trying to win my Kashet away from me. And I—I would like to show you what the world looks like from above. It is strange. There are no borders, you see—"

Kiron found himself smiling—then grinning—and had to swal-low to keep from whooping aloud, as Nofret leaned her head on Ari's shoulder. "I should like that, Ari. And please call me Nofret. There are no ladies here."

With a start, Kiron realized that his fingers had somehow got-ten entwined with Aket-ten's. "I think we should give them some privacy, don't you?" he whispered, hoping she could not hear how his heart pounded.

"That might be a good idea," she whispered back with a grin. "And you know, we might want to go see if there are dragon nesting places around here. It's going to be a while before Sanctuary can do anything about the Magi and the war. And we're going to need more dragon riders when we do."

"We certainly will," he replied, warmly, basking in their shared dream. Perhaps he was no Winged One, but the vision was clear to both of them. "We certainly will."